Seize the Day

366 tips from famous & 'extraordinary ordinary' people

Edited by
Stephanie Wienrich & Nicholas Albery

Assisted by
Mary McHugh

Chatto & Windus
London

Published by The Institute for Social Inventions
in association with
Chatto & Windus 2001

4 6 8 10 9 7 5 3

All royalties from this book are going to The Institute for Social Inventions, a charitable project for encouraging innovative solutions to social problems, and which runs the Global Ideas Bank on the web. The Institute gratefully acknowledges the kindness of all those who contributed their tips for this book.

First published in Great Britain by

The Institute for Social Inventions, 20 Heber Road, London NW2 6AA
(tel 020 8208 2853; e-mail: rhino@dial.pipex.com; web: www.globalideasbank.org)
in association with
Chatto & Windus, an imprint of Random House
20 Vauxhall Bridge Road, London SW1V 2SA

Random House Australia (Pty) Limited
20 Alfred Street, Milsons Point, Sydney,
New South Wales 2061, Australia

Random House New Zealand Limited
18 Poland Road, Glenfield,
Auckland 10, New Zealand

Random House South Africa (Pty) Limited
Eudulini, 5A Jubilee Road, Parktown 2193, South Africa

Random House UK Limited Reg. No. 954009

A CIP catalogue record for this book
is available from the British Library

ISBN 0 7011 69389

Papers used by Random House UK Limited are natural,
recyclable products made from wood grown in sustainable forests.
The manufacturing processes conform to the environmental
regulations of the country of origin.

Printed and bound in Great Britain by
Mackays of Chatham PLC, Chatham, Kent

Foreword

Anita Roddick, OBE
Founder and Co-Chair The Body Shop International

> "It is better to give than to receive – especially advice."
>
> *Mark Twain*

Seize the Day is packed full of useful, provocative and insightful tips for life, a distillation of the best advice from our contemporaries. I believe most of us will find here at least one or two of what the poet William Blake called 'minute particulars', the small and useful details that can make a difference to a person's quality of life. We are naturally social creatures and it is hard to manage entirely on our own: this sharing of advice is one way in which we can help each other out. Where advice from those we know – and who know us too well – often grates, advice from others' lives can sometimes get under our guard and touch us.

This book offers a wealth of experience from 366 'extraordinary ordinary', and not so ordinary, people, who have travelled a long way on their own experiential journey. From poets to philosophers, from psychologists to politicians, the range of contributors cuts across a wide swathe of age-groups, professions, political affiliations and social backgrounds. My own tip is about travel, a physical journeying into unfamiliar lands and new cultural experiences, as an essential rite of passage. This book will take you to new realms of experience without you even having to leave your seat; in some instances, hard lessons may have been learnt for you. It is affecting to find certain tips resonating powerfully in our own lives, connecting us at the most human level with people who have successfully articulated or realised their dreams.

Like the Institute for Social Inventions, the educational charity which will receive royalties from the sale of this book, and of which I am a patron, The Body Shop is dedicated to the pursuit of social and environmental change. I support wholeheartedly the aims and ideals of the Institute: to promote socially innovative ideas and projects, to encourage public participation in continuous problem-solving and to promote small-scale innovative experiments.

Just as Kew Gardens gathers every variety of seed for its Seed Bank, so the Institute of Social Inventions gathers and saves and respects a wide diversity of ideas in its Global Ideas Bank. *Seize the Day* is their Advice Bank, containing advice from contemporary people whose lives have made a difference. May its seeds bear fruit in your life.

Introduction

Brian Eno

Musician, artist and author

Sometimes I think that the most important thoughts of one's life appear at the most odd and inauspicious moments. They are the ideas that somehow stick, ideas that reappear at crucial junctures, and set you on one road rather than that other. They don't have to be even well thought out – they just somehow appeal. They sound true to you.

This is a book of ideas that sound true to the people who have been guided by them. In a sense, it's the distilled life-wisdom of 366 people – their comment about how to make your life more rich and fulfilled.

An Indian teacher once said "the fruit ripens slowly but falls suddenly". It's like that with ideas. You spend a long time quietly, and often unknowingly, getting yourself ready for a thought, and when it finally appears, everything is in place to receive it and understand it. It seems completely right and obvious, and you say "why didn't I think of that?" The fact is, you did – you just didn't put it into words yet.

So when you think: "that's exactly right", what you mean is that you've been getting round to thinking this thing yourself, and finally someone has put it into words.

I've had this feeling many times in my life, and I've always tried to follow it, to embrace the changes that would ensue. To accept a new idea is to reorganise your life around it, to change your priorities. You don't just parcel it off and render it harmless. New ideas are not harmless – they are the most powerful things we make.

John Fuller was born on January 1st 1937. He is a poet and writer of fiction. His latest collection of poems Stones and Fires *was awarded the Forward Prize in 1997. His* Collected Poems *were published in 1996, and the latest of his five novels,* A Skin Diary, *in 1997. For over thirty years he has been Fellow and Tutor in English at Magdalen College, Oxford.*

Reclaiming twenty years of your life
a tip from John Fuller

It is a tedious commonplace that we spend about a third of our lives asleep. Knowing this perfectly well, most of us do nothing at all about it. I'm not suggesting (God forbid) that you should sleep any less than you need to, but I am suggesting that you should try to reclaim some of this lost time by keeping a dreambook.

The procedure is simple: (a) anchor a pad of 3" x 3" Post-Its to your bedside table; (b) buy a pen that incorporates a light (my Light 'n Ink bought in the US by my wife clicks to produce a green glow around the ballpoint); (c) make notes the instant you wake, and write up the dream at breakfast. The resulting volumes are a useful resource, a commentary on your involuntary life, an indicator of irrepressible obsessions, a key to the dungeon of forgetting.

John Fuller adds: I have only been doing this for about three years, and regret not having done it earlier in life. However, I have always jotted down especially significant dreams in ordinary notebooks and have used some of my most lingering and serial dreams in short stories and novels. *Flying to Nowhere* exploits a number of them, and the core idea of *The Burning Boys* is a dream which I have used more than once and which still recurs. I hope that one day an examination of my dreambook will help to explain it to me.

January 2

Valerie Yule, who lives in Victoria in Australia, was born on January 2nd 1929. She was a late starter and, according to her family, "the cause of the Great Depression". She has worked as a clinical child psychologist, teacher, academic, researcher and writer, believes in the need for spelling reform and is the founder of the Australian Centre for Social Innovations.

Everyday resurrection
a tip from Valerie Yule

My tip concerns the concept of resurrection – that is, living again after you feel you are dead. It is a mercy of life that every day, however awful, comes to an end in sleep, and that there is a new dawn every morning, clean and untouched – your personal miracle. People vary in their best time of the day, and it is a healing discovery to learn to make the most of your own 'dawn time' each day and to forgive yourself the rest.

Each day's dawn resurrection is the time to attempt and re-attempt those things which need to be done in the world, before inspiration and courage ebb and the day becomes covered in one's usual snail-tracks and mistakes.

To be alive is to experience many little deaths. Resurrection is a hope and a grace. "I'll lay me down and bleed awhile, and then I'll rise and fight again" (Sir Andrew Barton, in the old ballad).

Valerie Yule adds: It was all right for Browning to say, "a man's reach should exceed his grasp or what's a heaven for?", but my eyes have always been too big for my uneven abilities. I can see what a heaven the world could be and what a hell we are making it, and want to join in helping to stop this, because "if I don't do it, who will?" (my second tip). I could give up and just do housework and the garden, rather than continually fail and be tiresome, but then there is also my third tip: that to keep on for the "last quarter mile" has a chance of making a difference. As I am a depressive, each day ends in darkness – so each new dawn is indeed new life.

Neville Shulman has undertaken a number of expeditions to faraway places and climbed a number of high mountains, mostly to raise monies for international and national charities. His books telling the stories of his adventures have been published in the UK and in the US and in several other countries. Neville Shulman is a Fellow of the Royal Geographical Society and a member of the Explorers Club. He is a journalist and writer and works in theatre and film, as well as business management, entertainment and the arts generally.

January 3

Never panic – life is never easy
tips from Neville Shulman, OBE

Never panic. We all experience a crisis at some time or other, either in our personal lives, professional activities or in my case, often on a mountain or in the jungle. The greatest piece of advice I can give is: Don't panic; try to avoid reacting immediately; first of all work out all possible options or alternatives. There is usually a way out or at least an opportunity to deal with the problem, no matter what it is. Often the problem itself can be the making of you and give you another chance to take another direction. (By the way, it's interesting to note that the derivation of the word 'panic' arises from the sight of Pan; the primal fear of meeting this half-man creature.) Sometimes you don't have so much time, but if possible, sleeping on a problem, waiting 24 hours, is all that is necessary to see things in a different and more acceptable perspective.

Maxim for the millennium. Life is never easy, even for those that seem to have more than most. I always remember Sylvester Stallone saying in one of his interviews that if he'd understood at the beginning that the downside of fame was going to be as it really is, he wouldn't have taken that rocky road. Perhaps then he would have muscled in on another profession! Always keep your mind open and above all learn from your mistakes. The philosophical tenet I would offer is: He who learns but does not think, is dead. He who thinks but does not learn, is in great danger.

Neville Shulman adds: On January 3rd 1997 I stood at the South Pole, a few metres from where two of the greatest polar explorers, Roald Amundsen in December 1911 and Robert Scott in January 1912, had stood 85 years earlier. It had always been one of my dreams to travel to the bottom of the world. Never more so than having reached the top of the world, the North Pole, on April 24th 1989. The adventures of these two totally different expeditions are recounted in my book, *Some Like It Cold*.

January 4

Rod Hackney was born on March 3rd 1942. He is an architect, past president of the Royal Institute of British Architects (RIBA), current Honorary Librarian of RIBA and President of the Snowdonia Society. He has written a book called The Good, The Bad and The Ugly *(1990) and a music play based on his own work entitled* Good Golly Miss Molly *(1991).*

Appreciate the opportunities afforded by diversity
a tip from Dr Rod Hackney

What is the definition of culture?

Our culture in its broadest sense largely determines:

whether our rites of passage involve circumcision, circumambulation or bungee-jumping

whether in our dialogue we use the anglophone, francophone or saxophone

whether we practice monogamy, polygamy or hierogamy

whether our madness is schizophrenia, spirit-possession or psychedelic

whether we love monologue, dialogue or paradox

whether our viewpoint is birds-eye-view, fish-eye-view or simply belle-vue

whether we love logos, mythos or chaos

whether our music is monophony, polyphony or cacophony

whether we dance clockwise, counter-clockwise or otherwise

whether we wear our clothes loosely, tightly or off-the-shoulder

whether our god is anthropomorphic, cosmogonic or binary

whether we consider nature a friend, a foe or a dump

whether our eschatology directs us to Utopia, Heaven or Nirvana

whether our suffering is lebensschmerz, infernal or Samsara

whether our time is linear, circular or recyclable

whether we accommodate, exterminate or incorporate our opponents

whether what really matters for our system is input, output or kaput

whether our life is dominated by bye-laws, in-laws or outlaws.

Rod Hackney adds: January 4th is around the time when most people, having enjoyed the festivity break, are getting back into gear for the new year, hopefully with renewed vigour. My tip – a prompt that we are fortunate to be living in a vital and multicultural world with all the positive opportunities afforded by diversity – is no bad start for the days ahead.

David Canter was born on January 5th 1944. He is Professor of Psychology at the University of Liverpool where he directs the Centre for Investigative Psychology. He is known for his work on the psychological effects of buildings and what people do in disasters; and, more recently, for developing the scientific basis for criminal investigations (which he has termed 'investigative psychology'). He often appears on radio and TV and writes pieces in the national press about 'offender profiling' and other developments in psychology. He married Sandra Lorraine in 1967.

Make major decisions from the heart
a tip from **Professor David Canter**

The few really important decisions in life, such as who to marry, what house to buy, career to follow or name to give your children, should always be made because they 'feel' right.

Intellectual analysis and careful reasoning are good for minor matters such as where to go on holiday, whether to demand an increase in salary or which tie to wear. But the decisions that shape your life have to come from deep down inside your being, even though you may need to explain them away.

David Canter adds: As a scientific psychologist constantly battling against the superstitions and prejudices of others who think they understand 'the mind', I am usually very sceptical of claims for the power of intuition and hunch. But I have been aware of a few moments in my life in which there was an emotional inevitability to the course I was considering. The most telling was when I just knew I would marry my wife, even though at that stage we were casual friends.

I think there are moments when all of our senses and understandings add together with such power that we are silly to ignore them. However, this powerful experience is only valid for really crucial decisions that involve all aspects of our selves. Too many people waste this capability and imply that they are using intuitive insight to make trivial day-to-day decisions, because that saves them the effort of careful thought and systematic analysis. That is prejudice masquerading as prescience.

January 6

Edward Lucie-Smith was born on February 27th 1933. He has written more than 100 books, most of them art books, but also poetry, a historical novel, and a biography of Joan of Arc. He is a member of the Académie Européenne de Poésie. He has also made a reputation as a photographer, with exhibitions in London and abroad. He travels widely. Joan of Arc was born on January 6th in 1412.

Passez outre
a tip from Edward Lucie-Smith

When confronted with a trap question at her trial, or one concerning matters which she considered private, such as the exact form taken by her visions, Joan of Arc often refused point blank to answer. She would say "Passez outre" meaning, literally, "Go on to something else".

In effect, it is often better to refuse to say anything at all than to become entangled in a series of prevarications and half truths.

Edward Lucie-Smith adds: I find it sometimes shocks people to learn that Joan of Arc may have been the originator of modern stonewalling techniques when dealing with intrusive questions. Yet it is always worth remembering that there are plenty of things about one's life which others have no right to know.

Amy Fletcher, born on January 7th 1950, is the mother of three children, all now independent. For the last twelve years she has earned a reasonable living as a self-employed garage mechanic specialising in the repair of Citroen 2CVs.

Spilling milk and clearing it up
a tip from Amy Fletcher

It's not until you've done something wrong that you really understand how to do it right.

Amy Fletcher adds: When I was training to be a mechanic, surrounded by blokes who knew it all, it became a matter of pride to make less mistakes than they did; I was afraid of the humiliation that I thought I might be subjected to. Looking back over my life, however, I see that the only times I have really learned anything or made any significant progress have been when I have done something wrong. Naturally, I am not referring solely to my professional skills.

January 8

Dominic Prince was born on January 8th 1961. He is an award-winning freelance writer, broadcaster and documentary producer. He has worked for all the national newspapers and produced films for Channel 4 (including The Totter*) and the BBC (including* The Big Deal*).*

Think about other people
tips from Dominic Prince

Think about other people.

When you are young, try and get on with your parents.

Be nice to trees and the countryside.

Don't smoke.

Don't worry.

Dominic Prince adds: When I was young I didn't think much about other people and I didn't get on with my parents until my thirties. I never really understood my father, didn't want to and when he was alive didn't much care for him – until he'd gone.

Trees allow us to breathe. England is a small country and we should preserve the countryside and think of other housing solutions.

I smoked 60 cigarettes a day for 25 years and I cannot recall a single benefit.

I worry all the time and yet I'm still here. I can't work it out.

Sir Christopher Lever was born in London on January 9th 1932. He is a naturalist, author and conservationist, and has written nine books, including The Naturalized Animals of the British Isles *(1977),* Naturalized Birds of the World *(1987) and* Naturalized Fishes of the World *(1996), and contributed to a further eight. He has travelled widely, especially in Africa, on conservation matters, and has often been interviewed on radio and TV.*

Always think twice before putting anything in writing
a tip from Sir Christopher Lever

Never put in writing anything you may subsequently regret. The written word is much more permanent than the spoken word, remains in the mind of other people for longer, and is far more difficult to either retract or forget.

Sir Christopher Lever adds: This piece of advice was given to me as a young man by my father, and whenever I have forgotten or ignored it – whether I have been writing a book, a letter, a review, a report or whatever – I have almost invariably regretted it.

January 10

Bo Lozoff was born on January 10th 1947. In 1969 Bo and his wife Sita were living a utopian lifestyle on a sailboat in the Caribbean, when their boat became involved in a drug smuggling saga which ended with a close relative being sent to jail for 40 years. Bo's response was to set up the Prison Ashram Project, which helps prisoners to treat their jails as ashrams or monasteries, as opportunities for meditation and spiritual growth – centres of human kindness. Bo and Sita's Human Kindness Foundation now sponsors this and other projects, producing and distributing free materials to prisoners and others. Bo's latest book is entitled It's a Meaningful Life: It Just Takes Practice.

You can do hard
a tip from **Bo Lozoff**

We have a saying around Kindness House: *You can do hard*. The reason we say this is that in modern times, the words 'it's too hard' have become an anthem for giving up. The message is: Have an ache or pain, reach for a pill; get depressed because you lose your job, take Prozac. A friend once confided to me that she regretted divorcing her husband. She said the only reason she did it was a prevailing attitude among her friends that "If it gets really hard, why make yourself suffer?" Maybe we have become convinced that we can't do hard things.

You can do hard is a way of reminding yourself that you need not run away in fear just because something is greatly challenging. You can do challenging. It might even be scary, but you can do scary. You can do hard. Really, you can. Don't let a shallow culture fool you into thinking you'll crumble when the chips are down. Human beings were designed for the chips to be down sometimes.

Bo Lozoff adds: I first grappled with this advice while waking up in hospital after a high-speed, head-on collision with a large truck. My face was disfigured, spleen removed, spine permanently damaged, a finger sewn back on, skull fractured. The tempting way was to shut down, close off from others, take drugs and grow bitter. The hard but hopeful way was to be humbled, open my heart to all suffering, and choose to have faith that this happened to help me become a wiser, more compassionate human being. Choosing the hard way accelerated my healing tremendously.

John Kennedy Melling was born on January 11th 1927. A chartered accountant and member of many British and American professional organisations, he is an author, critic, historian, editor and broadcaster on subjects ranging from crime to antiques and from Alfred Hitchcock to the theatre.

Be worth a six-inch obituary in *The Times*
tips from **John Kennedy Melling**

To be worth a six-inch obituary in *The Times*:

In life, as in marksmanship, you need B-R-A-S-S – to breathe, relax, aim, squeeze, shoot. If you miss the first time, shoot again. Don't give up until you know you're hopeless. Devote your energies and emotions solely to those matters you can affect, and ignore others. Decide early in life what you want – and don't be deflected. Be indispensable in your work and don't let your dislikes show. Have your experience acknowledged in more than one field.

John Kennedy Melling adds: I knew what I wanted to do in life at the age of 11 and I was never deflected. My father advised the indispensability and concealing the dislikes of people. I started two careers in parallel, concentrated only on what interested me and ignored everything else, like Dr Johnson – I always remember his dictum that no man ever lost his dinner over a revolution!

January 12

Jonathan Myerson was born on January 12th 1960. He was given a classical education in Cardiff, London and Oxford. He now writes novels, plays and film screenplays. Most recently, he wrote and directed an animated version of The Canterbury Tales *which was nominated for an Oscar and won the BAFTA and four EMMYs.*

Trust: a simple rule
a tip from Jonathan Myerson

Never trust anyone who likes neither cricket nor cats. Some people don't like sport, some people don't like pets. But someone who dislikes both cricket and cats is lacking a profound humanity; do not trust this person.

Jonathan Myerson adds: Since the death of religion, sport and animals have become the two great dividers. Cricket distinguishes those who can absorb humiliation, pain and the spotlight of criticism from those who cannot. The agony of walking back to the pavilion, no runs to your name, or spilling that crucial catch or being run out on ninety-nine are hardening experiences which no one should be allowed to avoid. Meanwhile, a cat will never let you off the hook: you have to meet it more than halfway and you give love long before you can hope to receive it. I have never lived without a cat or a cricket bat. Anyone who determinedly avoids both cricket and cats needs help.

Michael D. Howells was born on January 13th 1957. As a production designer, his films include Emma, Miss Julie, An Ideal Husband, Fairytale, *and* Ever After – a Cinderella Story. *He has designed sets for John Galliano at Christian Dior and Alexander McQueen at Givenchy. His work in the theatre has been mostly dance projects, including* MSM *for* DV8, Der Damon *at the Stats Oper, Berlin and* Toward Poetry *for the Royal Ballet.*

Success and failure
a tip from Michael D. Howells

Failure is no disgrace, low aim is.

Michael D. Howells adds: My father gave me this advice and it has fired me in my work. When undecided or nervous about a project, this simple advice has energised me to achieve the best.

January 14

Peter Barkworth was born on January 14th 1929. He has appeared many times on the West End stage, on television and in films. His plays include Siegfried Sassoon, *a one-man show of his own devising. He has been in episodes of* Maigret *and* Heartbeat. *His films include* Where Eagles Dare. *For his performances in the television version of* Crown Matrimonial *and Tom Stoppard's* Professional Foul *he has twice won the BAFTA Best Actor Award.*

Reply by return
a tip from Peter Barkworth

My GP for many years, Dr John Horder, was available on the telephone for all his patients between 8 and 9 o'clock every weekday morning. After that he left for his surgery.

I once asked him how he coped with that hour every morning. "Well," he said, "I sit at my desk and have my liquid-only breakfast. Orange juice and tea. That means I can get on with other things. When I'm not talking on the telephone, I do desk-type things and attend to that morning's mail. When I've opened a letter, I deal with it before I go on to the next. If it is a bill, I pay it. If it is a request, I answer it. Only if a letter requires a long and considered reply will I put it in the pending tray, which I keep as empty as possible. If you do this, it means that you have to read most letters only once."

Peter Barkworth adds: Since then, I've always done the same. I have a liquid-only breakfast and attend to the mail. It is an enormous time-saver. I don't get telephoned between 8 and 9 in the morning, but I do write my diary for the previous day. It's a delightful hour. It wakes me up and keeps my desk clear.

The humorist Ivor Cutler was born on January 15th 1923. He trained as an air navigator (grounded for dreaminess). Aged six, he sang 'My Love is Like a Red Red Rose' by Robert Burns and won a school prize. His first gig was at the Blue Angel, London, 1957 (unmitigated failure). He has written more than 270 songs. He started writing poetry aged 42 (he wasn't any good until 48). Author of Many Flies Have Feathers, Fresh Carpet, Large Et Puffy and Cockadoodledon't!!!. Quotes about Ivor Cutler include: "The demeanour and voice of the weariest human ever to be cursed with existence" (Music Week) and "Ivor Cutler spends a lot of time in his bedroom" (Observer Magazine).

Sticky labels
a tip from Ivor Cutler

I recommend my recreation to you, which is dishing out sticky labels to deserving persons (the labels are printed for me by Able-Label, Earls Barton, Northampton NN6 OLS). Here are some of the labels from my collection:

If you want to go from A to B, go to C.
You will then find yourself at B.

Chronological age is misleading –
and therefore irrelevant

silence and space –
the dark flowers of creativity

"Do as you would be done by"
(A universal ethical proposition:

Iuop Cvtlep	20th cent AD
Confucianism	6th cent BC
Buddhism	5th cent BC
Jainism	5th cent BC
Zoroastrianism	5th cent BC
Classical Paganism (Plato)	4th cent BC
Hinduism (Mahabharata)	3rd cent BC
Judaism (Hillel)	1st cent BC
Christianity (Jesus)	1st cent AD
Sikhism	16th cent AD)

Ivor Cutler adds: With hindsight, I realise I've gone blindly through life, steered by my unconscious. To my astonishment, my work seems to be therapeutic, both to myself and to audiences.

My most successful label is 'Changing your pants is like taking a clean plate'. I delight in the reaction that two square inches with a few black marks can produce. Women react faster than men: they frown with concentration, then explode and shower the air with happiness and relief and gratitude. Bus drivers' responses are the most elegant, but older drivers' faces are like a gate opening after thirty years, and I want to cry and comfort them.

January 16

Brian Patten was born on February 7th 1946. His work has been translated into many languages and his collections include Love Poems, Storm Damage, Grinning Jack *and* Armada. *To children he is best known for his humorous verse, with collections such as* Gargling With Jelly, Thawing Frozen Frogs *and* Juggling with Gerbils. *He has also written for the stage and his children's novel* Mr Moon's Last Case *won a special award from The Mystery Writers of America. January 16th was the day of Thomas Hardy's funeral in 1928 – his heart was buried in the village cemetery in Stinsford, Dorset and his ashes in Westminster Abbey. Hardy is one of Brian Patten's favourite poets.*

A cat does not converse with its fleas
a tip from **Brian Patten**

A cat does not converse with its fleas.

This tip should be self-explanatory: don't bother with people who annoy you.

Brian Patten adds: 'A cat does not converse with its fleas' is from a line in a poem of mine and has worked for me in a number of ways. If people irritate or annoy me, or are bores or put me down, I remember it's best not to empower them by engaging in argument with them. In 30 or more years I've never replied to a bad review of my work by trying to defend it, nor sought to win over those who seek to disparage me in day-to-day life. It makes for a much calmer life.

Monica Furlong was born on January 17th 1930. She has worked on a number of newspapers and as a religious programmes producer for the BBC and has written widely on issues to do with religion, as well as writing novels for adults and children. As moderator for the Movement for the Ordination for Women (1982–5) she worked to get women ordained as priests. She has recently completed a study of the Church of England.

Staying in balance
a tip from **Monica Furlong**

How should one use one's energy? There are roughly three divisions in life:

1. work, success, making money

2. caring for oneself in various ways, including having fun

3. caring for other people.

What seems to work best, and stop one getting either completely self-absorbed or so unselfish that one gets resentful, is to make sure that all three are given their proper space.

Monica Furlong adds: The late Huw Wheldon, of BBC fame, once said this to me. At first I disliked it, feeling that there was something too calculating about it, but again and again since, I have thought it was very good advice and have tried to practise it. Each of the three areas mentioned above can give us a lot of pleasure or, if indulged at the expense of the other two, can become a trap, using up all our energy and making us one-sided. Now, because of Huw, I try to notice when that is happening and correct the balance.

January 18

Paul Vallely was born on November 8th 1951. He is an associate editor of the Independent *and has also worked on the* Yorkshire Post, Daily Telegraph, The Times, *the* Sunday Correspondent *and the* Sunday Times. *His books include:* Is That It? *(with Bob Geldof);* Bad Samaritans: First World ethics and Third World debt; Promised Lands: Stories of power and poverty in the Third World; Daniel and the Mischief Boy *and* The New Politics: Catholic social teaching for the 21st century. *He is chair of the Catholic Institute for International Relations. John Hume, who gave Vallely his tip, was born on January 18th 1937.*

Project your desires as realities
a tip from Paul Vallely

Always tell people that what you want to happen already *is* happening. Then you stand a chance it will happen.

Paul Vallely adds: Originally I had intended to offer a different tip, one given to me early in my career by Louis Heron, the erstwhile deputy editor of *The Times*, who took me to lunch at the Garrick and passed on the advice he had been given as a young reporter in Washington by a distinguished American journalist. "When you are interviewing someone always keep this question at the back of your mind: 'Why is this lying bastard lying to me?'" But the date January 18th suggests the more prophetic tip, 'Project your desires as realities', which sums up something once said to me by John Hume, who later went on to win the Nobel Prize for Peace for his work in Northern Ireland. Over the years Hume had repeatedly offered journalists a more optimistic analysis of the situation in Ireland than events warranted. One day I asked him why he repeatedly did this. He replied: "Always tell people that what you want to happen already *is* happening. Then you stand a chance it will happen." It is a great antidote to cynicism.

Bettina von Hase was born on January 24th 1957 and is a media and arts consultant and freelance writer. She is creative consultant to Paul Allen and Dave Stewart's 'Hospital' project and writes for the Daily Telegraph, *the* Telegraph *magazine, the* Spectator, Vogue, *and the FT business magazine. She has been a foreign correspondent for Reuters, a news producer for CBS News, and head of development at the National Gallery. She sits on the advisory council of the German-British Forum. Chinese New Year tends to fall sometime between mid-January and mid-February.*

One billion Chinese know nothing about it
a tip from **Bettina von Hase**

Don't lose your head when you've made a mistake. Even if it's a whopper, remember it can happen to everyone and you can practise your ingenuity by trying to resolve it. It overshadows your plans momentarily, but in the grand scheme of things a mistake is not as catastrophic as you might think. One billion Chinese know nothing about it.

Make the most of your mistakes by learning from them – in my experience they are often more valuable than moments of success.

Bettina von Hase adds: My father made this comment to me when I told him about a mistake I had made at work. I was devastated, but when he said "one billion Chinese know nothing about it", it gave me immediate perspective and made me laugh. Whenever I make a mess of something I think about what he said, and it gets me out of the vortex of worry. Rather than fretting pointlessly, I carry a picture in my mind of bicycling Chinese, which makes me want to take a plane to visit China and eat dumplings. It always helps to resolve the problem.

January 20

Sebastian Coe was born on September 29th 1956. Before retiring from competitive athletics in 1990, he broke 12 world records including the 800 metres (which he held until 1997). He is probably best remembered for winning the Olympic Gold medal for the 1500 metres in Moscow in 1980 and again in Los Angeles in 1984. He now has a successful chain of health clubs within the Jarvis Hotel Group. He became Member of Parliament for Falmouth and Camborne in 1992, and Private Secretary to The Rt Hon William Hague MP, Leader of the Opposition, in 1997. Coe has also written five books including The Olympians (1984).

Make a difference
a tip from **Sebastian Coe,** OBE

"Ask not what your country can do for you,
ask what you can do for your country."

*John F. Kennedy's inaugural address as President
on January 20th 1961*

Sebastian Coe adds: This quote has inspired me many times throughout my life, in sport, business and politics. I cannot begin to describe the emotions and pride I felt when winning Olympic Gold medals for my country. I also felt deeply honoured to have been entrusted with the faith of my constituents when I was elected as a Member of Parliament.

Allen Sheppard, born in 1932 the son of a hard working engine driver and bank clerk, is now a double Knight and a Life Peer. Having graduated from the London School of Economics, he started work at Dagenham as a junior financial analyst with Ford on January 21st 1958. After 20 years in the motor industry, he joined Grand Metropolitan and became its chairman and group chief executive. A great believer in helping people to help themselves, he has been chairman of the Prince's Trust, Business in the Community and London First.

January 21

Never ask anybody to do anything you would not do yourself
a tip from Lord Sheppard of Didgemere

Never ask anybody to do anything you would not do yourself. Leading by example is the only way to achieve success. If one is unwilling to do something oneself then one should not ask someone else to do it.

Allen Sheppard adds: Unfortunately I was once voted 'the toughest manager in Britain' in a Sunday Times poll in the City. This, together with my once having jokingly described my management style as "a light grip on the throat", has given me the reputation of being a hard boss. However, anybody who works with me knows that whilst I expect people to work hard, to take sensible commercial risks and to enjoy what they do, I never demand from anyone more than I demand from myself.

January 22

Andrew Collins was born on March 4th 1965. He is a freelance writer, journalist and broadcaster who writes mostly about entertainment for the Observer, Q, Empire, Radio Times and GQ. He is the author of Still Suitable for Miners, the official biography of Billy Bragg, appears regularly on Radio 4's Front Row, moonlights as a scriptwriter for TV soap operas and works often with the BBC. January 22nd is the birthday of his wife, Julie Quirke.

Get dirty
a tip from Andrew Collins

Get dirty, especially when young. Scrub around in the dirt and walk in streams. Pick things up, regardless of where they've been. Scuff your shoes, muddy your knees, lick your hands clean. Don't be afraid of muck. Childhood is a time for being grubby and unclean – there'll be plenty of time for hygiene later!

Andrew Collins adds: This is scientific advice. A study by the Institute of Child Health at Bristol University found that children who bathe every day and wash their hands more than five times are 25% more likely to develop asthma than their dirtier peers. Dirt equals infection, infection when young equals a hardy immune system. No one actually gave me this advice as a child, but I adhered to it anyway, as all normal kids do. As a health-conscious adult and firm believer in holistic medicine, I now thank my parents for letting me roam and for not over-washing me. (I still developed asthma.)

Francis Gilbert was born on February 2nd 1968. He grew up in Cambridge, London and Northumberland and attended Sussex University and the University of East Anglia. On January 23rd 1993, he married Erica Wagner, who is currently the literary editor of The Times. *Originally trained as a teacher, he now combines teaching part-time with writing journalism and fiction. He is a great admirer of the Stoic philosophers.*

Always obey your wife
a tip from Francis Gilbert

Generally women know best. Men should follow their instructions. They shouldn't do this blindly – there should be plenty of discussion involved, arguments possibly – but in the end they should accede to their wife's wishes. Women are much less aggressive and impulsive than men and know when to make decisions for them and when to let them have the final say.

Francis Gilbert adds: This secret of a good marriage is probably one most men would hate to hear but, unfortunately, I think it's an excellent piece of advice. All the happily married men I have spoken to may protest in front of their beer-swilling mates that this tip is a load of old rubbish, but get them alone and they'll agree with you in whispered, slightly abashed tones.

I've been married to Erica since 1992 and she's known what's been best for me from the very start. She even knew that I would be far happier married than not – she proposed to me and wouldn't take no for an answer. But please don't think that I'm horribly henpecked: I have a lot of freedom – within certain parameters.

January 24

Jon Briggs was born on January 24th 1965, the very day that Winston Churchill died ("if only I had his powers of oratory"). Jon is one of the best known voice-over artists in the UK. Formerly, he was a BBC radio news anchor, presenting the breakfast show for Radio 5 for two years, and working on numerous programmes for Radio 4 and Radio 2. He is now managing director of the voice-over agency, The Excellent Voice Company, and is in international demand as a conference host and speaker.

Five hard lessons in life
tips from Jon Briggs

The hardest things in life are very simple:

Always take responsibility for yourself. I spent my twenties trying to avoid taking the blame. The moment I passed 30, I suddenly learnt to put my hand up and accept that I'd made the blunder. You'd be amazed how much simpler life is, and how much more respect you earn from others, if you take the rap (only when it's your fault of course!).

Always read the manual. I have destroyed too many of my many gadgets by thinking I knew what made them work.

Treat yourself. There's nothing wrong with being selfish. If you continually give to others and don't recharge yourself, then eventually you'll have nothing to give.

Always let the people in your life know how you feel about them. The greatest emotional need any person has is to be appreciated. Make sure that if you never saw that person again, they would always know exactly how important they were to you.

If you want it enough, you'll get it. Get out there and do whatever it is that you want to do. You can do it, but don't be afraid of hard work.

Jon Briggs adds: Finally, a tip that's not original, but true – as I've found out for myself only by getting it wrong. If you feel that all you do in your life is juggle things, take a note of the balls you're juggling with. As you keep your work, health, family, friends and spirit in the air, remember that work is a rubber ball and will bounce back if you drop it. All the rest are made from glass; drop one of them and it will be irrevocably scuffed, tarnished, or even smashed.

John Maurice Lindsay was born in Glasgow on July 21st 1918. He was first trained as a musician. The wrist injury that forced him to abandon a career in music also led to his becoming a staff officer in the War Office. Music critic of the Bulletin, *a Glasgow newspaper now defunct, for 14 years, and a regular BBC broadcaster from 1945 to 1961 on the arts and current affairs in Scotland, he became the first programme controller of the ITV station Border Television in 1961, first director of the Scottish Civic Trust in 1967 and honorary secretary-general of Europa Nostra from 1983 to 1990. He is a past president of the Association of Scottish Literary Studies. His books include* Collected Poems 1940-1990, The Burns Encyclopaedia, History of Scottish Literature *and, with his wife Joyce,* The Theatre and Opera Lovers Quotation Book. *Scotland's national poet, Robert Burns, was born on January 25th in 1759 and so this is traditionally Burns Night.*

Keep at it
a tip from Dr Maurice Lindsay, CBE

For some years during summer holidays, my father made me learn by heart a poem a day. What then seemed an imposition is, however, something for which I have latterly always been truly grateful. He stressed Shakespeare's line "Perseverance, dear my lord, keeps honour bright" (pronounced 'persévérance', with the accent on the second syllable, in Shakespeare's day and meaning 'keep at it').

In later life, forgetting the hero part – I don't believe in heroes and hero-worship – I have adopted Burns' favourite quotation:

"What makes the hero truly great
Is never, never to despair."

Maurice Lindsay adds: My life's motto – 'never, never to despair' – has not always been easy to live up to, but it encapsulates the Shakespeare line my father stressed.

January 26

Iona Opie was born on October 13th 1923. With her late husband Peter Opie she wrote many books about children's lore and literature, including The Oxford Dictionary of Nursery Rhymes *(1951, 2nd edition 1997) and* The Lore and Language of Schoolchildren *(first published 1959). Iona Opie's mother, Olive Chapman Cant, was born on January 26th 1892.*

Do a little every day
a tip from Iona Opie

"Do a little every day" was my mother's dictum for getting through a daunting task. It sounds boring, but my goodness it works like magic. There is never time in a day for a long job, but there is always time for a small one. It is easier to start if you have promised yourself you need only do a little.

Once you have picked up pencil and paper, or thrown away the first armful of cagmag from the garage, you have done the most difficult thing, and you think to yourself, "I might do a little more".

The 'every day' part establishes a habit; it creates a rhythm. It is important, though, not to think about finishing the job, but simply to believe that one day it will be finished.

Iona Opie adds: In this way, I have done various heroic-sounding tasks: clearing ground elder from a large area of the garden; digging a hole for a goose pond; cataloguing, with a friend, the bankrupt stock from a glass shop.

Alison Willcocks was born on July 22nd 1952. She is Head of Bedales, a co-educational public school in Hampshire famous for its progressive approach to educating teenagers. She has been a senior inspector of independent schools, chairman of HMC's Co-educational Group and a member of the National Standards for Boarding working party. She writes and lectures regularly on a variety of educational themes. She is married to a teacher and has two children and four stepchildren. Her first child was born on January 27th in 1980.

If you love something, set it free
a tip from **Alison Willcocks**

If you love something, set it free. If it comes back to you, it's yours. If it doesn't, it never was. We do not possess anything in this world, least of all other people. We only imagine that we do. Our friends, our lovers, our spouses, even our children are not ours; they belong only to themselves. Possessive and controlling friendships and relationships can be as harmful as neglect.

Alison Willcocks adds: This ancient Chinese proverb articulates a powerful truth about the importance of letting go. It had a profound effect on me when I first heard it, and it has guided me in both my private and professional life ever since. I have often quoted it as an excellent model for parenthood, which is a gradual, wonderful – and sometimes painful – process of letting go. It begins with the cutting of the umbilical cord and ends when you hand over the keys of your car. They will fly the nest, but if you freely and willingly let them go, then they will always come back.

January 28

Tim Heald was born on January 28th 1944. He is the author of more than 30 books ranging from the Simon Bognor series of crime novels to an acclaimed biography of Prince Philip. His journalism has appeared in newspapers and magazines around the world. He has been International Co-ordinator of the Writers in Prison Committee of PEN International, a guest speaker on the QE2 and a visiting fellow at the University of Tasmania.

Don't let the bastards get you down
a tip from Tim Heald

Don't let the bastards get you down. When things are going particularly badly, put on your best suit and overcoat; buy the biggest cigar you can find and walk up and down Piccadilly smoking it.

Tim Heald adds: This advice was given to me in the autumn of 1965 by Randolph Churchill, who often took it himself. It was mildly anachronistic even then, but the idea is sound. Never give your enemies the satisfaction of thinking that you have been defeated. Broadcast your defiance in the most public place possible. The cigar is optional but conveys an agreeable whiff of political incorrectness.

John Junkin was born on January 29th 1930. He was a schoolteacher who entered showbusiness at the age of 25. He has since been an actor with over 1,000 TV appearances; the writer or co-writer of roughly 1,500 TV and radio shows; and a speaker and lyricist. He currently contributes a column on 'things' to his county newspaper.

Take care of the children
a tip from John Junkin

Take care of the children – they're the only future anybody has.

John Junkin adds: I have always tried to behave and talk to my daughter as if she were a small adult. Now she is in her twenties, it may or may not help to turn her into a world beater, but it has helped make her an amiable, interesting human being with a humorous and inquiring mind. We do get along very well. I think if most parents could say the same, figures for juvenile crime would take a quite dramatic dive.

January 30

Claudia Egypt was born in Rome on April 19th 1950. She was raised in England, suffered in India and returned to be a global theatre practitioner. She is artistic director of the Buckminster Fuller Theatre in Bath. She also directs shows here and there, including the legendary WARP by Neil Oram, which was first performed, in a full-length version, on this day in 1979.

Be sure you have room for elephants
a tip from Claudia Egypt

Don't forget, if you make friends with an elephant trainer, be sure you have room for elephants in your home.

Claudia Egypt adds: This piece of advice I originally heard in Nepal where presumably it would be taken literally. I mention it to friends when they are about to launch with enthusiasm into new relationships or projects. I had a lover who was a keen motorcyclist; I ended up with dismembered bikes in my bedroom.

John Horder was born in Brighton in 1936. When a 14-year-old schoolboy at St Paul's School, he was the star of Junior Wranglers on BBC TV. He is now a hugging poet, performer, storyteller and freelancer for the Guardian *and the* Independent *newspapers. His most cherished experiences include the performances of his plays* Cakes and Carrots *and* The African Who Loved Hugging Everybody *and of his reinvention of* Rumpelstiltskin, *praised by Michael Palin and Meher Baba. He hopes to co-edit a book celebrating the centenary of Stevie Smith's birth in 2002. January 31st is the day, in 1969, when the 'hugging genius' Meher Baba died. He was famous for his words "Be happy. Don't worry" and for later remaining silent for 44 years.*

Lifelines
tips from John Horder

Lifelines that work for me: leaping and hugging friends and companions; walking across London's Hampstead Heath and Regent's Park; learning to love, honour, cherish and respect my own and other people's authentic stories; and, perhaps the most invaluable of the lot, writing what Julia Cameron in *The Artist's Way* calls 'morning pages'.

John Horder adds: Even if I feel depressed as hell – and I experience deep depression at life's chaos, pain and unpredictability – I still write my morning pages. This is a triumph for my authentic self and a lifeline I wouldn't be without.

February 1

Dan Cohn-Sherbok was born in Denver, Colorado on February 1st 1945. He was ordained a Reform rabbi in the United States and has served congregations on four continents. He is currently Professor of Judaism at the University of Wales at Lampeter and is the author and editor of over 50 books, including On Earth as it is in Heaven (1987), Atlas of Jewish History (1993) and Fifty Key Jewish Thinkers (1996).

Get a cat
a tip from Rabbi Dan Cohn-Sherbok

If you want to understand people, get a cat. Our cat Herod is totally selfish. He never thinks of anyone but himself. He wakes us up in the middle of the night when he's hungry. He won't eat catfood unless it's his favourite brand. He steals smoked salmon. He hates other cats. He thinks dogs are vulgar. He sleeps on my favourite chair. And he loves killing birds and mice for fun.

Underneath the surface, most people are just like Herod. But unlike our cat, they disguise their selfishness and nastiness, pretending that they're acting out of altruistic motives. Don't be fooled by such behaviour. Human beings are greedy, self-centred and cruel. If you want to know what people are really like, make a study of cat behaviour.

Dan Cohn-Sherbok adds: When I was preparing to become a rabbi, I continually read in Scripture and rabbinic sources that human beings are essentially good. I believed this and could not understand why I always seemed to have such difficulties with friends and acquaintances. But after I got married, my wife's ginger cat, Herod's predecessor, disabused me of all illusions. I realised that he acted in the way all human beings would like to behave. He didn't care about anyone else's needs or comfort. He was the centre of his own universe.

For example, every morning at about four he bit my feet, woke me up, and demanded to be fed. Half asleep I stumbled to the kitchen, opened the refrigerator and took out his smelly catfood. I then stumbled back to bed. When he finished eating, he hopped on to my side of the bed and slept at my feet so I had to curl up in a cramped position. Nobody will tell you the truth about how bad human beings really are. But if you want to know, live with a cat.

David Shepherd, OBE, FRSA, was born on April 25th 1931. He is known internationally as a wildlife artist and conservationist. His first one man exhibition in London in 1962 was a sell out and an exhibition in October 1999 sold out in the first two days. The David Shepherd Conservation Foundation has raised nearly £3 million for wildlife conservation since Shepherd set it up in 1984. His books include the autobiography The Man Who Loves Giants *(1975) and* David Shepherd – Only One World *(1995). He married Avril Shirley on February 2nd in 1957; they have four daughters.*

Don't leave success to luck
a tip from David Shepherd

Don't leave success to luck – use every hour that God gives you and never give up. Success is a mix of hard work and seizing every opportunity that comes your way.

David Shepherd adds: As a wildlife artist, my early life was a disaster, having been thrown out of art college as being untrainable, and it was entirely through luck that I met the man who trained me, to whom I owe all my success. He then taught me to use every hour that God gave me to work ever harder and never give up. So it wasn't just luck; I wouldn't have succeeded without taking his advice to heart and applying it to my working life.

February 3

Virginia Ironside was born on February 3rd 1944. She's been a journalist and agony aunt for 25 years and now has weekly columns in the Daily Mail, Independent *and* Sunday Mirror. *She has written several novels and also books on her special interest, bereavement.*

"This too will pass" and name-taking
tips from Virginia Ironside

1. Always say, whatever the situation you are in, whether good or bad: "This too will pass". The thought behind the statement encourages you to live in the moment.

2. Never speak to anyone on the phone without taking their name and extension number.

Virginia Ironside adds re Tip 1: I've found this very useful when I've been severely and clinically depressed, which has been frequently throughout my life. Although it seems, when one is very low, that the blackness is total reality, this phrase casts healthy doubt on what seems like a hopeless situation. Similarly if you say it when you feel good, it makes the present more alive and makes you enjoy it more.

Re Tip 2: Once you get someone's name, you have a personal relationship with them and they have to take responsibility for what they say or promise. This simple rule means that the time I spend dealing with the gas boards, phone companies or anyone in a service industry is halved.

Peter Jay was born on February 7th 1937. A former ambassador to the US (1977–79), chairman to the National Council for Voluntary Organisations (1981–86), presenter of A Week in Politics *(1983–86) and chief of staff to Robert Maxwell (1986–89), he is currently economics editor for the BBC. Jay says: "February 4th is the date my last child was born and I became a father for the seventh time."*

A patent remedy for jet lag
a tip from The Hon. Peter Jay

Jet lag can infallibly be avoided by following these simple rules:

1. Go West by day.

2. Don't go East.

3. If you must, go East by night.

4. Set your watch to the arrival time before take off.

5. 'Think' arrival time (never think what the time is where you came from).

6. On arrival behave as if you had been there all along, go to work, a party or whatever.

This way tiredness and 'body-time' cancel out.

Peter Jay adds: This has worked on more than 100 transatlantic trips and several trips around the world.

February 5

Russell Grant was born in Middlesex on February 5th 1951. He sprang to fame in 1978 when proclaimed as the British Astrologer Royal after presenting the Queen Mother with her astrological chart – the first time royalty had openly accepted astrology for 400 years. He is an expert on the geography and history of British places and local government. His favourite bestselling book was not astrological but The Real Counties of Britain *which became the basis for his television series* Russell Grant's Postcards.

Always be yourself
a tip from Russell Grant

Be true to yourself, but live and let live.

Whatever you do in life, be yourself so long as you don't hurt anyone else whilst doing so. But do not judge others by your standards, criteria or philosophy.

Russell Grant adds: I have spent most of my life wanting to please and gain approval from other people. Recently I realised that by doing so you can make yourself deeply unhappy, whilst not necessarily pleasing or gaining the approval of the people you set out to win over in the first place.

Dermot Bolger was born on February 6th 1959. He is an Irish novelist, poet, playwright and publisher, whose chief works include the books The Journey Home, A Second Life *and* Father's Music *and the play* The Lament for Arthur Cleary, *for which he has received many awards, including* The Samuel Beckett Prize. *He is editor of* The Picador Book of Contemporary Irish Fiction.

Leave every party a half hour earlier
a tip from Dermot Bolger

Close this book for a second. Then close your eyes and take a deep breath.

Think of all the fights you would not have got into, all the bores you would not have met, all the insults you would have not inadvertently thrown, all the mornings you would not have found yourself waking up with a hangover – naked except for one red sock, alone and lying on the floor of a strange flat in a country you never even knew existed – if you had simply left that party half an hour earlier.

Dermot Bolger adds: As a writer – and in the interest of professional research – I have always pondered this advice, but have steadfastly refused to take it.

February 7

Kevin Crossley-Holland was born on February 7th 1941. He is a poet, a Carnegie Medal-winning writer for children, a translator from Anglo-Saxon, a broadcaster and an elected fellow of the Royal Society of Literature. Home from teaching in Minnesota, where he held the Endowed Chair in the Humanities at the University of St Thomas, he now lives in north Norfolk and has two adult sons and two teenage daughters.

Don't say "Umm ..."
a tip from Kevin Crossley-Holland

When you say something, speak clearly, simply and without hesitation. Above all, never begin by saying "Umm ..." (or "Er ..." or "Erm ...").

Kevin Crossley-Holland adds: Sunday lunch with my grandparents: very long and very boring. I was eight and extremely impatient to say something, but I had to wait until my grandfather had delivered himself of some weighty opinion. When at last it was my turn, I began "Umm ... grandpa ..." Fatal!

My grandfather waved his cheese knife, and at once lectured me on the importance of saying what you have to say without humming or hawing. "Speak simply and clearly," he said, "and people will listen to you and have confidence in you. Are you listening?"

"Yes, grandpa."

My grandfather waved his cheese knife in the direction of my bemused five-year-old sister. "And that goes for you too!" he said. Thereupon, he cut himself another chunk of cheddar.

My grandfather's advice to an eager eight-year-old has become part of family legend. He was absolutely right, of course, and I'm surprised how many times I've thought of his words during conversations, lectures and broadcasts. Clean words are the children of a clear head; and no less important, I think, warm words are the children of imagination and empathy.

*Titus Alexander was born on February 8th 1952. He is a freelance community educator who coined the term 'family learning', founded the Self Esteem Network (now part of Antidote), wrote a book about world politics (*Unravelling Global Apartheid, *Polity Press), drafted the Charter for Global Governance and started Inspiring Change, an education process for change agents.*

February 8

Cut your debt
a tip from Titus Alexander

Debt enslaves you to banks and lenders. Always pay off your credit card monthly. (If you can't avoid debt, find the lowest-rate personal loan or borrow from relatives.) Pay your mortgage off as fast as possible. (If you pay £250 fortnightly instead of £500 monthly you may save thousands of pounds.) Shorten the term to ten years or less and increase what you pay now to save even more. Use spare cash or windfalls to pay off lump sums. Get a lodger if possible. Freedom day is when you really own your own home.

Titus Alexander adds: I have rarely had a steady income and got my first mortgage in my late thirties. I was able to rent out rooms, but the mortgage still seemed like a life sentence (*mort-gage* means a commitment until death). Then a friend gave me this tip and I couldn't believe how fast the amount I owed the bank came down when I shortened the term. A small redundancy payment gave me a lump sum to start the ball rolling. Debt payments to the bank are a form of slavery which force us to work harder and longer than necessary – read Michael Robotham's *The Grip of Death* (Carpenter Books, tel. 01608 811969 for a copy). Ending debt slavery is part of liberation.

February 9

Kevin Warwick was born on February 9th 1954. He is Professor of Cybernetics at the University of Reading. His main research interest is to discover what intelligence is all about in both humans and machines. His book In the Mind of the Machine *points to a dystopian future in which machines will be more intelligent than humans. He appears in the* Guinness Book of Records *for a robot learning experiment across the Internet. In 1998 he shocked the world when he had a silicon chip transponder surgically implanted into his arm. The chip caused lights to come on and doors to open automatically in his departmental building. His latest book* QI *defines intelligence in terms of an intelligence hypersphere.*

We know virtually nothing
a tip from Professor Kevin Warwick

Humans have always tried to understand how the world and all things in it, including other humans, function. At any point in time we tend to think we know everything and are exactly right. Yet only a handful of years later we realise just how wrong we were and laugh at our previous stupidity. Our present understanding will, in truth, in one thousand years be seen as very primitive, full of religious bias and hocus pocus and certainly very unscientific. So:

• Never completely believe established physical rules, particularly when they contravene what you yourself witness.

• Never believe that just because something has always been done in a particular way, that it has to be the right way.

• Never regard a feat as not possible.

• Every day attempt to be the first person to travel faster than the speed of light, or some slightly lesser feat, in order that you can upset the established view.

Kevin Warwick adds: I hated Physics during my school days, simply because I would not accept some of the rubbish I was being taught. For example, I was told that the earth travels round the sun, and not vice versa. What rubbish! We can all see that the sun travels round the earth, and hence both views are acceptable. I was also told that we cannot travel faster than the speed of light due to Einstein's Theory of Relativity. No theory ever stopped us doing anything.

Since then I have obtained a PhD and two DSc's. In my position as Professor of Cybernetics, I am able to explore a range of scientific and technical frontiers, yet I am still told how things are, often with no physical basis at all, but simply because the view is politically acceptable or provides a conclusion people want to hear. Now I can treat such comments with a pinch of salt and get on with discovering the world on my own terms.

Jane Butterworth was born on February 10th 1948. She is the agony aunt of the News of the World *and also writes health books. She has in the past worked as a health editor and writer for women's magazines and been the author of various teenage novels and handbooks. She lives with her husband, Brian, in rural Herefordshire and is working on her first adult novel.*

Make peace before sleeping
a tip from **Jane Butterworth**

If you've been rowing with your partner, be sure to make peace before going to sleep for the night. If you don't, you're likely to wake up feeling even more angry and resentful and to carry on the quarrel for the foreseeable future. Making up not only clears the air, it gives you the perfect opportunity to get closer by making love.

Jane Butterworth adds: This is something I learnt from my husband, although it is hardly original. I'm a natural sulker, whereas my husband has the sort of sunny disposition which prevents him from staying angry for long, no matter how immense the provocation. He made me realise that keeping a quarrel going overnight was the surest way of undermining our relationship and that sulking is utterly futile.

February 11

Vanessa Branson was born in 1959. After running a pioneering gallery in Portobello she now co-runs The Wonderful Fund, purchasing a contemporary art collection of dazzling genius. A mother of four, she prides herself on being a "champion of creativity". She says: "Nelson Mandela is top of my list of most admired, and 'truth and reconciliation' is a mantra of mine. The understanding that to seek justice is only going to continue conflict helped me enormously during the break up of my marriage. The thought that a man could be released from 27 years in prison with dignity and no bitterness made the task of an elegant emergence from divorce seem a doddle — well, maybe not a doddle but at least possible." Shortly after his release from prison on February 11th 1990, Nelson Mandela agreed to the suspension of armed struggle.

People are the size they make you feel
a tip from Vanessa Branson

People are the size they make you feel.

This is a good pointer to enhance confidence on first meeting people.

Vanessa Branson adds: When I was a trainee picture framer I hated asking the girls behind the front desks at the smart auction houses the way to relevant departments. They made me feel so lowly in my stained work clothes. A wise friend pointed out that they were only uneducated debutantes in search of socially acceptable husbands. From then on I realised that great people make you feel great, and those who make you feel small have something pretty small to hide.

D. E. Harding was born in Lowestoft, Suffolk, on February 12th 1909. Though he earned his living as an architect in private practice, his real work has been the inventing of experiments which conduct us from the conventional and often depressing fictions of our life to the scientifically verifiable and often delightful and reassuring facts. The neo-mystical Shollond Trust (www.headless.org) is the registered charity which exists to spread and develop his work. The last 50 years of his life have been devoted to practising these experiments, sharing them in workshops around the world, and writing articles and books about them. The best known of these books is On Having No Head, Zen and the Rediscovery of the Obvious *(Penguin). And the most comprehensive is* The Hierarchy of Heaven and Earth – A new diagram of man in the universe, *which C. S. Lewis described as "a work of the highest genius".*

Notice what you see
a tip from Douglas Harding

When we dare to doubt what we are told and take a fresh look at what's going on, we are in for lots of pleasant and fascinating and useful surprises. A new and more satisfying way of life begins to open up, just by *noticing* what we see.

For instance: If you find your travel in the rush hour to and from work tiring or boring, just notice that it's the scenery that's doing all the rushing about while you take a nice rest. If you find your eyes getting tired and tensions developing in that region, just notice that you are looking out of one huge and relaxed Eye, and not out of a pair of tiny screwed-up peepholes in a box. If you feel ill at ease with some people, shy or often too self-conscious, just notice that what you are looking out of is not a face but a huge and tranquil Space for taking in those faces. If you are scared of spiders, or the possibility of cancer, or of death, just notice that this Awake Space that you really are at centre is quite safe in all emergencies ... This is a small sample of the welcome surprises that are there for the noticing.

Douglas Harding adds: As a young man, my curse was morbid self-consciousness, with all its embarrassments and anxieties. I was cured by refusing to 'see' what I was told to see, and looking at myself for myself. And I went on to find, over the years, that the same medicine cleared up all the other big problems of my existence. Truly, I can't imagine a happier way of life – and you are warmly invited to participate.

February 13

Clive Barker was born in Middlesbrough on June 29th 1931. Throughout his career he has interwoven work in the professional theatre with university lecturing. His work on actor training, which has taken him to many parts of the world, is published in Theatre Games *(Methuen 1977). He is joint editor of* New Theatre Quarterly *and chair of the International Workshop Festival, which mounts master classes for professional actors. On this day in 1954, he realised that, "If I didn't take the risk and leave home, I would be trapped in soul-destroying routine for the rest of my life. I decided to leave."*

The world needs changing, change it!
a tip from Clive Barker

Most people are born into a world where they are expected to make as little fuss as possible and to wait for their 'leaders' to tell them what to think and what to do. At the end of this they are expected to wait patiently for the time to be peacefully cremated, which saves on the space taken up by memorials and leaves no trace of humanity of any sort. Reject this expectation totally.

Clive Barker adds: My father could always give 16 good reasons for not doing what you had planned. I should give up all my airy notions and get a good job, and settle down. Since the figures for male unemployment on a housing estate in Middlesbrough at one point reached 98.4%, this could be counted as the worst advice a father ever gave his son. Luckily, I rejected it. I haven't led a revolution, but at least when I go, I will have the satisfaction of having left some mark upon the world which will take time to scrub out.

Gwyneth Jones was born on February 14th 1952. An award-winning writer of science fiction and fantasy (her books include White Queen and North Wind), she has been a children's cartoon scriptwriter, has featured occasionally in radio and TV programmes about science fiction ("they're short of females for that sort of thing") and in the past was an avid long-haul rough traveller.

Stick with Plan A
a tip from Gwyneth Jones

When you've decided on a course of action, stick with it as long as humanly possible, or until you have got from A to B. Once you let yourself be ruled by secondary decisions, chaos will ensue.

This is a conclusion reached the hard way, in the course of rough travelling situations – where taking a likely looking short cut or alternative means of travel has led to unholy complications and hateful consequences. Remember, Plan A was the one you spent time, in tranquillity, working out. Plans B to Z are creatures of the moment.

Gwyneth Jones adds: In the course of several years of doing unlikely things in faraway places, long ago when the world was young, my travelling companion and I frequently exhorted each other to 'stick with Plan A'. And we lived. Since settling down in Brighton, I have applied this rule to my writing. Once I've embarked on a story, I go on until I've reached the end, and *then* I rethink the entire project, change the sex of the principal character, have the lovers kill themselves in a passion of nihilism instead of living long and happy lives – or whatever – if it still seems like a good idea. Frequently it doesn't.

February 15

Lady Cooksey was born on February 15th 1940. She dominated British women's fencing in Great Britain for over a decade, representing her country at the Olympics in 1964, 1968 and 1972. She is a picture restorer and art historian with wide and varied interests, and more recently has become a formidable fundraiser, leading both local and national appeals.

Stay alive
tips from Lady Cooksey

Stay alive. You can't achieve anything if you're dead.

"Do what you want to do first, and do what you ought to do after, if there's time" (from Pameli Benham).

Lady Cooksey adds: Every now and then, someone says something to you, at a moment that you are ready to hear it, which fundamentally changes how you behave.

Dorothy Schwarz was born on May 15th 1937. She is a writer and teaches Creative Writing in Colchester. In 1956 she married Walter Schwarz, a journalist, with whom she has recently written Living Lightly – Travels in Post Consumer Society. Her grandmother, Sarah Kramer, lived long enough to see Dorothy and Walter's first two daughters and elder son. Sarah Kramer died on February 16th in 1972, at the age of 93.

Do you *need* to go on holiday?
a tip from Dorothy Schwarz

My grandma used to say: "Why do you all need to go on holidays all the time? Don't you have houses?"

She was born in Whitechapel in 1878, the daughter of Romanian immigrants fleeing some pogrom or other. She never said which one. She lived for the last 25 years of her life in Golders Green, in a house bought for her by my businessman father. An unmarried son and a married childless son lived under her sway. She was firmly against globalisation before that word had any common currency. She couldn't see why you had to buy something you could make yourself. Nor did she see the use of throwing away a torn sheet when you could cut it in half and sew the two edges together. She spent her spare time, when she wasn't cleaning or cooking vast meals for any of the other six children and grandchildren who visited on holy days and holidays, sitting on a high stool by the front door (open in summer and closed in winter) reading the Talmud with a magnifying glass. For her, only the family and food had much reality. Amusement, entertainment and travel she thought a great waste of money. Money was a commodity to be saved in case of crisis and food was the way you stayed alive and expressed love.

Dorothy Schwarz adds: Grandma never truly bought into the consumer culture and her influence affects some of her descendents. For example, I can't bear to throw something away that still has some use in it.

I haven't always followed her example, having travelled for 25 of my 60-odd years, but I still retain a sense that stillness resides within you. It cannot be found through rushing about.

February 17

Maurice Pope was born on February 17th 1926 in London. He went to South Africa in 1948 where he eventually became professor of Classics and dean of the Faculty of Arts at the University of Cape Town. When the government imposed apartheid on the university in 1968 he resigned his chair and came to Oxford where he has lived ever since, writing articles and books – mainly on classical subjects, but most recently an update of his Story of Decipherment *with a chapter on the Maya glyphs (Thames and Hudson, 1999) and a book for parents,* The Non-Stop Reader *(Non-Stop Books 1997), on how to teach their children to read.*

Whom would you most wish to become like?
a tip from **Maurice Pope**

Tinker, tailor, soldier, sailor,
High court judge or county jailer?
Doctor? Dentist? Engineer?
What, oh what's, the right career?

What sensible advice is there? Only this. If you know what you want to do, do it. If you don't, look at older people in different walks of life. Whom do you have most in common with? Whom would you most wish to be or to become like? Theirs is the life most likely to suit you, the one you are likely to be happiest in and best at.

Maurice Pope adds: I remember being asked by a college porter at Cambridge when I was being called up into the navy whether I intended staying there when the war was over. "What?" I replied (arrogantly as I now realise) "And finish up as an admiral? Never!" So I must already then have been thinking along the lines of my tip. But it was reinforced later, at second hand, by a pupil of mine in Cape Town who had been to see an industrial psychologist and who told me that this same approach was the basis of the technique he had used. I have since given the advice to my own children, who have all acknowledged it to be good advice – even though it came from their father.

Prue Leith was born on February 18th 1940. She has variously been cookery editor, restaurateur, businesswoman, director of companies as varied as British Rail and Whitbread plc, novelist and chairman of the Royal Society of Arts.

Doggedness
a tip from Prue Leith, OBE

Starting things is easy – a business; a novel; a war; a baby. Keeping them going is a lot harder. I have a feeling doggedness is quite as important as imagination.

Prue Leith adds: Running a restaurant business is more a case of checking the loos are clean and the VAT forms are done rather than creating lovely dishes. I was boringly dogged about standards, which could help account for the restaurant still going strong after 30 years. On the other hand, I lost interest in the thankless task of catering for the public in Hyde Park, and that business failed.

February 19

Guy Dauncey was born on February 19th 1948. Guy is an author, thinker, futurist, activist and sustainable communities consultant. He lives in Victoria, British Columbia, Canada, where he works on ecovillage development, global solutions to climate change, building local community self-reliance, and whatever else seems important. He was co-founder of the Victoria Car Share Co-operative, and is author of After the Crash: The Emergence of the Rainbow Economy *(Greenprint, 1988) and other titles. You will find details of his work on his web home page: www.earthfuture.bc.ca*

Re-membering
a tip from Guy Dauncey

If you are struggling with something, be it a confusion, a difficult decision or just a generally tough time, don't forget to ask the larger universe for help. For some this 'larger universe' is God. For others it may be the Earth, the Ocean, or Nature.

By doing this, even if your request goes out in the most basic form ("Dear ★★★★, please help me"), you re-establish a connection to the greater whole that surrounds us, of which we are part – and things will begin to happen.

I like to think of this (and every kind of prayer) as 're-membering' – re-connecting the membrane that links us to the greater spiritual and cosmic whole of which we are part, the universe from which both our bodies and our spirits were born, and to which we shall always belong. It is only our forgetfulness that makes us think that we have to solve our problems on our own.

Guy Dauncey adds: During the 1980s, I was living in south Devon, on the edge of Dartmoor. I was writing a book at the time, and struggling with a deadline that my publisher had given me, not knowing how to deal with it. Instead of seeing clearly, I was getting caught up in a morass of self-judgement, and what felt like impossible choices – none of which helped me to complete the book.

Then one night (it was summer and warm) I decided to ask for help. I packed a blanket and a sleeping bag, drove onto Dartmoor, and walked out to one of my favourite look-out points. I was willing to stay the whole night, if need be. As the sun went down, I arranged my blanket, arranged myself, and then formally sent out a request for help and for clarity. I made my request to the sun, to the earth, to the air, and then to the distant sea and the water, speaking my words out loud to each in turn, asking for their help.

About an hour later, I packed my blanket and went home, having decided I didn't need to stay all night. About five days later, I mentioned my dilemma to a friend in a casual conversation, and he said "Why don't you just phone your editor and ask for three months' more time?". At that moment, I felt a shiver go down my spine, and I knew that this was my answer. In retrospect, it seems so small, but at that point in time, it was everything. I called, got the extra months and finished the book on time. Everything had slotted itself back into order.

Aideen McGinley was born on May 31st 1954 and was formerly chief executive of Fermanagh District Council. She is now permanent secretary of the Department of Culture, Arts and Leisure in the new Northern Ireland administration. She has been involved in a whole range of community and voluntary and statutory organisations both regionally and at UK level. Her tip is taken from George Bernard Shaw's play Back to Methuselah, *which was in the middle of its first London run at the Court Theatre on February 20th 1924.*

Why not dream?
a tip from Aideen McGinley

"You see things and you say, Why? But I dream things that never were and I say, Why not?"

George Bernard Shaw

Aideen McGinley adds: This quotation sums up my ethos in life. Maybe I am the eternal optimist, but I feel that you can look beyond what you see to a new and better horizon. So go ahead and dream and you never know what you may be capable of achieving.

An example from my working life is The Higher Bridges Project: a £5 million capital project symbolic of the vision of peace for Northern Ireland. It is creating an interactive technology centre on an old Orange Hall site which links across the River Erne to the Enniskillen bomb site. It will be a living memorial to the 12 people who died there in 1987 – a focal point in the community to raise their sights and to encourage them to strive for a better future for themselves and for those that they love. Adversity made us determined – the Millennium Commission turned down our project in 1996 because they said the site was not significant enough – but we applied the *Why not?* principle and have since convinced 18 other funders of our dream.

February 21

Jilly Cooper was born on February 21st 1937. She is a writer and newspaper columnist who has written for the Sunday Times *(1969–82) and the* Mail on Sunday *(1982–87). She has had over 36 books published including* Class, Riders, Rivals, Polo *and* Appassionata *(1996).*

Never miss an opportunity for kindness
a tip from Jilly Cooper

"I expect to pass through this world but once; any good thing therefore that I can do, or any kindness that I can show to any fellow-creature, let me do it now; let me not defer or neglect it, for I shall not pass this way again."

Attributed to Stephen Grellet (1773–1855)

Jilly Cooper adds: This is the only quotation I really mind about, and I have given it to many people. I think it's wonderful.

Tina Knight has won various awards and accolades for her success as an entrepreneur including the 1988 Women in Business award, one of the Top Entrepreneurs of the World in 1998 and UK Business Pioneer at the Global Summit of Women in London, 1998. She is also a regular contributor to business and current affairs programmes on radio and TV and is widely quoted in the national consumer and trade press. In addition to running her computer networking equipment enterprise, Nighthawk Electronics, she is a popular international keynote and after-dinner speaker. She speaks on a wide range of themes from entrepreneurial leadership and women in business to successful company start-ups and employee motivation. February 22nd was a pivotal date in her "personal growth and mature understanding of human nature".

Have the courage to apologise
a tip from **Tina Knight**

The first hint of my future as an entrepreneur came when I was six years old. I held a pantomime party in my garden and used my birthday present money to buy some orange juice. I then charged everybody an entrance fee of 3d and sold them orange juice for 3d a glass.

I made a fortune. Then my mother came home from work and made me give it all back. Later, she made me go round and apologise to all the children's mothers. But their fathers thought it was a great idea and most of them dropped me two whole shillings when they saw me out.

This taught me my first entrepreneurial lesson: never be afraid to apologise – it can pay dividends.

Tina Knight adds: No matter how high a position you attain, or how important you become, you can still make mistakes. Many successful people are loathe to admit it when they make a mistake, and instead try to cover it up. And over the centuries we have seen the unfortunate results of that in business, in politics, in the armed forces, and in many other walks of life. Always remember that it takes a brave and confident person to admit a mistake, and people will respect you for your honesty when you do. Covering it up or fudging the issue is the coward's way out and although you may not be discovered at the time, it will always catch up with you one day. Throughout my career of running several multi-million pound businesses, I have always had the courage to admit mistakes and apologise for them, no matter how embarrassing or difficult. Not only has this helped me to earn the respect of my staff, customers and peers, but also it has allowed me to sleep well every night.

February 23

Julian Spalding was born on June 15th 1947. He became director of Sheffield Art Galleries in 1982, then director of Manchester City Art Galleries, and, finally, director of Glasgow Museums (until this post was abolished, against his advice, in 1998). Among his many initiatives have been the world's first museum of Religious Life and Art and Glasgow's Gallery of Modern Art, which shocked the art world by including paintings by Beryl Cook. He spent a year advising on the development of museums in Denmark, and his book on the future of museums worldwide is called The Return of the Muses. *He has broadcast frequently and written books on the British industrial landscape painter, L. S. Lowry, and on modern British painting. L. S. Lowry died on February 23rd 1976.*

There is no *ought* in life
a tip from Julian Spalding

There is no *ought* in life.

If I catch myself about to say I *ought* to do this or that, such as invite so-and-so round, I always stop myself and think of another way of putting it, such as wouldn't it be great to have so-and-so round? *Ought* is like the Emperor's new clothes. It makes us spend our lives doing things we assume other people want us to, without thinking about whether we want to do them ourselves. I'm not arguing for selfishness, just self-expression. *Ought* is a nasty, grey nebula that smothers natural development.

Julian Spalding adds: I quickly discovered how pernicious *ought* can be. For example, we *ought* to have a meeting. Why? A meeting is a sign of management failure; there are usually more efficient ways of solving problems. It took me one marriage (and a bit longer) to discover that there's no *ought* in one's personal life, either.

Stephen Cang was born on September 22nd 1935. He is a psychologist, specialising in the fields of human ability, work and organisation. He was senior research fellow at Brunel University (1967–92) and research consultant at the London School of Economics (1992–94). His work has focused on how health services should be organised and the nature of the doctor–patient relationship. He is now working on the organisation of local government services in the Republic of Ireland. He also writes verse. George Moore, Irish poet, novelist and critic, was born on February 24th 1852.

Never refuse information
a tip from Stephen Cang

Never refuse information, and always record it in your diary.

Anything that catches your attention is likely to be wanted again – that name, the alternative phone number, the full postcode, the ISBN of a book, the name of that restaurant in Timbuktu, details of an hotel stayed in – even if you feel positive you'll never need it again. But never use scraps of paper to record such information on. Be sure to note it in your diary on the day you got it – it's then easier to find, because you'll remember "Oh, that would have been in early November, just before ..."

Stephen Cang adds: This tip has saved me tons of time and racks of frustration tracking back to get, for example, the phone number I was sure I'd not need any more because that particular business was finished; and having a good-enough sense of roughly when that item first came my way has made it easier to find because it was in the diary. The scrap-of-paper habit is curiously hard to ditch, but I've usually regretted not following this lesson of experience.

February 25

Alastair Niven was born on February 25th 1944. He is director of literature for the British Council. He was for ten years director of Literature at the Arts Council of Great Britain (later of England). He has also been director general of the Africa Centre in London and has lectured at the Universities of Ghana, Leeds, Stirling, Aarhus and London. He has written several books about modern novelists (including two on D. H. Lawrence and an anthology of commonwealth writing called Enigmas and Arrivals, 1997) and has been a judge of the Booker Prize.

Always make the effort to attend a funeral
a tip from Dr Alastair Niven

By their nature, funerals are arranged at short notice and it is easy therefore to convince oneself that it will be impossible to get along to one. The opportunity to honour a dead relative, friend or associate in this way only occurs once. By being at the funeral you give incalculable support to the closely bereaved. A funeral which almost no one attends is the most deeply depressing occasion, but by contrast, one where those present have clearly taken some trouble to be there is strangely uplifting. You will never regret the effort you made in going to pay your last respects.

You will show that even in a busy life you know when it is appropriate to pause and reflect. By being generous with your time you will bring something positive to a sad event.

Alastair Niven adds: I have reached the age when attending funerals happens more often than going to weddings. It was at my mother's funeral in 1993 that I really understood how much it meant to the bereaved family to see people come from far away to be at the service: people one had not seen for years, people who had had to travel since dawn, people who hardly knew her. A day which my brothers and I had dreaded turned into something uplifting and celebratory, as my mother would have wished. I realised that day how important it is to make time for such small acts of ritual.

The poet and novelist Robert Nye was born on the Ides of March, March 15th 1939. His first book of verse, Juvenilia 1 *(1961), contained poems written between the ages of 13 and 18; his latest, the* Collected Poems *of 1995, remains in print from Carcanet. His best known novels are* Falstaff *(1976), which won both the Hawthornden Prize and the Guardian Fiction Prize, and* The Late Mr Shakespeare *(1998). He also writes book reviews for* The Times *and* The Scotsman. *The first Grand National Steeplechase was run at Aintree on February 26th 1839.*

A horse-racing tip
from Robert Nye

For an infallible betting system:

Back the third favourite each-way in any long distance non-handicap hurdle race where the favourite starts odds-on in a field of between eight and 12 runners.

Robert Nye adds: This tip was given to me by a professional gambler as he lay dying behind the grandstand at Kelso racecourse. Its wisdom is that it exploits a weakness in the bookmakers' odds — when the favourite is odds-on, the third favourite is often slightly overpriced. Enough of these horses come second or third to give a small profit, and when they win it more than pays for any losers. All you need is patience and courage, plus several bookmakers.

PS: The dying gambler also told me to tell the truth but tell it *slant*. I think he must have been reading Emily Dickinson.

February 27

Sir Paddy Ashdown was born in New Delhi on February 27th 1941 into a family of soldiers and colonial administrators. When he was four years old, his family bought a farm in Ulster. He went to Bedford School, where his Irish accent earned him the nickname 'Paddy'. He saw active service as a commando officer in Borneo and the Persian Gulf. He won election as the Liberal MP for Yeovil in Somerset at four elections and was elected Leader of the Liberal Democrats in 1988, holding this position until his resignation in 1999. He was appointed a Privy Councillor in 1989.

An ounce of education
a tip from Sir Paddy Ashdown

An ounce of education is worth a ton of prevention.

Sir Paddy Ashdown adds: My grandmother used to say this to me. Jane and I have tried to follow this advice in bringing up our two children.

The son of an Italian painter, Barry Fantoni was born in London during an air raid, on February 28th 1940. He works mainly as a jazz musician, playwright and poet. In 1997 he became an Italian citizen, taking the post of visiting professor in English media and communications studies at the University of Salerno in Southern Italy. He has written and drawn for Private Eye since 1963.

Trust in the Lord and keep your bowels open
a tip from Barry Fantoni

Trust in the Lord and keep your bowels open.

I suspect this is an army expression, although I picked it up as a small child during the last war. There is a faultless logic in this advice, dealing with both mind and body, insofar as these can be separated. A belief in a spiritual saviour is sometimes the only aid for us through the experience of pain, and a healthy diet leads to a daily opening of the bowels, which is most important; not eating meat is a very good move from this point of view.

Barry Fantoni adds: I became a vegetarian in 1956, as a result of meeting a Hungarian refugee whose family had been vegetarians for generations. He was the picture of health as I was the picture of sickness, the result of too much beer and poor nourishment – I left home at 16 and as a struggling artist often went days without proper food. As a result of my present diet (mainly pasta, organic fruit and vegetables) I hardly ever suffer from digestive problems. I have been ill, as we all are in life, but not from bad eating habits.

My mind, on the other hand, is a constant mess and only a daily act of faith – praying – helps. I accept that suffering is universal, but for me Christ is a symbol of that suffering and moreover, took our suffering on himself. Pills don't help long term and therapy doesn't help in the short term. So there you are.

February 29

Alan Brownjohn was born on July 28th 1931. He has produced nine books of poetry, including his Collected Poems, *and two novels (*The Long Shadows *appeared in 1997). For many years he was a teacher and lecturer and he has worked as a freelance critic and literary journalist for various journals and newspapers, including the* New Statesman, *the* Times Literary Supplement *and the* Sunday Times.

Be different
a tip from Alan Brownjohn

Be different.

Try very hard (it won't be easy) to decline anything offered you because people are assuming you *will* want it as one of a large, undifferentiated mass of persons. It could be an item of clothing, a song, a fast food, an opinion or belief, an advertisement. Enjoy – without congratulating yourself, or being obstinate or snooty – the confidence (perhaps the sense of risk) it gives you to turn aside from what everyone else is doing. By refusing to be the dupe or victim of a mass society, you will be thinking – and, very importantly, you will be helping others to think by your example.

Alan Brownjohn adds: I chose February 29th for this tip as it puts me among the smallest minority of birthday-celebrators – thus I am different.

I can hear my parents' voice, repeatedly from when I was about seven, "Why must you be *different*? Why can't you be like *other* boys?" But there was a note of humorous pride in their voices. Whatever else he was, their son was not one of a thoughtless throng. I have done some foolish things because they were different, and there have been moments of distinct unpopularity, but I feel I have been able to resist mass pressure of various kinds, to my own – and I hope other people's – benefit. Being 'different' requires persistence, though ...

Lesley Grant-Adamson was born on November 26th 1942. She has written 15 novels; the acclaimed Writing Crime and Suspense Fiction; *and* A Season in Spain, *a travel book written jointly with her husband, Andrew. She formerly worked as a staff journalist on magazines, provincial newspapers and the* Guardian. *As a freelancer, her features appeared in the* Observer *and* Sunday Times *and she also wrote television documentaries. She appears on TV and radio to talk about crime fiction in general or her own work. March 1st is St David's Day. Lesley says, "As a Welshwoman I mark the day each year, with daffodils in the house and Welsh cakes for tea."*

Never be afraid to leave a job
a tip from Lesley Grant-Adamson

Never be afraid to leave a job. It's soul-destroying to waste so many of your waking hours doing a job you don't enjoy – so don't do it. It's easy to get demoralised and to lack the self-confidence to go after the work you want – but don't. If you have a talent you want to put to the test or a dream you want to chase – then wave goodbye to the boss and do it.

Lesley Grant-Adamson adds: I was given this piece of advice by my first editor, who hated his job but lacked the courage to make a change. There was a takeover the week I joined the magazine and he was sacked, to his great relief. I've remembered his advice at key points in my own career: when resigning from my job with a newspaper group that was dangling an editorship; and most momentously when leaving the shelter of the *Guardian* for the great gamble of trying to make a living writing fiction, something I hadn't even dabbled in until then.

March 2

Katharine Whitehorn was born on March 2nd. She is currently agony aunt for Saga magazine, but had a column on the Observer for over 30 years. She has written various How To books, such as How To Survive Children and Cooking in a Bedsitter, in print for 40 years. She is married to thriller writer Gavin Lyall, and has two grown sons and a grandchild.

Do the dreary things when you're fed up anyway
tips from Katharine Whitehorn

Do the dreary things when you're fed up anyway. As a student I learned that it's pointless, when you're feeling low or hungover, to waste what money or time you've got trying to make yourself feel better. A sounder plan is to use the time for some dismal chore that would make you feel lousy anyway.

Remember you get out what you put in. Small children, for example, aren't particularly interesting seen from a distance; but the more time you spend with them, the more their advances and quirks become absorbing. My garden looks a whole lot better now someone else is doing it – but I don't get anything like the same satisfaction.

Katharine Whitehorn adds re Tip 1: I have to say I never persuaded my children that if they were suffering from angst, rejection and a sore throat they might just as well tidy their rooms; but I did, when they were little, wait till they were crying about something else and *then* cut their toenails.

Tip 2: I suspect the same thing goes for jobs, marriages, friendships – and I know that people who don't make an effort at parties have a deservedly rotten time.

Mavis Cheek was born on February 25th 1948. She writes: "I failed absolutely everything: my 11-plus – twice – so that I failed to get into grammar school, the aptitude test for the A stream at my secondary modern, and the B stream during the years between 11 and 16 where they attempted to teach me shorthand and typing so that I could become a grateful clerk or typist. I failed extremely enthusiastically at this last. Instead I left school at 16 and became a humble receptionist in an art gallery, where I stayed, for 12 happy years, learning about contemporary art and finally running a gallery in London's West End. At 28 I took a degree in humanities and graduated with distinction. I have now published nine novels. The moral? Never believe it when they say you can't." Mavis Cheek's first novel, Pause Between the Acts, *was published on March 3rd 1988.*

Do as you would be done by
a tip from Mavis Cheek

Do as you would be done by.

Keep this in mind at all times and you will not go far wrong in your dealings with people.

It makes you kind and it deals with prejudice – how would *I* like it if someone punched me on the nose or spat at me because of the colour of my skin? How would *I* like it if I was in a wheelchair and everyone avoided me out of embarrassment? How would *I* like it if everyone sneered at my ignorance?

Mavis Cheek adds: It was understanding the value of this saying (I think I read it first in *The Water Babies*) that helped me formulate my political and social view of the world in my teens, so that now I have the confidence to go anywhere and meet anyone and feel good (though never smug) about myself.

March 4

Sir Patrick Moore was born on March 4th 1923. He is an astronomer, broadcaster and author of over 150 books, mostly on astronomy. He has also been vice president of the British Astronomical Association.

Two simple questions
a tip from Sir Patrick Moore

If you want to do something, ask yourself:

1. Is it sensible?

2. Does it harm anybody or anything?

If you answer Yes to the first and No to the second, do it. If not, don't!

Sir Patrick Moore adds: I believe that came from my mother, when I was very young.

Christopher Hibbert was born on March 5th 1924 and has been writing books since 1959. These include Benito Mussolini *(1962),* Agincourt *(1965),* The London Encyclopedia *(ed. 1983) and* Wellington *(1997). He is married with three children.*

Never wear a kilt south of the Tweed
a tip from Christopher Hibbert

When I was in the army a friend of mine told me that his father, an elderly Scottish laird, had told him always to be guided by three rules on going out into the world:

Never hunt south of the Thames

Never wear a kilt south of the Tweed

And never drink port after champagne

... "Then you won't go far wrong in life, dear boy."

Christopher Hibbert adds: On meeting my friend again recently, he told me that he was proud to say that, at the age of 76, he could honestly say that he had obeyed his father's advice in every particular.

March 6

Clive Debenham, born on April 3rd 1946, is a general dental practitioner at No. 1 Harley Street, London. He graduated from Guy's Hospital and Northwestern University, Chicago. Married with four children, he combines a busy practice with some international lecturing and the organisation of dental societies. March 6th marks the birth of his second child.

Ignore your teeth and they will go away
a tip from Clive Debenham

Ignore your teeth and they will go away.

Dentistry really is painless in the 21st century. With all the techniques available to the dental profession you should expect and demand pain-free treatment. That is one side of the coin. The other is that there are no excuses for neglecting your oral health.

Clive Debenham adds: Every week in practice, the terrified sit in the chair: grown men in tears, people forced by pain, patients who have not been for ten years. Each week they walk out saying "Is that all there is to it?" If this is on your conscience, and fear is your enemy, ask a good friend, find a good dentist, and go.

Dei Hughes was born on March 7th 1938. He is a poet, a sculptor and a shaman. He has many sculptures exhibited in private and public commissions all over the world. He is currently finishing off his third book of poems to be called Standing in the Shadow of Love *and completing a novel entitled* Bonegathering. *He is also a grandfather to 11 grandchildren with a twelfth on the way.*

Chop wood and carry water
a tip from Dei Hughes

Before enlightenment 'chop wood and carry water'. After enlightenment 'chop wood and carry water'.

There are so many times when we concentrate in an egotistic way on our higher goals or achievements that we miss the beauty in the ordinary little daily tasks that we have to perform to survive.

Dei Hughes adds: This was a piece of advice that I was given by a Zen Buddhist monk who used to stay with me in the 1960s. Over the years I have thought deeply and applied the advice in practical terms. There have been times when I have tasted and seen enlightenment and this has had a profound effect on my life. But I also appreciate that the daily tasks of washing, cooking and seeing children off to school have an equal value to those brief glimpses of enlightenment that I've had the courage and the gift to work through.

March 8

Mayer Hillman was born on October 30th 1931. He has been engaged in research at Policy Studies Institute (of which he is now Senior Fellow Emeritus) since 1970 on transport, health, energy and environmental policy. He was the author of the 1992 BMA report published by Oxford University Press, 'Cycling: towards health and safety'. SUSTRANS, formed to create safe cycle and walking routes for recreation, was inaugurated on March 8th 1984.

Take up cycling
a tip from **Mayer Hillman**

Overcome your initial fears and take up cycling.

It is a unique way of keeping fit and healthy, feeling good and getting about conveniently on far more of your journeys than you realise.

Statistics show that, on average, for every life year lost in cyclists' fatalities on the roads, about 20 life years are gained from cyclists' improved health leading to their greater longevity.

Mayer Hillman adds: My paternal grandparents had five grandsons, all male. With one exception, a faulty heart gene has led to their premature death or serious incapacity following major heart surgery. What distinguishes the exception from the others is that, for the last 30 years, I have made cycling my primary means of travel as part of my daily routine.

Vadim Jean was born on December 9th 1963. He is an established director of feature films and commercials. Winner of the Chaplin Award at Edinburgh, the International Critics Prize at Venice and the Evening Standard Award for best newcomer for his first feature film Leon the Pig Farmer, *Vadim Jean went on to direct a horror film he can't quite remember the name of and* Clockwork Mice, *which won every award at the Giffoni Film Festival. His following feature,* The Real Howard Spitz, *starring Kelsey Grammer of* Frasier *fame, was released in 1999, winning Best Film at the Cinemagic Film Festival, Belfast. His fifth film,* One More Kiss, *won the audience prize at the Atlantic Film Festival in Canada. Jean says, "March 9th was the first day of shooting on* Leon the Pig Farmer, *which throughout its making required daily suiting up in the Rhino gear."*

Zip up your Rhino suit
a tip from Vadim Jean

Every morning put on your Rhino suit, zip it up nice and tight all the way to the top – and charge! Then keep on going and going, until you bash into the side of the Land-Rover of your choice.

The Rhino suit is perfect for deflecting the tranquilliser darts of any and all stupid, ignorant, negative people who might wish to divert you from your purpose in life.

Vadim Jean adds: My producer Paul Brooks, who is probably the only person on the planet that I've met with as much positive energy as myself, taught me this one. His Rhino suit is a particularly fine example, although it has no hair on its head.

March 10

His Holiness the 14th Dalai Lama, Tenzin Gyatso, is the head of state and spiritual leader of the Tibetan people. He was born Lhamo Dhondrub in 1935, in a small village, Taktser, in northeastern Tibet and recognised at the age of two as the reincarnation of his predecessor. Tibetans often refer to him simply as Kundun – The Presence. In 1959, His Holiness escaped from Tibet to India where he was given political asylum. Some 80,000 Tibetans followed him into exile. Since 1960, he has resided in Dharamsala, the seat of the Tibetan government-in-exile. In 1989 he was awarded the Nobel Peace Prize.

Never give up
a tip from His Holiness the Dalai Lama

Never give up, no matter what is going on,
Never give up.
Develop the heart – too much energy is spent these days in developing the mind instead of the heart.
Be compassionate – not just to your friends, but to everyone.
Be compassionate.
Work for peace in your heart and in the world.
Work for peace and, I say again,
Never give up.
No matter what is happening,
No matter what is going on around you
Never give up.

The Dalai Lama adds: In all our lives, whatever we choose to do, we must first decide whether it is something that can be done. When we are convinced that it is possible, if we persist steadily, patiently, never losing sight of our goal, we will ultimately achieve it and even if we do not, we will have no cause for regret. The most important thing is – never give up.

March 10th, Tibetan Uprising Day, commemorates the occasion in 1959 when, after nearly a decade of Chinese occupation, the Tibetan people stood up to protest. The subsequent oppression was brutal, so today Tibetans also remember the 1.2 million of their compatriots who have given their lives for Tibetan freedom. I firmly believe this can be achieved by peaceful non-violent means, that the cause is just and that Tibetans will indeed never give up.

David Gentleman was born on March 11th 1930. He draws, paints in watercolour, engraves on wood, makes lithographs and writes and illustrates his own books about places and countries. He also designs – big things such as murals on the underground, middle-sized things such as posters, and small things such as stamps. He works on his own because it's fun, he can work at home or wherever he chooses, and it's the quickest way to get things done.

Draw something now and then
tips from David Gentleman

Don't commute – and don't drive if you can avoid it.

Draw something now and then: it makes you look at it and reminds you that it's good to be alive.

David Gentleman adds: The beginning of the day is my best working time and I would hate to have to use it up travelling to work. Besides, drawing and driving require the same amount of concentration, but drawing makes you look searchingly at things and driving stops you doing so.

March 12

Candida Crewe was born in London on June 6th 1964. She has written six novels, but since starting out in journalism with a weekly column in the Standard in 1985, she has also contributed extensively to The Times, the Telegraph, the Guardian and the Spectator among other publications and currently has two columns in the Times Magazine. She has won the Catherine Packenham Award and was shortlisted for the John Llewellen Rhys prize for her novel Falling Away. Married with two children, she lives in London. Her stepfather, James Howard-Johnston, mentioned below, was born on March 12th 1942.

Never underestimate the value of anticipation
a tip from Candida Crewe

Never underestimate the value of anticipation.

Anticipation is a guaranteed means of eking out the pleasures of life. To look forward to something is to extend its very existence. It is often thought that anticipation is a dangerous thing because it can bring about disappointment. Sometimes, maybe, but so often not – think of the times when anticipation has been too modest, and nowhere near matched the reality of the thing. But even on those occasions when the reverse is true, you can bet your bottom dollar that the happy anticipation lasted longer than the anticipated, disappointed thing itself. Anticipation, a pleasure in itself, is always worth the risk.

Candida Crewe adds: My stepfather, James Howard-Johnston, a man for whom I have greater respect than almost anyone I can think of, has always been a great champion of anticipation, as well as a master of it. It was with enormous pleasure that I saw James, on holiday in Norfolk a couple of summers ago, observe my son, Erskine, not yet two at the time, being offered a chocolate biscuit. Erskine grinned such a huge grin as I have rarely seen, and his whole body doubled up; slowly, slowly he picked the biscuit up from the table and performed a sort of contemporary dance with it. He touched his eyes, his nose, his eyes again, and then his chin with the biscuit. Delicately as a butterfly, he then touched his lips with it, and quickly took it away again. The ritual went on for what must have been a good seven minutes, before, at last, he tentatively allowed himself to take his first nibble. James was dazzled, in awe. Never before had he seen such a blatant example of the pleasure of anticipation. None of us who witnessed Erskine's extraordinary display that day could have been in any doubt: it is a wonderful thing.

David Nobbs was born on March 13th 1935 and has been a full-time professional writer since 1963. His thirteenth novel Going Gently *was published in 2000. He has written many TV series including* The Fall and Rise of Reginald Perrin, Fairly Secret Army, A Bit of a Do *and* Love on a Branch Line.

March 13

Live on two levels at once
a tip from David Nobbs

Live on two levels at once. Always remember those less fortunate than yourself. Always think of those whose problems are worse than your own. But don't get any less angry when the repair man makes a complete cock-up of things.

David Nobbs adds: Recently our expensive food centre packed up, and it took several visits by two repair men to put it right. What could it matter if I couldn't get instant ice or chilled water when most of the world hasn't any clean water? So I kept very calm deep down. However, we had paid more than £2,000 for the blessed thing so I didn't ring the insurance company and say, "Never mind. Worse things happen at sea." But as I made my vehement complaints I was thinking, "Never mind. Worse things happen at sea." I was living on two levels at once. If you don't, it's difficult to remain both sane and decent if you've any degree of prosperity in this hard old world.

March 14

Sean Mathias was born in Swansea in Wales on March 14th 1956. After several years as an actor he started to write for the theatre and later for film. For the past ten years he has directed plays at the Royal National Theatre, in the West End and on Broadway. He recently directed his first feature film Bent, *and his latest film,* Cape High, *is set in his new home, Cape Town, South Africa.*

Never shut the door on change
a tip from Sean Mathias

If change is in the air it can seem natural to run and hide from it. But I think one should open all the windows and doors and let it blow right through your house, with all its trailing chaos and confusion.

Sean Mathias adds: I suppose because I have lived on three continents, Europe, America and Africa, I have had to learn to adapt to different circumstances; but it is in the instability of my life that the most powerful and provocative developments have materialised. If I was told tomorrow to leave showbiz and make my way to Tibet I wouldn't ask too many questions.

Tess Stimson Sadler was born on July 17th 1966. She is a writer and freelance journalist. Her books include the biography of Beirut hostage, Jackie Mann, and the novels Hard News, Soft Focus *and* Pole Position. *She has in the past worked for ITN, CNN and most UK broadsheet and tabloid newspapers. She is currently writing a new novel set in Lebanon, from where she has recently returned to London. She comments: "March 15th is the date that I learned the first man I ever fell in love with had died; and by strange coincidence, the date that, ten years later, I met and fell in love with someone else."*

No relationship is ever wasted
a tip from Tess Stimson Sadler

Everyone is searching for their perfect partner, their soulmate. Sometimes the butterfly-flitting from one relationship to the next means that, when one fails, we discard it and move on, still searching.

But because the relationship failed it does not mean it was a *failure*. There is always plenty of good, even if it ends up outweighed by the bad. These moments should be treasured and hoarded in the memory.

Don't ever see a past relationship as a waste. It always brings you something, even if it is only self-knowledge.

Tess Stimson Sadler adds: It is too easy, in these days of high divorce rates, to junk a relationship that ended in acrimony, to be a revisionist historian and start a new page with a new relationship as if the past never happened. But that is like ripping up your childhood photographs because you are no longer seven years old. It is as if you are saying the destination is all important, and the journey is just a means to this end.

Every relationship I have ever had is important to me because it made me part of who I am now.

When I think back to the start of each I can still feel the excitement, the anticipation, the thrill, no matter how that relationship eventually ended.

March 16

Jean Thow was born on December 20th 1928. Her career in schools began in 1950 among 'displaced persons' in north Germany and finished in 1980 in a school in Scotland which was approaching its tercentenary. She writes: "I have something of a superstition about the Ides of March and am always glad when they have passed and the 16th day of the month dawns new and normal."

First things first
a tip from **Jean Thow**

First things first.

Match your energies to the activities which face you each day and create thereby order and priorities in your life and a feeling of being in charge of it.

Jean Thow adds: I learned about energy as a teenager on the golf course. It was no good expecting to play well after expending energy on too many other ploys. This lesson was invaluable in professional life, and in retirement it is a sine qua non. What is not done early in the day, may not be done at all.

Wendy Richard was born on July 20th in Teesside. She was educated at the Royal Masonic School for Girls and the Italia Conti stage school. She is an actress who is most famous for her TV work in Are You Being Served?, Eastenders, On the Buses *and* Give Us a Clue. *She has also worked on radio and appeared in the* Carry On *series of films. She was married on this day in 1990.*

Keep promises and be charming
tips from Wendy Richard

Never make a promise you cannot keep, especially to a child.

Always be charming to folk. You never know when you will meet them again.

Wendy Richard adds: And always look behind you before you put on the washing machine. There will be a sock ...

March 18

Desmond Banks was born on June 6th 1946. He worked at Release from 1968 to 1971 and qualified as a solicitor in 1973. He has run his own general legal practice from Notting Hill since 1985. He is also the honorary solicitor to the Fourth World Education and Research Association Trust. He lives in North Kensington with the artist Di Livey and their two daughters. His father Stephen Banks, a naval officer, was born on March 18th 1914.

Listen to reason
a tip from Desmond Banks

My father would say – "Don't confuse me with facts, my mind is made up" – as a pointed and ironical rejoinder to anyone who would not listen to reason.

My tip is to keep an open mind; sometimes you can be absolutely certain that you are right only later to discover that you were wrong. Better to have learned this sooner.

Desmond Banks adds: In 1964 my housemaster, R. C. J. 'Bunty' Hunter, offered to me and my fellow pupils two pieces of advice. I have never forgotten them because they seemed to make no sense. He said "No excuse is better than none" and "If a job is worth doing, it is worth doing badly". It took many years for the meaning of these to sink in and for me to apply them to my own life. I would not like to risk spoiling their effect by seeking to explain them.

Shaun Usher was born on May 18th 1937. During three decades on the Daily Mail *he has been New York columnist, foreign correspondent, TV critic and film reviewer. An award-winning short story writer, he has also written for TV and radio. His son Peter was born on this day in 1963.*

It's all raw material
a tip from Shaun Usher

"It's all raw material" means that any experience, good or bad, may be of use in some way, once one gets over it.

Shaun Usher adds: My father, author-columnist Gray Usher, raised me on that. The advice became especially valuable in Beirut in the 1980s, when a lunatic PLO gunman was threatening me with summary execution. (Only in hindsight did I twig that if he had shot me, I couldn't have used the experience.) Still, it was a great comfort at the time, and in my adult life, it has consoled me over reverses, or put victories into context.

March 20

Herbert Lomas was born on February 7th 1924, has published ten books of poetry and 13 books of translation from Finnish and is a regular critic for London Magazine *and other journals. He has received Guinness, Arvon and Cholmondeley awards for poetry, and his* Contemporary Finnish Poetry *won the Poetry Society's biennial award for translation. He was made Knight First Class, Order of the White Rose of Finland, for his services to Finnish poetry. A former lecturer at the universities of Helsinki and London, he lives in Aldeburgh, Suffolk. March 20th is the feast day of another Herbert, St Herbert of Derwentwater.*

Always follow your own nose
tips from Herbert Lomas

Whenever you fall in love with someone who reminds you of your mother or father, don't.

Don't listen to any advice about love, including this.

Try not to fall asleep while you're awake.

Always follow your own nose.

Never give advice.

Herbert Lomas adds: I've not always followed all these extreme precepts, but I wish I had. A poet is necessarily an autodidact, since his job is to listen to himself, speak what he hears and use his own voice. But the world would be both more interesting and, I think, happier and better if more people trusted themselves.

"Follow your own nose" is the last line of 'Many Happy Returns' by W. H. Auden. A surprising number of people don't smell anything if they're told there's no smell.

Once childhood is over, which can be very early, all of us can be sleepwalkers a lot of the time.

Shirlie Roden was born on March 5th 1948. She is a composer, lyricist, writer, performer and sound therapist, author of the book Sound Healing *and co-writer of the West End musical* The Roy Orbison Story. *Shirlie's music is focused on creating healing energy for personal and environmental awareness. She is an international workshop leader and also co-teaches with rock star Suzi Quatro. Shirlie Roden comments, "To me March 21st, the Spring Equinox, when the light and dark are equal, signifies accepting the light and dark in ourselves and embracing our new beginnings with the onset of Spring."*

Sound yourself alive
a tip from Shirlie Roden

Sound yourself alive.

Sit quietly where you won't be disturbed. Close your eyes, focus on your in and out breaths. Now bring into your mind any situation or person currently upsetting you. Feel the emotion in your body. As you breathe out, begin to make a sound – high, low, angry, sad, horrible. Keep holding the situation in your mind, and gradually increase the volume and the intensity. Don't worry about the neighbours – this is for you! Fill the sound with your feelings and continue until you have released all that pent-up emotion and stress.

Shirlie Roden adds: This is a process I've used on myself for years to clear situations and relationships. Through my work with sound vibration, I discovered that the cells of the body also hold memory – particularly of difficult situations from childhood – and that when people 'push my buttons', it's usually because their behaviour towards me mirrors the way someone treated me negatively as a child. Using sound in this way, I have managed to contact and release many of the unhealed, unresolved feelings I held within the cellular structure of my body and to become much more my real self.

March 22

Caroline Coon was born on March 23rd 1945. She is an artist who, on leaving Central St Martin's School of Art and Design in 1967, co-founded Release – the drugs charity with a 24-hour emergency helpline and a special interest in ensuring that young people are well-informed about drugs and civil rights. She is a campaigning feminist who believes in the need to combat the lingering prejudices against women that hamper full economic and sexual equality. March 22nd is the birthdate in 1808 of Caroline Norton, a passionate writer who inspired Caroline Coon and whose fight to keep custody of her three sons resulted in the first-ever feminist legislation in 1839.

Visualise each step needed
a tip from Caroline Coon

Visualise yourself succeeding at whatever it is you want to do.

Caroline Coon adds: I was first taught to visualise as a child by Madam Nicolaeva-Legat, my Russian ballet teacher. When instructing her class how to impress audiences with the height of our jumps she would say, "Imagine you are hovering in mid-air like humming birds!" I discovered that the same visualisation techniques worked whatever I did. For years, before I go to sleep at night, I have visualised each step needed to complete whatever it is I'm working on. Visualising success helps me to overcome self-doubt.

Graham Watson was born in Rothesay on the Isle of Bute on March 23rd 1956. He was the first UK Liberal Democrat ever to be elected to the European Parliament. A qualified interpreter, banker and yachtsman, he works on issues of economic and monetary policy and on human rights in China. He lives with his Italian wife and two children in the small market town of Langport, Somerset.

Survival
a tip from **Graham Watson,** MEP

It is better to arrive twenty minutes late in this life than twenty years early in the next.

Graham Watson adds: Shortly after my election to the European Parliament in 1994 I was given the simple piece of advice above by a person who understood the pressures of travelling around a large rural constituency with many small roads and little public transport. It has kept me and possibly others alive and in good health. No meeting or engagement is so important that it is worth a road accident. I am fortunate to have been spared one since my election.

March 24

John Rowan is a psychologist who attended Birkbeck College in the 1960s. He has presented workshops on group and individual psychotherapy in 12 countries and helped to found the Association for Humanistic Psychology Practitioners. He has written a number of books, including The Reality Game, Subpersonalities, The Transpersonal in Psychotherapy and Counselling *and* Ordinary Ecstasy: The Dialectics of Humanistic Psychology *(3rd edition). He is a Fellow of the British Psychological Society and of the British Association for Counselling. He has four children and three grandchildren, and has published six slim volumes of poetry. His father's birthday is on March 24th.*

Always go from the known to the unknown
a tip from John Rowan

"Always go from the known to the unknown" was a tip from my father. He says he got it from a schoolmaster who taught him algebra and impressed him greatly. In algebra this is the basic way in which we solve equations.

My father used this tip to travel all over the world and talk to people such as yogis, and to do detective work in India. He was incorrigibly curious about the world and the people in it. He patented an invention. For him this tip meant incessant exploration.

John Rowan adds: I have used this tip myself to approach different theories and different practices in humanistic and transpersonal psychology. The question has always been: "What is on the other side of that?" If we don't ask that question, we never discover anything new. In my case it was mainly about self-exploration. It also came in useful in meeting my muse and *shakti*, Sue, something which could not have been predicted. In 1976 she was a mature student in one of my extra-mural psychology classes. I gave her a lift home one rainy night and it all started from there. She was too young, had the wrong political opinions, had no background in therapy, was too commercially oriented, knew little about philosophy or psychology – obviously thoroughly unsuitable, as I intolerantly thought. But here we are now happily married. We have both changed.

Michael Patterson was born on March 25th 1959 and lives in Minneapolis in the States. He has written or edited over 30 manuals and guides for community development during his employment by the US Department of Housing and Urban Development. He has been a statewide Federal Employee of the Year, twice, and is a recipient of Vice-President Gore's Hammer Award for excellence in government service. He does Storytelling and Stone Age Technology presentations in schools, and is interested in every aspect of sustainable communities, from permaculture and appropriate technology to indigenous design and education. He is a certified Ericksonian hypnotherapist.

Questions create your reality
a tip from Michael Patterson

A very common question, asked or unasked, when I work with people in communities, is "Why doesn't anybody care about our problems?" What a worthless question! What would you do with the answer to that question, even if you got it?

You always get answers to your questions. QUESTIONS CREATE YOUR REALITY.

Wouldn't it be more fun to focus your attention on more exciting questions? Such as:

What would our community be like if it were perfect?

What's missing? How can we have fun, creating some of that, right now?

What's stopping us? How can we have fun working around that, creating beautiful things in our neighbourhoods?

Michael Patterson adds: Jeannie Dewey attended an empowerment workshop I ran. She asked questions such as those above. She created a computer centre from nothing, as her answer.

In December 1998, she invited me to the grand opening of her Neighborhood Network computer centre (described at www.NeighborhoodNetworks.org) in Holyoke, Massachusetts, which has a reputation as a problem city, where nothing good happens.

In the centre it was standing room only, there were so many people. There were 20 networked, recent model computers. At least 80 per cent of the centre was donated.

Jeannie, as resident services co-ordinator for Marken Properties, was the seed around which this centre crystallised, with help from many others. It looked like a $140,000 centre. It was gorgeous, better than any I've seen to date.

I asked her how she did it. She said, "Well, it's hard to put in words. I just loved everyone who walked through the door. We never asked for donations; we just invited people to come down and see what we were doing. Somehow, as soon as they came through the door, they wanted to help us out, however they could. And they did, and they do."

March 26

William Hague was born in Rotherham, Yorkshire on March 26th 1961. His family ran a soft drink business. At the age of 12, he sold his toy soldiers and became devoted to politics. At the age of 16, he gave a televised speech at the Conservative Party conference. At the age of 26, he became the Conservative MP for Richmond, Yorkshire. At the age of 34, he became a Cabinet Minister. At the age of 36, he became leader of the Conservative Party and leader of Her Majesty's Opposition.

Look at each other without mistrust
a tip from **The Rt Hon. William Hague, MP**

Pope John XXIII once said, "Let us look at each other without mistrust, meet each other without fear, talk with each other without surrendering principle."

William Hague adds: These words have stood me in good stead throughout my political career.

John Bayley was born on March 27th 1925 in Lahore, Pakistan, then British India. He served in the army for four years, got a scholarship to Oxford, and has been there ever since, working as teacher and professor of English. He has written three books about his late wife, the writer Iris Murdoch. He is now married to Audi Villers, an old family friend and widow of Boris Villers.

How to ignore being married
a tip from John Bayley

My tip is about marriage. Find someone who is as untidy as you are and likes to go to bed at the same time (getting up doesn't matter: my wife used to get up at 7, I stayed in bed and worked till 9). Then marry and pay your spouse no further attention beyond normal civility, cuddling in bed and enjoying together jokes, eats and drinks.

Apartness in marriage is a blessed state. Don't bother about it: just let it happen. And never work on your marriage.

John Bayley adds: Iris and I lived happily in this way for 44 years, even after she developed Alzheimer's Disease during the last four.

March 28

Frank Ashcroft Judd was born on March 28th 1935. He served in the RAF from 1957 to 1959. From 1966 to 1979 he was Labour MP for Portsmouth West (later Portsmouth North following a boundary change). He has been parliamentary under secretary of state for defence (Navy) (1974–76), minister for Overseas Development (1976–77) and minister of state (FCO) (1977–79). He has also been a director of VSO (1980–85), director of Oxfam (1985–91), president of YMCA since 1996 and chair of International Alert. His books include Radical Future *(jointly, 1967),* Fabian International Essays *(jointly, 1970) and* Purpose in Socialism *(jointly, 1973).*

Progress not kudos
a tip from Lord Judd of Portsea

In the fight for humanitarian values, it is necessary to decide whether you want results or the kudos. To make progress it may frequently be important to forego kudos – at least for the time being. Conversely, to insist on kudos may block progress.

Frank Judd adds: This advice, given to me by my father who was a lifelong worker for international understanding, justice and peace, has seemed to me increasingly wise in the light of my own experiences. Too often in life, I have been sad to see brilliant ideas screwed up because the person concerned was determined to get the kudos as well as the results.

David Puttnam was born on February 25th 1941. He is the Academy Award-winning producer of the films Chariots of Fire, The Killing Fields, Midnight Express, Memphis Belle *and* The Mission. *He was chairman of Columbia Pictures from 1968 to 1988. In 1997 he was appointed to the House of Lords and now devotes much of his efforts to the field of education. He is chairman of the General Teaching Council and of the National Endowment for Science, Technology and the Arts (NESTA). On March 29th 1982,* Chariots of Fire *won the Oscar for best film.*

Free advice
a tip from Lord Puttnam of Queensgate

Be careful about taking free advice, it is usually worth roughly what you paid for it.

David Puttnam adds: Assume that the world is on your side, but never trust an architect's timescale, a lawyer's estimated costs or a film star's definition of 'value for money'.

March 30

Ruth Fainlight was born on May 2nd 1931 in New York City, but has lived in England since the age of 15. She cannot remember a time when she did not write poetry, and during the past 30-plus years has published more than a dozen collections of poems as well as two books of short stories and translations from French, Portuguese and Spanish. She has also written libretti for three chamber operas, one of which, Erika Fox's The Dancer Hotoke, was nominated for a Laurence Olivier Award in 1992. Ruth Fainlight's son, the photographer David Sillitoe, was born on March 30th 1962.

You're absolutely right!
a tip from Ruth Fainlight

Always preface an unpleasant or contradictory statement with the phrase: "You're absolutely right!"

Ruth Fainlight adds: A piece of advice given to a friend by her father, which impressed me greatly when she told me about it, and for years has remained in my memory as an ideal of suavity and diplomatic behaviour which, alas, I rarely, if ever, achieve.

Steve Grand was born on February 12th 1958. He is a self-taught scientist and engineer, studying the nature of life and intelligence by trying to give these qualities to machines. His book, Creation – Life and how to make it, *explores this topic. He was awarded an* OBE *for his work on an artificial life computer game called* Creatures. *He lives in Somerset, with his wife, occasionally his student son and a robot orangutan called Lucy. Sir Isaac Newton, mentioned in the tip below, died in London on March 31st 1727.*

March 31

Peer through the legs of giants
a tip from **Steve Grand,** OBE

Isaac Newton once spoke of having seen a little further than most by standing upon the shoulders of giants. He may have been poking fun at his rather short enemy, Robert Hooke, but mostly he meant that his work was simply an extension of the ideas of other great people who had gone before him. This was laudably modest for such an immodest man, but happily for us he never did any such thing. After all, what if the giants had been looking in the wrong direction?

My best advice to you is to do what geniuses such as Newton really do: learn to think things through for yourself, from first principles, and only listen to what other people think when you get stuck. People often lay great store by being 'educated' – by being able to recite the wisdom of our forefathers. But sometimes it's best to stay on the ground and peer through the giants' legs. Then, like Newton, you may spy something that nobody else can see. Life is a great search for the truth, and what's the point of us all searching in the same place? Let's spread out and cut our own paths – that way we will cover more ground.

Steve Grand adds: The snag, of course, is that you can't take this advice without ignoring it. If you listen to my opinion then you are doing exactly what I advised you not to do. Go figure it out for yourself! The main reason it works for me is that I was born with a memory like a whatsit. I can't remember my name half the time, let alone any facts about who said what. So I have always been forced to work things out for myself, and this has taught me to look for the essence of things – the smallest amount I need to know in order to understand everything. Luckily, the universe turns out to be remarkably elegant and parsimonious – everything seems to run on the same small set of principles. I'll leave it to you to discover what those principles are.

April 1

Christina Gorna is a barrister, writer and broadcaster and the first woman to set up and head her own chambers in the West Country. A pioneer in demystifying the law through the media, the achievements of which she is most proud are surviving Question Time, starting young lawyers on their careers, and her two children Samantha and Caspar. She is known for her colourful fashion sense, especially the hats (her reaction to years of wearing black in court) and she has recently painted her London patio mauve. She has chosen April 1st "for the fun of thinking up crazy April Fool jokes to play on all my long-suffering friends".

There's never a foul face
a tip from **Christina Gorna**

"There's never a foul face, but there's a foul fancy for it" was a favourite saying of my best friend's mother. She came from the North and had a robust turn of phrase.

I find it most encouraging in that however imperfect one may be, somebody out there will think you absolutely wonderful.

Christina Gorna adds: This happened to me when my dear and extremely handsome late husband spotted me at the local rugby club, pursued and married me. Lucky me – and how I miss *his* words of wisdom.

Esther Freud was born to Lucian Freud and Bernardine Coverley on May 2nd 1963. She is a writer whose novels include Hideous Kinky, Peerless Flats *and* Gaglow. *Her first novel* Hideous Kinky *was made into a film starring Kate Winslet in 1998. Her latest book is called* The Wild. *She lives in London with her family. Her first child was born on April 2nd.*

Don't waste the best hours of the day
a tip from Esther Freud

Don't waste the best hours of the day doing the washing up.

Every one has a time when they feel most driven and creative. Work out when this is and use it to do what you most want. The other things will get done somehow, or if you leave them long enough someone else might even do them.

Esther Freud adds: For years I didn't seem to have the self-discipline to write, and waiting for inspiration to strike wasn't working. Eventually it occurred to me that I always felt at my best first thing in the morning, so I made a decision that I would work between breakfast and lunch and at no other time. Instead of sweeping the floor, putting the washing in and taking out the rubbish, I went straight to my desk. So now my house is much less tidy, but I have written four novels and I've stopped wondering how people have the discipline to sit down and write.

April 3

Canon Michael Saward was born on May 14th 1932. He is Canon Treasurer of St Paul's Cathedral, an author, journalist, broadcaster and hymn writer. He has been a Church of England clergyman for 43 years. He was the Church's radio and television officer and served on the General Synod for 20 years and as a church commissioner for 15. In 1999 he published his autobiography A Faint Streak of Humility. *He was married on April 3rd 1956.*

Never say never and never say always
a tip from Canon Michael Saward

Far too many people and organisations stifle creativity by saying 'we've never done this' or 'we've always done that'. They are the ultimate killer phrases, proving that the speaker has a mind that is set in concrete.

Michael Saward adds: When I became a clergyman in the 1950s the lay leaders of my first parish used these phrases interminably. The church was dominated by a 'nothing changes here' mentality which made the under-30s totally frustrated. I swore a mighty oath that I would never let myself, or any church of which I was the vicar, get stuck in such a rut. I've tried hard to keep that promise.

Maya Angelou was born Marguerite Johnson in St Louis, Missouri on April 4th 1928. She is the author of a five-part autobiography: I Know Why the Caged Bird Sings, Gather Together in My Name, Singin' and Swingin' and Gettin' Merry Like Christmas, The Heart of a Woman *and* All God's Children Need Travelling Shoes. *Her collected poetry includes* And Still I Rise *and* I Shall Not Be Moved. *Maya Angelou is Z. Smith Reynolds Professor of American Studies at Wake Forest University in North Carolina.*

Honourable surrender
a tip from Professor Maya Angelou

Surrender, in its place, is as honourable as resistance, especially if one has no choice.

Maya Angelou adds: At 15, life had taught me undeniably that this was true.

April 5

Michael Bryant, CBE was born on April 5th 1928. He is an actor who has been a National Theatre player since 1977.

The sound of silence
a tip from Michael Bryant, CBE

"We need a reason to speak, but none to keep silent."
Pierre Nicole

Michael Bryant never gives interviews or talks about his work, because he has nothing to say about it — it's just his job. He believes that the idea that 'it's good to talk', as propounded in BT ads, is nonsense, so he says he shouldn't really be giving this advice.

Sir Edwin Leather was born on May 22nd 1919. He has been a Conservative MP (1950–64) and the governor of Bermuda (1973–77). He is also a broadcaster, an Anglican lay reader (since 1951) and the author of The Vienna Elephant, The Mozart Score *and* The Duveen Letter *(1980). On this day in 1977 Sir Edwin Leather retired from politics.*

Two brilliant things
a tip from Sir Edwin Leather

I only did two brilliant things in my life: marry my childhood sweetheart at age twenty (both of us); and retire from politics two to three years *before* the term became an insult.

Sir Edwin Leather adds: In my early twenties I spent much time trying to do a critical self-analysis. The conclusion: my main quality was that I seemed to have more energy than most people. So I tried working on it until it became a habit. I have found that three things are vital: plenty of exercise; sensible eating and drinking (and enjoy them); specialise in being a cockeyed optimist.

April 7

P. J. Kavanagh was born on January 6th 1931. He is a poet and his Collected Poems were published in 1992. He has been an actor, a broadcaster and a journalist. From 1983 he was a columnist with the Spectator and from 1994 a columnist with the Times Literary Supplement. He also edited the Collected Poems of Ivor Gurney (1982). Gurney served in the First World War and was wounded at the Front on Good Friday, April 7th 1917.

Always look up
a tip from P. J. Kavanagh

Whenever you are in a High Street, or anywhere there are shops, look *above* the shop-fronts. These are often set in houses older than the shops below them, and you will often be surprised by decorations, window-placements, ornate brickwork, which takes you back to the past, and you learn how much of it survives.

P. J. Kavanagh adds: This tip was given to me years ago by an architectural friend and I've often been grateful for the lift in spirits you can get merely by lifting your eyes. (It doesn't work in a custom-built shopping mall, which is why it is best to avoid such places.)

Nigel Rees was born on June 5th 1944. He is the author of over fifty books, mostly about the popular use of the English language. As a broadcaster, he is best known as the deviser and presenter of BBC Radio 4's Quote ... Unquote *and for appearing in* Dictionary Corner *on TV's* Countdown. *Sir Harold Mitchell, who gave Nigel Rees this tip, died on this day, April 8th, in 1983.*

Cut your losses
a tip from Nigel Rees

Cut your losses – not only with regard to money but also when it comes to moving on from any defeat. Don't dwell on the past and attempt to rectify something that nothing can be done about, but put it behind you and get on with the next thing.

Nigel Rees adds: This is a piece of advice that I often find myself recalling. It is the only thing I remember from a radio interview I once did with Sir Harold Mitchell, an extremely wealthy Tory bigwig who pulled out of Britain when the coal mines were nationalised in the 1940s. He was referring to financial losses, but I think the advice applies to any don't-cry-over-spilt-milk situations. It accords with one of my favourite quotations – what André Maurois wrote of Balzac: 'In defeat he thought only of future victories.'

April 9

Monty Roberts was born on May 11th 1935 in Salinas, California. Before he had reached his first birthday he had been in the saddle. When he was 13 years old he went off on his own to the deserts of Nevada to watch Mustangs in the wild. He developed a deep love and understanding of horses and gradually acquired his knowledge of their language. He then developed methods that enabled him to train and tame wild horses. He says that his unique 'join up' methods are not only applicable to horses, they contain a far wider message. He published the story of his life The Man Who Listens To Horses *in 1996. In April 1989, Roberts spent time at Windsor Castle working with the Queen's horses. His approach inspired the film* The Horse Whisperer *with Robert Redford.*

The gentle touch
a tip from Monty Roberts

Don't use coercion to train horses or humans. By getting a horse to trust that it won't be harmed it is possible to overcome years of abuse. Domination, coercion, pain and restraint are no way to train horses – and the same message applies equally to humans.

Monty Roberts adds: The sheer range of horses I have ridden means I have the ability to read and understand problem horses. It is necessary to learn what is troubling the horse through observing their actions and reactions. I developed an inner ear. A good trainer can hear a horse speak to him, a great trainer can hear him whisper. By whipping horses or humans into submission, no respect or allegiance is won, but only reluctant obedience and instilled fear.

Mitchell Symons was born on February 11th 1957. After working as a director at BBC TV, he became a writer and journalist. He has contributed to most national newspapers and to many magazines and has also written 23 non-fiction books, including The Chip and Fry Diet *(with his wife Penny, 1992) and* The Man Who Short Circuited the Electric Chair *(1996). His first novel,* All In, *was published by Headline in 2000. He has created many television formats and has been a regular presenter of* What The Papers Say. *His wedding anniversary is on April 10th.*

Never tell a friend anything wounding someone else has said about them
a tip from Mitchell Symons

Never tell a friend anything wounding that someone else has said about them. They don't need to know – honestly they don't – and besides, they'll hear it from someone else soon enough.

This tip is based on a Mark Twain quote: "It takes your enemy and your friend – working together – to hurt you to the heart: the one to slander you and the other to get the news to you", and since he was extremely wise, it has to be good advice.

Mitchell Symons adds: I've learned this through bitter experience – from both sides. I once told a friend something thoroughly nasty that a mutual acquaintance had said about him and he was so upset that it almost jeopardised our friendship and, on another occasion, I was very distressed about a comment (made by someone who had only met me once) repeated to me (by someone I considered a friend) that I wouldn't otherwise have heard.

April 11

Heather Pinchen was born on January 31st 1963. She has a background in journalism and psychosexual therapy and, apart from assorted projects, is currently working hard at being a good mother. Her daughter Isabella was born on April 11th 1998.

The child is father of the man
a tip from Heather Pinchen

At a party I once met an unlikely-looking guy (well, men in skirts aren't that common) who, in stark contrast to the other merry-making singletons, was there with his seven-year-old son. We got talking on the subject of children and he said to me, in tones of awe and profundity, "The child is father of the man." I suppose I must have nodded sagely in agreement, but didn't actually have the foggiest idea what he meant. In fact, it was only some years later – with a daughter of my own – that I finally found out.

Having a child marks a rite of passage into mature adulthood which you are only really aware of once you have passed through the initiation process. Suddenly, like a character in a film, you see your own life from a completely different perspective. The experience tends to be marked by numerous humbling revelations. You realise that your own parents probably knew you rather well, after all ... It slowly dawns that yes, you too were once a helpless baby ... As does the sorry realisation that your own offspring will one day probably regard you as some incompetent oldie with absolutely no idea ... And so the circle of life goes on.

Heather Pinchen adds: Having a child has reaffirmed my belief in the sacredness of sex – the wonder of creation. She has given me a huge amount of joy, despite the weariness that being a mother entails. Having her has made me softer – I have become less focused on achievement and more in touch with living. For me, no amount of creative endeavour could possibly rival the delicious satisfaction of motherhood which comes from nurturing the extraordinary potential of a new human being.

Geoffrey Cannon was born on April 12th 1940. He founded the Serpentine Running Club and the Caroline Walker Trust, and for many years was chairman of the National Food Alliance. His books include Dieting Makes You Fat, The Food Scandal, The Politics of Food *and* Superbug. *He was chief editor of* Food, Nutrition and the Prevention of Cancer. *He has worked in journalism and won a number of awards as a writer, designer and editor. He was an assistant editor of the* Sunday Times, *editor of* Radio Times *for ten years, rock'n'roll correspondent for the* Guardian *and a founder member of staff at* New Society. *He has three children and four grandchildren.*

Face your loss
a tip from Geoffrey Cannon

All your life you will love people: some you keep, some you gain, some you lose. As life continues, losing members of the family is inevitable – grandparents, parents, others of your generation. And you will also lose people who have come into your life, some of whom you want very much to keep as friends or lovers.

The pain of such losses is at first so bad, that you will be tempted to avoid it, with distractions or drugs or denial. Do not do this. Remember that in traditional societies where grief is expressed, they understand that this is the first necessary stage of the healing process, in which the person who has left you is teaching you that you can and will love again. So:

1. Face your loss. Feel your pain. Avoid any anaesthesia.

2. Express your pain. Cry out loud. Shout. Scream.

3. Trust people to be your companions in this process.

4. If you are alone – and in any case – write how you feel.

5. Be aware of what happens to you in the following months.

Geoffrey Cannon adds: At Oxford I had one intimate friend. We had won scholarships a year before our classmates at school, and so felt we had come together at a wonderful time in our lives. We had the same name. After a year we were as one, sharing thoughts, secrets, beliefs, ideals. We trusted 'us'. Then when we were both 22, he died from bone cancer. I could not face the pain and instead promised myself never again to trust, to be so open; a promise I forgot – and yet kept for 35 years. I found this out when eventually I loved a woman completely. In this context I dreamed of my friend and was able to send a gift to his brother, whose letter in reply, touching on his own grief, released mine.

When students, Geoffrey and I and others had driven to Yugoslavia, and then, without car or cash, we hitched back to Britain. I took a picture of him drinking wine on the road to Paris, waiting to get lucky. I found the negatives recently, made a new print and framed the picture. It's on my mantelpiece now. I will always remember Geoffrey. He guides me.

April 13

Stuart Prebble was born in London on April 15th 1951. After many years as a producer and commissioning editor of factual programmes on ITV, he is now Chief Executive of ONdigital. April 13th is his father's birthday.

Make sure that everyone you love, knows it
tips from Stuart Prebble

Make sure that everyone you love, knows it.

And, if you want to put your small problems into perspective, get a big one.

Stuart Prebble adds: Recent years of my life have been shaped by having a daughter with an incurable illness, who eventually died aged 14. It taught me to make the most of whatever time you have. It also taught me to be on good terms with those around you – because you never know which will be your last meeting with them. Most of all, our daughter knew that she was loved – and there's nothing more important in the world.

Angela Lambert was born on April 14th 1940 — a very good day (early spring) in a very good year in which to start life as a feminist and a writer. Her mother was German, which as well as making her bilingual gave her an outsider's perspective on life and an insider's view of Europe. She has worked as a TV reporter for News at Ten and Thames TV, and as a freelance journalist. With her partner Tony Price, she now spends four months of every year in a small French cottage where she writes her books — eight so far, including Unquiet Souls, A Rather English Marriage *and* Kiss and Kin. *The rest of their time is spent in London where Angela writes for the* Daily Mail *and other papers, and sees as much as possible of her children, grandchildren and friends.*

Never neglect a good impulse
a tip from Angela Lambert

Pride is the source of so much regret and selfish or immature behaviour. As soon as the impulse to mend a quarrel or make an apology or give a present occurs to you, act upon it, before you have time for second thoughts.

If you see a job advertised and think, "*I* could do that" — apply! You probably could. If someone looks interesting or funny or even lonely or sad — go and talk to them, at once, before you can think of reasons for not doing so.

Act on impulse: instinct is often right.

Angela Lambert adds: Oddly enough this tip came from my mother, though she herself was a sulker of great stamina. She could keep up a silence for days, during which I would agonise about what I had done wrong (probably nothing) and how to coax her out of it. As a result I can honestly say I have never sulked: I find it childish, futile and cruel.

April 15

Emyr Humphreys was 80 on April 15th 1999. He has written 21 novels, a number of volumes of poetry and many scripts for television in both Welsh and English. He is a past winner of the Somerset Maugham award, the Hawthornden prize, and the Welsh Arts Council Non-Fiction and Book of the Year prizes.

Don't be afraid of being earnest
tips from Dr Emyr Humphreys

Establish contact with the starry heavens above and the moral law within. Take an hour, take a lifetime to do this.

Avoid cheap jokes and cheap wine.

Watch less television.

Walk when you can no longer run.

Read the New Testament twice a week.

Learn another language; preferably Welsh.

Emyr Humphreys adds: Most of these tips are a recipe for *un*-success in my experience. This doesn't mean they have no value. We belong to an ingenious species, designed, one would hope, "to strive, to seek, to find, and not to yield".

Sir John Harvey-Jones was born on April 16th 1924. He is retired, having started his working life, at a very young age, in the Royal Navy. In his early thirties he joined ICI, where he finally became chairman. He subsequently became chairman of The Economist and has been involved with numerous good causes. He has appeared on television and radio and is probably best known as the BBC Troubleshooter.

The best is the enemy of the good
a tip from Sir John Harvey-Jones, MBE

The essence of this is that it is far better to do something to the best of your ability than to spend a great deal of time and effort making sure that what you do accomplish is absolutely perfect.

Time is the one irrecoverable asset, and nothing changes without action. To defer or delay action is a form of cowardice and ultimately we all have to take responsibility for our own actions.

John Harvey-Jones adds: This was something I learned in my very early days in industry. Particularly in large hierarchical organisations there are infinite excuses for inaction. There are always more people who are happy to say no than there are who are prepared to say yes to any action – no matter how badly needed it might be. I decided fairly early on that I would rather be faulted for making a mistake than for not having the courage to 'have a go'.

April 17

Natalie d'Arbeloff's mother, Blanche, was born in Paris on April 17th 1904. Natalie's father, Prince Alexander 'Sacha' d'Arbeloff, was born in Georgia and died in London in 1996 aged 101. He was a filmmaker, publisher, entrepreneur and writer. In 1951 he wrote The Word Accomplished, *a poetic exploration of the Christian message, under the pseudonym A. B. Christopher and 20 years later his daughter published an illustrated hand-printed edition of extracts from the book. Natalie's other books include* Augustine's True Confession *and* For a Song. *Michel Seuphor, born in 1901, was a French artist, author and critic with whom Natalie corresponded until shortly before his death in 1999.* Seuphor à Natalie *is a book of extracts from their letters illustrated with Natalie's etchings.*

Make something each day
tips from Natalie d'Arbeloff

Make something, produce something, anything, but
something each day. Put aside, don't judge: make.
Even if you repeat the same thing day after day.
To build one's nest, twig by twig.

When you have found what you love best, you must
immediately subordinate it to all the rest.

Both of the above from Seuphor à Natalie *by Michel Seuphor*

Do not blame your brother for an unloving action.
Try to cancel it by performing a loving action in its place.
Do not preach moral principles; sow only deeds of love.
From there all the rest will follow as if by enchantment.

From The Word Accomplished *by A. B. Christopher*

Natalie d'Arbeloff adds: These words are guiding principles in my life and I am wholly convinced of their truth. The constant struggle is to teach one's self to apply them in daily life and to remain faithful to them.

Dick Davis was born on April 18th 1945. He is Professor of Persian in Ohio, USA. He has published poetry, translations from Persian and Italian, and scholarly works on literary history.

Immerse yourself in a different culture
a tip from Dick Davis

My tip isn't perhaps for everyone, and it's probably still easier for a man to act on than for a woman, but for those for whom it works it transforms their lives:

Don't believe people who tell you the sky is the same everywhere: it isn't. Give yourself to another culture, immerse yourself in it, let it reinvent you.

This doesn't mean denying yourself, it means finding out what you're really like and what you really care about; it means broadening and deepening yourself. And it gives you a sense of the world's cultural plenty which you will never otherwise have.

If you can't travel you can do it to some extent at home, but probably the most profound experiences of difference only come if you actually leave home – and by home I mean country, language, everything. As the Persian poet Sa'di says: "For lands and seas are broad, and vast the human race."

Dick Davis adds: I've lived and worked in five different countries and travelled in many more. In each one I learned new things about the world and about people and about myself. I married someone from another country. My professional life is now devoted to a culture I came to as an adult, and which has enriched my life immeasurably. I feel very lucky to have lived in a time when this is possible. I know that if I'd stayed within my childhood's cultural horizons, my life would be very impoverished compared to what it now is.

April 19

Professor Ian Brown was born on February 28th 1945. A playwright, he is professor of drama and dean of the Faculty of Arts at Queen Margaret University College, Edinburgh. As drama director of the Arts Council of Great Britain from 1986 to 1994, he served for the second longest period ever in that post and was the only director in many years not to have closed a theatre building. His first play, Carnegie, *premiered on April 19th 1973.*

Hear the meaning
a tip from Professor Ian Brown

Language slips – between genders, generations, social groups.

What we say is shaped by what we've been, where we come from. Too often we fight with family or friends because we react to the surface of what they say, not hearing why they speak that way.

Hear what people mean to say.

Ian Brown adds: At Edinburgh University I learned about social influences and historical changes in language; this then seemed arid. Starting to write, I saw that we each speak differently. As I moved around, I learned familiar words used by other English-speakers differed subtly in significance, sometimes not so subtly. Still I could argue needlessly with family, colleagues and friends over misunderstandings. To communicate clearly, we must recognise and respect differences. Thankfully, my family remain my best friends.

Christopher Pilling was born on April 20th 1936. His final teaching post was as head of French at Keswick School. His first collection of poems Snakes & Girls *won the first New Poets award in 1970. His recent collections are* Foreign Bodies, Cross Your Legs & Wish, *and two collections about paintings:* The Lobster Can Wait *and* In the Pink *(all on Matisse). His translation of Tristan Corbière's* Les Amours Jaunes *(These Jaundiced Loves) is the only complete one in English.*

Ask a question or two
a tip from Christopher Pilling

Most people are only too happy to talk about themselves, which is fine if the conversation is two-way. Those who only want to talk and show no interest in anyone else are few and far between, but there are many who hold the floor too often or for too long, seeming to believe their listeners are fascinated by their least thoughts and doings. If only they would ask a question or two, show a real interest in the other person's enthusiasms, and learn to listen more.

Christopher Pilling adds: I have realised, because I often find it difficult to find my words in a group or even in one-to-one conversation, how much I appreciate those who ask questions and give one space to reply. Genuine interest in another's thoughts, ideas and activities can lead to that vital two-way relationship.

April 21

Peter James was born on August 22nd 1948. He was educated at Charterhouse and then at film school. He lived in North America for a number of years, working as a film-maker (his projects include the award-winning Dead of Night*), before returning to England. He has written 14 novels which have been translated into 22 languages. Three have been made into TV films and mini-series:* Prophecy, Host *and* Alchemist. *He was also an Internet pioneer, co-founding Pavilion Internet plc, one of the first UK Internet service providers, and has written and broadcast extensively on his interests in technology, science, medicine and the paranormal. He married Georgina on April 21st 1979.*

Try anything once, except incest and folk dancing
a tip from Peter James

"Try anything once, except incest and folk dancing."
Borrowed from the late Sir Arnold Bax

Always bear this quotation in mind when you have doubts about embarking on some new experience. Always think of it when you've done something that has gone disastrously wrong. Don't lie on your deathbed filled with regrets about all the things you wished you had done — and left too late to do.

Peter James adds: The only difference between a rut and a grave is the depth. Life is dangerous — no one gets out alive — so I've always believed in taking risks. Trying not to hurt people in the process is the only real rule I apply when making a decision to go for something.

Jane Henry was born on April 22nd 1951. She is a psychologist who chairs the British Psychology Society's Consciousness and Experiential Psychology section and the Open University Creativity, Innovation and Change course. Her books include Creativity and Perception in Management; Creative Management; Managing Innovation and Change *and* A-Z of Parapsychology *(Routledge, 2001). She likes walking on the South Downs and in Marin, California.*

Work with your foibles
a tip from Jane Henry

Western personal development rhetoric leads people to expect personal growth and the possibility of curing their neuroses. Studies of twins and advances in genetic and psychological research suggest that a lot of our behaviour is heavily influenced by genetics. Furthermore, personality research suggests that though we can learn to cope better as we get older, fundamental traits (such as extroversion and introversion; a preference for considering possibilities or working with concrete details; being organized or more spontaneous; preferring a logical approach to tasks or one that takes account of people's reactions) change little over our lifetimes.

The answer? Don't waste your time going to a therapist and trying to change your basic make up. Work with your foibles. Are you an owl who works better at night? Forget the 7am alarm call, arrange afternoon meetings wherever possible, do your shopping and cleaning in the morning and your serious work when you are at your mental peak later in the day. Do you get bored with small talk at parties? This is unlikely to change. Save hours of boredom by stopping going or leaving early. Do you tend to do things at the last minute? Don't chide yourself and try to change, congratulate yourself for being so efficient and cease to spend any time worrying about the task until the last minute. You'll come through – your unconscious is almost certainly more on top of the situation than your conscious. There are numerous other weird and wonderful habits we have. If they work for you, stick with them, there's probably a good reason for it.

Jane Henry adds: I spent years trying to work regular hours, but now accept that I write better after 4pm and so I start my serious work then. It is equally important to accept others' foibles. A colleague in the habit of arriving at workshops 45 minutes before they began (to check everything worked) spent years worrying when I would arrive (generally a minute before kick-off). Our workshops went much better when he eventually accepted that I was not going to change; I did come and we got good ratings anyway.

April 23

James Kirkup was born on April 23rd 1918 and has had a long career as a poet, novelist, dramatist, teacher and translator. He has spent most of his life as far away as possible from Britain, mainly in the Far East. Since 1988 or so, he has contributed obituaries about people in all walks of life and from all lands to the Independent *and the* Guardian *newspapers. His motto for the writing of obituaries is 'reanimate the inanimate'. He pays special attention to those who have sought 'voluntary death'. His autobiography is entitled* Me All Over: Memoirs of a Misfit.

Find your own mantra
a tip from Professor James Kirkup

Whenever I feel my life is running out of control emotionally or financially I repeat "Let not your heart be troubled, neither let it be afraid" which is a sentence I remember from my Christian childhood. (I long ago discarded that religion and became a Buddhist.)

I find this mantra the perfect cure for any kind of mental or physical distress. Whenever I am assailed by bigots, busybodies and the big bores of literary and artistic officialdom, I repeat my mantra and they all vanish in a puff of stale wind.

James Kirkup adds: When I was very small, my parents proudly informed me that I was born on Shakespeare's birthday. I took this quite literally, and for many years I believed I had been born in 1564. It was something of a shock when I finally realised I had been born in 1918. So I was born old, which has helped me to stay young in heart and mind, if not in body. I am a pacifist, and spent six years in the labour camps of Britain, doing my bit for peace and common sense. When I was released at the end of the war, I deducted six years I considered wasted from my real age. On my 80th birthday, I suddenly felt I was starting a new life, and count my present age from April 23rd 1998. This is my demonstration that time is an illusion, and that the millennium should be called the sillennium.

Lt-Col. Sir John Baynes was born on April 24th 1928 and served with the Cameronians (Scot Rifles) from 1948 to 1968 and with the Queen's Own Highlanders from 1968 to 1972. He is the author of numerous books, including The Jacobite Rising of 1715, Urquhart of Arnhem *and* For Love of Justice.

Cool cheek
a tip from Lt-Col. Sir John Baynes

Cultivate the ability to treat both people and occasions with 'cool cheek'. Never be overawed or over-impressed by other people or great events. Always a combination of politeness and cool cheek will give you the advantage in any situation.

Lt-Col. Sir John Baynes adds: At the age of 16, in 1944, an elderly captain in the army serving in my father's staff gave me this piece of advice, which I thought at the time was a joke; but I have been shown during a longish lifetime that it was meant seriously. The captain was a wartime officer and in civilian life was the successful proprietor of several newspapers in the north of England.

April 25

Richard Lindley was born on April 25th 1936. He is a television news and current affairs reporter and presenter. As an ITN reporter he travelled the world looking for trouble to film. Later, for current affairs programmes like the BBC's Panorama *and ITV's* This Week, *he tackled the politics and the issues of life and death that concern us all. Now, with his partner Carole Stone, he makes television and radio programmes as an independent producer.*

Don't let fear frighten you
a tip from Richard Lindley

Don't let fear frighten you into doing nothing. Don't become so paralysed by fear that you can't respond in any given situation. Don't be so frightened of being frightened that you don't take on anything difficult, for fear of failure.

Richard Lindley adds: During National Service, I'd lead my platoon through the Malayan jungle and be much more frightened about failing in the mission than getting shot. Then, as an untrained and very inexperienced reporter, I found myself in Africa faced with covering Southern Rhodesia's Unilateral Declaration of Independence for ITN News. I was terrified I'd fail the test. I stayed up night and day, trying to build on the gossip I overheard and pick up the basic journalistic skills I should have had but didn't. Somehow I managed to convert a potentially paralysing fear of failure into action. And it's been the same on every story I've ever covered. I always have to use my fear of failure as the spur to get me out and about in an effort to survive the latest test. And quite often I do.

Bashir Ahmad Orchard was born on April 26th 1920. He accepted Islam while serving with the Indian Army during the Second World War. After demobilisation in 1946, he served the cause of his faith both in the UK and abroad. He is the author of two books, Life Supreme *and* Guide Posts *(The London Mosque, SW18).*

Better relations
a tip from Bashir Ahmad Orchard

"Give so much time to the improvement of
yourself that you have no time to criticise others."

James Allen

Ahmad Orchard adds: Constant reflection on this advice has enabled me to become acutely aware of my faults, thereby helping me to adopt a positive attitude towards those that I used to censure. As a result, my relationship with them has improved and ties of friendship with friends have grown stronger.

April 27

Kevin Kelly was born on April 27th 1952. He is the former publisher and editor of the counter-culture bible Whole Earth Review *and former executive editor and now editor-at-large for* Wired, *the visionary technology magazine.* Wired *won the National Magazine Award for General Excellence twice during Kelly's tenure. Kelly's latest book is* New Rules for the New Economy *(1998). The full text of his first book,* Out of Control, *can be read at: www.well.com/user/kk/OutOfControl/ His next project is to list the 30 million or more known species of life on the planet – a full genome of all life,* The All Species Inventory. *Kelly lives in California and is married with three children. He has no college or university degrees.*

Pronoia
a tip from Kevin Kelly

Professor Albert Einstein said many amazing cool things, but my favourite is this piece of advice, which I find myself telling to my two daughters:

"The single most important decision any of us has to make is whether or not to believe that the universe is friendly."

I, of course, think the universe is chiefly on our side. You know what paranoia is, right? The belief that the universe is out to get you. Well, what Al is talking about is pronoia – the belief that the universe is out to help you.

It costs nothing more to wear the pronoia spectacles, and all I can say is that everyone who is wearing those filters is having a much better time on earth! Try it on.

Kevin Kelly adds: I've never had the pleasure of meeting Albert Einstein, but I am sure he is not the person we think he is, certainly not the fuzzy, sweater-wrapped professor we hold in our minds. I'm betting he was a coyote trickster – a guy who was both brilliant and mischievous, who pulled our leg while making a perfectly serious point.

Professor Cary L. Cooper was born on April 28th 1940. He is the BUPA professor of Organizational Psychology and pro-vice chancellor of University of Manchester Institute of Science and Technology, and is currently the president of the British Academy of Management, the Institute of Welfare Officers and the International Society for the Investigation of Stress. He holds fellowships in the British Psychological Society, the Royal Societies of Arts, of Medicine and of Health, and the American and British Academies of Management. He has written over 80 books and hundreds of academic articles and appears regularly on TV and radio programmes.

Never say why something can't be done
tips from Professor Cary L. Cooper

Never say why something can't be done – be positive.

Be yourself, not what others or the situation expect you to be.

Maintain close friendships throughout your life.

Remember your roots in good times and bad.

Work is a means, not an end in life.

Cary L. Cooper adds: My father was not well educated in a formal way, but taught me one of the most important lessons in life – don't be negative or jealous of others; always see the positives in others. When I do feel jealous of others or try to prevent something from happening because it wasn't my idea, I visualise my Dad, feel guilty, and try to make amends – remembering his words, "no one gains from hurting others".

April 29

John Cavanagh was born on December 27th 1964. In his time with the BBC, he has covered everything from rock on Radio 1 to opera on Radio 3 (in fact he's played rock on Radio 3 as well) to documentary presentation for the World Service and even providing the voice-over for TV's classified football scores (though he knows nothing about football). On April 29th 1996 John made his first experimental recording, which was effectively the spontaneous formation of the band Electroscope, with Gayle Harrison. Electroscope have now made three and a half albums.

Try to keep an open mind
a tip from John Cavanagh

During an interview about my life, I was once asked my ultimate ambition. Without thinking, I immediately replied, "To keep an open mind". Later I thought about this spontaneous answer. Perhaps in a few words it summed up a lot about my motivation and outlook. Perhaps it was an ambition worth keeping alive.

John Cavanagh adds: I have seen people quite suddenly change their lives – it often seems to happen in their early- to mid-twenties – in a studied effort to become serious and adult. I remember one example: a friend who told me that, at the age of 23, she was too old to listen to a new album by Neil Young. It sounds like a small point on the surface, but it concerned me that my friend had already closed her mind to a new idea whilst Young (who was old enough to be her father) still had a sense of wonder in trying something fresh. Often this change is motivated by the perceptions of others and the ugly concept of the peer group. Each day holds a potential for new adventures, but by concentrating on what you think you should be, you can easily lose sight of these worlds of possibility. Some people feel that I don't live in the real world. True: I really don't have a line in conversations about no-claims bonuses and mortgages, but my attempt at maintaining an open mind has revealed a world of constant evolving scenes, new things to learn and ideas to experiment with. Why rely on a limited number of 'good old days' when the best times may lie ahead?

Ronald Blythe was born in Acton, Suffolk on November 6th 1922. He became a full-time writer in 1955 and has spent all his life in East Anglia. He has written poetry, short stories, history, essays and literary criticism. His books include The Age of Illusion *(1963),* William Hazlitt: Selected Writings *(1966),* Akenfield *(1969, filmed by Sir Peter Hall 1973),* The View in Winter *(1979),* The Stories of Ronald Blythe *(1985) and his latest,* Out of the Valley *(2000). His writings have won him the Heinemann Award and the Angel Prize. He is president of the John Clare Society. April 30th is his brother Harold's birthday.*

Have close friends of all ages
a tip from Ronald Blythe

Have close friends of all ages in these long-lived times. So many people are left all alone after surviving their contemporaries. To stick only to one's own age-group is among the uncivilised customs of the present.

Ronald Blythe adds: I came to this conclusion after writing *The View in Winter* – a philosophical glance at old age – when I was constantly discovering the distress caused by the loss of contemporaries, and having no one to take their place.

May 1

George Monbiot was born to Raymond Monbiot, CBE and Rosalie Vivien Gresham, OBE on January 27th 1963. He is a producer and broadcaster, a columnist for the Guardian *newspaper and an environmental and social justice campaigner. He is the author of the books* Poisoned Arrows: An investigative journey through Indonesia, Amazon Watershed *(which won the Sir Peter Kent Award in 1991),* No Man's Land: An investigative journey through Kenya and Tanzania *and* Captive State. *He has been voted one of the 25 most influential people in Britain and named as one of the 40 international prophets of the 21st century. For Monbiot, May 1st is significant as the traditional day of protest and revolution.*

Live according to your conscience
a tip from George Monbiot

Live according to your conscience.

If you attach your morality to the law, then when the law becomes unjust, you become immoral.

Good citizens are law–abiding only when the law is fair.

George Monbiot adds: As I became interested in discovering why there is so much wealth and yet so much poverty, and such potential for good yet so much destruction, I came to see that many aspects of the law exist to defend injustice. It's hardly surprising, as our legal framework predates democracy. I have learnt that in order to do what is right, sometimes you have to break the law, carefully and selectively.

Daniel Cohen was born on March 12th 1936 in Chicago, Illinois. He has been a freelance writer for over 30 years and has produced articles, reviews and over 170 books on a wide variety of subjects, including animals: What Kind of Dog is That; *the supernatural:* Civil War Ghosts; *history:* The Manhattan Project; *and, most recently, a personal account written with his wife:* Pan Am 103: The bombing, the betrayals, and a bereaved family's search for justice. *Daniel and Susan Cohen's 20-year-old daughter, Theodora, was killed in the bombing of Pan Am flight 103 over Lockerbie, Scotland in 1988. Jerome K. Jerome, quoted below, was born on May 2nd 1859.*

Thirst is a dangerous thing
a tip from Daniel Cohen

"Throw the lumber over, man! Let the boat of life be light, packed with only what you need – a homely home and simple pleasures, one or two friends, worth the name, someone to love and someone to love you, a cat, a dog, and a pipe or two, enough to eat and enough to wear and a little more than enough to drink, for thirst is a dangerous thing."

Jerome K. Jerome, Three Men in a Boat

Daniel Cohen adds: I first ran across this bit of wisdom many years ago and it went right by me. Recently re-reading Jerome's book I came across the quotation again. This time the wisdom was obvious.

May 3

Peter Marshall was born on August 23rd 1946. After travelling around the world as a cadet in the merchant navy and teaching English in Africa, he took a DPhil in the History of Ideas and became a tutor in philosophy. Since 1980 he has been a full-time writer and occasional TV and radio broadcaster. His many works include Nature's Web: Rethinking our Place on Earth, Demanding the Impossible: A history of anarchism, Riding the Wind: A new philosophy for a new era, Around Africa *(also a TV series),* Celtic Gold: A voyage around Ireland, *and most recently,* The Philosopher's Stone: A quest for the secrets of alchemy. *May 3rd is his daughter's birthday.*

Take sweets from strangers
a tip from Peter Marshall

Take sweets from strangers. Trust people until they prove untrustworthy. It is better to risk being friendly with people you don't know than go through life always being afraid of others. By trusting people you often make unreliable people worthy of your trust and in the long run make the world a safer and better place.

Peter Marshall adds: I suggested this advice to my son and daughter from an early age, adding that they should not do anything with strangers they did not feel like doing. I have followed the same advice myself throughout the world in some of the most difficult situations. As a result, I have never come to harm and have made some very good friends.

Christopher Packham was born in Southampton on May 4th 1961. Having trained as a zoologist he embarked on a career as a wildlife photographer and film maker. This led him into broadcasting where he has communicated his enthusiasm for wildlife to both children and adults in a wide range of programmes for BBC and ITV, including the BAFTA award-winning The Really Wild Show *(BBC, 1986–95). He is also vice-president of Wildlife Watch and president of the London Wildlife Trust.*

Judge books by their covers
a tip from Chris Packham

Life is short. Develop a moderate degree of intolerance. This will prevent you from wasting your all-too-valuable time on those who are undeserving.

Decide precisely what you want and avoid at all costs that which you don't. Remember that one day a word, a single word, may be all you have left to utter – make sure you whisper it into the right ear!

Chris Packham adds: As we age, we develop and shape our tastes: from music and art, to those with whom we share our lives. I realised some time ago that I had wasted much of my life with those not really on my wavelength. Now I have almost too few friends to make a circle – but the nature of that friendship is understood and honed, wholly honest, invaluable and enduring.

May 5

Canadian-born Suzan St Maur is a professional writer across a wide range of business communications – including speechwriting for a number of the UK's 'captains of industry'. She also writes articles for several business publications and equestrian magazines in the UK and the USA. She is the author of five published books and speaks at conferences and on the radio. Having moved to the UK with her family as a child, she now lives in Bedfordshire with her young son, two dogs, four cats and a horse. May 5th is Suzan St Maur's birthday.

Never forget that we are animals
a tip from Suzan St Maur

In our hi-tech world it's all too easy to forget that, despite our intelligence and 'civilised' environment, we are animals too, just like the humble dog and cat. A great deal of human behaviour has developed from basic instincts akin to those of many other animal species.

A bullying boss at work is like a wolf marking out and defending his territory ... someone losing their temper is like a dog fighting over a bone ... a protective mother is like a lioness who hides her cubs ... men showing off their flashy cars are like peacocks strutting and fanning their tails ... the list goes on. And when you feel stressed or angry, it is probably your innate 'fight or flight' response – nature's way of preparing you to react, just as a horse runs away from a frightening noise, or a dog snaps at a seemingly-threatening postman's ankle. So observe the animal kingdom – it helps to ease the strains of our own lives by putting many issues into perspective.

Suzan St Maur adds: I have lived with dogs, cats and horses since I was a child. I owe them all a huge debt of gratitude for teaching me the essential things in life – how to love unconditionally, how to trust, how to nurture babies, how to be loyal, how to defend myself without unnecessary aggression, how to value my family and my possessions, how to conquer fear of the unknown, and much more. In recent years we have seen an upsurge of interest in communication with other animal species, from the mountain gorillas of Africa to horses, with the advent of 'horse whisperers'. Many people who learn horse whispering techniques or other forms of communication with animals say that doing so is spiritually moving and uplifting. I believe this is so because through understanding other animals, we get back into contact with our inner selves and with the animals that we really are.

Tony Blair was born in Scotland on May 6th 1953. He read law at Oxford University and qualified as a barrister in 1976. He has been Labour MP for Sedgefield since 1983, Leader of the Labour Party since 1994 and Prime Minister since 1997. At 44 years, he was the youngest person to be elected Prime Minister since Lord Liverpool in 1812. He is married to Cherie Booth, QC. They have one daughter and three sons.

Seize the day
a tip from The Prime Minister, The Rt Hon. Tony Blair, MP

Seize the day.

Tony Blair adds: This is the best advice I could offer anybody, particularly a young person.

May 7

Roger Scruton was born on February 27th 1944. He is a writer and philosopher whose books include: Art and Imagination, An Intelligent Person's Guide to Philosophy *and* England: An elegy *(2000). He is also Grand Panjandrum of Horsell's Farm Enterprises, Britain's leading post-modern rural consultancy, specialising in musicology, hedge-laying, log-cutting, logic chopping, sheep, straw and dreams. Scruton comments, "May 7th is the Saint's Day of S. Stanislas, bishop of Cracow, and martyr (1530), protector of the poor and castigator of the great, epitome of the Polish Catholic spirit to which we are all (whether we know it or not) indebted."*

On being judgemental
a tip from Professor Roger Scruton

The goodwill of people who make no adverse
judgements is not worth having. Remember this
when people criticise you for being 'judgemental':
for it is a sign that they wish your friendship to be as
cheap and worthless as theirs.

Roger Scruton adds: I have applied this tip in my own life, and it has helped me to bear unjust hostility, to discover true friendship and to know the meaning of forgiveness.

Angela Farmer was born on March 22nd 1944. In her early career she worked with the International Wool Secretariat and was in public relations within the fashion industry. Then together with her late husband, a Royal Marine colonel, she started a Business Transfer Agency. Since 1990 she has successfully developed a school uniform retail business in Surrey. Her first of three sons was born on this day in 1971.

May 8

Instant availability
without continuous presence
a tip from Angela Farmer

Instant availability without continuous presence is perhaps the best role that a mother and business executive can play. I have combined both for the past 30 years and found that children and work can be complementary. The frustrations felt in one area can be lessened by successes in the other.

Angela Farmer adds: Children can learn by example from a working mother. The reason many parents no longer lead their children in the right direction is because the parents are not going that way themselves. Lessons learnt as a mother can be applied to business practices and vice versa. Long ago I realised that it was important not to let anyone walk away from me without a smile on their face. Perhaps there are really only two lasting bequests we can hope to give our children and those we supervise at work: one of these is roots (a successful mother and manager should create a comfortable environment), and the other is wings (children and work colleagues should develop sufficient independence to cope on their own wisely). Lastly, at the end of each day it is a good exercise to think of the best and worst events that have occurred that day and determine how they can be repeated or prevented in the future.

May 9

Richard Adams was born on May 9th 1920. He was educated at Bradfield and at Worcester College, Oxford and served five and a half years in the army from 1940 to 1946. After taking his MA in 1948 he served 25 years in the higher civil service which he left soon after the publication and success of Watership Down *(published 1972, filmed 1978). He then became a fulltime novelist and has published seven novels, including* The Plague Dogs *(1977, filmed 1982) together with an autobiography* The Day Gone By *and various other works. In 1949 he married Elizabeth Acland. They have two daughters and six grandchildren.*

Never get into bad company
a tip from Richard Adams

Never get into bad company; that is to say, with anyone who has a criminal record or with anyone whose past life will not bear scrutiny by honest people.

Richard Adams adds: During the war, when I was a very young and inexperienced officer, I was ordered to serve as escort to an older officer under arrest and awaiting court martial. I allowed this man to lead me into bad company – he seemed to know so much more about life than I did. There was trouble and I was lucky not to be cashiered.

Albert H. Friedlander was born on May 10th 1927. He is dean of Leo Baeck College in London, training rabbis, and was the rabbi of Westminster synagogue for 27 years. He has also been a visiting professor at various European universities. He has written more than ten books on history and theology and has published articles in the Independent, The Times, *the* Guardian *and various German newspapers and magazines. He has also written songs with Donald Swann and Malcolm Williamson and sometimes appears on TV.*

Always speak out
tips from Albert H. Friedlander

Don't walk away from public situations when someone is getting hurt. Don't avoid controversy (you'll hate yourself and life will get dull). Don't tackle a bunch of heavies who will murder you – but do try to get help.

At a party, don't shut up when you hear racial slurs or you'll be an accomplice. At work, don't nick things – you'll rarely use them anyway. And look for fairness.

Albert H. Friedlander adds: It took me a long time to speak out. I lived in Nazi Germany for my first 11 years, saw books burned on my birthday, was questioned by the police and learned to lie. Later, in Mississippi, I kept quiet when my classmates talked about 'niggers' – I was still afraid. Years later, I took my students at Columbia University to the South and marched with Martin Luther King. There I stopped being afraid. In London I found my best friends at demonstrations. I still march: Amnesty, CND. Come join me.

May 11

Lady Rachel Billington was born on May 11th 1942. She has published 15 novels, two books of non-fiction and six books for children. She is president of English PEN and co-editor of Inside Time, *the national newspaper for prisoners. She is married to Kevin Billington and they have four children.*

Weeding with love in your heart
a tip from Lady Rachel Billington

When overwhelmed by the weeds in your garden — e.g. ground elder, nettle, dandelion, thistle, grasses of various sorts — encourage them to grow and, where possible, flower. Look at them with proper love and attention and appreciate the wonders of nature. In this way, you will learn to avoid grinding your teeth at their appearance among your roses and delphiniums. You may eventually decide to reduce them a little, but you will do so with sympathy rather than with soul-destroying rancour.

Rachel Billington adds: I consistently follow my own advice and lie relaxing in the sun while all my neighbours are bent double over their flower beds, cursing.

Robert Matthews was born on May 12th 1940. He was in the Heretics Society when at Cambridge University. Having studied physics he became a hospital porter. Later he was absorbed into big business, but after tripping along the hippy trail to India, he became part of an eco-community in Britain. Through that he became interested in house building and now writes about self-build.

Look at a proposed change in reverse
a tip from Robert Matthews

It is sometimes initially not clear whether some proposal – either for society, an organisation or for yourself – would be beneficial. I find it useful to imagine that the proposal has been completely implemented and accepted and then the suggestion is made to reverse the proposal.

If the suggestion to reverse the proposal would seem stupid, then you know the proposal is a good one. Making the leap in imagination to a situation in which a proposal has become the norm enables you to cut through the obscurities due to habit, dislike of change and so on.

Robert Matthews adds: For example, is it a good idea to metricate the system of measurements used in Britain? Well, this is quite a controversial issue and opinions about the matter differ. Applying my tip, imagine that Britain has completely metricated. Would anybody suggest that Britain changes that system for an imperial one? No, it would be daft. Therefore metrication is probably a good idea.

I used this tip myself in group discussions at the eco-community. All sorts of rationalisations would be put forward why some proposal was undesirable. Using the tip tended to bring clarity.

May 13

Paul Foster was born on June 15th 1976 in Lancashire. He studied at the University of Leeds, then trained at the London Academy of Music and Dramatic Art before embarking upon an acting career. His latest film, Living in Hope, was released in 2001. He lives in north London.

Remember why we're like diamonds
a tip from Paul Foster

Remember why we're like diamonds.

A diamond starts its life as a piece of grit. Only after it has been pressed down and crushed for thousands of years does it become fashioned into an object of precious, lasting value to others. Similarly, as human beings, those events which seem so hard to bear are the very things which ultimately teach us about ourselves and shape us into soulful, multi-dimensional people.

Paul Foster adds: The wonderfully humane American author Maya Angelou has offered many inspirational insights into why we are who we are. I heard her say this in a television interview around the time when my eldest brother died suddenly on this date when I was seventeen. At a time when I felt bereft of comfort and reason, Angelou's words suggested that a path was open for me to come to terms with this loss; that the memory of my brother's vital spirit could actually allow me to move on and adjust, rather than despair and decay.

Professor Angus George Dalgleish was born on May 14th 1950. He is a foundation professor of Oncology at St George's Hospital Medical School and visiting professor at the Institute of Cancer Research. In the past he worked at the Clinical Research Centre at Northwick Park in Harrow as well as the Royal Marsden Hospital. Upon qualification from University College Hospital, London, he became a flying doctor to the Mount Isa Flying Doctor Service, following which he trained in general medicine and oncology in Brisbane and Sydney.

Never do anything the same way twice
a tip from Professor Angus Dalgleish

Never do anything exactly the same way twice.

Constant repetition without minor change is boring and leads to dumbing down. This can be applied to any field of human activity from travelling between A and B, to playing a piece of music or giving a lecture.

Angus Dalgleish adds: Constant and minor variation is the key to life and adaptation. Minor changes in routes, whether walked or driven, can reveal pockets of unsuspected beauty in country or town. Indeed, some of my favourite places have been discovered by this very means. One of the best ways to master pieces on the piano is to play them slightly differently, thereby discovering hidden tunes and nuances, otherwise unsuspected. The best way to learn is to teach; and constantly changing the delivery and emphasis of a subject leads to a much greater understanding of the subject, at least for the lecturer.

May 15

Brian Eno writes: "I was born on May 15th 1948, in Woodbridge, Suffolk, a small market town near the east coast of England. My father was a postman and my mother a Belgian immigrant. I grew up in Woodbridge, and my mother, brother, sister, aunts, cousins and other relatives still live there or in the area. I went to a Catholic grammar school and then to Ipswich Art School. After a Diploma in Fine Art at Winchester School of Art, I left Winchester in 1969 and moved to London. Shortly afterwards I joined Roxy Music and began making and producing records. In the late 1970s, I picked up my visual art activities again and began making installations with light, video, slides and sounds."

Pay attention to what you're noticing
a tip from **Brian Eno**

Pay attention to what you're noticing. That's to say, when you find yourself noticing something, look at it again. If something takes your interest, even if you can't understand why it's important, and even if no one else thinks it is, don't dismiss it. Trust yourself as an antenna.

Brian Eno adds: This idea came into sharp focus for me when reading a book about Chicago detectives. One of the particularly successful ones was asked how he'd developed such an accurate nose for trouble. He said: "If you find yourself doing a double take, do a triple take." So don't say "Ah ... it's probably nothing important" and rationalise yourself out of looking at it. Say instead "If I noticed it, it must be important. Now in which way is it?"

Isn't this what all the best science comes from – someone deciding to take seriously something that millions of other people could also have noticed but didn't?

Oriah Mountain Dreamer was born in 1954. She is a teacher and writer living in Toronto with her two teenage sons. She is the author of the piece 'The Invitation', which has been shared by word of mouth, quoted (and misquoted) on the Web and read by thousands, if not millions, of people all over the world. Her books include The Invitation *(Thorsons, 1999) and* The Dance *(Harper San Francisco, 2001). She notes, "May 16th is around the time I wrote this piece – an anniversary of my dear friend Catherine having a brain aneurism; something which reminded me that none of us know how much time we have and so must use all the precious time we are given."*

An invitation
tips from Oriah Mountain Dreamer

It doesn't interest me if the story you are telling me is true.

I want to know if you can disappoint another to be true to yourself:

If you can bear the accusation of betrayal and not betray your own soul;

If you can be faithless and therefore be trustworthy.

From 'The Invitation'

Oriah adds: In the spring of 1994 I went to a party and I made an effort to be sociable. I asked and answered the usual questions: What do you do for a living? How do you know the host? Where did you study? And I came home with the familiar hollow feeling of having gone through the motions. So, I sat down and did what I often do to sort out what is going on – I wrote. I wanted to express what I really wanted to say to the people I had encountered.

A week later I included the piece, exactly as it had been written that night, in a newsletter I send to my students. 'The Invitation' was copied and shared – in e-mails, or handed out at weddings, or read aloud at conferences – and I began hearing from hundreds of people I didn't know. The piece seemed to have a life of its own.

People have the strongest reaction to this extract above. 'Faithless' is an uncomfortable word. It was meant to be. We should be uncomfortable when we break an agreement, or a promise or a vow, but sometimes it's critical for us to be able to do so to stay true to ourselves. For instance, I hear people say that people get divorced too easily these days, and I always come right back to them and say, "Who?" Everybody I know who has been divorced went through hell. But the alternative is not a good one, which may be to stay and to keep closing down. That's unacceptable.

Life is hard and life is wonderful. 'The Invitation' is about finding what we need – the inspiration, the intimacy, the courage and the commitment to live fully, every day.

May 17

Sarah Anderson was born on May 17th 1947. She started the Travel Bookshop in 1979, and while still maintaining an interest in it, now spends much of her time writing. She has had three books published, the most recent being Inside Notting Hill *(co-edited with Miranda Davies), and she is currently working on an autobiography. She has also written book reviews and travel pieces for the* Financial Times, Guardian, Times, Telegraph, Independent, Spectator *and* Literary Review.

Nothing is boring
a tip from Sarah Anderson

Nothing in life need be boring. You will be surprised how there is almost always a chink of interest in potentially boring people or situations. Adjust your attitude, think laterally. You'll be amazed.

Sarah Anderson adds: When I was a child my father, who didn't like football, asked me why I was turning off a football match on the television. I told him that I found it boring and he told me that although I was perfectly free not to like something, nothing in life was boring. As a result of his words I believe I have got an immense amount more out of life and out of bizarre situations than I would have done.

Denise Danks was born on May 18th 1953. She is a novelist, screenwriter and journalist and was the first and only woman to win the Fulbright Raymond Chandler Award for the most promising crime fiction writer (1994/95). Before this, she was managing director of the first technology news agency and founding director of one of the first daily newspapers for the computer industry.

There is no substitute for excitement
a tip from Denise Danks

"There is no substitute for excitement" (*The Female Eunuch* by Germaine Greer).

To which I add: be bold, be imaginative, speculate and, if you lack a little confidence, remember, what one fool can do, so can another.

Denise Danks adds: Books have always guided me or given me confidence in my beliefs and none more so than *The Female Eunuch*. I read it when I was 23 and, looking back, it was much underlined where I had either agreed (mostly) or engaged in argument. Professor Greer was referring to sex in this sentence and she is absolutely right in that context, but I think it covers just about everything in life – in which case, beware: it is both the key and the lock.

May 19

Claire Rayner was born on January 22nd 1931. A writer, broadcaster and public speaker, she was formerly an advice columnist on the Sun, Today *and the* Sunday Mirror *newspapers. Her book titles, numbering over 90, include* A Time to Heal, The Performers *(12 volumes, translated into several languages) and* The Poppy Chronicles. *She is married with three children. In her tip, she quotes Ogden Nash, the humorous versifier, who died on May 19th 1971.*

The trouble with a kitten
a tip from Claire Rayner, OBE

"The trouble with a kitten is that
Eventually it becomes a cat."

Ogden Nash, 'The Kitten'

Claire Rayner adds: In other words, that small thing you agree to do for someone because they happen to call you one morning may turn out at the end of the year to be the most enormous job you've ever hated having to do. (A particularly useful thing for freelancers to remember.)

Tim Albery was born on May 20th 1952. He directs operas and plays in Europe and North America. His opera productions include Billy Budd *and* Peter Grimes *for the English National Opera,* The Trojans *for Opera North,* The Merry Widow *for the Metropolitan Opera, New York and* Das Rheingold *for Scottish Opera and the Edinburgh Festival. His theatrical work includes* Hedda Gabler *for London's Almeida Theatre,* As You Like It *for the Old Vic and* Wallenstein *for the Royal Shakespeare Company.*

In praise of meetings
a tip from Tim Albery

You might think that you are wasting time meeting people, but you aren't. One meeting in ten will pay off in some unpredictable way and at some entirely unexpected time in the future.

Tim Albery adds: This is a tip I still haven't taken entirely to heart. Work meetings that have no immediate purpose beyond 'you should know them, they should know you' or 'keeping in touch' seem such an unnecessary burden in this all too short and busy life. Yet the tip remains true. For example, one recent project happened solely because I called in to say a dutiful hello to an opera management I was certain would not employ me again. However, they'd lost a director for a show two days earlier and I got the job. If I hadn't bothered, they'd never had thought of me. Or, another example, two years after I had pitched an idea to a management I'd never worked with, I got a phone call out of the blue saying was I still interested? They'd like to do it.

May 21

Richard Downing Freeman was born on September 28th 1936. Now a part-time consultant, he has worked for BP, Melbourne University, HM Treasury, OECD and most recently as Corporate Chief Economist of ICI. He has chaired CBI and Chemical Industry Association committees and Economic and Social Research Council boards. The author of many articles and chapters in books, he has been a regular columnist for several newspapers. He was awarded an OBE for services to industry in 1995. He married on May 21st 1960.

Avoid false economies
a tip from **Richard Freeman, OBE**

Always avoid false economies. Don't try to save five or ten per cent on building a house, an industrial project or a public sector building. Avoid trying to save on transport safety. Don't accept any proposal which supposedly offers a cheap way to do things.

Richard Freeman adds: Throughout my adult life I have been struck by the folly of trying to do things on the cheap. When building my first house, the so-called savings on cutting corners were soon swallowed up several times over on putting things right. The same was true in industry with large capital investments. So many of our public buildings are ugly and impractical because governments put economy before aesthetics and ergonomics. Having been in the Clapham rail crash, I know only too well the costs of false economies in transport safety. I have learnt to my advantage that avoiding false economies always pays handsomely.

Hugh David was born on May 22nd 1954. Since leaving London University he has worked in the theatre, as a teacher and lecturer and as a writer and journalist. His books include The Fitzrovians, *the definitive history of bohemian London, and* On Queer Street, *a social history of British homosexuality. He is currently working as a charity consultant.*

What happens if it works?
a tip from Hugh David

Whatever you are doing, whether in business or in your personal life, think hard about the possibility of success. It sounds like the least of your worries; but have you really thought about the consequences if the deal comes off, they accept your proposal, she or he actually says Yes ... or you win the Lottery?

Hugh David adds: Naomi Sargent (Lady MacIntosh) taught me how vital it is to consider the possibility of success years ago, when she was a commissioning editor at Channel 4 Television. Hearing those words that evening, over a bottle of chilled Chardonnay, was probably the last part of my growing-up process. I can't remember what crisis in my personal life we were talking about – it doesn't matter – but the question has stayed with me. It has a universality and a resonance which, happily, has haunted me ever since.

May 23

Werner Pieper was born on March 2nd 1948. Since the 1970s he has been a leading writer and publisher of fringe information under the name, Die Grüne Kraft (publishing, among others, Julian Cope, Heathcote Williams and John Michell in German). Pieper introduced 'green' as a political colour in Germany. He also organised the first international conference on prisoners of the war on drugs and wrote an introduction to the German edition of Howard Marks' Mr Nice. Every few years, on May 23rd, he shaves his head completely; "there is nothing like the feeling of the Spring sun on your head". May 23rd is also the day when the Federal Republic of (West) Germany officially came into existence in 1949.

On the importance (and the fun) of having godchildren
a tip from Werner Pieper

Being a godfather means you can have all the fun with children that their real parents might avoid: sharing silly and exciting adventures with them, such as letting off stink bombs. It is a chance to relive your youth, or, in my case, a youth I never had.

For a long time I used to say, "It's better to be a good uncle than a bad father". Being a godfather actually helped me to become a good father, if only through watching my friends make what I saw as mistakes with their children.

Werner Pieper adds: When in those hippie years our traditional family ties disintegrated, I tried to develop an alternative net of chosen relatives rather than traditional ones. When two couples asked me, 25 years ago, if I would like to be the godfather of their kids, I first thought about the responsibilities that would come with the job if something happened to the parents – and then about the honour of being asked.

A quarter century later, I have to confess that I never had an idea how important these kids (two boys) would become in my life.

When the boys grew up, I started travelling with them and we shared some fun, not all of it good and clean. Now they are old enough to have kids themselves. My job with them is done, but now it's their turn to take care of me as I get older. They have to keep me informed about the music and what's happening with their generation. Later they may have to smuggle some noisy or exciting disturbances into my old people's home.

Bubble Miller-Lodge was born on May 24th 1964. She was the first female manager for Stoll Moss theatres before becoming the general manager of the Shaftesbury Theatre and then chief executive of the Everyman Theatre, Cheltenham. She is now an independent commercial theatre producer and director of The Sound Company. In May 1998 she married her business partner Jon on a Gloucestershire farm in a North American Indian Ceremony.

Druid vow of friendship
a tip from Bubble Miller-Lodge

I try to live in accordance with the teachings of this Druid vow of friendship:

I honour your Gods

I drink from your well

I bring an unprotected heart to your meeting place

I hold no cherished outcome

I will not negotiate by withholding

I am not subject to disappointment.

Bubble Miller-Lodge adds: Although I do not know anything about the Druids, when I read this vow for the first time, it touched me deeply. The more I respond to it, the more it reveals of itself. I believe that as we begin to love ourselves, we stop being separate from others and therefore find a deeper and lasting peace. All changes begin within.

May 25

Sir Ian McKellen was born in Lancashire on May 25th 1939. He has been a professional actor since 1961, working all over the world on stage and on screen. He famously played Iago in Othello for the RSC, winning the London Evening Standard and the London Critics' Awards, and Richard III in a film version of the play, which won the Evening Standard Best Film Award in 1997. In 1989 he was knighted for services to the performing arts.

Timing
a tip from Sir Ian McKellen, CBE

Always make your toast *before* you scramble the eggs.

Sir Ian McKellen adds: Life management, like cooking and acting, is all a matter of timing.

Sheila Steafel was born in South Africa on May 26th 1935. She says that at a very early age, she discovered that she could "defuse difficult situations by amusing people – especially my parents – so I did. This led me to try my luck at the age of 16 as a comedy actress in the UK. Fate was reasonably kind, and after a long hard haul, I finally made it. Is this it? It can't be!" Her theatre work includes Billy Liar (1960), Salad Days (1976), Twelfth Night (1983), Much Ado About Nothing (1989) and Faust (1995). Her films include Baby Love (1969) and The Waiting Room (1976).

It's always the person in the wrong who loses their temper
a tip from Sheila Steafel

It's always the person in the wrong who loses their temper. Try it. If you confront someone with something and they're immediately on the defensive, you can bet your bottom dollar they're in the wrong.

Armed with this knowledge, it's easy to stay cool and watch their temperature rise.

Sheila Steafel adds: I noticed this first when as a kid I quite innocently asked my brother if he'd seen my bicycle pump ... and got a mouthful of angry protesting in return. I slunk away feeling bewildered and upset. It was only later that I found the broken pump hidden in the umbrella stand, and got him to admit what he'd done.

May 27

Simon Brett was born on May 27th 1943, and is a wood engraver. He works principally as an illustrator for private presses, the Folio Society and commercial publishers such as Reader's Digest and Cambridge University Press. He has also been chairman of the Society of Wood Engravers and has published a number of books and articles on the subject.

Excellence is congruous
a tip from Simon Brett

Excellence is congruous ('congruous' as in 'consistent').

The saying means that whatever is really good will go with whatever else is really good. It implies that beyond each deadlock is a resolution, if only we can look higher and do better.

It is a craftsman's version of that religious statement of hope, that the Spirit will lead us all into truth.

It applies to everything – architectural styles, philosophical systems, political arguments and irreconcilable theories.

Simon Brett adds: This was a saying of a man called Ernst Auerbach, an itinerant silversmith whom I knew in New Mexico in the 1960s. Ernst lived in a caravan in which he summered in New Mexico, wintered on the Gulf of Mexico and travelled to Maine in between. He read Thucydides and *The Economist* and ate off a silver plate – because that is what he made.

Matthew Engel was born on June 11th 1951. He has worked for the Guardian *since 1979, covering everything from tiddlywinks championships and underwater hockey ("the notebook gets wet") to the Gulf War and Princess Diana's funeral. He now writes a column every Tuesday. For many years he was the editor of* Wisden Cricketers' Almanack. *May 28th is his son's birthday.*

Always have a nap after lunch
a tip from Matthew Engel

Always have a nap after lunch. Failing that, have one before lunch, or if necessary after breakfast. But take any opportunity that presents itself to take the tiredness out of your eyes and relax completely – even if it's only for a few seconds.

Matthew Engel adds: The British have an outrageous prejudice against the siesta, more appropriately called the power nap. I think a quick zizz can make all the difference to people's health, safety and productivity. In a work-obsessed age, it's more urgent than ever – especially for anyone who spends hours staring at a screen or the road.

May 29

John Chittock was born on May 29th 1928. He is a media eclectic – that is, his career has covered most aspects of film and television: for 24 years a Financial Times correspondent and columnist; driving spirit and often chairman of numerous media industry activities; writer and editor for a wide range of media publications; and founder and past-chairman of Screen Digest. *He has also produced over 30 documentary films, lectured extensively about film, video and television and is currently chairman of the Grierson Memorial Trust (annual documentary award) and the Kraszna-Krausz Foundation (media book prizes and grants).*

Man's reach should extend beyond his grasp
a tip from John Chittock, OBE

Man's reach should extend beyond his grasp ... or what's a heaven for, as Robert Browning wrote. Like the long-distance runner, it is vital in life to have objectives at least slightly beyond your capacity. If you are fortunate enough to find a partner in life who will share these objectives with you, and both of you are tolerant of each other's shortcomings and honest about your own, then happiness can be yours. Striving to fulfil yourself is the secret of a successful life. Carl Jung summed it up: "Most of my patients are not sick but aimless."

John Chittock adds: My wife and I found a common interest in photography, then film, when first we met. We soon made it our career – working together, running various media projects. Far from being a terrible challenge to peaceful coexistence in our marriage, as some people would imagine, work has been the epicentre of our lives. In consequence, our profession became our hobby and our raison d'être. But we (not just I) have come to learn that there is nothing simple or easy about life: it is difficult and you have to work at it hard and very patiently. Tolerance has helped, whenever we could muster it. The world is sadly lacking in tolerance – so, too, understanding. Yet to achieve ultimate happiness, we have striven (not with total success) to follow that classic mantra: "God give me the serenity to accept the things I cannot change, the courage to change the things I can, and the wisdom to know the difference."

Ray Cooney was born on May 30th 1932 and began his career as an actor as soon as he could leave school, aged 14, in 1946. He is probably best known as a playwright (his most recent London productions are Run for your Wife, Funny Money, It Runs in the Family, Out of Order *and* Two into One*), but he has also found the time to produce over 30 West End productions — most of which he directed — and to appear in the majority of his plays around the world.*

Eyebrows up!
a tip from Ray Cooney

As a comedy actor "Eyebrows up" is the most helpful piece of advice that can be given. It is almost impossible to say a line incorrectly with your eyebrows up. It is also the way to go through life.

Ray Cooney adds: I can't remember now who gave me this most valuable piece of advice. It was probably during my stint in weekly Rep during the early 1950s. This simple 'note' – eyebrows up – has stood me in good stead for nearly 50 years and I will certainly have passed it on to all the actors I've ever directed. You can tell any actor who has ever worked with me by the heavy lines on his or her forehead caused by constantly having their eyebrows up.

May 31

Terry Waite was born on May 31st 1939. Although many people think that he is a clergyman, he is not; though he has worked within the structures of the Anglican Church for much of his life. For 12 years he worked as a member of the private staff of the Archbishop of Canterbury. In the 1980s he founded Y Care International, an agency to assist young people in the developing world. He is the UK president of Emmaus, an organisation for the homeless, and he does a great deal of work within prisons in the UK and abroad. While negotiating for the release of hostages in the Middle East, he was captured and spent 1,563 days in captivity – almost four years of which were spent in strict solitary confinement. He has written about this experience in a book entitled Taken on Trust. *Today he divides his time between writing, lecturing and engaging in different humanitarian activities.*

Thoughts from a prison cell
from Terry Waite

When I was captured, I was placed in an underground prison. I was angry and afraid, but I was also determined that I would not be defeated by the experience. During the first week of captivity three points came to mind which were of considerable help during the long days alone. They were:

No regrets

No self-pity

No over-sentimentality.

Terry Waite adds: Although I had been captured I did not regret attempting to work for what I believed to be right. Before captivity I had counted the possible cost and when things went badly wrong I was determined not to fall into the trap of regretting my actions.

I imagine that from time to time all human beings feel sorry for themselves. However, constant self-pity can and does destroy. When I felt self-pity coming on, I reminded myself that there were thousands of people throughout the world who were in a worse situation than I was.

By 'no over-sentimentality' I mean that it is easy to look back on life and say, 'if only'. If only I had done things differently, spent more time with the family, been more considerate to others. I had to remind myself that the past was the past and I could not change it. Now I had to look to the future and maintain hope.

Margaret Chisman was born on June 1st 1917. She is many years retired after a working life spent in the civil service, but still going fairly strong. She is a director of the Institute for Social Inventions and sits on several other committees. She spends much time writing books – a book of Haiku poems, her autobiography and currently a novel set in the future. Her great passion is seeking patterns in nature and human artefacts.

Know when to stop
a tip from Margaret Chisman

Recently I began to feel that I was getting past cycling everywhere – we have no car. Yet I did nothing about it. Then one night I had a dizzy turn – and these continued for a week.

I decided to act on my own Haiku:

> "Life will tell you when
> To stop the old, start the new
> If you will listen"

or even:

> "To do nothing is
> A decision in favour
> Of the status quo"

I stopped cycling, put my bike away and adapted myself to walking and the occasional bus.

Margaret Chisman adds: Only a few weeks after this decision I heard of an old friend, slightly more than my 81 years, who fell off his cycle and broke his hip.

June 2

Diana Armfield, RA was born on June 11th 1920 near the New Forest. After her war work she became a freelance textile and wallpaper designer elected to The Chartered Society of Designers. After marrying Bernard Dunstan, RA and bringing up three sons, she moved over to painting and was elected a Royal Academician herself (on this day, June 2nd in 1991). She has her work in many a public and private collection, including that of HRH Prince of Wales, and she shows regularly with the Browse & Darby Gallery in London. She paints what she is fond of and what she admires and learns from in the world of her experience.

Poems at bedtime
a tip from Diana Armfield, RA

Bring on the night's sleep with newly-learnt poems.

In this way I have learnt more poetry than I ever believed possible or ever achieved at school. I'm nearly always asleep before I'm through reciting the lot.

Diana Armfield adds: My mother, in her 99th year, was learning 'The Windhover' by Gerard Manley Hopkins. I, who had never managed to learn poetry by heart, thought to help her by learning it as well, by reciting it together, and by saying it over and over again before sleeping, letting sleep slowly overtake. Once learnt, I needed another and then another poem for blessed sleep to come. Now I have six, including Psalm 23. All of them I choose for their wonderful imagery:

"cross and recross the strips of moon-blanched green"

"The earth lies all Danae to the stars"

"ringed by the azure world he stands"

are but three memorable lines taken from three of the poems.

The only drawback to all this is that I can only recite with a proper flow when my head is on the pillow; by day the words can escape me.

Stephen Bayley was born on October 13th 1951 in Cardiff, educated in Manchester and Liverpool, but now lives in London. He built London's Design Museum. He has written many books, including Sex, Drink and Fast Cars, Labour Camp *(about the* Millennium Dome*) and* General Knowledge *(his collected writings on design issues). He is married with two children – his son Bruno was born on June 3rd 1985.*

June 3

A modest proposal
a tip from Stephen Bayley

Treat everyone you meet as if you have *just* heard that they are about to become amazingly rich and famous.

Stephen Bayley adds: I'm afraid I have never been able to follow this advice.

June 4

Dr David Clutterbuck was born on June 4th 1947. He is a management thinker, writer and entrepreneur, and author of 40 books including The Power of Empowerment and Mentoring in Action. He is a world authority on mentoring and one-to-one development, and he learns a new sport every year.

Don't take yourself too seriously
a tip from Dr David Clutterbuck

Don't take yourself too seriously. If you can laugh at yourself, it's easier to learn from your mistakes.

David Clutterbuck adds: It's very hard to get pompous or self-important for long if you make a habit of laughing at yourself. I often take the perspective of an outsider, to look for the ridiculous in what I'm doing. It helps me recognise what's really important, to be more sensitive to other people's needs and feelings and to defuse tension in meetings. A question I often ask both myself and other people about their work is: If it isn't fun, why are you doing it?

Mike Alfreds was born on June 5th 1934. He is the artistic director of the theatre company Method & Madness. He was the founder and first artistic director of Shared Experience and has been an associate director at the Royal National Theatre. He has worked extensively abroad, particularly in the United States, China, Israel, Canada and Germany. He has made many translations and adaptations for the stage and teaches acting and directing.

Don't cling to false security
a tip from Mike Alfreds

In a situation where you are unhappy or even merely dissatisfied, don't allow yourself to stay just because it is the line of least resistance or because you are frightened of the unknown.

Mike Alfreds adds: When I was in my early twenties, a friend of mine left a boring but safe, quite well-paid job with a large dress manufacturer. He had no other job to go to. I was appalled: "How can you take such a risk?" and so on and so forth. Within six months, he had his own fashion house and had become one of what was then known as 'The Top Ten'. This made a huge impression on me. Not long afterwards, I decided to leave a safe, pleasant enough teaching job that had little opportunity for development. I too had no prospects, but after a couple of nail-biting months, my whole life turned around in an exciting way and, as they say, I never looked back. It seems that taking strong, decisive action creates a very positive energy in oneself — an energy that communicates with others.

June 6

Leonard Pearcey was born on June 6th 1938 and educated at Christ's Hospital and Corpus Christi College Cambridge. He is a musician, writer, broadcaster, producer, presenter and administrator, who has over the years covered a wide range of topics on radio, TV, in print and in public presentations. He enjoys combining business and showbusiness. He has always done all he can to help young musicians.

Never forget the benefits you have received
a tip from Leonard Pearcey

"I charge you never to forget the great benefits that you have received in this place, and in time to come according to your means to do all that you can to enable others to enjoy the same advantage."

From Christ's Hospital leaving service

Leonard Pearcey adds: The words of this Charge, delivered at my school leaving service (already an emotional enough occasion for me as I'd been very happy at Christ's Hospital), have stayed with me ever since; and while I have certainly applied them to the best of my ability for that fine school, I have remembered them in *all* areas of my life. And just as I have benefited from help and advice, so have I tried to share my experience with and offer guidance to others, most especially young musicians – who in turn I counsel to acknowledge not just the fine establishments where they completed their music studies but also the teacher who very early on first inspired them to follow that path.

Martyn Goff was born on June 7th 1923. He has written 19 books; has been the administrator of the Booker Prize for 30 years; was a Daily Telegraph *fiction reviewer for 12 years; was chief executive of the National Book League for 18 years; and is chairman of Henry Sotheran Ltd, the oldest antiquarian booksellers in Europe. He served in the RAF during the Second World War.*

Sleep on it
a tip from Martyn Goff, OBE

My father, somewhat Victorian and puritan, encouraged his children to write letters of complaint when things went wrong and not to pull punches. But, he would emphasise, never post the letter on the day it is written. Put it under your pillow and reread it on waking. If it still reads well and fairly, post it. Otherwise, tear it up.

Martyn Goff adds: I adhered to this tip and applied it in other ways. So, in 1991, when Nicholas Mosley disagreed with his four fellow Booker judges and said he was resigning, I begged him to put the resignation on hold, sleep on it and then withdraw or confirm it next morning. Initially he agreed, then changed his mind and resigned that evening. Literary gossip has it that he regretted that resignation.

June 8

Chris Mullin was born on December 12th 1947. After working as a freelance journalist, he was the editor of the Tribune *from 1982 to 1984. He has been Labour MP for Sunderland South since 1987 and chairman of the Home Affairs Select Committee from 1997 to 1999. He is now a minister at the Department of the Environment. His books include* A Very British Coup *(1982),* The Last Man Out of Saigon *(1986) and* The Year of the Fire Monkey *(1991). Mullin, a veteran exposer of injustice (his book on the Birmingham Six helped secure their release from prison), writes: "Thomas Paine, journalist, author of* The Rights of Man *(1791) and champion of liberty and justice, died on June 8th 1809."*

Avoid pointless activity
a tip from Chris Mullin, MP

Avoid pointless activity.

Do not waste time on feuds; always consider the possibility – however remote – that you may be wrong.

Persistence in a good cause is a virtue, obsession a vice.

Chris Mullin adds: Life is short. You only come around once. You, therefore, have to make the most of it. In politics there is a huge amount of pointless activity. Some of my colleagues burn up their lives by rushing around in circles. When I receive an invitation I always ask, "Will my presence or absence make the blindest bit of difference?" Usually, the answer is "No" and I, therefore, decline.

Deidre Sanders was born on June 9th 1945. She has been the problem page editor of the Sun newspaper since 1980 and with her team of five counselling-trained letter-answerers, she sends personal replies to around 1,000 readers each week. She is a trustee of the National Parenting and Family Institute, patron of Youth Access and the National Association of People Abused in Childhood, a forum member of the Royal Society of Medicine, honorary council member of the NSPCC, and a member of the British Association for Counselling and of the National Commission of Inquiry into the Prevention of Child Abuse. She has been married for over 30 years and has two daughters, Susan and Phoebe.

Someone's got to do it
a tip from Deidre Sanders

If there is some job or role in life you long for, but worry you are aiming too high or would be thought presumptuous for aspiring to it, or if you have been given a responsibility you fear you will not be up to, just keep reminding yourself "Someone's got to do it".

Deidre Sanders adds: When I was a student in the 1960s and at a party confided in the editor of our university newspaper (whose knee I was sitting on at the time) that I aimed to be a journalist on a national newspaper, he laughed and said something along the lines of "you and a thousand others".

I wasn't mega-talented, but by being willing to learn subbing and starting at the bottom – the TV listings – I was on a national newspaper 18 months later. Someone had to do it.

When appointed agony aunt at the *Sun* in 1980, I did worry – frenziedly – about how I was going to cope with the responsibility of all those thousands of readers turning to me for advice. "Someone's got to do it" me and my team remind ourselves, and we do our best.

June 10

George Wedell was born on April 4th 1927 and is professor emeritus of Communications Policy in the University of Manchester. He was the founder and director-general of the European Institute for the Media (1983–93); founder of the Manchester Symposium of Broadcasting Policy (1969–); and first head of the Board for Social Responsibility of the Church of England (1958–60). June 10th is George Wedell's parents' wedding anniversary.

Bis dat qui cito dat
a tip from Professor Emeritus George Wedell

Bis dat qui cito dat. Twice gives whoever gives quickly.

If you are going to give some person or organisation some help, money or grant, do it quickly, without delay. It is twice as valuable to them now as later.

George Wedell adds: This was a piece of advice about generosity which my father gave me as a young man. It has often been proved right. I believe the author is one Publilius Syrus (c. 85–43 BC), a Syrian-born Latin writer.

Hunter Davies was born on January 7th 1936, "a real boring, draggy time of the year to have a birthday. I blame my mother. I changed it once for about twenty years, to August 7th, and my mother was not at all amused. June 11th is my favourite day, it was the day I got married [to Margaret Forster] in 1960 – the best thing I ever did. So far." Hunter Davies is "still alive, shifting words, articles, books for a living, for a pleasure – around ten million at the last count". His books include Here We Go Round the Mulberry Bush, Living on the Lottery *and* Born 1900.

Don't get it right, get it written
a tip from Hunter Davies

Don't get it right, get it written.

This doesn't mean get it wrong, or do it badly, but get it done. Just stop messing and mucking around, saying you are going to do it, whatever it is. Once you've got something down, it can be improved, cut, altered – or abandoned. But at least you got it done.

It need not be a piece of writing, just anything which you are telling yourself, and others, you are going to do.

It's partly because with many people their critical faculties are greater than their creative ones. In which case they shouldn't go around saying, oh, I could write a novel one day ...

Hunter Davies adds: I'm not sure where I got this phrase from, but I like it because I can justify myself.

June 12

Gillian Reynolds was born in Liverpool on November 15th 1935. She is the radio critic of the Daily Telegraph. *Before that she was the first woman programme controller of a commercial radio station in Britain, Radio City in Liverpool, and before that she was radio critic of the* Guardian. *She read English at St Anne's, Oxford and did graduate work at Mount Holyoke College in the US. She has three sons, one granddaughter and 15 radios. June 12th 1960 is the birthday of her eldest son.*

Always tell the truth
a tip from Gillian Reynolds

Always tell the truth.

Telling the truth is practical. Lies, even well-meant, lead to more lies. Before long, you will be in such a tangle you won't remember what was true in the first place. At this point other people begin to realise that somewhere there's a lie and begin to seek it out. When it's found, it will look much worse for you than the truth would have been in the first place.

Gillian Reynolds adds: This tip was given to me by my friend, the poet and critic Edward Lucie-Smith. I was in the middle of a horrible custody case for my sons and was outlining a possible course of action which involved a mild degree of misleading. "Tell the truth," he said, "It's easier in the long run." I did and it was. As a matter of fact, it always is.

*Leon Lewis was born on February 5th 1952. He is a vegetarian caterer and author of two successful books (*Vegetarian Dinner Parties *and* More Vegetarian Dinner Parties, *1998). He provides food for 14,000 people each year, largely at music festivals. He travels regularly to wine growing areas in France, Australia and New Zealand. He has built up a knowledge of the world's best wines and has a cellar to match. He also enjoys collecting, preparing and preserving wild mushrooms and takes groups of people on informative forays into the woods close to his home in Brentwood, Essex. He says, "About this time of year, I start serving thousands of healthy meals at summer festivals."*

Eating for a purpose
a tip from Leon Lewis

It is by listening hard to your body that you will best understand, and therefore be able to respond to, its needs. A handful of pumpkin seeds each day will provide zinc, sesame seeds will give calcium, and olive oil will help reduce cholesterol levels. In general, a high fibre diet of whole grains, fruit and vegetables will ensure a regular and healthy body. Good red wine in moderation will add pleasure to your meals and increase longevity.

Leon Lewis adds: In life you should consume only the finest ingredients. I now have the privilege of providing gourmet vegetarian food for thousands of people while they are enjoying themselves at celebrations and festivals. Their enthusiasm and appreciation of my food helps me feel good about my way of life; I hope it inspires them to eat and drink well, with respect for their environment and fellow creatures.

June 14

Margaretta D'Arcy was born on June 14th 1934. She is an Irish playwright (for stage and radio), publisher, feminist activist and runs a women's pirate radio. Her published works include: Tell Them Everything, Awkward Corners, Galway's Pirate Women *and* Collected Plays *(with John Arden). She is also a member of Aosdana, the Irish artists' parliament.*

A daily reminder for all women
a tip from Margaretta D'Arcy

We women do two-thirds of the world's work, invisible, unrecognised, unwaged; and by telling ourselves about it whenever we need to, we can strengthen ourselves immeasurably. For example, if a man tries to intimidate us, to put on superior airs, to come over us all heavy, we just step back and visualise all the women's work without which he wouldn't even *be*.

Margaretta D'Arcy adds: I have lived with five men: four sons and a husband. I was their planner, manager and maintenance worker and never got a day's pay or recognition. In the end I got myself to the United Nations Women's Conference at Beijing in 1995, where millions of women from all over the world persuaded the governments of the world to commit themselves to measuring and valuing the unwaged work we do. Our next step is to see that this is implemented, and to put in our bill for the Day of Reckoning.

Peter Carr was born on June 15th 1947. A conventional childhood and education in the south of England did not persuade him to follow a predictable career. For 25 years he has lived on Knoydart peninsula in north-west Scotland, a remote place only accessible by boat. He is a prawn fisherman, but has worked in the past as a scallop diver. He has three children and one grandchild. A widower, he is now in a new relationship.

On matters of health, don't delay
a tip from Peter Carr

If you have some concern about your health don't just wait to see how things progress but go and get a professional opinion right away. Many conditions are easier to treat and have better outcomes if they are diagnosed at an early stage.

Peter Carr adds: In 1996 I became aware that one of two small brown blotches on my face had started to look very subtly different from the other. I asked my GP within a couple of days and was referred to a consultant by the end of the next week, who was flexible enough to remove it there and then. It turned out to have been a melanoma, but thanks to the speed it was dealt with, I appear to have got away with it.

Not only does early diagnosis potentially make a huge difference to the patient, but it should also make things easier and therefore cheaper to treat. Of course it's better to stay healthy in the first place, so try not to do stuff that's obviously bad for you such as smoking. My personal message would be to take good care of your skin.

June 16

Julia Neuberger was born on February 27th 1950. She was ordained a rabbi in London in 1977 and served the South London Liberal Synagogue from 1977 to 1989. She was a visiting fellow at the King's Fund and then at Harvard Medical School (as a Harkness Fellow) and then chaired Camden and Islington Community Health Services NHS Trust from 1993 to 1997. In 1997 she became chief executive of the King's Fund, a charity that works for the health and welfare of Londoners, and was until recently chancellor of the University of Ulster. She also writes and edits books, including The Story of Judaism, The Things That Matter *and* On Being Jewish *(1995). Her first child, Harriet, was born on June 16th 1979.*

Doing two things at once
a tip from Rabbi Julia Neuberger

If you have to sit through a lot of meetings which you are not chairing, take with you, for the moments when you have nothing to contribute, small pieces of correspondence and a great deal of paper for making lists. You can manage to write your thank you letters and short notes to draw friends' attention to things and you can also write lists of things to do – a sort of 'pending' pile – whilst still listening to what is going on.

Julia Neuberger adds: On the whole, this means that I get my personal correspondence done whilst still focusing on the meeting. However, I was once so busily engaged in writing a friend a witty note of thanks for something that I completely missed the fact that we had moved topic and that I had to present a paper. So beware!

Jane Northcote was born on June 17th 1955 and lives and works from her small flat in Soho, central London. She enjoys the parks and the people and does her shopping at the Berwick Street vegetable market. She earns her living as an independent management consultant, which means helping teams of people in large organisations to change the way they work.

Learn a technique for going to sleep
a tip from Jane Northcote

Being able to go to sleep is a very useful skill. It's the best way to relax. It takes no equipment and can be done anywhere. However, sometimes it takes an effort, especially if you are under stress, or in an unfamiliar or unpleasant place, yet these are often the times when you need sleep most.

So my tip is: learn a technique for going to sleep. There are books on the subject, or you can make up your own relaxation techniques. Learn and apply the technique at a time when you DON'T need it, then it will work better when you do need it.

Jane Northcote adds: A long time ago, during a difficult time, a sympathetic person called Mike Bere said to me "Are you sleeping?" and saw that I wasn't. He lent me an ordinary book on meditation techniques. I found that the meditation techniques sent me to sleep, which was very useful. Sleep is my antidote to stress. Now, in happier times, I can get a good night's sleep before important events, on trains, in daylight and through most sorts of noise. This is important, and enables me to live here in Soho, where the noise in the street reaches a crescendo at 2am when the nightclubs close.

June 18

The late Mike Ockrent was born on June 18th 1946; he died on December 2nd 1999. He was a theatre and film director and novelist. His award-winning theatre productions (including Me and My Girl, Crazy For You, Passion Play *and* Educating Rita*) played in the West End and on Broadway.*

Smile as the sun comes up
a tip from **Mike Ockrent**

Every day the sun comes up and you can smile, be thankful. Never waste a moment of that day. Never say "I'm bored". Never forget to smile at those you love and those that love you.

As the sun goes down, look forward with a smile to the next day the sun comes up.

Mike Ockrent wrote: In February of 1998 I was diagnosed with leukaemia. For a year and a half I have been receiving treatment. On most mornings I have been fair and able to understand the beauty of seeing and smiling as the sun comes up.

*Professor James E. Lovelock was born on July 26th 1919. He is an honorary visiting fellow of Green College, Oxford and has been awarded honorary DSc degrees by the universities of Exeter, Plymouth, East London, Edinburgh, Kent, East Anglia, Colorado and Stockholm. An independent scientist, he is best known for propounding the Gaia hypothesis, the theory that life on Earth regulates its environment to keep itself healthy. He has written numerous books (*Homage to Gaia *is his latest) and has several successful scientific inventions to his name. Novelist William Golding, Lovelock's friend and neighbour, suggested the name Gaia (after the Greek Earth goddess). Golding died on June 19th 1993.*

Seek the flaw in everything
a tip from Professor James Lovelock

Seek the flaw in everything orthodox and accepted.

It is only through rigorous questioning of accepted values and truths that human progress can be achieved.

Everything that happens in the great Earth system is the result of some individual somewhere doing something slightly different. If it succeeds and it's improving the environment then it will take over its part of the ecosystem. If it fails, it dies out. So it's down to individuals ultimately.

James Lovelock adds: After having worked with the Medical Research Council for 20 years, I decided to break free and become an independent researcher. It wasn't easy. My first submission to the journal *Nature* since becoming independent (a paper about detecting life by measuring entropy reduction) was returned with a curt note: "We don't take papers from private addresses." Over the last 40 years I have maintained that every individual action is part of a network of dependency and interconnectedness which it influences in turn. I have put my trust in Gaia. It is comforting to think that I am a part of her and that my destiny is to merge with the chemistry of our living planet.

June 20

Guy Claxton was born on June 20th 1947 and educated at King's School, Worcester and Cambridge and Oxford. His prolific writings on psychology, education and spirituality include the books The Heart of Buddhism, Hare Brain, Tortoise Mind: Why intelligence increases when you think less, *and* Wise Up: The challenge of lifelong learning. *For several years a follower of the controversial Indian mystic Osho (Bhagwan Shree Rajneesh), he was a founding teacher at Schumacher College in South Devon, where he now lives, and is visiting professor in the University of Bristol Graduate School of Education.*

Learn to loaf
a tip from Guy Claxton

Learning the art of loafing is absolutely essential for creativity, productivity and peace of mind. It is vital to spend time every day dozing, doodling and goofing off. You should never ignore feeling sleepy: it is literally dangerous habitually to keep on going when your body is telling you to rest. The faster the pace of life, the more you need to make time to meander, drift and do things that have no point or product. Flyfishing with all its busy swishing misses the point. Sitting on the canal bank, mindlessly watching the float, lost in reverie, having totally forgotten the fish – that's the state that feeds the soul. Find your equivalent form of inactivity, cherish it, and give yourself to it as regularly as you can.

Guy Claxton adds: One of the ways I learn things is to write a book about them – and then gradually realise the 'truth' in my own life of what I have described. Since I wrote *Hare Brain, Tortoise Mind* I have been learning to practise what I had been drawn to preach. I have slowed down. I doze and potter. I have shed the old voice from childhood that kept telling me I ought to be 'being productive' and 'fulfilling my potential'. I feel better. And, strangely enough, I think that I'm thinking (and writing) better than I ever did before. I work very productively in bursts, usually between breakfast and lunch. And then have a good rest and don't feel at all guilty. It works!

Dennis Barker was born on June 21st 1929. He had a disastrous Second World War education, but in the 1950s became one of the first journalists in Britain to win the National Diploma in Journalism, introduced by the National Council for the Training of Journalists as the higher, degree-standard qualification in the days before journalism degree courses existed. After being a reporter, theatre, radio and film critic in the provinces, he joined the Guardian, *for which he was successively reporter, writer of various columns and media correspondent. He has written eight non-fiction books, including three on each of the British armed forces, and three novels. He was also a founder panel member of the favourite BBC Radio 4 chat show,* Stop the Week.

If deceived, blame your own faulty judgement
a tip from Dennis Barker

Never blame other people for the results of your own faulty judgement of them. Blame yourself and resolve not to make the same mistake twice. Save the energy you would have wasted on recriminations for taking productive counter-measures.

Dennis Barker adds: My father, a self-made industrialist, and a shrewd politician as head of his trade's national association, often had need of his own advice, which he passed on to me. I have found it equally apt. It can serve you well in circumstances as various as an unhappy love affair or a workplace betrayal. If you are ever deceived, blame your own faulty judgement of the person who has deceived you. Not least, this advice stops you feeling victimised by making you see yourself firmly as the (inevitably fallible) manager of your own life.

June 22

Lord Wakeham was born on June 22nd 1932. He served 18 years in the House of Commons, holding a number of distinguished posts including leader of the House of Commons, Lord Privy Seal and Chief Whip. He has been a member of the House of Lords since 1992 – and was for two years its leader, making him only the fourth person in British history to lead both Houses of Parliament. He is currently chairman of the Press Complaints Commission and of a number of companies. In 1999 he chaired the Royal Commission into reform of the House of Lords, which reported at the start of 2000.

Only argue if you can win
a tip from **Lord Wakeham**

Never get into an argument unless you know you can win it. Far too many people begin debates that they haven't a chance of winning. But if you always lose, you become a far less worthy adversary in any future battles. Always make sure you are on solid ground, have all the facts to hand, and know what other people think before you engage in combat. If you always win the debate, people will be far less likely to take you on and will also come to respect your judgement.

Lord Wakeham adds: My years working for Mrs Thatcher taught me never to go unprepared into discussion or debate with her. She loved argument and she didn't mind losing, but she was wary of people who argued with her and had not thought things through.

Claudia Rosencrantz was born on June 23rd 1959. She is Controller of Entertainment for the ITV Network where she was responsible for commissioning Who Wants to be a Millionaire. *Before that she produced Dame Edna for over ten years both in the UK and the USA. She was also a journalist and has produced and directed various documentaries including Elton John's* Tantrums and Tiaras.

Walk gently on the earth
a tip from **Claudia Rosencrantz**

The highest compliment a native aboriginal can pay someone who has died is to say that they walked gently on the earth; that they have done no harm or damage to the earth or to the people on it.

Claudia Rosencrantz adds: My other tips are: Know who you are. Treat people well. Tell the truth. Don't drink. Never be bored. Laugh a lot.
My father (and mother) taught me all the above and much much more.

June 24

June Thomson was born on June 24th 1930. She has published 18 novels featuring her series detective Jack Finch and his sergeant Tom Boyce. She has also published a collection of short stories and four volumes of Sherlock Holmes pastiches, together with a 'biography' of Holmes and Watson. Her books are published in the UK, the US, France, Russia and Japan.

Get the happiness habit
a tip from **June Thomson**

Being happy can become a habit. You can get hooked on happiness as you can on nicotine. It's just a question of taking in a regular daily dose of the stuff.

June Thomson adds: When I first heard the phrase "Being happy can become a habit", I thought it rather simplistic. However, it must have had some effect, because over the years it has come to mean more and more to me.

Professor Charles Arnold-Baker was born in Berlin on June 25th 1918. He learned French, besides English and German, and has been a hospital administrator, soldier, practising barrister, manager of a local government pressure group, professor, traffic commissioner, publisher and author of the book The Companion to British History, *which he and his family published.*

Have overlapping jobs
a tip from
Professor Charles Arnold-Baker, OBE

Time is the only asset which, once lost, is irrecoverable, but a single day-in, day-out job can drive you round the bend. Address both problems by keeping two, or several, paying or merely fun activities going side by side so that when one is interrupted (by you or circumstances) you simply take up another until you are ready to return.
It makes life more useful, lucrative and interesting, and sometimes you can fix things so that one activity helps another.

Charles Arnold-Baker adds: When I became secretary of the National Association of Local Councils in 1953, I had an enormous correspondence giving varied advice to thousands of councils on mostly legal subjects of which I knew little. So, over a period of four years I worked it all into a book called *Local Council Administration*, published it and persuaded many councils to buy it. Result: I knew more and could cope more easily; some bought the book and wrote me fewer letters; and I increased my income. The book is now in its fifth edition. *The Companion to British History* took 30 years. It overlapped both activities and was fun to write. It now makes money too.

June 26

Richard Reoch is an international human rights activist. Born in Canada, in 1948 he came to London to join the International Secretariat of Amnesty International where he headed the organisation's worldwide media operations. He has travelled widely, working with human rights groups around the world. June 26th is the day that the International Convention Against Torture entered into force in 1987.

Inspired leadership
a tip from Richard Reoch

See everything
Overlook a lot
Correct a little

This was the advice given by Pope John XXIII when he addressed the historic Vatican Council. It is the key to inspired leadership for anyone in charge of anything, from a huge organisation to a home.

Richard Reoch adds: When I had my first leadership position I fell into the common trap of trying to accomplish everything and worrying about every little detail. My whole approach changed when I encountered these three simple sentences. My understanding of their wisdom is that the starting point of great leadership is a completely open mind. Allow people to see the world in their own way and let things unfold according to their own logic. Save your energy: be precise about what matters most and focus your life-force on that.

Alan Coren was born on June 27th 1938. A former editor of Punch *and the* Listener, *he has written 30 books for adults and 10 for children. He currently writes a Wednesday column for* The Times, *and appears daily on BBC1's* Call My Bluff *and weekly on Radio 4's* The News Quiz.

People like US
a tip from Alan Coren

I offer you two American heroes. Though both were professional cynics, do exactly what the first hero says, but do the exact opposite of what the second hero says.

From that towering comic journalist H. L. Mencken: "When I am gone, and you have a thought to please my ghost, forgive some sinner, and wink your eye at a homely girl."

And from that towering comic actor W. C. Fields: "Never give a sucker an even break."

Alan Coren adds: Succour the weak, strengthen the sucker, and since all life is a joke, laugh at it.

June 28

Alasdair Hutton was born on May 19th 1940. He is the narrator and writer of the world-famous Edinburgh Military Tattoo and many similar shows around the world. He has been a European parliamentarian, broadcaster, journalist and TA Paratrooper. He is also director of a weather forecasting company, and crafter of CVs for people who have lost their jobs. June 28th is the birthday of his elder son.

Always go the extra mile
tips from Alasdair Hutton, OBE

Always go the extra mile. Make what you do memorable. Don't only do what you are asked to do, but do what is needed. Make an effort to help anyone who asks. Go out of your way to support someone who has lost their spirit.

Alasdair Hutton adds: You cannot foretell what any of your actions could lead to, so it is always worth making everything you do special rather than routine. Your effort will be returned many times and in unexpected ways. Trying to make every big show memorable has led to my being asked to present a wide variety of fascinating events around the world.

I attempted to help everyone who came to me as a politician. Long afterwards I am still in touch with many of them. They have given me interesting work as well as rewarding friendship.

Once upon a time Benjamin Zephaniah was born in Birmingham, England. As a teenager he became well known in the Handsworth area of the city for his lively performances which were full of social commentary and observations of the political scene. Since then he has gone on to write nine books of poetry. He has composed eight records and has made numerous appearances on TV. His hobbies, he says, are "collecting money and kissing". June 29th is his mother's birthday; he does not know his own.

Try to love everyone
a tip from Benjamin Zephaniah

Try to love everyone. Even racists and bigots need help.

Try to 'overstand' those that you don't agree with and try to be 'overstood' by those that don't agree with you.

Benjamin Zephaniah adds: I once moved into a house and had a racist as my new neighbour. He proudly proclaimed his racism to me when I moved in. I listened carefully to his views and carefully challenged him on them. I got so much joy as I watched him slowly changing his views.

June 30

Alex Lester was born on May 11th 1956 in Walsall. He is a radio and TV presenter, with his own daily show on BBC Radio 2. Over the years he has worked for Radio 4, satellite TV and local independent and BBC local radio. On June 30th 1987 he joined Radio 2 as a trainee announcer – "my first ever national radio job and very frightening. Little did I realise at the time that I would eventually have my own daily show."

Keep your tubes clean and you'll live for ever
a tip from **Alex Lester**

I met a man in a pub who was a clear-eyed 86-year-old and he told me the secret of eternal life. Keep all your tubes clean.

So don't ingest or insert anything unhealthy. No drink, drugs, tobacco or bizarre sexual practices. He also added that a daily diet of prunes helped too.

Alex Lester adds: I have managed some of the above but I am afraid not all. He spoke extreme common sense but I must admit that living on a diet of prunes did put me off the idea of being around for the next millennium.

Vicki Robin was born in Oklahoma in 1945, raised near New York City, and schooled academically at Brown University, but experientially through 30 years of light living, travel and service. She is co-author with Joe Dominguez of Your Money or Your Life, *a US bestseller, and president of the educational and charitable social profit organisation, the New Road Map Foundation. She is a leader of the 'voluntary simplicity' movement in the US and has done thousands of radio, TV and print interviews about the joys of frugal living. July 1st is declared Freedom Day for Vicki. She says, "It was the day in 1969 I put all my furniture on the sidewalk outside my Brooklyn NYC apartment, got into a van and went on the road. I never 'returned', but rather engaged in a lifelong journey of exploration – inner and outer. 'The road' has been my metaphor for being 'in the world, but not of it' ever since."*

"It seemed like a good idea at the time"
a tip from Vicki Robin

"It seemed like a good idea at the time."

We aren't bad people. We mostly do the best we can with what we know. So don't waste too much time dissecting the past, especially if your explanation is really blame in disguise. Just know that whatever you or someone else did, and whatever your opinions of the outcome, the act, when performed, seemed like a good idea at the time. If you assign lessons or meanings beyond this, test them out in the future, but don't use them to pick at the past.

Vicki Robin adds: I was raised to be guilty and depressed – who knows why. It took a long time to realise that no one but me wanted me to wallow in misery over past errors (if they were errors at all). Or, if someone did want me to suffer, I didn't have to co-operate. It has helped me with everything from "why did I eat all those brownies?" to "why did I start (or end) that relationship?" to "why do politicians lie?" to "why is there something instead of nothing?" It assisted me in distinguishing between misery and meaning. It led me to inquire instead of obsess. The gentle chuckle behind "it seemed like a good idea at the time" liberated me for both enjoying my life and applying myself to larger issues in the world than assigning blame. My friend Tom Atlee has added to this wisdom his own general theory of explanation: "There's always more to it than you think." And a third sage has added: "Or not." So the final inquiry into why anything happens is: "It seemed like a good idea at the time. But there's always more to it than you think. Or not."

July 2

Nina Petrova was born on June 9th 1913. She is a writer, broadcaster and once acted at the Gate Theatre during the war – in a Chekhov play called The Bear. Nina Petrova is distantly related to Chekhov through her third cousin in Taganrog. Anton Chekhov died on July 2nd 1904.

Don't spit in the well
a tip from Nina Petrova

Don't spit in the well, you might need a drink of water.

This Russian proverb means: Do not discard people who have upset you or behaved badly – workmen, friends or others – as you might need them later.

Nina Petrova adds: I was told this proverb by a Russian friend many years ago and I thought it rather dirty and funny at the time. But it has worked for me. I have an old friend who upset me by recommending a bad builder who cost a lot of money, did a bad job and did not finish the work. This affected my health. I wanted to drop her several times but she happens to be one of the few friends left with whom I can talk about old times and old friends at my age. So I am glad that I took this advice and made the decision to remain in touch.

Susan Penhaligon was born on July 3rd 1949. She is an actress best known for A Bouquet of Barbed Wire *and many theatre and TV appearances. She has also had a book of her poems,* A Two Hander, *published along with Sara Kestelman.*

Small changes can be effective
a tip from Susan Penhaligon

Judi Dench used to say in rehearsal "If a director asks you to change something, only change it by that much" – and she'd hold her thumb and forefinger an inch apart.

Susan Penhaligon adds: I've always found this very useful both in work and play.

July 4

Christopher Monckton was born on St Valentine's Day 1952. He is a former Downing Street special adviser to Margaret Thatcher and is the inventor of the bestselling ETERNITY jigsaw puzzle. For the past 15 years he has run a successful consultancy business advising small governments and large corporations on how to overcome problems with bureaucracy. He appears regularly on TV and radio and also writes for the newspapers. He is a former consulting editor and chief leader-writer of the London Evening Standard. He writes: "I first discovered the joys of capitalism on July 4th, American Independence Day, at a party thrown by American friends."

Never give advice unless you've been paid for it
tips from Christopher Monckton

I

Never, never give advice
Unless you've first been paid your price:
There's no more canny tip than this 'un –
The more you charge, the more they'll listen.

II

Never, never take advice
From just one mouth: ask twice and thrice –
But take advice without compunction
If your adviser's Mr Monckton

(Except on how to make things rhyme:
He isn't very good at that).

Christopher Monckton adds: Part I of my tip comes from Tony Peck, an immensely competent and successful consultant from whom I learned a great deal. He grew rich on charging well for good advice, and so in turn did I. Part II comes from observing Ministers at close quarters. The ones who did well were the ones who were humble enough to listen and wise enough to consult widely. The ones who failed were the ones who were either too proud to listen at all or (still more disastrous) too dim to listen to anyone but their civil servants.

Musa Moris Farhi was born on July 5th 1935 in Turkey. He came to England to study drama and stayed on. A graduate of the Royal Academy of Dramatic Art, he worked for some years as an actor. He took up writing professionally in the early 1960s and wrote numerous scripts for television and films. In the mid-1980s, he decided to devote himself to writing novels. His works include: The Pleasure of Your Death *(1972),* The Last Days *(1983),* Journey Through the Wilderness *(1989) and* Children of the Rainbow *(1999). He has also published many poems.*

Finding your way with onion and garlic
a tip from Musa Moris Farhi

Always travel with an onion and a bulb of garlic.
(If these prove cumbersome, carry photographs instead.)

Those of you who can't tell which side is right and which left, keep the onion in your left hand – or pocket – and the garlic in your right hand – or pocket. Those of you travelling in areas where magnetic fields play havoc with compasses, do the same. And those motorists who have a poor sense of orientation or are bad navigators, place the onion and the garlic, respectively, on the left and right side of the dashboard. Whenever you ask for directions, whether on foot or in a vehicle, always ask the person to indicate 'left' and 'right' as 'onion' and 'garlic'. If need be, make a map where turnings are marked by icons of an onion and a garlic bulb. Don't throw away these maps; some turn out to be great paintings.

Musa Moris Farhi adds: I received this advice, in my youth, from my wrestling coach, Süleyman Ağa, the wisest and gentlest person I have ever known. Stranded in a desolate terrain, in the wake of General Allenby's rout of the Ottoman Army in Palestine, in the First World War, Süleyman Ağa set out to regain his country. Illiterate at the time and unable to differentiate between his left and his right, he accomplished his odyssey after a shepherd gave him an onion and a bulb of garlic and taught him how to use them when asking directions. This measure not only saw him home, but also brought him luck: he became one of the most celebrated wrestlers of his time. Luck is another blessing garlic bestows. In my case this tip worked infallibly, on many occasions, during my travels in the wilds of Africa, South America and the Balkans.

July 6

Writer and broadcaster Colin Larkin was born on December 15th 1949. In 1989 he set about creating the Encyclopedia of Popular Music (EPM), *a multi-volume work that was to become the popular music equivalent of the* Grove Dictionary of Music. *With three editions and over 40 spin-off titles, the* EPM *is now the leading music encyclopedia in the world. July 6th 1975 is the birth date of Colin's late son, Ben.*

A song a day
a tip from Colin Larkin

Popular music has made us all cry, shiver, whoop, laugh, scream, blush, smile and dance. That is its prime duty. Never let a day go by without listening to a complete song, preferably in the morning or last thing at night. Make sure it's something that you are familiar with or something that you may learn to love.

A good song buzzing around your head throughout the day is better than any vitamin pill, special diet or yoga. Music is as important to existence as life itself.

Colin Larkin adds: Whatever has happened in my life, popular music has always been my saving grace. Since the age of three, I have been aware of the exhilarating effect of a great pop song, sometimes unashamedly crying over a song that makes me feel so good. This happened to me with 'Cathy's Clown' in 1960 and continues with many other songs to this day. Sad, melancholy or happy, popular music has got me through broken marriages and the death of one of my children. It continues to inspire me every day.

Rowland Morgan, journalist and author, was born in Brighton of Welsh parents on July 7th 1945, the day after the allied victory parade through the ruins of Berlin. Nine days later, on July 16th at Alamogordo, USA, the atomic structure of the world was rearranged by the atmospheric splitting of an atom. About 60,000 nuclear warheads were subsequently produced, and 1,900 test explosions occurred, many of them 40,000 times as powerful as the first bomb. Since he was born, 3,500 holes have been blasted in Earth's protective ozone layer by rockets launching satellites. The human population has increased by nearly 3,000,000,000.

Believe in the potential for change
a tip from Rowland Morgan

At any given time, about 1,800 million people are asleep and dreaming. At each revolution of the earth, humans sleep for a total of five million years, hooking up to we know not what mothership. When we reawaken to civilisation, we remain about 90 per cent unconsciously run, because a tiny percentage of the mind is used by consciousness. In other words, humans, like fractals, function at a narrow margin of chaos, more or less sleepwalking through life, subject to hypnotic forces far beyond our ken.

As dreamers, we forget the massive convulsions of unexpected transformation that have happened to us in the past.

For example, women took up ovulating every 28 days, against the practice of all other mammals, without consulting a single doctor. Five thousand languages were launched without a day of research or development. Cannibalism and incest were outlawed without a scrap of legislation. Christianity swept the western world in a decade without any advertising. So we know that spontaneous changes in human behaviour have been far beyond the power of science, commerce or government to affect. There is no reason why they should not be again.

Rowland Morgan adds: Residents of Sussex, my home county (motto: We won't be druv), lived without automobiles for nearly 20,000 generations. (We know, because a human tibia was found in Boxgrove, dating from 498,000 BC.) The rich now own a fleet of over 500 million cars that would stack to the moon and beyond. Wealthy air travellers, who know they are the single most climate-wrecking users of transport, are set to double in number in a decade or so. Rich investors are eradicating the primeval forests that function as Earth's lungs. Despair looms before such facts, yet somehow, ideas like the above have come along to help me avoid despair. As an existentialist, sworn to gaze unflinchingly at the state of the world, I have found this tip to be a reasonable basis on which to hope for miracles. It also works as a joke. At least on friends of mine.

July 8

Colin Ward was born on August 14th 1924. He has written for the anarchist paper Freedom *since the 1940s, and edited* Anarchy *in the 1960s and* BEE *(Bulletin of Environmental Education) in the 1970s. His 30 books range from* Anarchy in Action *(1973) and* The Child in the City *(1978) to* Reflected in Water: A crisis of social responsibility *(1997). A book in his honour,* Richer Futures, *edited by Ken Worpole, was published by Earthscan in 1999. July 8th is the birthday of his partner, Harriet Ward.*

As the threshold of competence rises, so the pool of inadequacy widens
a tip from **Colin Ward**

As the threshold of competence rises, so the pool of inadequacy widens.

Harriet made this remark round about 1970, and the more I see of the widening gulf between the affluent and powerful and the poor and powerless, the more I reflect on how wise she was.

Today you have to be far smarter to get by, and if you aren't, we penalise your children.

Colin Ward adds: One third of the children in Britain grow up in poverty – with all that this implies about their attainments, behaviour and attitudes – while the gulf between the incomes and opportunities of the affluent and the poor has widened continuously over the past 20 years. The number of households with less than half of the average income has risen during that period from four million to eleven million. Meanwhile the confident and competent can rejoice in their instant communication by internet or e-mail or fax. It enables them to ignore those fellow citizens who lack a telephone or bank account and haven't even a toe-hold in the world they take for granted.

The late Dame Barbara Cartland was born on July 9th 1901. A world-bestselling authoress, she wrote more books than any other Briton (723) and sold over one billion copies in 36 languages. Twice-married herself, she believed that married couples should take a honeymoon every year and retire to bed for the afternoon ("when men are at their best"). In 1931 she carried the first glider airmail in her own sailplane from Manston airport to Reading. She joined the Women's Voluntary Services during the war and later lobbied for a wage for stay-at-home mothers. She was also the step-grandmother of Princess Diana. Barbara Cartland died peacefully in her sleep on May 21st 2000. Her body was buried, at her request, in a cardboard coffin in the grounds of her estate in Hertfordshire.

Live every minute to its full
a tip from **Dame Barbara Cartland,** DBE

"Live every minute to its full" has always been my motto, but then I was born in July and those people always want everything done immediately – if possible, yesterday!

Barbara Cartland believed that her many life achievements (only a few of which are detailed here) were the direct result of her living life to the full, every minute of every day.

July 10

Charles Shand was born on July 10th 1945. He is a businessman, creative entrepreneur, engineer and writer. Best known for his work as a designer, he willingly admits to being unable to draw a straight line even with the aid of a ruler, but as a team leader he has inspired younger colleagues to produce acclaimed product, graphic and environmental design work. His work developing products such as the Toyota Lexus, and corporate identities for organisations including the Museum of the Moving Image and Harrods, has won international awards.

Be bold and mighty forces will come to your aid
a tip from Charles Shand

Be bold – and mighty forces will come to your aid.

Whenever you're facing a tough decision and doubts set in, remember these words. Confidence is a cumulative thing and while boldness in itself is no guarantee of anything, the person who tries and fails will always be better off than someone who tries to do nothing and succeeds. Always try to live a bit beyond your obvious capacities.

Charles Shand adds: It's amazing how words can illuminate. These (from a rather free translation of Goethe: "Boldness has genius, power and magic in it", *Faust*, Part 1) made me see that when I had fallen short in an undertaking, it was often because a fear of failure had stopped me from trying too hard at all. However, this is no exhortation to be reckless and foolhardy. Boldness should be a deliberate decision, taken from time to time, to bite off more than you can chew. Moreover, there is nothing mysterious about the forces at play here. They are the latent powers we all possess: energy, skill, sound judgement, creative ideas – yes, even physical strength and endurance in far greater measure than most of us realise.

The Bishop of London, The Rt Revd and Rt Hon. Richard Chartres, was born on July 11th 1947 and was ordained in 1973. He was chaplain to the Archbishop (1980–84), Bishop of Stepney (1992–95) and Gresham professor of divinity (1986–92). He is also dean of Her Majesty's Chapels Royal.

Never be cynical
a tip from The Lord Bishop of London

A very fresh and spirited octogenarian said to me, when I was a very depressed and elderly 15-year-old, "Never be cynical", because people tend to conform to one's expectations of them.

Two people moved into the same community on one day. They both looked into a local café during the exhausting business of humping furniture and they both found an old resident sitting at a table in the window.

The first person asked, "What's this community like?"

"What was it like where you came from?" said the elderly resident. The newcomer replied that it had been a place which he had been glad to leave, full of snobbery, competition and unkind gossip. "Alas," said the elderly resident, "I have bad news for you. This place is even worse."

A little while later, the second newcomer looked in and posed the same question to the elderly resident. When asked to describe the place he had left, the newcomer said that he had been very sorry to leave and that it was full of people always ready to lend a neighbourly hand and that there was a real spirit of solidarity about the place. The elderly resident beamed, "You could be describing this place."

The Bishop of London adds: I have not always lived up to this peremptory advice, but I see more and more clearly how important it is not to be cynical.

July 12

Michael Norton was born on July 10th 1942. He was the founder of Directory of Social Change, the UK's leading provider of information and training to the voluntary sector. In 1995, he started the Centre for Innovation in Voluntary Action to develop and launch new projects that encourage voluntary action and community involvement. This centre operates in the UK and overseas, with an emphasis on India. He is also the chair of Changemakers, which encourages young people to become active citizens, and of Transform, a training and support programme for non-governmental organisations in Africa. July 12th is his parents' wedding anniversary and his middle child's birthday.

The worst case scenario
a tip from Michael Norton

You may be faced with a problem that seems just too difficult to deal with. You can run away from it, of course. Or you can sit there paralysed, unable to do anything to make things better. The problem will then continue to confront you, and will cause growing aggravation. Either way, you are not doing anything to sort out the problem.

One way of unblocking the situation, that I have found useful, is to consider the worst thing that could happen. If you can come to terms with this, and even be comfortable with it, then anything you do to improve things will be an advance. Instead of feeling oppressed by your inability to do anything, you begin to feel enthusiastic that you can actually do something to make things better. And you may even go on to find a solution that works.

Michael Norton adds: In 1996, I was setting up a specialist publishing operation in India to produce and distribute books that provided information and ideas to people and organisations working on poverty and development. I had found a partner to work with me, who was a successful Delhi publisher, and arranged the funding which would sustain the operation for the first five years. Then my partner suddenly dropped dead at the age of 47 from a heart attack.

I tried to proceed without him, but found the going impossible. Setting up something on your own in a country that is over 4,000 miles away is not simple. In India it's impossible. Although I appointed three people to help me, and found three more who were prepared to be trustees, no progress was being made and the money was beginning to haemorrhage away. I wasn't sure what to do and was getting increasingly depressed about the chances of rescuing things. But then I applied the principle of 'worst case scenario planning' which I had just invented.

The worst thing that could happen would be to give up. My funders would understand that I had tried my best and that I hadn't spent too much of the money by then anyway. Giving up was a realistic option. So I set myself a deadline of five months to find a partner organisation to work with, and if I couldn't then I would call things a day. I did manage to find one, although it took a further nine months to negotiate how we would work together. Books for Change is now a flourishing operation based in Bangalore.

Godfrey N. Brown was born on July 13th 1926. He is Emeritus Professor of Education at Keele University. He has been successively an Intelligence Corps officer, an international civil servant at UNHQ in New York, a schoolmaster, an academic in Ghana, Nigeria and Zimbabwe and, since retiring from Keele, the director of an art and antiques gallery.

Try to live in the present, past and future
a tip from **Godfrey N. Brown**

Try to live in the present, past and future.

There's no avoiding living in the present, but disregarding the past and the future impoverishes the process. It removes the enhancement of historical reference and the excitement of historical discovery; it means failure to look ahead realistically, and makes setting objectives and planning impossible. Living 'for the day' is essentially living for an unending night.

Godfrey N. Brown adds: This advice seeks to put into practice Einstein's belief that "the distinction between past, present and future is only an illusion, however persistent". The longer I live the more true this seems. Having read history at university, been concerned to conserve an historic house and having tried to plan an interesting life, I believe Einstein got it just right.

July 14

Claude Martin was born on July 20th 1945 and appointed director general of WWF International in October 1993. Before this he had been director and chief executive of WWF Switzerland for ten years. His career with WWF started in the early 1970s, when he lived in Central India, studying the ecology of the threatened Barasingha deer in Kanha National Park. From 1975 to 1978 he served as director of protected areas in Ghana, West Africa. He is the author of The Rainforests of West Africa (1991), a comprehensive study examining the ecology, utilisation and conservation of these forest areas. Martin notes that "July 14th is the National Day of France (and of Iraq) – a day when all nationals are asked to sing national anthems with doubtful success."

Never ask a pig to sing
a tip from **Claude Martin**

Never ask a pig to sing.

Claude Martin adds: The grandmother of a friend of mine produced this piece of wisdom. I have found it useful in not trying to force my views on unwilling staff members, who will always find a way to resist your strategic thinking – a lesson I have seen few professional managers take seriously. Most are stubborn in their pursuance of unconvincing ideas – and fail.

Carmen Callil was born on July 15th 1938 in Melbourne, Australia. She came to live in London in 1960. Except for a few years in Italy and many divided between France and England, she has lived in London ever since. As a book publisher, she founded Virago Press in 1972 and was publisher of Chatto & Windus and The Hogarth Press from 1982 to 1994. She is now a writer and critic. The Modern Library: The 200 best novels in English since 1950, *written with Colm Toibin, was published in 1999 by Picador. Her latest book is about Vichy France.*

Answer back
a tip from Carmen Callil

I came from a family who never put up with anything much. This is an inherited trait that can get you into trouble, but it can be a good trait – in a modified form – for the English to develop. As follows:

If you are not happy with the education your child is getting at school, make a sensible fuss. If British Telecom send you a bill full of incomprehensible charges, which they do, object to it. If you don't like what your local politician is doing, object. And so on.

Carmen Callil adds: I certainly misapplied this trait, but then I was indoctrinated with it along with my mother's milk. As the years have gone by, though, I have discovered that a bit of iron in the backbone is a good thing and helps change the world a little. I would avoid using it on an hourly basis though, which used to be my problem.

July 16

John Spurling was born on July 17th 1936 in Kisumu, Kenya. His first play MacRune's Guevara *was produced by the National Theatre in 1969. Since then he has written some 30 plays for the stage, radio and TV, the most recent being* King Arthur in Avalon *for the 1999 Cheltenham Festival of Literature. His first novel was* The Ragged End *and his second* After Zenda *(1995). He was art critic for the* New Statesman *from 1976 to 1988 and still sometimes writes about art. He also reviews books for the* Sunday Times *and the* Times Literary Supplement.

Hello and goodbye
a tip from John Spurling

Always let the driver hanging on your tail get past as soon as possible. He's obviously not yet had an accident or even a near miss and so he's dangerously inexperienced as well as impatient and aggressive.

Perhaps this applies to life in general. Impatient, aggressive people tend to lack experience and therefore character, and are not worth spending too much time with.

John Spurling adds: I'm naturally impatient and aggressive myself and used to drive sports cars until we had too many children and cats to fit behind the seats. One excellent remedy for impatience is to smoke a pipe (yes, I know it's incorrect, but just staying alive kills you in the end anyway). Another is to avoid irritating places like roads, railways and airports, to stay at home and read very good books (don't try gardening – that's for naturally patient people).

Venerable Ajahn Khemadhammo was born on July 17th 1944. Formerly an actor, he has been a Buddhist monk since becoming a novice in Bangkok in 1971. Full ordination followed in North-East Thailand on May 26th 1972. He has been visiting Buddhists in prison since 1977 and is the spiritual director of Angulimala, the Buddhist prison chaplaincy organisation which he helped launch in 1985.

Kindly stand your ground
a tip from **Ajahn Khemadhammo**

By all means be firm, stand your ground and don't give up easily, but do so with a smile on your face and loving-kindness in your heart.

Ajahn Khemadhammo adds: I was taught that I should regard as my meditation practice whatever I am doing at that moment. Trying to apply this to my prison visiting, and the seeming implacable negativity you can find in such places, I eventually discovered the value of combining the two Buddhist principles of loving-kindness and determination.

July 18

Fay Weldon was born on September 22nd 1931 and spent half of the intervening years writing. Her books include Life and Loves of a She Devil (1984), Big Women (1997) and Rhode Island Blues (2000). Weldon says, "July 18th is my second son's birthday. But I don't wish the other three to feel excluded." (Daniel, the second son, was born in 1963. Nicholas was born in 1954; Thomas in 1970; and Samuel in 1977.)

Tips for those who can't help writing
from Fay Weldon

Tips for writers:

Beginners: Try not to be too grateful to your publisher. Don't do things for next to nothing on the grounds that you like doing it anyway. This is bad for your income and for that of other writers. Women writers in particular should be offered classes in ingratitude by the Society of Authors, who you must join at the first flash of a contract.

Established: Remember that, love them as you may, the interests of your publishers overlap yours, but do not fully coincide.

Advanced: If you want to win the Booker Prize, keep your sentences long and never make jokes. I speak as one who has judged it but never won it.

Fay Weldon adds: I come from a family of novelists – mother, uncle, grandfather – and always understood that writing was a practical matter, very little to do with literature, and a risky way of paying the rent besides. You are only ever as good as your last book. If you want to 'be a writer' the advice is, don't. If on the other hand you want to write a particular novel, play, film or whatever, because you have something to say, and the talent to say it, carry on and good luck to you. Nothing will stop you anyway.

Peter Birrel was born in Vienna (his parents were English) on July 19th 1935. After a false start reading Law at Cambridge – "I'd seen myself in wig and gown being dramatic at the Old Bailey" – and National Service in the RAF, he went to the Bristol Old Vic Theatre School and has been a professional actor ever since.

A tail to lions rather than a head to foxes
a tip from Peter Birrel

This tip isn't actually from me, it's from Rabbi Matithya ben Cheresh, quoted in the *Pirkë Avoth*, the Jewish 'Sayings of the Fathers'. The Rabbi says: "Be rather a tail to lions than a head to foxes."

I specially like this advice as I take it to mean that it's never satisfactory to settle for second best, even if the price is acknowledging your own limitations.

Peter Birrel adds: This advice has been very apt to my career as I've mainly played supporting roles (if not always tails).

July 20

Paul Brown was born on July 20th 1944. He has been environment correspondent for the Guardian newspaper since 1989. He was previously an investigative reporter and worked for the Sun and a number of provincial newspapers. He has written books on Antarctica and global warming.

Caister men never turn back
a tip from Paul Brown

"Caister men never turn back" means if you have made a decision to do something, do not give up when the going gets tough. It is the motto over the lifeboat station at Caister-on-Sea in Norfolk where in times past many of my ancestors were crewmen. It was one of the first sentences my father was able to read as a child and, whenever life got difficult, he quoted it and it seemed to give him strength. Strangely I find myself doing the same and for some reason it always makes me smile.

Paul Brown adds: It could be a dangerous motto if it meant being inflexible in changing circumstances, so it should not be an excuse for being pigheaded or foolhardy. But in journalism and in many daunting situations, such as rowdy public meetings when I have to speak, it has stood me in good stead. I feel generations of lifeboatmen are giving me courage.

Sidney Brichto was born on July 21st 1936. He was director of the Union of Liberal & Progressive Synagogues. He has written many articles for the national and Jewish press, and two books: Funny ... You Don't Look Jewish *and* The People's Bible *(vol. 1, Chatto, 2000).*

Be nicer to your family than to strangers
a tip from Sidney Brichto

Be nicer to your family than to strangers.

Be generous in your praise. Only criticise when you have no alternative.

Don't believe what your partner says in anger.

Never hit your child.

Sidney Brichto adds: These tips are based on my own experiences. Even when I have not been able to live by them, they have been a good benchmark for judging whether I have grown wiser as I have grown older.

July 22

U. A. Fanthorpe was born on July 22nd 1929, and taught English for 16 years before deciding that teaching was no substitute for learning. A brief flurry of temping jobs led finally to a permanent job as receptionist in a small Bristol hospital. Here she discovered that poetry was the only way of managing her feelings about brain-damaged patients. So she wrote poetry, and still does – seven collections to date (the most recent being Consequences, *published by Peterloo Poets) and three audio-cassettes (the most recent,* Double Act, *with R. V. Bailey, produced by Penguin).*

Don't overlook Now
a tip from U. A. Fanthorpe

It's very easy to waste time and energy in fretting about the past and the future. Those who really get a kick out of this contrive never to think about Now at all – there's always 'What I did yesterday', 'What I'm going to do tomorrow', and endless variations on these themes.

Of course, sometimes escape from Now is what we most want – and then past and future are most helpful. But what more often happens is that we miss the immediate pleasures of Now. For all we know, there may be no tomorrow, or it'll be quite different from what we expect. It would be a great pity therefore not to relish being alive Now.

U. A. Fanthorpe adds: I was late for a seminar at Swansea University. It was a fine, blue-skied day, and I was driving down the road towards the sea. Unfortunately, so were half the other inhabitants of Swansea. The queue hardly moved at all. I kept looking at my watch. I was quite new on the course and the only woman, and I didn't want to create a bad impression by being late. The tutor was an intimidating person. I was sweating; the car engine smelt hot. Unexpectedly, and almost as if someone had thrown a switch, I saw things differently: it was a lovely day; the scenery (apart from the cars) was beautiful; the sky was blue, so was the sea. I was feeling well and happy, and enjoying the course. But my own decision to worry had obscured all these things. I settled down to enjoy where I was. When, eventually, I reached the seminar, I told my tutor about this mini-revelation. Kind man that he is, he said that such an experience was true learning, and far more important than getting to a seminar on time. The tip still helps me, but I'm sorry to say that I've completely forgotten the seminar.

Sir Nicholas Barrington was born on July 23rd 1934. He spent 37 years as a career diplomat, ending up as British high commissioner in Pakistan. For three years in the 1970s, he was a political counsellor in Tokyo. Since retirement in 1994 he has been involved with a number of cultural and educational charities.

Minimise worry
a tip from Sir Nicholas Barrington

Developing certain simple habits can minimise worry: Touch your pocket to check you have keys before you go out and slam the front door. Always put your train ticket in the same pocket. Similarly, have a special pocket for your cloakroom ticket.

Unless you're just going round the block, always take with you:

A handkerchief, a comb, a small pencil, some paper, a box of paper matches for bonfires, candles and ladies' cigarettes, and a small nail file to keep nails clean, to cut string, prise up drawing pins and serve as a screwdriver.

As instructed by a Zen monk in Kyoto:

Don't worry about the past: it is over. Don't worry about the future: if something needs to be done, do it. Concentrate on doing as well as possible the activity of the moment.

Sir Nicholas Barrrington adds: One of the most remarkable and impressive men I have met in my life was the Reverend Kobori San, a senior Zen monk in Kyoto. He emanated positive goodness and harmony with the world and could talk about anything, humorous or serious.

July 24

The poet and author Robert Graves was born on July 24th 1895. His best known prose works are Goodbye To All That, The Greek Myths, The White Goddess *and* I, Claudius. *Graves was born in London, but lived most of his adult life in Majorca, where he died in 1985. His daughter Lucia, who offers this tip, is an author and translator.*

Pour fearlessly!
a tip from Lucia Graves

Whenever my father, Robert Graves, saw that I was about to pour something which required a steady hand he would say: "Pour fearlessly!" He was right, of course: once fear has been removed, not a drop will spill.

Lucia Graves adds: Fearlessness and self-confidence were promoted at many levels by my father in our family life, and that went hand in hand with his belief in the power of the mind, which he often referred to as 'magic'.

Though I am timid by nature, I can remember two instances when I felt that I was making use of this power. One was when I succeeded in getting a night porter to open a department store in High Street Kensington, back in the 1960s, because I simply had to retrieve my driving licence, which I had forgotten by a counter. The other was sailing past customs in Franco's Spain with a copy of Hugh Thomas' banned book *The Spanish Civil War*, and being quite convinced that by holding my nerve I had cast a spell on the Civil Guards.

Throughout my life, my father's advice to 'pour fearlessly' has always helped me (with varying degrees of success) when I am about to face something unnerving.

Charles Handy was born on July 25th 1932, the son of an Irish archdeacon. In flight from Ireland and the church, he joined Shell in Singapore in 1956. Having been, he says, "a lousy manager", he turned to teaching management instead and became a professor in the early days of the London Business School. In despair at the futility of educating managers, he turned to writing, which he now does full-time, with books such as The Empty Raincoat *and* The Hungry Spirit.

Compliments from friends
a tip from Charles Handy

If you are wondering what you could do other than your current work, ask ten people whom you know and respect to tell you just one thing which they think you do rather well. Put those positive aspects of yourself – those compliments – together and you will have the outline of the next step in your life.

Charles Handy adds: After 25 years of a varied career I was still unsatisfied. My wife took me in hand and got me to list the things she and I thought I was good at. Writing and public speaking featured large, so she persuaded me to leave everything and concentrate on those. It has made all the difference.

Formalising the idea, I then started to suggest to those who came to me for counselling that they should ask ten friends to give them just one compliment each. Initially they often find this too immodest, but once started it becomes very revealing. It surfaces aspects of oneself that have been neglected or overlooked in the past.

July 26

Robert Wyatt was born on January 28th 1945. He is a well-known musician whose albums include Ruth is Stranger than Richard. *He says that he makes just enough records to earn a living from it (for further information see: www.rykodisc.com). Robert is married to Alfie and July 26th is their wedding anniversary.*

Avoid arguments
a tip from **Robert Wyatt**

Avoid arguments. People don't really win arguments. They're as often as not quite pointless and only serve to entrench people in defensive positions.

Robert Wyatt adds: I was once having a heated debate with a Trotskyist about Chinese foreign policy. And it suddenly occurred to me: why was I wasting my throat muscles when I could have been having a nice quiet think? We saw things differently, that was all.

Get used to the loneliness. If somebody asks your opinion and you can be bothered, give it, but you won't get a more sympathetic hearing if you rise to the bait of a threatening challenge. I wish I'd understood that decades ago and saved myself and others a lot of aggravation and millions of uselessly burnt-out brain cells. You may not agree with this tip. Well, I'm not going to argue with you.

Valerie Grove was born on May 11th 1946. She writes for The
Times *and has published two books of interviews:* Where I Was
Young, *about London childhoods, and* The Compleat Woman,
*about women who, like herself, have had four children, a job and
stayed married for 25 years. She has also written two biographies:*
Dear Dodie, *the life of Dodie Smith, and* Laurie Lee, The well-
loved stranger. *Valerie Grove notes: "It was about July 27th
1967 when I first started in Fleet Street, with a vacation job on the*
Londoner's Diary of the *Evening Standard."*

The pillow book
a tip from Valerie Grove

Take a nice, fat, square, empty book and write things
down in it. The ancient Chinese called it a pillow
book: it is not a diary, which is just a tyranny, but a
place to put your random thoughts whenever the
whim takes you. Over the years it presents a whole
picture of your life and you will always be grateful to
have it.

Valerie Grove adds: I kept an embarrassing diary from the ages of 13 to 18, but stopped just when my life
became really interesting. A decade remains sadly unrecorded and therefore consigned to oblivion. Then
I read *The Pillow Book of Eleanor Bron* and realised that even occasional jottings – lists of 'nice things',
'annoying things', 'a bad day', 'a good day' – give a vivid snapshot of life without creating guilt for
unwritten days.

As a biographer, I overflow with gratitude for my subjects' diaries and commonplace books. You never
regret having written things down; you only regret what is lost in the mists of fallible memory.

July 28

The late Nicholas Albery was born on July 28th 1948. He was the founder of the Institute for Social Inventions in London. Projects launched by this Institute include an Encyclopedia of Social Innovations, a Global Ideas Bank (www.globalideasbank.org), the Natural Death Centre (to help with 'green' funerals), the Befriending Network (volunteers who sit with those who are dying at home), the ApprenticeMaster Alliance (finding jobs for people in small and one-person businesses) and www.DoBe.org (bulletin boards for events and meetings). Nicholas died in a car accident on June 3rd 2001.

20 main pleasures in life
a tip from Nicholas Albery

If you have a job, but occasionally need extra money, or if you have no job and want one, or if your present work is not sufficiently satisfying, my advice is to try a ten-minute exercise devised by Leonard Orr (the guru who started the Rebirthing movement in the States). The exercise assumes that since life is short, one might as well have a job that is as pleasurable and satisfying as possible – ideally a job that one would do even without being paid for it. So:

1. Write down your 20 main pleasures in life. Then:

2. Write down ten ways to make money from your pleasures (ideally from a combination of your pleasures).

3. Explore one of these ways, trying it out, if you can, in reality.

Nicholas Albery wrote: In 1984, my student grant for a polytechnic course came to an end, after three delightful years, and I was becoming anxious about how I was going to earn a living. I did the above Leonard Orr exercise. My pleasures included hot sand, warm sea, walking off the beaten track, brainstorming, starting projects and working with my friend Nicholas Saunders.

I found that the design for an Institute for Social Inventions in London, with an annexe in the Canary Islands, grew naturally from my pleasures, combining 17 of the 20. I decided that I would give this ambitious scheme a try and that if it didn't work I would take any job going. So I appointed myself Institute chairman, persuaded Nicholas Saunders to become a director and the Institute was launched in London in 1985. It has more or less prospered to this day, although the Canary Island annexe has yet to happen, alas.

Elspeth Barker was born on November 16th 1940. She has written many reviews and articles for the Independent on Sunday, *the* Guardian, *most other broadsheets and glossy magazines. She tutors regularly on Arvon creative writing courses. Her award-winning novel,* O Caledonia, *is published by Penguin and her next novel is published in 2001. Barker notes: "I have chosen July 29th because it was my wedding day, which for technical reasons had been put on hold for 26 years. So it was a specially joyful occasion, attended by our grown-up children, grandchildren, and, in my husband's case, great-grandchildren." Elspeth married George Granville Barker, the poet, in 1989. He died in 1991.*

Always be ready to talk about dogs
a tip from **Elspeth Barker**

Always be ready to talk about dogs.

Even dog haters will join in this and you can convert them. If the worst comes, you must put up with their cat stories, finally trumping these with an unbeatable dog anecdote.

Elspeth Barker adds: Dog dialogues defuse tricky situations, loosen the tongues of the shy, divert delightfully.

An icy lady, receiving my very long overdue rent, melted into sunshine and rainbows when offered a cue to talk about beagles. All forgiven and forgotten.

Recently I suffered the humiliation of a pedicure (therapeutic, not cosmetic). I asked the smiling sadist in his Dr Scholl white coat what had led him into the world of feet. Dogs, he said. He had been a poacher in Ireland, but he wasn't any good at it because of his awful dogs. Lurchers, deranged and uncontrollable, fading like ghosts into the ceaseless drizzle. So he had turned, as one does, to something completely different. He still kept one lurcher to remind him that they had sent him in out of the rain to this new and happy life. His tales of lurcher treachery were so beguiling that I forgot to scream when he plunged a scalpel thing into my middle toe. Dentists might learn from this.

Dogs in literature can be helpful too. See Thurber's *Book of Dogs*. See the bulldog Jaw Jaw, who passes from generation to generation through Salman Rushdie's *The Moor's Last Sigh*. At some point he dies, but stuffed and mounted on castor wheels, he is able to maintain his starring role. That's the way to do it. One could go on and on; one often does.

July 30

Brian Clemens writes: "I was born on July 30th yonks ago, but I'm younger than Sean Connery." He created, wrote and produced The Avengers *and* The Professionals *series. He has written many movies, including* Golden Voyage of Sinbad, Highlander Two *(story only),* Dr Jekyll's Sister Hyde *and* Captain Kronos *(which he also directed). Most recently, he co-created* Bugs *for the BBC.*

Give the other person a way out
a tip from Brian Clemens

Always give the other person (no matter how moronic) a way out. If the bank misplaces millions of your dosh, do not start your angry letter, "Look here dick-head". The same goes for all confrontations, social or professional – defuse the situation up front. The soft voice is better than the big stick, no matter how much you are in the right, or how angry you are. Remember that other person is human too.

Brian Clemens adds: I used to write those 'dear dick-head' letters and get nowhere. I have found it is much better to give the other person an escape route, such as "I know it is probably a computer glitch, but ...", "I appreciate you have a difficult job, but ...". You get the picture? It has served me well – *and* gone a long way to correcting problems (and has reduced the threats to my life).

Dr David Landau was born on April 22nd 1950. He has been, he says, a doctor specialising in cardiology who lost his faith in orthodox medicine, a fellow in Renaissance Studies at Worcester College, Oxford, who decided he wanted to make money, the co-founder of an ice-cream business which went belly-up, and later chairman of Loot – the classified listings paper. Landau is now a multi-millionaire and Loot has won awards for its ergonomic workplace where the staff are offered free massages and fresh fruit. On July 31st 2000, Loot was sold to Scoot.com for £189m.

Be honest in business
a tip from Dr David Landau

When I asked my mother if it was possible to make lots of money without exploiting people she replied that, in fact, honesty was the only way of ensuring the longterm success of a business. Our family had been for many generations successful diamond merchants, she said, successful because of their honesty. If they had cheated their customers, it is unlikely that they would have kept many of them.

David Landau adds: I was a Marxist at university and was always rather sceptical about the ethics of making serious money. But my mother's timely advice greatly affected me and I would venture that she is in part responsible for the success of *Loot*. It is only through being honest with its customers and staff that *Loot* was so successful.

August 1

Shirley Marie Jacobsen was born on August 1st 1944. She is a poet, writer and artist, specialising in gospel music and photographic and pencil art displays. She has won awards for poetry from the National Library of Poetry (USA) and music and biographical awards from Airplay International and Around the World promotions; and from The International Biographical Association and The American Biographical Institute.

Hold a little back for yourself
a tip from Shirley Marie Jacobsen

Lift the anchor of your soul and sail on to greater waters.

Believe in yourself and develop your own individual talents and initiatives. Remember you are your own person. Hold a little back for yourself. Be mysterious and in control of your destiny. Weigh the advice of others carefully.

Shirley Jacobsen adds: This advice took me a while to learn. I discovered that the advice of others is sometimes self-seeking, so I learned to look at the purpose and content and intent of the heart, and to forgive instantly. On the other hand, there have been times when others have given me their 'best' and I learned valuable lessons from their counsel. This particular advice has saved me many heartaches.

Sam Llewellyn was born on August 2nd 1948. He is a sailor, musician, poet and the author of more than 25 novels for adults and children, including Wonderdog, The Sea Garden *and* Hell Bay. *His books have been published in 12 languages. He says he is proud to declare that he has not had a steady job since 1973.*

Neither make nor accept excuses
a tip from Sam Llewellyn

Excuses are a waste of time – yours and other people's.

If you neither make nor accept excuses, you become completely reliable and ultimately useful to other people.

Sam Llewellyn adds: I seem to remember that this was the principle which led Lord Carrington to resign as Foreign Secretary and return to his garden. His version was: "In the Guards, excuses are neither offered nor accepted." While I have (thank God) never been a soldier, my experiences at sea have shown me that situations slithered away from invariably become worse. If physical and mental distress result from facing life head on, too bad. I realise that this is an unfashionable principle, contrary to the practice of all current politicians and most people in business. But if you adopt it, life becomes immeasurably more straightforward.

August 3

Nick Drake was born on August 3rd 1961. He is a poet. The Man in the White Suit was published in 1999 by Bloodaxe Books. He translates Spanish drama, including Lope de Vega's Peribanez (Oberon Books, 1999). He has also worked in theatre, commissioning plays at the Bush Theatre and for the National Theatre's Connections project, a six-year epic involving hundreds of youth theatre companies, 34 playwrights and many theatres. Recently, he has also worked in the development of film projects.

Make it up as you go along
a tip from Nick Drake

Jump!

Always make the choice you fear. Take the risk. Choose the unknown. Follow your desire. Make it up as you go along. Find out what is in the dark forest of your heart.

Nick Drake adds: All the best things in my life have come from choosing to do the thing I feared the most. Leaping into the unknown is the best way to find out who you are and who you might become. Fear holds us in the same place, desire questions fear. When desire wins, then the unexpected happens. So jump whenever you can.

Colin Shindler was born in Hackney on September 3rd 1946. He is currently a fellow in Israeli Studies at the School of Oriental and African Studies, University of London. He has been concerned with human rights issues in many areas of the world and is a member of the standing commission on Disarmament and Security of the World Conference on Religion and Peace. He has edited several periodicals and his last book was a political history of the Israeli Right.

Be on your guard against the ruling power
a tip from **Colin Shindler**

"Be on your guard against the ruling power, for they who exercise it draw no man near to them except for their own interests; appearing as friends when it is to their own advantage, they stand not by a man in the hour of his need."

From Ethics of the Fathers *by Rabban Gamliel*

Colin Shindler adds: I have always appreciated this 2,000-year-old comment which seems to personify for me not only the sense of Jewish dissidence down the centuries, but more universally the instinctive willingness of a few courageous human beings to ask awkward questions in difficult circumstances and not simply to blow in the wind with the majority.

On August 4th 1914, ordinary people put their trust in the ruling power and the First World War commenced, in which millions lost their lives in the cause of futility. From this, both Stalinism and Nazism sprang. The legacy of the First World War was the Gulag and Auschwitz.

August 5

Ann Henning Jocelyn, Countess of Roden, was born in Göteborg, Sweden on August 5th 1948. She was educated in Sweden, then became resident in London, where she still has a home. In 1986 she married the 10th Earl of Roden and now spends most of her time with the family in the west of Ireland. As an author, writing as Ann Henning or Ann Henning Jocelyn, she is the author of Modern Astrology *and* The Connemara Whirlwind Trilogy. *Her stage plays have been produced in Sweden, Ireland and Bulgaria. She is artistic director of the Connemara Theatre Co. Ltd and broadcasts regularly on Irish and Swedish radio and TV.*

Offer what you've been given
a tip from Ann Henning Jocelyn
Countess of Roden

Don't base major decisions on your own needs and ambitions: that's like looking at the world through the wrong end of a telescope. Forget what you want; develop and offer what you've been given.

Ann Henning Jocelyn adds: This tip marked my coming of age. I was in my early twenties and had just finished an interesting but not very marketable arts degree. Vacantly I stared into the abyss of my future. So many possibilities, so many perils; endless potential for success as well as failure; irrevocable choices waiting to be made. I was caught between fear and desire, in a paralysing dilemma.

This advice was given to me by an old family friend who had made a great success of his own life. Thanks to him I became aware that to take the step into the truly adult world, you must look beyond your own person: accept that we are all components consigned to playing our parts in a large universal structure.

It was by contributing what I had, to the best of my ability, that I found the strength, courage and confidence I needed to go forward. If I didn't achieve all that I had hoped for, I discovered that the effort brought as much satisfaction as the result. Away from personal gratification, choices are easy. There are no anxieties, no frustration, no regrets. Just the inner peace of knowing that, whatever happens, you did your best.

Mary Ann Sieghart was born on August 6th 1961. She is an assistant editor of The Times, *and also writes political leaders and a weekly op-ed column. She has in the past also worked for* The Economist, Today *newspaper and the* Financial Times. *She appears occasionally on TV and radio programmes such as* Question Time, Any Questions *and* Start the Week.

Never do anything irreversible
a tip from Mary Ann Sieghart

Never do anything irreversible. Don't get a criminal record. Don't have an unwanted child. Don't take a lift from a drunken driver and end up scarring your face. Don't get addicted to alcohol, nicotine or drugs. Think hard before having a tattoo.

Mary Ann Sieghart adds: This was one of the best pieces of advice my father gave me. It helped me hugely in my teenage years. I managed to resist serious peer pressure to start smoking at 13 and to take heroin at 16. I was never cavalier about contraception, as many of my teenage girlfriends were. I have been tempted by a tattoo, but haven't yet succumbed. If I did, I'd have it done somewhere on my lower back where I didn't have to look at it in later life if I grew embarrassed by it.

August 7

Matthew Parris was born on August 7th 1949. He was educated in Rhodesia, Cambridge and America before going to the Foreign Office. He entered parliament in 1979 and left to take up an appointment in television in 1986. When that ended, he became parliamentary sketchwriter for The Times, a post he still holds. He also writes for the Spectator and is the author of several books, including Read My Lips and I Couldn't Possibly Comment.

Make important decisions irreversible
a tip from **Matthew Parris**

When you have taken an important decision and you are resolved to go through with it, make it irreversible. Burn your bridges. In this way you guard against subsequent failures of nerve.

Destroy material objects which have become an encumbrance. End relationships you know you want to end in a manner which admits of no reconciliation. Do not look back. Do not hesitate half-way.

Matthew Parris adds: I had an antique cup and saucer given to me by someone of whom I had once been fond. I sort of wanted to keep them, and sort of didn't. One day I lost the saucer; flew into a rage about the loss, then into a rage with myself for letting it get to me. So I smashed the cup. Later on I found the saucer and was able to smash that too with a much easier mind.

Connie Stevens was born on August 8th 1938 and was a teenage icon in the 1960s. Since the 1950s, her career as an actress, singer and entertainer has encompassed film, television, stage, recording and concert performances. She is also the mother of Joely and Tricia Fisher, a volunteer for charitable causes, including her project Windfeather which provides college scholarships to Native American youth, and chief executive of Forever Spring, a skin care and cosmetic line and The Garden Sanctuary, a day spa and boutique in Los Angeles.

Be the person your dog thinks you are
a tip from Connie Stevens

When you are in doubt as to how to act in a given situation, always be the person your dog thinks you are.

Connie Stevens adds: After a bad day of ranting, raving or feeling sabotaged and out of sorts or just plain tired, I have always found the unconditional love that comes from an animal energising and a gentle reminder to treat others as you would like to be treated.

August 9

Michael Young was born on August 9th 1915. He has founded some 50 charities since 1957. He has been a Labour peer in the House of Lords, director of the Institute of Community Studies since 1953 and chairman of the School for Social Entrepreneurs since 1996. Author of The Rise of the Meritocracy, Social Scientist as Innovator, Your Head in Mine *(poetry, 1993) and* A Good Death *(1996).*

Make use of the opposition
a tip from Lord Young of Dartington

I agree with many other pessimists that we probably have about the least bad system of parliamentary democracy we could have; and it is not as bad as it could be because there is an Opposition. The Opposition is often even more tiresome than the Government, but when it is working with zip, it really does make a difference. All sorts of decisions become a little less threadbare if they are subjected to intelligent opposition.

This also applies to anyone in their ordinary or fairly ordinary life. If you think of starting something – or stopping something which at one time you considered worth starting – or writing an article or a book and you don't feel completely clear about the theme of it, then the best thing to do is to find someone who will think what you are doing is daft. Ideally, they should be sympathetic as well as caustic in their criticism. But not everyone has that gift. If you have a friend like that, or can find one, then do ask them if they are willing to help you over the many stiles you are bound to meet.

Michael Young adds: I have found, when starting new charitable enterprises, that it is the critics rather than the creators who have made the difference. I tried to follow my own advice when taking the first steps to set up the Open University, or the University of the Third Age, or the Tower Hamlets Summer University, or almost anything I have done.

Susan Greenfield was born on October 1st 1950. She is a neurobiologist, Oxford professor, broadcaster, and writer of over 100 research papers and books, including The Human Brain: A guided tour and Private Life of the Brain. In 1994, she became the first woman to be invited to give the Royal Institution of Great Britain Christmas lectures. She was appointed director of the Royal Institution in 1998. Her husband, the chemist Professor Peter Atkins, was born on August 10th 1940.

Focus on what you think of others, not on what they think of you
a tip from Professor Susan Greenfield

It is much more important to know what you think about other people than to worry about what they may or may not think about you.

Susan Greenfield adds: My mother told me this when I was still quite young. It is a particularly helpful piece of advice for a woman working in a male-dominated environment.

August 11

Anthony Barnett has published many volumes of poetry and prose, including Blood Flow, Fear and Misadventure, The Resting Bell, Carp and Rubato, *and* Anti-Beauty. *He has published works on the history of the violin in jazz. He is editorial director of Allardyce, Barnett publishers.*

Tip the British Isles over
a tip from Anthony Barnett

Try to tip the British Isles over so that the Highlands and Islands are to the South, the Downs to the North, the Valleys to the West and the Wetlands to the East.

If there is ever anything about your country that you are not happy with, its climate, its culture, its literature, its art, its music, its politics, its history – it doesn't matter what – try to tip it over starting each year 'On the 31st of July'. That's my tip.

Anthony Barnett adds: This is what I wanted to do in a story entitled 'On the 31st of July', which was the day in 1999 on which I began to write it. As the story turns out it didn't happen that night but on the 11th of August, the day of the 1999 eclipse. Why did the writer who appears in this story want this to happen? Because he wished his country were other than it is.

Bernice Rubens was born on July 26th. She won the Booker Prize in 1970 for her novel, The Elected Member. She is the honorary vice-president of International PEN. Her other novels include Madame Sousatzka, Sunday Best, A Five Year Sentence, Spring Sonata, Birds of Passage, Mr Wakefield's Crusade, A Solitary Grief and The Waiting Game. She lives in London and loves playing the cello. Her grandmother was born on August 12th.

You are too young to count your blessings
a tip from Bernice Rubens

Some years ago, say about 20, my husband left me and I was deeply depressed. My grandmother, aged 94, had come to London to stay with me. She was consoling. I tried to cheer myself, and I said, "No matter, I am blessed with two beautiful daughters."

And at the age of 94, she said to me, "It doesn't matter how old you are, you are always too *young* to count your blessings."

Bernice Rubens adds: It is a phrase which has stayed with me ever since. To count one's blessings is to abdicate. My grandmother's advice resulted in a clutch after life. What a gift she gave me!

August 13

Howard Marks was born on August 13th 1945. He grew up in South Wales, and spoke only Welsh for the first five years of his life. He read Physics at Balliol College, Oxford. By the mid-1980s, he had 43 aliases, 89 phone lines and owned 25 companies. He was smuggling consignments of up to 30 tons of marijuana. He was caught by the Drugs Enforcement Agency and sentenced to 25 years in prison at Terre Haute Penitentiary, Indiana. He was released in April 1995 after serving seven years of his sentence. In 1997, he published his autobiography, Mr Nice. He now campaigns vigorously for drug legalisation.

Control your attitude
a tip from Howard Marks

It is impossible to control what happens to you. The only thing you can control is your attitude to it.

Howard Marks adds: For a long time when I was in prison I was really down, then I realised that I was taking myself too seriously. I should just help people as much as possible, keep fit and well, and take what comes. So I spend the next decade in prison. Big Deal. So what? What next?

Ken Taylor was born on November 10th 1922. He is a television writer, winner of several TV awards, including a Writer's Guild award for best original screenplay and the Royal Television Society's award for his screenplay The Jewel in the Crown. *He is married, has four children and lives in Cornwall.*

August 14

Never wish time away
a tip from Ken Taylor

Never wish time away, it's shorter than you think.

In childhood when days seem to last for ever, we form a habit of living for what is yet to come. Letting that spread into adult life is the trap, because the less time that you have left, the faster it runs away.

Ken Taylor adds: August 14th was the day that Japan's surrender ended the Second World War and was the day for which I wished six years of my life away.

I've spent far too much of my life wishing time away – impatient for an objective such as the end of the war, that holiday, the big event, the deadline for a script. The final, unstoppable deadline coming towards you every day is your own – so make the most of now.

August 15

James Tucker was born on August 15th 1929. He is an author who writes crime novels under the pen names Bill James, David Craig and Judith Jones; and other novels and literary criticism under his own name. He was previously a journalist working for various newspapers and magazines, including the Daily Mirror, *the* Sunday Times *and the* Spectator; *and for TV and radio. His latest novel as Bill James is* Kill Me; *as David Craig,* Bay City; *as Judith Jones,* After Melissa.

Shun television
a tip from James Tucker

As Noel Coward or someone said, television is for being on, not for watching. It is designed to capture you by instilling a habit. It has been appallingly successful at this. The 'art of programming' is one designed to paralyse your power to operate the off switch.

Should people start talking to you in the pub about what they viewed last night, fall down as if they have struck you a low blow.

Avoid people who claim to watch only wildlife programmes. They think that their familiarity with the lair-building skills of the lynx validates all their other viewing.

Do not watch weather programmes: the most tedious topic in the universe is presented with ham gestures, silky smiles and mad confidence, as if it were entertainment. These programmes will make you believe weather is a fit subject for conversation and turn you into a bore as big as the people who front them.

James Tucker adds: My father argued that a great deal could be learned from television and so I decided to have little or nothing to do with it. I watch *Frasier* only. I therefore have time for my own pursuits. These are sleeping, drinking and falling down in pubs.

Allegra Taylor was born on December 23rd 1940. She is the author of several books, including I Fly Out With Bright Feathers, Acquainted with the Night *and* Ladder to the Moon. *She is also a practising healer and workshop leader. She is married to filmmaker Richard Taylor and they have six grown-up children and 11 grandchildren. August 16th is their wedding anniversary.*

Loving the distance
a tip from **Allegra Taylor**

My tip is taken from Rainer Maria Rilke's *Letters*:

"Once the realisation is accepted that, even between the closest of human beings, infinite distances continue to exist, then a wonderful living side by side can grow up – if they succeed in loving the distance between them which makes it possible for each to see the other whole against the sky."

Allegra Taylor adds: I have given this tip to quite a few young friends starting out on the relationship path. I'm sure it is a major contributory factor in my enduring love for my partner Richard and his for me in our 40-odd years of marriage.

August 17

Selima Hill was born on October 13th 1945. She is a writer, mother, ex-wife, doting grandmother; and the only poet to be nominated for not only the Forward prize, but also the T. S. Eliot and Whitbread prizes. V. S. Naipaul, mentioned below, was born on August 17th 1932 in Trinidad.

Avoid making too much money before you're 40
tips from Selima Hill

Avoid making enormous amounts of money before you're 40. (This from V. S. Naipaul.)

Nobody gives you the power: you just take it. (This one for women and for writers in particular.)

Never go to bed angry: stay up and fight.

And finally, if you want the rainbow, you gotta put up with the rain!

Selima Hill adds: When I reached 50, I realised I took it all too seriously – dutiful daughter, dutiful student, dutiful wife, or tried to be – and I decided just to enjoy myself and write. Margot Fonteyn is the last person I would expect to agree with, but who can argue with her when she says, "Taking your work seriously is imperative; taking yourself seriously is disastrous." Finally, I am grateful to my late father for his 50 years of advice and what it taught me: ignore it.

Brian Wilson Aldiss was born on August 18th 1925 in Norfolk ("I left in rather a hurry"). His first book was published in 1955, since when he has published a volume almost every year. He writes science fiction and contemporary novels. For several years, he toured an evening revue round the country. He is a member of the Royal Society of Literature ("I prefer it to work").

When depressed, pull a lever
a tip from **Brian Aldiss**

If we are to believe the polls, a high percentage of the population is depressed. This must stop! Advances in the study of the brain indicate that all intellectual decisions have an emotional basis. Thus we understand that intellectual decisions can influence emotional matters.

So when one is depressed one must decide intellectually not to be. Think of it in terms of imagery, as *pulling a lever*.

There are many considerations which can help if the lever is a bit stiff. For instance, consider how beautiful the view is from your bedroom window (even if it seems not to be); how kind your family are (even if they seem not to be); how delightful your friends are (even if they seem not to be); how fascinating your own character is (even if it seems not to be); how lucky you are to be alive (even if you seem not to be).

Lean on the lever. Soon everything will change. Far from being depressed you will become quietly elated. You'll have won. Remember Hamlet's words: "There is nothing but thinking makes it so." Pull that lever today.

Brian Aldiss adds: When my wife died, I became one of the walking dead. But I had to tend the garden, which was beautiful, as I realised. I was astonished by the support my family gave – and needed; I found good new friends; I even became interested in discovering how resourceful I was. I realised I could live on without my dear wife. One day I perceived that grief was self-indulgence and not a duty. I should try to make others happy. So – *I pulled the lever!*

Of course there are times when I slip back into the old despair. Then I dispel all those negative thoughts which do no one any good (least of all the dead). And – *I pull the lever again!*

August 19

Lady Valerie Solti was born on August 19th 1940. She has been an actress, journalist and broadcaster. She appeared for many years on BBC TV– on Face the Music and other programmes. Valerie was married to the conductor Sir Georg Solti and she promotes and writes on music and works in the arts. She is also currently the chair of the development appeal at Sadler's Wells Theatre.

Make the family your priority
tips from Lady Valerie Solti

Don't look back, look forward.

Make the family your priority.

Oh, and don't eat airline food or pierce your ears.

Valerie Solti adds: Since my husband died, I realise you have to look forward. You can take the memories with you, but if you look back too much you can't move forward.

My husband always underlined the value of the family. The greatest help and comfort I have ever had in my life has come from my parents, my husband and my children. The family is a great institution and its value should never be underestimated.

I don't eat airline food; I was once poisoned by a delicious shrimp sandwich on a Scandinavian Airlines flight with horrible consequences, alarming both for myself and for everyone around me. And I've never pierced my ears; I don't like the thought of open, suppurating sores.

Heather McHugh was born on August 20th 1948 to Canadian parents residing in the US. A poet, essayist, translator and teacher, she is a chancellor of the Academy of American Poets, and has served since 1983 as Milliman Distinguished Writer-in-Residence at the University of Washington in Seattle. Her most recent books include the collection of poetry The Father of the Predicaments *and a translation,* Glottal Stop: Poems of Paul Celan *(with her husband Nikolai Popov as co-translator).*

Him you do not teach to fly, teach to fall faster
a tip from Heather McHugh

Nietzsche's insight 'Him you do not teach to fly, teach to fall faster' lies in counter-intuition.

Not everyone is born to soar. Your star may lurk underwater, your worth may be a shoveller's reward, your diadems may lie at the earth's blind heart.

Heather McHugh adds: My father died on my birthday in 1999. On that same day 40 years earlier, he gave me my first book of poetry: an edition of Dylan Thomas ("Rage, rage, against the dying of the light"). But my father came to welcome his own death. He loved language, but was leery of life, and I offer my tip in honour of those whose relations to life and death are not the conventionally comforting ones.

Most readers construe the Nietzsche quotation as dispiriting for the majority of humans who cannot soar. But my tip comes with a sub-tip: anything readable should be read as many ways as possible. The less apparent reading of the Nietzsche I find helpful – indeed, a kind of antidote to despair. Ultimately each soul's genius may lie in its capacity to refine and apply its own weaknesses. (My father's lay in a faced fatality.) One's great force arises from one's greatest peculiarity: the mole who moons about wishing to be a thrush may miss his own best senses.

August 21

Carlo Gébler was born in Dublin on August 21st 1954. He is a writer of novels and plays and occasionally a director of documentary films. His film Put to the Test *won the 1999 Royal Television Society Award for the best regional documentary. He is currently writer-in-residence HMP Maghaberry, County Antrim. His latest book,* Father and I, *was published in 2000. He is married with five children.*

Write to stay healthy
a tip from Carlo Gébler

Write something every day. It doesn't matter what. It can be a description of something you see or overhear, it can be a letter or it can be a thought. Just write something every day in the same spirit as you take a walk or brush your teeth. Do it and don't worry. Regard it as part of what you have to do to stay healthy.

Carlo Gébler adds: I take my exercise by writing a diary every day. It takes ten minutes. Sometimes I write rubbish but that doesn't matter: it's the process that counts because in the doing I exercise the part of the intelligence that I use when I write. And it works; practice increases facility. I am a writer, but I believe we should all do this, non-writers as well as writers. Why? Because some day, one day, we will all need to write something that might change our lives, even if it's only a love letter. And when that day comes, if you've practised, then you will be strong and ready.

Mary Allen was born on August 22nd 1951. Her first career was as an actress. From the stage she moved to an oil company, for which she devised and managed a programme of arts sponsorship. After a decade of arts consultancy, she took over as director of Watermans Art Centre in 1990, moved to the Arts Council in 1992 and became its secretary-general in 1994. She left the Arts Council in 1997 for a brief but invigorating stint as chief executive of the Royal Opera House.

Career change through floor scrubbing
a tip from Mary Allen

If you are trying to change direction in your professional life, take every opportunity offered to you, however mundane. Sometimes these might seem to be more junior than your previous occupation, or beneath what you perceive to be your abilities. If you are asked to 'scrub floors', do it as well as you possibly can and without complaining. You never know when someone for whom you have done a small job well might be in a position to recommend you for something bigger.

Mary Allen adds: In the late 1980s, after a time of great change and difficulty in my life, I accepted a job that required me to adopt a much more junior role as an arts consultant than I had become accustomed to and to report to someone who had been my secretary ten years earlier. I had been given this tip a few months earlier. The tip, together with the enormous ability of my new boss, helped me to put all my energy into the job and, as a result of one of my assignments, I was offered a directorship of Watermans Arts Centre, an important break for me into arts administration.

August 23

Fred Emery was born on October 19th 1933. He was a longtime foreign correspondent for The Times, *which he left as acting editor. He was then a presenter and reporter of BBC's Panorama and wrote the book* Watergate: The corruption and fall of Richard Nixon *which inspired the BBC TV series. August 23rd is the date of his marriage, a date which, he notes, is "apposite to this tip as it is conveniently surrounded by the summer holidays".*

Take your holiday
a tip from **Fred Emery**

No one ever thanks you for not taking your holiday.

Fred Emery adds: This advice was given to me at the outset of my career by John Buist, then foreign news editor of *The Times*. I suspect his main interest was to avert holiday pile-ups that could cause holes in coverage. But I took it literally and never missed a day of my holiday, and so – though working hard – never became a workaholic. This way I preserved family life and health and, I hope, sanity – unlike some American friends who, even in retirement, crave an office to go to.

Ali Smith was born in Inverness on August 24th 1962. To date she has written two collections of short stories, Free Love and Other Stories and Other Stories, *and two novels,* Like *and* Hotel World *(2001).*

An easy-to-memorise tip
from Ali Smith

Only believe.

&

Remember to breathe.

Ali Smith adds: 'Only believe' is the phrase written on the back of a 1713 catechism coin given to me by a friend who found it under the Forth Rail Bridge. It's been a useful talisman, a useful phrase to keep about my person; as Robert Creeley said, "we believe in a world, or have none". Also, you can tell a lot about yourself from the state of your breathing. So remember to breathe. (If you don't, you'll faint.)

August 25

Desmond Morris was born on January 24th 1928. He is a zoologist and the author of 50 books on animal and human behaviour, including The Naked Ape, The Human Zoo, Animal Days *and* The Human Sexes. *His television shows include* Life, The Human Race *and* Animal Country. *He is also a surrealist artist and has had one-man shows in London, Paris and New York. August 25th is the most important date of his year – his wife's birthday.*

Work is the failure of play
a tip from Desmond Morris

Work is the failure of play. If you do not enjoy your occupation so much that it feels like play you are in the wrong job. Change it before you lose your curiosity and your imagination.

Desmond Morris adds: I have tried all my life to remain a childlike adult and to refuse to follow a set routine or do boring things like sitting on committees or attending formal functions. Life is too short to waste any of it.

Gillian Tindall was born in 1938. She has published novels (including the award-winning Fly Away Home*), volumes of short stories, a couple of biographies, and historical studies of London and Bombay and, most recently, of 19th-century France. For many years she contributed feature articles to national papers, but now finds she needs to save her energy for books and feels she has been very lucky in having been mostly able to write what she wants and to get paid for it. She reviews a little, contributes now and again to the* New York Times *and writes the occasional documentary drama for BBC Radio. She has been married since 1963. August 26th is both her son's birthday and the anniversary of the Liberation of Paris in 1944, which has been an important reference point for several of Tindall's books.*

Work out your priorities in life
a tip from Gillian Tindall

There is no general recipe for a good life: it depends on your priorities. The trick is to try to work out what these priorities are before the greater part of life has gone by. Often you do manage to get what you most profoundly want – but you are unlikely to get your second choice as well. There is a cost to everything.

Gillian Tindall adds: I also think that indiscriminate personal confessions are best avoided. Writers, in particular, put their own experiences, dreams and fears in disguised form into their work, and that is where they should stay.

August 27

Andrew Marshall was born on August 27th 1954. He is a lifelong comedy writer — "despite all counselling to the contrary" — first working with David Renwick on The Burkiss Way *for Radio 4, the award-winning* Whoops Apocalypse, Hot Metal *and other projects, and latterly on his own series* Health and Efficiency, DAD *and* 2point4 children.

Try not to say it
a survival tip from Andrew Marshall

Try not to say it.

You may want to say it, you might ache to say it, it may be funny, it may be the truth, it may be justice, it may be vengeance; but it might be better to Just Shut Up.

Andrew Marshall adds: In the far-off days of the 1970s when we all had widely-flared nostrils, platform underpants, cheesecloth teeth and spent lazy afternoons fingering the loons in Biba — and I don't refer to the trousers — I was an innocent immigrant to the capital from the wastes of East Anglia. I discovered that I soon got a reputation for saying what were believed to be devastatingly rude things to anyone to whom I was introduced. In fact this was simply an extraordinarily innocent habit of saying the thing that actually came into my head at the time.

Once, when a distinguished producer greeted me by saying "Andrew Marshall — I've always wanted to meet you!" I replied "Why?" I was actually wondering how on earth he'd ever heard of me, but of course it sounds as if it's a withering put-down. Really I should have *just kept that thought to myself.*

On another occasion after a particularly long and elaborate verbal riff by a newly-encountered Oxbridge wit, I said "Exactly *who* are you?" He seemed so confident that I assumed he must indeed be some very distinguished person I was unaware of. This sort of thing used to happen over and over again.

Unhappily, just a few short months ago, I was standing at a glittering media party adjacent to a Very Important Executive when another rather self-promoting writer said to him "We must have lunch again soon." As I had the stinging thought of my peer constantly carousing with the God in some half-timbered Oxfordshire hideaway over foaming mugs of balsamic vinegar, I found myself turning to him and saying "I'd like to have lunch with you too", whereupon he folded his arms, went something akin to the Dulux Matchmaker shade of 'Bruised Mango' and never spoke to me again ... and I mean *never.* So what I'm saying is — when it comes into your head *Try Not to Say it* ... you'll thank me for it one day.

Donald Adamson was born on March 30th 1939. He is an author, historian and translator. His written work includes books on Balzac, Pascal and Maupassant. He has edited the travel journals of John Byng, Viscount Torrington and written the history of a City livery company. He is married to Helen and they have two sons, Richard and John. August 28th was the date of Tolstoy's birth in 1828 (though the same date in the West was September 9th).

August 28

Read Tolstoy
a tip from Donald Adamson

A great book by Tolstoy has the simple title: *What Then Must We Do?* Life is no dull unquestioning routine. Every day we should ask ourselves what it is all about – and read Tolstoy.

Donald Adamson adds: I enjoy practically all of the 'good things' of life but hope I have never been bowled over by them (maybe that has happened now and again).

Tolstoy's writings are close in spirit to the New Testament. Other rather similar writers – prophetic and questioning – are Rousseau and Pascal.

August 29

Angela Huth was born on August 29th 1938. After working as a freelance journalist for national newspapers, she became a BBC TV reporter in 1967. She wrote her first novel in 1970, since when she has written eight more, also two stage plays, six plays for radio and TV, and three collections of short stories. In 1998 the film of her book The Land Girls *was released.*

Learn to love solitude
a tip from Angela Huth

Learn to love solitude. This is immensely useful. It means you never dread being bored or being alone. It's one of the most important things we should teach our children – to cultivate their own resources, so that they never fear spells of aloneness.

Angela Huth adds: In a very busy life, my means of restoration is to go away for a few days alone – preferably to my favourite place on the Norfolk coast. There I have uninterrupted time to think, read, walk and listen to music. I have a blessed silence and – selfishly – a small time in which others don't have to be considered. During this perfect break, the thought of returning to normal, peopled life becomes wonderfully reburnished.

Sir Peter Parker was born on August 30th 1924. He learned Japanese in the Second World War. He served in Burma, then went into Japan with the occupation forces soon after the surrender. He has chaired a wide variety of businesses, including British Rail from 1976 to 1983, and was chairman of the London School of Economics from 1988 to 1998. He has been a director of the UK-Japan 2000 Group since 1986 and in 1991 was awarded the Grand Cordon of the Order of the Sacred Treasure.

Rules for good management
tips from Sir Peter Parker

Eat and drink less, and laugh more. Don't think you have to be unpleasant to be strong.

Somehow find a way of sleeping twice a day.

Do all your sums, look hard, but don't forget you have to leap.

Hire people cleverer than you are and delegate more than you think is good for you. And take the blame.

Learn one other language at least; appreciating another culture will help you understand your own, and it's never too late.

Find things to praise in people but don't too easily trust yourself about yourself – you're such a flatterer.

If you're in a hanging mood, hang people like pictures – in the best light.

One minute of your time could be somebody else's day, good or bad, courtesy or curse.

Round tables for meetings do make a real difference.

Take your problems home – the family has shrewdly sized them up in general terms anyway, but without the detail it is even more worrying for them.

Organise into the smallest group you can – that way people are real to one another.

Ask people to do what they do best – don't ask Sinatra his view of the atomic bomb.

Sir Peter Parker adds: I have always used these simple rules (which appear in my autobiography *For Starters*) to underpin whatever professionalism I have. I want managers to renounce the stereotypes. There is no need to be half a man, or woman, to be a manager. As Hamlet said to Horatio, "every man hath business and desire".

August 31

Carol Royle was born on February 10th 1954. She is an actress and mother. She has worked extensively in television and theatre, appearing in such things as Life Without George, Blackeyes and plays with the RSC. She won the London Drama Critic's award for most promising actress for Ophelia in 1980. August 31st is her daughter Talitha's birthday.

Don't expect too much from people
a tip from Carol Royle

Don't expect too much from another human being.

If one expects certain behaviour from other people one places oneself in a very vulnerable position, liable to disappointment and indeed annoyance. If one does not expect too much, then one is not disappointed and one can be joyous when one discovers, as one so often does, that others can be wonderful.

Carol Royle adds: This is an especially useful tip on the roads, when expecting good, or even normal behaviour could be fatal. Back in 1973, my driving instructor said, "*You* always be the one to give way, because then you can be sure of the outcome."

Paul Godfrey was born on September 16th 1960. He is a playwright and director. His first play, Inventing a New Colour, *was produced at the Royal Court in 1988 and he later directed two of his own plays at the National Theatre (*Once in a While the Odd Thing Happens, *1990 and* The Blue Ball, *1995). He received the Arts Council playwrights award in 1989 and again in 1992. In 1999 he wrote* Tiananmen Square *for the BBC to commemorate the 10th anniversary of the Beijing Spring. The first volume of his collected plays is published by Methuen. September 1st is the date he reached Santiago in 1994 after walking 2,000 miles.*

September 1

Go out for a walk
a tip from **Paul Godfrey**

If you are confused, go out for a walk. If you don't know what to do next, go out for a walk. If it's all too much, go out for a walk. Walking releases the mind and I guarantee that you will come back feeling better. (Of course you might never come back.) And who knows what you might find on a walk?

Paul Godfrey adds: When I first began to write, I used to go out to think. Often now when I feel strong emotions I go for long walks across London. Once I walked 2,000 miles to Santiago de Compostella. No one would describe me as a religious person, but I think that any long walk becomes a tangible metaphor of your life. When I arrived in Santiago, two words came into my mind: "Everything passes".

September 2

Donald Holden was born in Beverly Hills on April 22nd 1931, when it was still a shabby neighbourhood. He is a painter and he sometimes writes about painting. His book Whistler Landscapes and Seascapes *(still in print after 30 years) is an attempt to tell art history from the viewpoint of the working artist. His watercolours have been exhibited in New York and London and are in the basements of museums on both sides of the Atlantic. Donald says: "I like September 2nd because (I think) that's the date when a wonderful kid named Roland Wojciechowsky took me to a museum for the first time. The year was 1942. I was 11. It was probably the most important day of my life."*

Boredom can lead to inspiration
a tip from Donald Holden

Like everyone else, artists often get bored with their work – although they don't like to admit it. The process of making art can be tedious. Your mind wanders. You find yourself on automatic pilot. You wonder: "Should I stop for the day?" But those periods of boredom can be amazingly productive. You have to force yourself to keep on working.

Astonishing things can happen when you just don't give a damn. The muse has a quirky way of stepping in when your mind drifts off and you stop thinking about what you're doing. Boredom can become that inspired state of 'no mind' that puts you in touch with the great forces that produce real art.

Donald Holden adds: I have a modest talent for doing small things well. But I also have a talent for sustained work. I'm tenacious and I don't give up easily. So my small watercolours – which are *not* a serious threat to Turner – have gradually got better over the years and have won me more attention that I ever expected. Most of us are not geniuses, but we can get pretty far with sheer perseverance.

Irma Kurtz was born on September 3rd 1935 in New Jersey. She took a degree in English Literature at Columbia University and, after a rackety youth on the road, settled in London. In the late 1960s she became a contributing editor to Nova magazine. In her subsequent freelance career, she has written for many publications, and broadcast widely on TV and radio. She is the author of several books, including a travel book, The Great American Bus Ride, *and a memoir,* Dear London. *She is the agony aunt for* Cosmopolitan *magazine in the UK and the USA.*

September 3

Love makes no prisoners
a tip from **Irma Kurtz**

Love is acceptance; to accept the unacceptable is slavery.

Love accepts its object and expects nothing more than the beloved is able and willing to deliver. However, when acceptance stretches to include abuse and perversion, love ceases to be free and joyous, and turns into its very own opposite.

Irma Kurtz adds: I learn this every day from countless women, who, when I say, "Leave the brute ..." reply, "But I love him ...". Sorry, no. Love makes no prisoners and takes no "buts".

September 4

John Bowen was born on November 5th 1924. He is a novelist (his books include A World Elsewhere *and* The MacGuffin*) who has also written plays for the theatre and for television (including* Heil, Caesar, *which won the Tokyo prize) and who writes occasional reviews. He has taught drama students at the London Academy of Music & Dramatic Art and sometimes gives talks to writers' groups.*

Trust your unconscious
a tip from John Bowen

A tip for writers. Whenever an image, a voice, a character comes unbidden into your mind – was not there at all at one moment, and suddenly is the next – go with it. And all of us, writers or not, should heed our dreams, because in dreams the unconscious mind tells us what we really want.

John Bowen adds: This advice was given to me by my agent, the late Peggy Ramsay, who died on September 4th 1991. "Trust nobody in this business, dear," she said, "Not even me. But always trust your unconscious." The image that comes out of nowhere has helped me many times, and I have always found that what comes easily to the page works better than what has needed labour.

Karen McCosker was born on January 10th 1948. She lives in Northern Maine and lectures at the University of Maine at Presque Isle. Her work has appeared in Harvard Review, *the* Wisconsin Review, Many Mountains Moving *and the* South Carolina Review. *She is the US editor of* A Poem a Day, *an anthology of poems meant to be learnt by heart. Karen writes: "September 5th is my mother's mother's birthday. Her life as a Slavic immigrant in the United States has directed my life in ways for which I am grateful."*

Follow directions
a tip from **Karen McCosker**

Follow directions.

When you think about it, we're living without a script, so why not make use of what little guidance we do receive.

Karen McCosker adds: The practical applications of this tip seem obvious. After all, who wants to be left with a fallen soufflé or singed eyebrows? Road signs help us reach our destination in one piece. Consulting a map may provide a measure of equanimity en route.

I remember hiking in the Rockies with a friend. I had violated a basic rule of the outdoors and gone on ahead, assuming my friend would be close behind. After some time, I realised she wasn't in sight. I called. I doubled back. I arrived at our destination without her. Eventually I spied her in the distance and apologised for having been so thoughtless. I told her that I assumed the cairns would keep her on the right path. "What are cairns?" she asked. To some, a pile of stones; to others, a less circuitous route.

I believe we carry inside us wise voices, and if we listen, their direction will mark our introspective path, just as cairns exist in strategic junctures on any physical journey. Even as physical frontiers are rapidly diminishing, there will always remain the turning inward, the journey of reflection and self-understanding. Though my friend was unaware of a certain type of guidepost, I was the more ill-prepared. Though I read the language of rock piled on rock, I failed to take another human being's journey into account, and I put us both at peril. What's the hurry? Where's your patience, your sense of responsibility to the person you're with? Questions asked by the voices I ignored in my haste.

I grew up in a small town in central New York State and at 17 I fled, graduated from a nearby college four years later, took an advanced degree and arrived in Greece, a country where, when asking for directions, natives will offer every manner of insight even though they haven't a clue, if only not to appear rude. As I stumbled on my way, often into cul-de-sacs, ships taking me to islands I never intended to go, I listened and learned how to read the cultural subtext of what I heard; only then did my sense of frustration diminish and the anger that was consuming me subside. Then did strangers, the other, the foreign, become human.

As a writer, I did not think I would be as astonished as I was to hear someone say that a poem should give the poet who writes it directions first into her or himself. All these years, I wrote with the emphasis on others, paying little heed to how those poems might better explain me to myself, as if writing the poem excused any further personal reflection.

On my wall is a photo of the Dalai Lama. Looking at it today I speculate what directions a wholly compassionate one might give: Look at the fields, at the whiteness of the daisies, at their yellow centres which you can't see from this distance but know are there. Recognise that you are one among the multiplicity of all living things. Act accordingly. Wait for others.

September 6

Anthony Rudolf was born in London on September 6th 1942. His published work includes poetry and literary criticism, monographs and anthologies, autobiography and fiction. He has also published translations of drama, poetry and fiction from French and Russian and (in collaboration) from other languages. His journalism includes book reviews, obituaries and art criticism. He runs Menard Press and is advisory editor to Modern Poetry in Translation. Anthony Rudolf has recently completed a novel and a book of short stories.

Read less, write more
a tip from Anthony Rudolf

Read less, write more.

Anthony Rudolf adds: My tip is so short and, I hope, so sweet that it is identical to its title. It was given to me, tellingly, by a painter not by a writer and I'll repeat it: *read less, write more.* In my experience all writers read an enormous amount, whether consciously directed by the demands of a work in progress, or to keep up with the books of friends and rivals, or to reread old favourites, sometimes for pleasure sometimes talismanically. Perhaps the only bad reason for reading is its use as an avoidance tactic — more plausible than drinking whiskey or making love — when one should be writing. Anyway, my painter friend gave me the advice when I told her that I had in mind to write a book inspired by Walter Benjamin and Jorge-Luis Borges (two of the greatest readers of all time), a book which would have involved processing every scrap of paper, journal and book in my flat. She was appalled and said I should just sit down and *invent* some stories from my head without reference to anything. *Read less, write more.* I took her advice and 18 months later had a book of stories – only one of which involved research. (That particular story, appropriately enough, may be the least successful. Even if it isn't, it belongs in another book.) Writing a book exclusively from my head (and arse★) was a new experience and a turning point. I know I would never have done it without that piece of advice. And the unwritten book? Well, I wrote a story about a man who processes every book, journal and scrap of paper in his flat ...

★ 'Arse' refers to the occasion when a friend of mine, the writer Z. Kotowicz, was asked by a wannabe author how to set about it: "Nail your arse to the chair."

James Stevens Curl was born on March 26th 1937. He is Professor of Architectural History and Senior Research Fellow, The Queen's University of Belfast. His books include the much-acclaimed Oxford Dictionary of Architecture *(1999). He has contributed to numerous journals, including the* Architectural Review, Bauwelt, *the* Literary Review, *the* Spectator *and the* Guardian. *He has made broadcasts on radio and television and is an international speaker. His tip comes from Schiller, who first met Goethe in 1794. On September 7th of that year, Schiller, who had serious health problems, wrote to Goethe: "With pleasure I am accepting your invitation to Weimar, but ... I ask for the unfortunate freedom that I may be ill at your house." Schiller died in 1805.*

Death is inevitable, so don't waste life
a tip from James Stevens Curl

Remember that death is the only certainty in life, so live each day as though it were your last. Don't waste your time, or anybody else's, for time is a finite commodity. For the truly creative person a lifetime is never long enough to get everything done, so each minute is precious. Therefore avoid watching pap on television (most of it is pap), for television is the greatest waste of time. Think for yourself: eschew received opinions, for the majority is *always* wrong. Never believe one word uttered by any politician.

James Stevens Curl adds: The gist of this advice comes from Goethe and Schiller, authors whose works have been an enormous influence on me. Like many in their teens, I wasted time too, and wish I could have back the years I foolishly misused then. I feel I could still accomplish certain tasks if only I could regain the lost times squandered in thoughtless profligacy when life seemed long and the days stretched endlessly ahead.

September 8

Elisabeth Hoodless, CBE was born on February 11th 1941. She is executive director of Community Service Volunteers, having joined the founder, Alec Dickson, in September 1963. She has helped establish youth action programmes in Jamaica and the United States. She believes everyone has something to give to others: time, skill and love. She lives in Islington where she chairs the Youth Court.

There is nothing the right volunteer cannot do
tips from **Elisabeth Hoodless, CBE**

1. There is nothing the right volunteer cannot do.
2. The enemy of my enemy is my friend.
3. It is easier to get forgiveness than permission.

Elisabeth Hoodless adds: 1. Too often people equate a salary with expertise, commitment and reliability, but few paid doctors are more expert than Médecins Sans Frontières. And many volunteers will work around the clock to complete a task or will care for a person in need long after the professionals have gone home.

2. Although a somewhat uncomfortable thought, it is well worth bearing in mind when trying to make something happen. For a whole range of different reasons, people may be able to work together to achieve a single purpose although they would not normally be friends.

In working towards a nationwide programme of citizens' service by young people, CSV built a coalition of ex-military traditionalists who believed in the value of service; youth leaders who aimed for more recognition for young people; and politicians who recognised the value of getting services delivered at non-market prices. Few of these people would normally have worked together, but in this instance they made common cause.

3. In the early days of CSV, we moved from 15 Trinity Square to the backyard of Toynbee Hall. I wanted to invite the Secretary of State for Education to open our tiny office and I knew that if I asked permission, the committee would say there was no point, he would not accept. I sent the invitation, he accepted and the committee was so delighted that nobody pointed out that I did not have permission to make the invitation in the first place.

Dennis Smith was born on September 9th 1940. His first book, Report from the Engine Co. 82, *sold more than two million copies and was translated into 12 languages. His recent book,* A Song for Mary, *is a memoir about growing up on New York's East Side in the 1950s and has been a Book of the Month club selection. It is his tenth book.*

Be fair and wear a clean shirt
tips from Dennis Smith

My mother, Mary, was a turn-the-other-cheek kind of woman and whenever she confronted unfairness, as happens often to people without money, it made her even more resolute in being fair to all people.

"Fairness", she used to say, "will count in the great and final tally at the gates of heaven. And remember," she would add, "they'll always think better of you if you're wearing a clean shirt."

Dennis Smith adds: I keep this advice handy whenever I sit at my desk to write, and also whenever I sit down to dinner with friends and associates. It is much easier to be unfair, for unfairness is unbridled and gives us great leeway to smear or tear down. Fairness, on the other hand, is tied to the straight and narrow and is normally constrained by the truth.

September 10

Sandra Billington was born on September 10th 1943. After working in the theatre, including a scholarship to RADA and working with Mike Leigh, she went to Lucy Cavendish College, Cambridge where she became fascinated by disorder in the Middle Ages. She is now a reader in the University of Glasgow and was made a fellow of the Royal Society of Edinburgh in 1997. Her books include A Social History of the Fool, Mock Kings *and* Midsummer *(2000).*

Humans can bounce
a tip from **Dr Sandra Billington**

Plans can go seriously wrong for many reasons – some, like injustice, have to be fought against. But it can also be hard to accept that it has happened, and that you must start again: it's hard to get rid of the feeling of doom or anger. Simple things can sometimes help. One is to examine your face in the mirror and say: "This is where you are. I forgive you."

Sandra Billington adds: From time to time I have had to deal with my inability to deal with this chancy world. The responsibility can feel crushing, but forgiving myself has been liberating. Another thought which I find works is Scarlett O'Hara's "Tomorrow is another day."

Roger Newman Turner was born on April 29th 1940. He is a naturopath, osteopath and acupuncturist who has practised in Letchworth Garden City and London for almost 40 years. He is the author of a number of books on diet and health and has lectured and broadcast on naturopathic medicine in many parts of the world. September 11th was Roger's father's birthday.

September 11

Waste not want not
a tip from Roger Newman Turner

Waste not want not. This little homily was oft repeated by my maternal grandmother during our school holiday trips to her home in Cornwall. She invoked it partly to justify eating up the leftovers of our beach picnics, even on one occasion taking a sip from the herb-beer bottle which had been used by one of my brothers when taken short in the car on the way home.

Roger Newman Turner adds: This piece of advice from the organic upbringing which our parents gave us – emphasising recycling everything possible to preserve the environment – has served me well. In my professional life, effective healthcare has meant making the best use of our natural resources. In everyday life it has made me something of a hoarder, but on the other hand I do manage to get an extra couple of weeks, use out of a toothpaste tube that my wife has consigned to the bin.

September 12

Frederick Charles Jones was born in the Potteries on September 12th 1927 ("a chronological absurdity as I am sure that I am in fact a degenerate 42"). He claims that he "dreamt away 28 years of his life", then trained and became an actor. He has worked in the theatre playing, amongst other roles, Sir in The Dresser *and Malvolio in* Twelfth Night *for the RSC; on film, in Fellini's* E la Nave va *(And The Ship Sails On), Far From the Madding Crowd, The Elephant Man and Cold Comfort Farm; and on TV, in Uncle Vanya, Pennies from Heaven, Inspector Morse, the lead in Zola's Nana, and Claudius in The Caesars, for which he was awarded the Monte Carlo Golden Nymph Best Actor.*

Never trust first impressions
a tip from Freddie Jones

"I always trust my first impression of someone" is a classic piece of arrogant rubbish. A first impression – or a third, or a tenth – provides only a tiny manifestation of a tiny part of the infinitely complex and constantly changing whole. Subject as it is to mood, metabolic variations and the shifting chemistry of social encounters, a first impression can only ever be a partial truth.

The initial exchanging of superficial clichés acts as a sounding board to discover mood, social standing and so on – for all the world like the opening of a fencing match with foils. Add to all this the inadequacies of language, and the problem deepens. Most importantly, the stress of an introduction very often induces a degree of aggression, however unintentional.

I believe it was an American president who, to alleviate the superficiality of introductions, always muttered "I just shot my grandmother." Only once did he get the response "Well, I guess she had it coming to her, Mr President."

Freddie Jones adds: One first encounter left me so humiliated, socially demeaned and angry, that I was subject to violent fantasies of revenge for days. Subsequently we began a golden friendship for life.

Jessica Mann was born on September 13th 1937. She is the author of 17 crime novels (the latest is The Survivor's Revenge, Constable*), a freelance journalist (writing for the* Sunday Telegraph, *the* Daily Mail *and others) and a broadcaster (*Question Time, Any Questions, Round Britain Quiz*). In her married name of Jessica Thomas, she has held a variety of public appointments on health authorities and employment tribunals. At present she is chair of the office of water services committee for the south west of England and a board member of South West Arts.*

Get the job over and done with
a tip from Jessica Mann

When you need to answer a letter, respond to a query, check a reference or simply buy the week's groceries, don't keep reminding yourself about it. Don't forget about it altogether – just save trouble by getting the job over and done with straight away. It's quicker in the long run and avoids guilt, anxiety and other people's reproaches.

Jessica Mann adds: This was something I learned when my mother, in her fifties, set up a one-woman solicitor's practice and decided that instead of beginning every letter – as most lawyers did – with an apology for the delay in replying, she would simply clear her in-tray by the end of each day. It was a good example, though I admit that I don't always manage to live up to it.

September 14

John Michael Francis was born on May 1st 1939. He is a former nuclear scientist who, following a Damascus Road conversion in 1970, became a campaigning environmentalist and the leader of a project on society, religion and technology based in Edinburgh. He acted as a scientific advisor to the World Council of Churches from 1971 to 1983 before being appointed as the director of the Nature Conservancy Council in Scotland. He now supports the John Muir Trust and is a member of the Global Look-Out Panel, Millennium Project, United Nations University. He describes himself as a futurist with concerns about ethics and values. September 14th is his wedding anniversary.

Life's a smile, if you can manage it
a tip from Dr John Michael Francis

"Smile awhile – and while you smile, another smiles – and soon there's miles and miles of smiles – and life's worthwhile because you smile!"

(From a great-aunt who was akin to someone out of Dickens. She belonged to a different era, but was capable of detecting something a little sad about the pace and struggles of contemporary life.)

John Michael Francis adds: This piece of advice was conveyed to me at an early age by a great-aunt called May and has always registered as a worthwhile maxim. It still strikes me as something helpful to carry forward to another generation because it reflects a certain idealism about the nature of personal relationships which is probably no longer expressed in such simplistic terms. However, it also restates a profound truth about the value and power of non-verbal communication and face-to-face interaction which currently we are inclined to neglect while sitting in front of high-speed networked computers in depersonalised work settings. To smile is a means of putting the other person at ease and thus encouraging and enabling the words to flow. Eyeball-to-eyeball meetings continue to be the stuff of corporate negotiation and international diplomacy alike, and the quality of the exchanges count a great deal. We should all aspire to smile a little more – even in the face of adversity.

John Julius Norwich was born on September 15th 1929. He is the author of a number of books on history (the Normans in Sicily, Venice, Byzantium) and several on travel (Mount Athos, the Sahara). He has also made some thirty television documentaries for the BBC; on radio he used to chair My Word and for three years he presented the Evening Concert on Classic FM. He produces an annual anthology known as A Christmas Cracker and plays nightclub piano for fun.

September 15

Having it both ways
a tip from John Julius Norwich

When I was a child my Nanny – though not, I think my parents – used to tell me over and over again that I couldn't have my cake and eat it. I never understood why not, and the older I get the more certain I become that this was a doctrine of rank defeatism. Not only is it perfectly possible, more often than not, to have one's cake and eat it; one should make a point of doing so at every opportunity.

John Julius Norwich adds: By never accepting that two desirable options are alternatives when in fact they are nothing of the kind, I have managed to achieve – and to enjoy – any number of things that would otherwise have been out of the question.

September 16

Ken Coates was born on September 16th 1930. He worked in Nottinghamshire as a miner between 1948 and 1956. He is now a Member of the European Parliament and a special professor in the Department of Continuing Education at the University of Nottingham. He writes and campaigns for the local environment, for full employment and for human rights. He is a member of the Bertrand Russell Peace Foundation and has written several books, including Think Globally, Act Locally *(1988) and* Dear Commissioner *(1996).*

What would the teenage-you do?
a tip from Ken Coates, MEP

When you are in doubt what to do, try to remember what you would have done as a teenager. You probably won't want to do the same – and if you do this might indicate arrested development. But if your present self is actually in conflict with your own youth, then something has gone wrong.

You may say that something has gone wrong in society, not in you. But then you have to ask yourself: what are you doing to straighten out the society which is putting your older self at odds with your younger self?

Ken Coates adds: The irreplaceable Bertrand Russell, who died in 1970, gave me a similar tip. It was written by his grandmother on the flyleaf of a bible which she presented to him at a tender age. It said: "Thou shalt not follow a multitude to do evil."

I have assiduously followed these tips and they have always got me into trouble. However, they have always imbued me with sufficient arrogance to think that I was in the right!

Tamasin Day-Lewis was born on September 17th. She is a film maker and co-director, with her brother, Daniel Day-Lewis, of Day-Lewis Productions Ltd. She is also a food writer, author of West of Ireland Summers *(1999) and has a weekly food column in the* Daily Telegraph's *Weekend section. She is the mother of Miranda, Harry and Charissa.*

Never offer the young negatives
a tip from Tamasin Day-Lewis

Instead of negatives ('do nots'), offer young people concepts, such as:

"The magistrate sits in your heart that judges you."
Arthur Miller

"We write in order to understand, not in order to be understood."
C. Day-Lewis, my father

Tamasin Day-Lewis adds: Apparently abstract ideas such as these may help young people make sense of the world.

September 18

Richard Harries was born on June 2nd 1936. He became Bishop of Oxford in 1987 after being dean of King's College, London. He has done a regular 'Thought' on the Today programme for many years, as well as other radio and TV work. He is the author of many books and has been elected a fellow of the Royal Society of Literature. His current responsibilities include chairing the Church of England's Board for Social Responsibility and the Council of Christians and Jews. He was a member of the recent Wakeham Commission on the reform of the House of Lords. September 18th 1709 was the birthday of Dr Samuel Johnson, the famous lexicographer and conversationalist (mentioned below).

When to give things up
a tip from the Rt Revd Richard Harries

If you want to give up anything or change the direction of your life, timing matters. It is no good simply saying you will do something with the top of your head. It needs to feel the right time to do it with your emotions and spirit as well as your mind and will. Otherwise you will quickly get knocked off course. You also need to look at your diary and anticipate points of difficulty. It is no good trying to give something up if you are going through a bad patch. Then you need to pamper yourself with little treats.

Richard Harries adds: Dr Johnson was once asked whether he would like a little wine and he replied "Certainly not. I would like a lot or none at all." For this reason I find it difficult, for example, to try to give up alcohol for Lent if I allow myself a number of built-in exceptions. Nor can I enter into the spirit of Lent unless the whole body is ready to be more disciplined. I also need to look at the diary and ask myself whether I am really prepared to forego delicious wine on a number of agreeable social occasions. But the church's rhythm of feast and fast is a great help and adds enormously to the richness of human existence. As well as Lent, I find it helpful to try to give up alcohol for Advent. It is such a relief not having to drink anything at those pre-Christmas parties.

Barbara Ward was born in 1937 and has worked in business, health education and education. She is also a psychosynthesis therapist and works part-time as an employee counsellor for Devon County Council. She is at present training as an Interfaith minister and spiritual counsellor. She is the author of Good Grief *and* Healing Grief. *September 19th is the day her husband died in a car accident on the way back from their second honeymoon in Scotland.*

Life is a mystery
a tip from Barbara Ward

"Life is a mystery to be lived, not a problem to be solved."

Charles Roland

Barbara Ward adds: This advice was given to me by my second father, Charles Roland, and is helpful when life doesn't make sense. It helped me after my husband died nine months after we were married and I had to rebuild my life – none of the religious platitudes worked and all I wanted was to die too. It started my path as a religious seeker – I have followed shamanism and Buddhism, as well as Christianity and particularly Quakerism, and am now training as an Interfaith minister to help others in similar situations.

September 20

Barbara Hardy was born in Swansea on June 27th 1924. She is Professor of English in the universities of London and Swansea, a literary critic, novelist, autobiographer and poet, fellow of the Royal Society of Literature and the Welsh Academy and honorary member of the Modern Languages Association. Her books include London Lovers *(1996) and* Shakespeare's Storytellers *(1997),* Thomas Hardy: Imagining imagination *and* Dylan Thomas: An original language *(both 2000). In 2001, Shoestring Press published a selection of her poems. Her first daughter, Julia, was born on September 20th 1955.*

When you're poor, act rich
a tip from Professor Barbara Hardy

When you're poor, act rich. If you have an overdraft or debt or lose money, treat yourself to a luxury, not something grossly or ruinously expensive, but something enjoyable, desirable and unnecessary. (Wine and food may help, but for this particular therapy I like less transient treats.)

Barbara Hardy adds: I happened on this solace when I had an income tax debt that was keeping me awake at nights. Passing an antique shop in London's Tottenham Court Road, I fell in love with a Victorian brass and green glass double-headed desk-lamp, bought it on impulse and overdraft, cured my anxiety and never looked back. In times of financial stress, the lamp tells me that money troubles come and go. A dateless black velvet doublet with gold quotations from Shelley – my poetry jacket – and a leather Edwardian sofa are other relics of Extravagance Distraction. Debts usually get paid sooner or later and the delightful objects remain as 'solid pleasures' – to quote a childhood hymn – and symbols of hope and recovery.

Candy Atherton was born on September 21st 1955. She represents Falmouth and Camborne in Parliament and is the first woman MP in Cornwall since the 1920s. She is also a journalist. When in London, she lives on a narrow boat called The Honourable Lady, *moored in an old canal basin in Chelsea.*

Self-preservation
a tip from Candy Atherton, MP

On your way up, never tread upon those whom you may need on your way down.

Candy Atherton adds: As one of the few women who have made it to the House of Commons, I feel a particular responsibility towards those who wish to follow in our footsteps. Many women MPs helped me to become one myself, and now I must help others.

In the past I have been a councillor, a mayor and served on health authorities and find that everything in life eventually returns – usually to haunt you. Thus if you cause grief to another, then boy oh boy you'll surely meet again on the day you lose your seat or are on your uppers.

September 22

Dannie Abse was born on September 22nd 1923. He is the author of 11 books of poetry and four novels, as well as plays and autobiographical works. He practised medicine in a chest clinic for many years. His most recent book is Arcadia, One Mile, *published by Hutchinson in 1998.*

Financial advice
a tip from Dannie Abse

If you have two pennies to spend, spend one on bread that you may live; spend the other on a flower so that you may have a reason for living.

Dannie Abse adds: This old Chinese saying seems sensible, though sometimes in my life I've been greedy and tried for three pennies.

Jenny Joseph was born on May 7th 1932. She is a poet, writer and lecturer. Her books include The Unlooked-for Season, Persephone *(a story in prose and verse),* Selected Poems, Ghosts and Other Company, *and* Extended Similes. *Her latest book is a selection of poems for children,* All the Things I See *(Macmillan Children's Books, 2000). She says of this date: "September 23rd is more or less the Autumn solstice and therefore the official onset of the wintry half of the year which people dread, and so it should be a comfort then to think that everything, even Winter, has an end."*

A snake has two ends
a tip from Jenny Joseph

Everything has an end, and a snake has two.

Jenny Joseph adds: This is perhaps more a saying than a tip, but has various possible uses:

a) You might lighten those stuck in gloom by making them smile;

b) Can also be used as a polite form of "Go and jump in the lake" to persistent moaners to whom one's sympathetic words of wise advice have not been helpful.

I first heard it in a Danish version. It was a couplet with something like ' ... ange' '... schlange' as the rhyme.

September 24

Richard Hoggart was born into the Leeds working class on September 24th 1918. He was orphaned at eight. "From then on I had three main aids: the love of my grandmother and her daughters; the disinterested help of others at key points all the way (English teacher, headmaster, the visitor from the Leeds Board of Guardians, my professor at Leeds University and, of course, my wife); and the discovery of the power and beauty of language and literature." He was the Reith lecturer in 1971, vice-chairman of the Arts Council from 1976 until 1981 and is the author of many books, including The Uses of Literacy, An Imagined Life *and* The Way We Live Now *(1995).*

Swallow your own smoke
tips from Richard Hoggart

Personal relations: Give promising personal relations time and space to bed themselves in; don't nit-pick and push any disagreement too far. Leave room for them and you to back off; swallow your own smoke – don't take offence too quickly; roll with the blows; learn to live with uncertainty, the unfinished – especially in yourself.

Society and work: Don't join any fashionable intellectual or literary club; never seek advance blurbs of your own work, broadcasts, reviews or public occasions; stay with it, die with your boots on; if you *are* outraged on a matter of principle and can't summon up sufficient moral courage to oppose it, make do with stubborn bloody-mindedness.

Richard Hoggart adds: I picked up all the above along the way, as one usually does. I learned some of it painfully, from my own failings and, sometimes, successes. I learned the rest from the experiences, good and bad, of friends; and of some who never became friends but were examples, again, good or bad. But now I try to make them my guidelines.

Professor Stafford Beer was born on September 25th 1926. He was the founder of managerial cybernetics, and remains an international consultant in the management sciences – working at government level in 25 countries. In Chile he directed the project to reorganise the social economy for President Allende. He has published 11 books (one of poetry) and 250 papers. He preaches holism and practises it through philosophy and science, but also through recitals of his poetry, exhibitions of his paintings and his teachings of meditative yoga.

Do not do what you hate
a tip from Professor Stafford Beer

Jesus the living says:
do not do what you hate
for that is a lie
made manifest in the face of heaven

from the apocryphal gospels discovered in Upper Egypt

Stafford Beer adds: In 1974 I took stock of my life. I had been twice married and had eight children. In the course of my business career I had commanded large staffs of professionals and was well-known internationally both as a cybernetician and as a management scientist. I had owned five (heavily-mortgaged) houses and my lifestyle had escalated accordingly. I had owned a swimming pool and a Rolls-Royce, and had employed at times a gardener and a chauffeur. Well-known in London restaurants, I was a wine connoisseur and smoked 30 cigars a day.

The wickedness of the destruction of constitutional government in Chile, and the murder of Allende and other friends, shook me profoundly. Although I had left the institutional church – perhaps because I had – Jesus became newly real to me. It had always seemed likely that he actually *meant* the parable of the rich man who could as readily enter the kingdom of heaven as pass through the eye of a needle, but I had "gone my way sorrowing".

During this year of meditation, the passage quoted above insistently recurred – *do not do what you hate.* And I had to face it: I hated absolutely everything about the life in which I was now entangled.

In 1975 I renounced possessions, except for a primitive stone cottage in mid-Wales and a 20-year-old Land-Rover, both of which I bought. I gave almost everything else to my estranged wife, who bought her own house with the money.

I now have a third spouse and we are based in Toronto. But I still live in the Welsh cottage for about six months a year, and am celebrating its Silver Jubilee by installing a water supply.

September 26

Anne Robinson was born on September 26th 1944. She is a columnist for The Times *and presents the* Watchdog *programme and* The Weakest Link *for the BBC.*

Pearls of parental wisdom
a tip from Anne Robinson

I quote my mother, who politically was very much of the Harvey Nichols tendency, and who, on the eve of my first wedding, declared that to ensure a happy married life there were just two things I must remember: "To have a facial once a month and to get plenty of help in the house."

Anne Robinson adds: Another pearl – when my friend Eric went up to Oxford in the 1950s, his father said there were only two things his son needed to know: never to put apple in fruit salad, and never, ever to bounce a cheque on a tart.

Robert Patrick was born on September 27th 1937. He has published over 60 plays, including Kennedy's Children. *As a pioneer of underground and gay theatre, he claims that his novel* Temple Slave *is the only book about those movements by a participant. Awards he has received include: the Glasgow Citizens Theatre World Playwriting Award, the ITS Founder Award for services to theatre and to youth, a Rockefeller grant, and the Show Business Best Play Award. He lives in Los Angeles and writes television and screenplays.*

How to hold a man, but not why
a tip from Robert Patrick

Have a special smile
Only he can foment.
Then, once in a while,
Withhold it for a moment.
He'll dare hell and fire
To restore your pucker.
You'll have your desire,
If you still want the sucker.

Robert Patrick adds: Note too that human males are mere competing machines. Uncritically, they vie with incredible energy and invention for any goal society sets – a grail, a gold medal, a throne, a laurel wreath, a lady's favour. The modern fallacy that men have free will has left them helplessly competing for the most primitive prizes. Properly motivated, they made jungles into cities; left to themselves, they're making the cities into jungles.

September 28

The Duke of Buccleuch, KT was born on September 28th 1923 and was brought up in Scotland. He served in the Second World War with the Royal Navy, going from ordinary seaman to lieutenant commander. In 1953 he married Jane McNeill and they have three sons and a daughter. When Earl of Dalkeith, he was an MP for Edinburgh North from 1960 to 1973. He was Lord Lieutenant from 1974 to 1998, was made Knight of the Thistle in 1978 and has been chancellor since 1992. He is also president of the Royal Association for Disability and Rehabilitation.

On choosing a wheelchair
a tip from The Duke of Buccleuch

• The wheelchair should be as light as possible, mainly for the sake of a spouse or companion, when lifting into a car. 28lbs should be the maximum.

• 20 inch wheels rather than 22 inches. They roll just as well and make sideways transfer easier with less risk of bruising. Also they save space in a car. 20 inch wheels with a 1 inch hub instead of the usual 2 inches or 2.5 inches. This can reduce the overall width of a chair by a good 2 inches, thus making accessible many rooms without the huge cost of altering doorways.

• Detachable footrests, main wheels and armrests essential. Must be able to fold flat.

• A fabric shelf underneath the seat for storage of briefcases, books, paper, etc. (I have managed to carry seven bottles at a time.)

• As an accessory, a briefcase with a board inside it for use as a lap table, small enough to fit between the armrests.

• For someone living in a house with narrow doorways or likely to travel to hotels with narrow bathroom doors or lifts, it can make all the difference to have detachable handrims on the main wheels. It is possible to have this done, but obviously at extra costs. This can save another 2 inches.

• I personally prefer solid small wheels to pneumatic after twice having front wheel punctures.

The Duke of Buccleuch adds: I broke my back in a riding accident in 1971 and have experimented with wheelchairs ever since, ending up with a Newton special design. This makes it possible to enter lifts and bathrooms in foreign hotels that are impassable with standard wheelchairs. The light weight saves wear and tear on my wife, and it is possible for me to enter my car, remove the wheelchair's main wheels and footplates, fold the chair chassis and pass it over to the passenger seat in two minutes. This gives a sense of independence, for which wheelchair users yearn.

Eric Avebury, born September 29th 1928, formerly an engineer, unexpectedly won the Orpington by-election in 1962 and switched to a political career. He held the seat at two subsequent general elections, but the Tories regained it in 1970. The following year he inherited a peerage and has worked full time at politics since then, apart from a few years in the 1980s when he ran a computer company. He became a Buddhist in his seventies and, as patron of the Buddhist Prison Chaplaincy, Angulimala, he is actively concerned with the welfare of prisoners of all faiths and none. He founded the Parliamentary Human Rights Group in 1976 and spends most of his time on situations of internal unrest and conflict which are the cause of human rights violations.

Time and information: the most valuable commodities in the world
a tip from Lord Avebury

Time and information are the most valuable commodities in the world.

My grandfather said that you could learn a foreign language in the time it took to do up your shoelaces. He did speak French and German fluently, and had a fair grasp of Latin, though he had left school at the age of 16.

A publisher asked him to choose the Hundred Best Books, and, when he had completed the task, he was asked how he managed to read them all. He replied that he lived on the southeast railway line. He always took a book on the train, and even to the theatre so that he could read during the intervals.

If my grandfather had been alive today, he would have been an assiduous user of the World Wide Web. Access to information of every kind has been made easier than ever before, and as the technology gets cheaper, few people are deprived by the cost barrier.

Lord Avebury adds: In my own work, the World Wide Web is indispensable, and I can hardly think back to the days before it existed. I can read this morning's *Jakarta Post*, *Times* of India or *Washington Post*. Through the BBC's Summary of World Broadcasts, I have yesterday's broadcasts on Sierra Leone radio or Moscow TV. The latest resolutions of the UN General Assembly, Security Council and Human Rights Commission are all there, as are the reports of the Secretary-General and the various human rights rapporteurs and working groups. The publications of Amnesty International, Human Rights Watch, Index on Censorship or the US State Department are available, as well as a host of specialist materials on every country from Algeria to Zambia and every issue from arms sales to the World Bank.

September 30

Harry Keating was born on October 31st 1926. At his christening his father gave him the names Harry Reymond Fitzwalter. The second of these, spelt with an 'e', would, his father is reported to have said, "look well on the spines of his books". It was, however, not until 1959 that a publisher accepted the third detective story he had written, "by which time," he says, "alas, my father was dead." Since then he has written more crime novels, other novels, works of literary comment and criticism and, in his seventies, a crime novel in verse, Jack, the Lady Killer. September 30th is his only daughter's birthday.

Find your dharma
a tip from H. R. F. Keating

Each of us has, I hazard, a dharma, a role in life.
The trick is to find one's own and to stay with it.
As far as I can make out, you find your dharma by
doing what comes most happily to you, and
observing yourself when you do it or anything
connected to it. So your dharma could be, not
your job, but an absorbing hobby.

Harry Keating adds: I came to realise only gradually, despite my father's christening hint, that my dharma was to be a writer of fiction. It is a wonderful life to be living, even if the financial rewards have been at times highly precarious. I think about it all the time. But what if I had found my dharma had been to be a dustman? I hope I could still have been as content with my lot. That's the secret.

Charles Howard Stirton was born in Pietermaritzburg, South Africa, on November 25th 1946. He is the first director of the £46 million Millennium landmark National Botanic Garden of Wales that opened in west Wales in 2000. He is a botanical scientist, the author of 100 scientific papers and four books. He has travelled on all continents and in many countries. He is fascinated by languages and cultural and biological diversity and loves to exchange postcards with people from around the world. The first postcard was issued on October 1st 1869.

October 1

Start collecting
a tip from Charles Howard Stirton

Start collecting when you're very young and when you retire you will be a world expert. Collecting ephemera, objects and artefacts when you are young opens you up to a lifetime of enjoyment, new friends and acquaintances, and builds a collection over a lifetime that can be of either economic, social, cultural or spiritual value. The collection can be handed to the next generation, sold to provide for retirement or donated to a museum for the benefit of others.

Charles Howard Stirton adds: My daughter, Elishka, has begun a collection of small dog ornaments as it focuses her passionate interest in dogs. My mother collects ornamental owls. I have bought them both scores of these wherever I have travelled and this has enriched my own life. My interest is in Czech and modern art and in political satire postcards from around the world. For example, it is fascinating to see through 120 different postcards of Margaret Thatcher how she is perceived by her foes and friends. It is a snapshot of her history and of contemporary British life.

When my daughter was very young we used to take out a pack of postcards and sit together and look at them one by one. As she got older she became more and more curious about the contents, asking questions about the world, cultures, nature and politics. I believe that it has enriched both our lives: hers in expanding the domains of her known world and aspirations, and my own in sharing in her growth and discovery.

October 2

Colin Dexter was born on September 29th 1930. After Christ's College, Cambridge, he spent his life in education. He also wrote detective stories featuring a certain Chief Inspector Morse, for which he was fortunate enough to win several awards (including the Cartier Diamond Dagger Award in 1997). His novels include: Service of all the Dead *(Silver Dagger Award, 1979),* The Wench is Dead *(Gold Dagger Award, 1989) and* The Way Through the Woods *(Gold Dagger Award, 1992). On October 2nd 1999, Colin Dexter said of the death of Inspector Morse in* The Remorseful Day: *"I'm sad to see Morse go, but in the end it was the only way to end the era and I am quite content with the final result."*

The beginning is one half of the deed
a tip from Colin Dexter, OBE

If you are faced with a difficult or lengthy assignment, do something about it immediately. Get started.

Almost every language has its own variant on the Latin proverb *Initium est dimidium facti*: 'The beginning is one half of the deed.'

Colin Dexter adds: It was in particular as a writer that I found this as good a piece of advice as any I ever received. When stuck with starting a book, a chapter, an essay, an article – anything – I learned to forget about writing the finest sentence ever penned, and learned instead to write the worst sentence ever penned. Provided that I *started*, provided that I did *something*, the gods seemed generally to smile upon me and show me the way forward.

Tom Burke was born on January 5th 1947. He currently advises BP Amoco and Rio Tinto on environmental policy as well as being a council member of English Nature and a visiting professor at Imperial College. He was previously a special advisor to three successive Secretaries of State for the Environment and before that was the director of the Green Alliance and of Friends of the Earth UK. He has written and broadcast extensively on environmental issues for 30 years. In 1997 he was awarded a CBE for services to the environment. St Francis of Assisi, patron saint of the environment, died on October 3rd 1226.

Changing outcomes
a tip from Tom Burke, CBE

Changing outcomes matters more than winning arguments.

One of the greatest dangers facing those who believe in something important is that they want to persuade others to share their belief rather than to change their behaviour. This is a consequence of insecure belief and confuses causes and religions. If you really believe in your goals it matters far more that others behave in ways that are consistent with them than that they agree with your reasons for believing. Far too many environmentalists would rather be told they are right than make a difference to what actually happens in the world. It is reassuring to be told you are right, but it rarely changes much.

Tom Burke adds: This tip is the product of hard experience. There are few more claustrophobic places to be than the ghetto of a good cause. Stokely Carmichael's provocation at the Politics of Liberation conference held in London in the 1960s was to ask repeatedly "What have you done? What have you done?" It was a very good question even if his own answer was inconsequential. A pragmatist is only someone who wants to make his dreams real in this world rather than the next – that is what distinguishes him from a priest. What matters is the difference you make in the world, the rest is vanity.

October 4

Tessa Keswick was born on October 15th 1942. She has been the director of the think tank, the Centre for Policy Studies, since 1995. Previous to that she was special advisor to the Rt Hon. Kenneth Clarke at the Departments of Health, Education, the Home Office and the Treasury. She contributes to the newspapers and appears occasionally on television and radio, including the World Service and programmes such as Question Time *and* Any Questions. *On October 4th 1985, she "got married (happily)".*

Remember King Robert
a tip from Tessa Keswick

When the fortunes of King Robert the Bruce, in his valiant attempts to win back the throne of Scotland, were at a particularly low ebb, he found himself sheltering in a cave wondering whether to throw in his hand. His attention was taken by a spider which was desperately trying to climb the dank walls and kept falling back. The spider kept on trying. Eventually through sheer determination it managed to reach its goal. This success hugely encouraged the forlorn King Robert and he pulled himself together. Thus renewed, he went on to revive his fortunes.

Tessa Keswick adds: I hope that the rather corny old chestnut to 'keep on trying' is still taught to every schoolchild because confidence based on endeavour and achievement is what counts throughout life. It is only by trying that each of us learns where one's ability lies and no one can be good at everything – what is important is to discover which talents have been given to us. So, through successful endeavour we gain confidence and in our occasional failures we learn, I hope, a useful measure of humility.

Russ Lindsay was born on July 12th 1961. He is the co-owner and managing director of the James Grant Media Group Ltd which manages a number of TV and radio personalities, including Phillip Schofield, Anthea Turner, Zoe Ball and Lindsay's wife, Caron Keating. Russ and Caron live in Barnes, London, with their two sons Charlie and Gabriel. October 5th is Caron Keating's birthday.

Always find time to sharpen your axe
a tip from Russ Lindsay

Two woodcutters are in a race to cut down as many trees as possible in a day. They are fairly equal by lunch time when one of the woodcutters sits down and unwraps his lunch. Seeing his chance to get ahead, the other woodcutter keeps chopping as hard as he can and fells dozens of trees while his opponent relaxes. However, come the middle of the afternoon his heart is not in it and his arms are heavy from the blunt axe. He looks over at his opponent singing away as he chops down tree after tree in an effortless style, going on to win the competition. Wearily he inquires as to the man's strength and stamina.

"It's not strength and stamina that enabled me to chop down the trees so easily this afternoon," replied the woodcutter. "Whilst you were chopping away at lunchtime, I went off and sharpened my axe."

Russ Lindsay adds: Take good quality breaks as often as you can, as no one benefits if you're worn out. Also, when you are making important decisions, find time to think them through thoroughly. Be prepared to say to people "Give me 24 hours on that" or "I'll let you know tomorrow". Sure, we all have to make decisions on impulse because of the pace of life today, but where possible, find time to analyse your initial thoughts – and never be afraid to change your mind.

October 6

Stephen Hearst was born on October 6th 1919. He has worked in broadcasting since 1954, first as writer and producer of documentaries, then as Head of Arts Features, BBC and Controller, Radio 3. He has also written essays and contributed articles on broadcasting issues.

Don't lose your capacity for doubting
a tip from Stephen Hearst

Faith is the distance spanning belief and evidence.

Sod's law tells us that what can go wrong will.

The law of unforeseen consequences says that effects of deliberate actions are unpredictable.

Doubting helps us to bear the burden of both laws.

Stephen Hearst adds: As a rough contemporary of Hitler, Stalin, Mao Tse Tung and Pol Pot, doubting their fanatical ideologies made it easier for me to resist them and to think that democracy, with all its weaknesses, would eventually prevail. The moment somebody, in public or private, says "Let me make it absolutely clear", start doubting at once.

Sir Andrew Derbyshire was born on October 7th 1923. During the war he worked as a physicist for the Admiralty on anti-submarine systems. He qualified as an architect at the end of the war and, after a period in local government, joined the architectural practice of Robert Matthew Johnson-Marshall and Partners (later RMJM Ltd). Until 1998 he was chairman and then president of this firm of 450 architects, engineers and planners working in six different countries. The work for which he would most like to be remembered is his contribution to the planning and building of the University of York. He now works from home as a freelance consultant on architectural and planning matters.

If you don't like the people you work with you're in the wrong job
a tip from **Sir Andrew Derbyshire**

If you don't like the people you work with you're in the wrong job.

The truth of this was borne in upon me when a journalist came to see me to talk about my career move from science to architecture. After listening to the story of my life he declared that I fitted very nicely into a hypothesis he was developing as a result of many interviews: that the chief motivator for people to make a career change was that they found that none of their colleagues were friends. I don't know if he ever published an article on this subject, or even the book which he said was in his mind, and I can't remember his name. But he set me thinking.

Andrew Derbyshire adds: Like many people I was bedevilled at school by the enforced choice between the arts and science sixth forms. I liked drawing and was fascinated by buildings, but I was also good at physics. At the beginning of the war I was advised that nobody would find a use for architects whereas science would bring us victory. So I allowed myself to be conscripted to Cambridge to read the Natural Sciences Tripos.

I now realise that what I thought was an aptitude for physics was in fact my response to a brilliant teacher. Although it didn't occur to me as significant at the time, none of my friends at Cambridge were reading my subject. And later, when I was drafted into operational research for the navy, the same thing happened – I couldn't relate to my fellow scientists. I found them narrow and uninterested in the things that excited my imagination.

This has gone on happening. My move from public to private practice in architecture was driven by the same need to work with people who share the same aspirations, dream the same dreams about a better world, believe in the same politics and like the same books and music.

There is more to job satisfaction than this, and there are many reasons for moving on in these days of insecure employment, but I would always take a lack of real chums at work as a strong signal to look elsewhere.

October 8

Celia Brayfield was born on August 21st 1945. She is the author of seven novels, including Heartswap *(2000) a modern romantic comedy based on the opera* Così Fan Tutte; Sunset, *a story of love and volcanoes; and* Harvest, *a black comedy. Her first novel,* Pearls *(1995), is an international bestseller about an aristocratic family in post-colonial England and Malaysia. Brayfield has also written non-fiction books, including* Bestseller *(1996) about the art of popular fiction. As a journalist, she contributes to many publications, including* The Times. *Her daughter Chloe was born on October 8th 1980.*

No good deed will go unpunished
a tip from **Celia Brayfield**

"No good deed will go unpunished."

This is cynical, but true – and often also comforting.

Celia Brayfield adds: This is a favourite admonition of one of my friends. We take it as a warning against calculated altruism, hardly a growing phenomenon, but still a problem to those who are kind of heart. The meaning is that if you want to do good, you have to do it for its own sake and accept whatever result your action brings. If you do good and expect to benefit from it, you're not acting in the true spirit of virtue and the universe may send you a bad experience in return. So you learn to do good not for the sake of looking good, being admired, having control, gaining advantage, not feeling guilty or whatever, but just because it's the good thing to do.

Joe Ashton was born on October 9th 1933. He has been a Labour Member of Parliament representing Bassetlaw for over 30 years. He is a director of Sheffield Wednesday Football Club and chairman of the All Party Football Group, which has 150 MPs and Lords in its membership. He was the winner of the What the Papers Say *award for Columnist of the Year in 1984 and is the author of a novel,* Grassroots, *and a play,* A Majority of One.

Distress, not stress, is the killer
a tip from **Joe Ashton**, MP

It is not *stress* that kills you. It is *distress*.

Enjoy the stress. Realise that distress is the killer.

Joe Ashton adds: The job span of an average football manager is about two years – highly paid, but totally dependent on the performance of other people in a highly competitive business where league table statistics don't lie and are the only criteria.

All new managers are told that it is distress, not stress, which brings on heart attacks. Stress is when their team is playing at Manchester United and winning by 1–0 with five minutes to go.

Distress is playing at Manchester United and losing 5–0 with half an hour to go.

October 10

Charles Osborne was born on November 24th 1927. He worked in Australia in literary and musical journalism and in theatre before coming to England in his mid-twenties. He was a director of the Arts Council of Great Britain for 20 years and has written a number of books on musical and literary subjects. He contributes regularly to the Telegraph, *broadcasts for the BBC and lectures in Europe and America. He is a fellow of the Royal Society of Literature. He is also an authority on the operas of Verdi. Verdi was born on October 10th 1813.*

Steer clear of religion
a tip from Charles Osborne

Do your best to avoid religious instruction periods at school. If your parents object, tell them you'll consider adopting a religion only when you have reached the age of 14 and can think clearly about the subject without undue pressure being placed on you. Only then should you, if you still want to, sample the various religions on offer, and decide which of them, if any, you wish to take up.

Charles Osborne adds: Fortunately, my parents were both agnostics, and connived at my being excused from religious instruction at school. When I was 14, my father offered to take me to services at the local Catholic and Protestant churches, synagogue, mosque and so on. But by this time I had come to realise that religion had been (and, indeed, still is today) responsible for much of the violence and mass slaughter in the world. I had been taught by my parents that one should try to make life as pleasant as possible for oneself and for others, and I felt no need to lean on a religion.

Peter Wadhams was born on May 14th 1948. He is reader in Polar Studies, and formerly director, at the Scott Polar Research Institute in Cambridge University. His research work covers the polar oceans, their sea ice cover and the role of the polar regions in global climatic warming. He has led more than 30 expeditions to the polar regions. His books include The Arctic and Environmental Change *(co-editor, 1996). He married Maria Pia on October 11th 1980.*

Give a child an inquiring mind
a tip from Dr Peter Wadhams

The most important thing that you can give a child is an inquiring mind.

Peter Wadhams adds: My father told me this. He believed that it is vital that a young person should actively seek to investigate the unknown, to learn new things and to approach every question with an open mind. One should acquire the habit of thinking things out for oneself instead of passively accepting received opinion. It was thanks to my father's example that I became a scientist, which ought to be one of the most open-ended and inquiring professions that there is. If I had taken his advice fully, however, I would not have become a scientist in a conventional field where a safe career is possible, but would have risked my reputation by working in frontier regions where the most important future advances in knowledge will be made, but which at present, owing to the intense conformity in science, are regarded as beyond the pale. Examples are phenomena such as telepathy, precognition and psychokinesis, powers of the mind which are completely inexplicable but which have been demonstrated to occur.

October 12

Norman Tebbit was born on March 29th 1931. An airline pilot by profession, he later served 22 years in the House of Commons, eight years as an MP and six in the Cabinet. He was secretary of state for employment (1981–83), secretary of state for trade and industry (1983–85), and chairman of the Conservative Party (1985–87). He is now a journalist and columnist. His books include Unfinished Business (1991).

So long as you survive
a tip from **The Rt Hon. Lord Tebbit**

Remember, no experience, however awful, is entirely bad – so long as you survive.

October 12th 1984 was the day of the Brighton bombing, when Norman Tebbit and his wife, who remains wheelchair-bound, were seriously injured in the IRA attempt to murder Margaret Thatcher and her Cabinet.

Edwina Currie was born on October 13th 1946. Educated in Liverpool and at Oxford University, she was Conservative MP for Derbyshire South from 1983 to 1997, and Minister for Women's Health from 1986 to 1988. She was voted Campaigner of the Year in 1994. She is also the author of four novels, including A Parliamentary Affair (1994) and The Ambassador (1999).

If you find yourself redundant
a tip from Edwina Currie

If you find yourself redundant:

(i) Take whatever is on offer – you have no idea what you can do;

(ii) Get a makeover – be a new man! (or woman).

Then you are ready for a new life.

Edwina Currie adds: And do something completely mad – that you couldn't do before. Run a marathon; do a bike ride for charity; climb a mountain. Does wonders for the psyche.

October 14

Martin Palmer was born on October 14th 1953. He is secretary general of the Alliance of Religions and Conservation which works worldwide on religiously-based environmental projects. He is also religious advisor to World Wildlife Fund International, director of the International Consultancy on Religion, Education and Culture and regular broadcaster on the BBC. He has written over 30 books on all aspects of religion, including Faiths and Festivals *and* Sacred Britain *(co-author, 1997), and is a particular expert on Chinese religion. He notes that October 14th is also the date of the Battle of Hastings.*

Let your soul catch up with your body
a tip from Martin Palmer

Never leave for a journey without sitting still for a few minutes to let your soul catch up with your body.

This piece of traditional Russian Orthodox wisdom was given to me by a dear friend in Moscow. I spend a great deal of time travelling, leaping from one country and culture to another. His advice means that as you are about to leave the hotel room, or home, to travel and your bags are packed, sit down and stop for just a minute or two.

This has two wonderful consequences. It does allow your soul to catch up with your body. You focus and rest and prepare all at once. The other useful consequence is that you often suddenly spot something you meant to pack.

Martin Palmer adds: This works, believe me. It may seem crazy to stop and sit at exactly the moment you feel you should be rushing. But perhaps the reason this works and leaves you feeling a little more relaxed is because it reminds you of what is important in life – your well-being – and puts all those pressures of time and life in a slower perspective. I just wish I always remembered this tip – but I don't.

Janni Howker was born on July 6th 1957. Among the many accolades she has received for her books for young people are the Whitbread and the Observer young people's fiction award. A life member of the Arvon foundation council, she is a confirmed educationalist and lecturer, and holds creative writing workshops throughout Britain and abroad. She is the only writer for children to be presented with a Somerset Maugham award. October 15th is her wedding anniversary.

Walk at the pace of a good conversation
a tip from Janni Howker

Do what the day brings and never no more.

Don't put off paying that bill, visiting that old aunt, writing that letter.

Don't worry about the future or regret the past.

Walk at the pace of a good conversation with a friend.

Janni Howker adds: This piece of advice was given to me by an extraordinary wandering musician, the Galloway fiddler who strolled into the pages of my novel *Martin Farrell*. Anxiety, depression, insecurity and ecological destruction are all connected to a lack of quiet attention to the moment. Don't go crazy, go fishing.

October 16

Hugh Scott writes children's novels and short stories, including The Plant That Ate The World *and* The Grave-Digger. *He won the children's category of the Whitbread Book of the Year Award in 1989. He is also an artist, and teaches writing and art to adults. He gives talks to adults and children. October 16th is his birthday.*

Eschew political correctness
a tip from Hugh Scott

Political correctness is evil parading in fine clothes. It says, "I am clever. I am right. I am good. Listen to my wisdom." Then it points out the wickedness in its own mind, saying, "You cannot refer to a little girl as a little girl in case a paedophile is listening. You cannot call that foreigner a foreigner in case he is offended at the truth. You cannot refer to the colour of someone's skin in case he believes that you think less of him."

Every thought and remark of the politically correct arouses precisely those fears it purports to quash.

Hugh Scott adds: The examples of 'little girl' and 'foreigner' are actual examples of political correctness put to me by an editor. Needless to say, I refused to change my perfectly innocent phraseology.

Alan Garner was born on October 17th 1934 and was educated at Alderley Edge Council School, the Manchester Grammar School and Magdalen College, Oxford. A classicist by training, he works in whatever form is appropriate: mainly as a novelist, but also as a playwright, librettist, and maker and presenter of documentary films. He has also contributed to the worlds of history, archaeology, anthropology and folklore.

October 17

If the other fellow can do it, let him
tips from Alan Garner

Tip one: If the other fellow can do it, let him.

Tip two: Always take as long as the job tells you, because it will be there when you're not, and you don't want folks saying, "What fool made *that* codge?"

Alan Garner adds: Joseph Garner (1875–1955) was a smith and my grandfather. Of all his wisdom, these two statements, which he put upon me when I was seven years old, were the wisest and have directed my life. They have enabled me to live a life of spiritual and intellectual freedom by making me assume conscious responsibility for my actions and to see them through. They have also made me understand the purpose beyond, which is to bring about the Future.

October 18

Diana Lamplugh was born on July 30th 1936. She is the mother of Suzy who disappeared from her workplace in 1986. Suzy has been presumed abducted and murdered. Diana set up the Suzy Lamplugh Trust in December 1986 and is now its director. This trust has become Europe's leading authority on personal safety. Diana is also a speaker, broadcaster and writer. She sits on the British Transport Police Committee and is a member of the Penal Affairs Consortium and the Forum on Violence and Children. Diana has been awarded three university doctorates. Diana and her husband Paul, who were married on this day in 1958, have three other grown-up children and two dogs and a cat.

Living through tragedy to charity
a tip from Diana Lamplugh, OBE

"Don't waste energy dwelling on the past and wallowing in sorrow, look forward and wonder what you can do to improve the world."

My mother's governess

Diana Lamplugh adds: After Suzy's disappearance, thinking "Why me? Why my daughter?" nearly destroyed me. Remembering Suzy with joyful love and considering how to work towards a safer society restored me.

Maxim Jakubowski was born on October 19th 1944. Once a publisher, he now divides his time between running Murder One, the world's largest mystery bookshop, and editing imprints for various publishers and writing. His novels range from mystery to erotica. He says: "I have been described as the king of the erotic thriller, but prefer to describe my work as romantic pornography." He is a frequent broadcaster, a columnist for London's Time Out magazine and a winner of the Anthony award.

Live now, pay later
a tip from **Maxim Jakubowski**

You only have one life, so live it to the full.

There may be regrets, heartbreak and deep sorrow, but at least you'll still have the memories. Experience everything once, to the limits of legality and morality, because who cares what others might say; it's your life, not theirs. And as for payment or divine retribution, well, if you can live with melancholy and an expanding waistline, it's worth the price.

Maxim Jakubowski adds: No, I am not going to reveal here to what extent I have followed my own tips in real life. But I will admit to moments of epiphany and glorious food (hence the fact that I am no longer the skinny man my wife married all those years ago). And regrets, of course; but then I'm only human.

October 20

Douglas Rushkoff, born February 18th 1961, is the author of books including Cyberia, Media Virus, Ecstasy Club, Playing the Future, Coercion, *and the novel,* Bull *(http:// www.rushkoff.com/bull.html), a black comedy about how a society can fall into 'market fascism'. Rushkoff is a commentator for American National Public Radio's* All Things Considered, *a professor at New York University's Interactive Telecommunications Program, and a frequent television guest and lecturer around the world. He lives in New York with his "fearsome beta fish, Claude". October 20th is the birthday of Rushkoff's niece, Rebecca.*

Are you having a good time yet?
a tip from Douglas Rushkoff

Chances are, if you're reading this book you will never have to worry about finding your next meal or getting a roof over your head. And if your survival needs are taken care of, then the rest is about fun. Play. Self-actualisation. Even if you decide to go to Africa to help feed the starving – for them it's survival, but for you it's fun.

No matter how terrible things are, or how little time you might have left, there's no good reason not to start having as much fun as possible, right now.

Douglas Rushkoff adds: Some day, you're going to die. And when you're lying there on your deathbed, you won't look back on your life and count how much you accomplished, how much money you earned or even how you'll be remembered. The only thing that will matter is how much fun you've had – how much true, deep, intimate fun. So, ask yourself: Are you having a good time yet?

Margaret Dawes was born on September 10th 1918 in Singapore and lived her earliest years in remote Malay villages. She graduated from Somerville College, Oxford, in 1939 and worked at Bletchley Park in the war — the secret headquarters of the government's codebreaking operations. Since being registered blind, she has been an enthusiastic member of a ceramics group for the visually impaired. Her first book, on private provincial bankers in England and Wales, was published in October 2000. On this date, October 21st 1991, over 400 codebreakers were brought together for a farewell party at Bletchley Park, which was about to be destroyed to make way for a housing development. As a result of the stories told on that day, a decision was made to keep Bletchley Park for posterity. It has since been restored and is now open to the public.

Be to his faults a little blind
a tip from Margaret Dawes

"Be to his virtues ever kind; be to his faults a little blind."

My uncle, Ernest Rowe-Dutton, somewhat in loco parentis after my father's death, gave me his much-read copy of *Handley Cross* by Robert Surtees in which I first met Jorrocks, respectable London grocer and renowned Surrey Master of Foxhounds, and his wonderful collection of eccentrics. Among many precepts for living, the above, used of his horse Xerxes, seemed a useful brake on a hot temper.

Margaret Dawes adds: After I met my husband during our first term at Oxford, and we exchanged our respective schemes for life, by mutual application of Jorrocks' apophthegm we contrived more than 55 years of marriage. Jorrocks also kept me from extremes in politics, having been, in the immortal words of Mrs Thatcher, a wishy-washy Liberal. In some situations, however, his influence proved less effective, as for example in dealing with recalcitrant machines or with that greatest temptation to intolerance, another driver.

October 22

Julian Rathbone has been a full-time writer since 1973, and before that was a teacher of English. He has published over 30 books in a variety of fiction genres, short stories and even poetry. He has won several awards and twice been short-listed for the Booker, for King Fisher Lives (1976) and Joseph (1979). He has also written screenplays for TV movies and films. He was born on February 10th 1935, but born again on October 22nd 1996 – the day he survived burst oesophageal varices, had eight bags of someone else's blood pumped into him and stopped saying yes to booze. He survived to go on saying yes to everything else.

Say yes
a tip from Julian Rathbone

Whatever crops up, whatever is offered, whatever opportunity occurs – say yes.

This probably needs qualification. Generally speaking don't do something if it's going to cause long-term serious hurt to someone else – but remember that people are resilient. A yes for one person may seem to mean a no for someone else and yet turn out all right in the long run.

Criminal activity should generally be eschewed unless you a) object to the law that criminalises the activity, and b) can get away with it.

But all this is negative. Never been to the US? Go there. Fancy sky-diving? Try it. Is the sun shining? Go for a walk. Remember the cliché that this life is not a rehearsal, it's all we get.

Julian Rathbone adds: In the first half of my life I drifted into teaching almost by accident, and before I was 40 found myself high up the ladder with good prospects of getting to the top and dying of stress-related illness before 50. Then I dropped not out but in. I took an 80 per cent cut in income, travelled, wrote and said yes to anything and anyone who came along – including the person I'm still with, and I said yes when she said she wanted to start a family. I'm still not sure where the next penny comes from, but that's now the Inland Revenue's worry not mine. Through saying yes for the last 30 years, I've had a full, varied and happy life. I hope I've got the habit, so that when the fell sergeant fingers my collar, I'll be able to say yes to him too.

Anita Roddick was born on October 23rd 1942 in Littlehampton, on England's south coast. In 1976 she opened The Body Shop, a small shop in Brighton where she sold naturally-based cosmetics inspired in part by ingredients she had come across on her world travels. Over two decades, The Body Shop has grown into a global business with over 1,700 shops in 48 countries. It campaigns internationally on behalf of human rights and animal protection.

Travel: a university without walls
a tip from **Anita Roddick**, OBE

Get out of your chair and move.

Travel turns your whole life into an experiential education. It makes you think for yourself and helps you challenge everything you've been taught in school. Travel is an essential rite of passage for the activist.

Anita Roddick adds: I trained as a teacher. In 1962 I won a scholarship to study on a kibbutz in Israel to complete my thesis. My experiences in Israel convinced me that teaching was never going to be enough for me. I had a bad case of itchy feet. I worked for the United Nations in Geneva for a year and saved enough money for a ticket to Tahiti. Then I roamed around the Southern Hemisphere for a while.

It was a seminal time in my life. The people I met, the things I saw, became the foundation for everything I subsequently did. Plus, I learned how truly advantageous fearlessness is.

October 24

Timothy Lachlan Chambers was born on February 11th 1946. He trained as a doctor, specialising in paediatrics, and says that he is still learning from patients and their families. This learning he holds in higher esteem than all the representative offices he has held in medicine at home and abroad. A Room of One's Own, by Virginia Woolf (mentioned below), was first published on October 24th 1929.

Keep a diary and write letters
a tip from **Dr Timothy Chambers**

Writing a diary allows time for reflection and clarification of one's thoughts and impressions. A diary is useful for this – provided you do not write with an eye to eventual publication.

Write letters too, including ones in longhand. There are few greater pleasures in life than receiving a personal letter with a stamp on the envelope.

Timothy Chambers adds: This was a wise piece of advice from Virginia Woolf. Communication is the bedrock of human relationships – provided you keep certain letters in a drawer for a few days before deciding to send them.

Renée Asherson graduated from the Webber-Douglas Academy of Dramatic Art and her first big break was to play the part of Princess Katherine in the Laurence Olivier film of Shakespeare's Henry V *– hence the placing of this tip on St Crispin's Day, the anniversary of Henry V's victory at the Battle of Agincourt on October 25th 1415. Renée Asherson married the actor Robert Donat and is still active in the theatre after a long career in theatre, film and television.*

To thine own self be true
tips from Renée Asherson

First, Polonius' instructions to Laertes (*Hamlet*, Act 1, Scene 3), especially the final words:

> "To thine own self be true,
> And it must follow, as the night the day,
> Thou canst not then be false to any man."

And secondly, perhaps as an antidote, from Gilbert and Sullivan's *Iolanthe*:

> "Nothing venture, nothing win."

Renée Asherson adds: This advice comes from a not naturally bold person. I have to admit that I have only learnt this from long experience, and in retrospect I see that I have sometimes followed these life instructions – and often failed.

October 26

John Arden was born on October 26th 1930. He originally trained as an architect, but has earned his living as playwright and novelist since 1958. His best-known plays are probably Sergeant Musgrave's Dance *(1959) and* The Non-Stop Connolly Show *(written with Margaretta D'Arcy, 1975). His novel,* Silence Among the Weapons, *was shortlisted for the Booker Prize in 1982. He lives in Galway in the west of Ireland.*

Carry a pencil and notebook
a tip from John Arden

Carry at all times a pencil and notebook and thereby avoid enslavement to complex technology – never mind your computer, never even mind your typewriter (now totally, so it seems, obsolete). For the notebook, if need be, use a small piece of folded paper. And the pencil, if need be, can always be sharpened with one's teeth and fingernails. Theoretically it would be possible to compose *War and Peace* with such resources. We are, after all, but one step from the Stone Age and it's dangerous to forget it. Any machine, anywhere, can always go wrong. Maybe I should have recommended a piece of flint and a slate?

John Arden adds: I do carry my pencil and paper; I often need them, I often use them. But I can't quite convince myself about avoidance of slavery. As I write, I look back on a fortnight containing: (1) a ruined bicycle tyre, (2) an intermittently faulty fridge, (3) a central heating system breaking down because of a bird's nest in the kitchen chimney, (4) a computer printer that has been failing to print, even when sworn at and sung to. I have worried myself sick about all these nonsenses.

Ari Badaines writes: "I made my entry into the world on October 27th 1941 – a gorgeous morning in Maine. From there it was all uphill (or downhill depending on your perspective). I am a playful character who can also be serious and caring. I have led personal growth workshops in many countries and love life and baseball (probably in reverse order). I am concerned about the environment and the psychosocial relationships among individuals and groups."

If you *have* to decide, it's too soon
a tip from Ari Badaines

There you are, desperately trying to decide on some key issue: get married? take the job? move somewhere else? change careers? You have spoken to umpteen people seeking their opinion, made lists of the pros and cons, debated it in your head back and forth, and still you can't decide. Here comes the tip:

Stop trying and drop *having* to decide. Let all the thoughts, opinions, excitements, fears drift around – don't exclude anything, don't force anything. Just stay open to whatever is happening, and by the time you need to know what you're going to do, the decision will arrive – you'll know without ever having to decide. Sometimes the clarity will arrive at the last possible moment, but it will arrive as long as you stay open to all possibilities. These will be your truest decisions because they were not forced.

Ari Badaines adds: In 1985 I had a visa to live in Australia (not easy to obtain back then) and I couldn't decide whether to move to Sydney or stay put. I carefully weighed the advantages and disadvantages, consulted with friends, and did all the other stuff that anyone does in making a major decision. "Time is running out, I have to decide," I kept telling myself. Then I remembered hearing somewhere: "If you *have* to decide it is too soon." I stopped trying to decide, let my feelings and thoughts run free, leave me, create havoc, but experienced a huge relief that I didn't *have* to decide.

About a week later, on a Friday morning, I awoke feeling anxious and depressed and these feelings persisted throughout the weekend. On Monday, I wondered aloud to a friend, "I bet I'm going to Australia and I just don't know it. The anxiety is about the future and the depression is grieving for the past." Tuesday I knew I was going to Sydney – no decision forced, just a calm knowing – and I'm still there.

Now I sometimes think that a decision won't come, but I've learnt to trust that it will, and it always does.

October 28

Bill Gates was born on October 28th 1955. He attended Seattle High School and then Harvard University. He wrote his first software program, for playing tic-tac-toe, when he was 13 years old. In 1976 he co-founded the Microsoft Corporation. He has published The Road Ahead *and* Business – The speed of thought. *He married Melinda French in 1994 and they have a daughter.*

Learn to learn
a tip from Bill Gates

Learn to learn. Great educators have always known that learning is not something you only do in classrooms, or only under the supervision of teachers. The information highway is going to give us all access to seemingly unlimited information, any time and any place we care to use it. It's an exhilarating prospect. The highway will alter the focus of education from the institution to the individual.

The ultimate goal will be changed from getting a diploma to enjoying lifelong learning.

Bill Gates adds: Some fear that technology will dehumanise formal education. But anyone who has seen kids working together around a computer, the way my friends and I first did in 1968, or watched exchanges between students in classrooms separated by oceans, knows that technology can humanise the educational environment.

Paul Tyler was born in Devon on October 29th 1941, his mother having emigrated from Cornwall and married a Devonian. Through her, he is a direct descendant of Bishop Jonathan Trelawny, on whose behalf '20,000 Cornishmen' threatened to march to London against the tyranny of King James II in 1688. Through his father, Paul is descended from Oliver Cromwell. Paul has been involved in the public life of the West Country since he was elected the youngest county councillor in Britain in 1964. MP for North Cornwall since 1992, he is now the Liberal Democrat Chief Whip and Shadow Leader of the House.

Remembering names
a tip from Paul Tyler, MP, CBE

If you have embarrassing memory lapses (as I do) make sure that your mental retrieval system has plenty of data to provide connections: design your own system to suit your personal idiosyncrasies. I try to associate people with places, especially if they are constituents. In the early days of the telephone, my grandmother connected up names with the then three figure numbers and the relevant hymn tunes in *Ancient & Modern*. Whatever sparks your memory, go for it.

Paul Tyler adds: So many of my MP colleagues possess photographic memories – or give the impression of doing so. I have so often nearly stumbled into a social or political calamity, that I work hard to recreate these connections. No system is infallible, for sure. However, your own personally adjusted remembrancer is less likely to let you down – and what pleasure is caused (for them as well as you) when it does work.

October 30

Patty Dann was born on October 30th 1953. Her most recent book is The Baby Boat: A memoir of adoption. *She has also written a novel,* Mermaids, *which has been translated into five languages and has been made into a movie starring Cher and Winona Ryder. She teaches memoir and fiction classes in New York.*

Never hitch your wagon to a star
a tip from **Patty Dann**

Never hitch your wagon to a star, or you will remain a wagon.

Do not be impressed by status or fame. Seeking your own will only make you sick, and trying to be close to someone who has it will sap your energy. Do your work, nobody else's. You have no other choice.

Patty Dann adds: My father told me this when I was a child, and I never understood what it meant until I was offered a job answering fan mail for a world-famous ballet dancer. At first I was lured by his name and the thought of being in the same room with him, but I heeded my father's words and became a teacher, which I love, and which also gives me time for my own writing. If I had done the other, I would have gone to more dinner parties and had nothing to show for it but some extra weight.

Stephen Gallagher was born on October 13th 1954 and is a novelist, screenwriter and film director specialising in contemporary suspense. His works include Chimera, Oktober *and* Nightmare, with Angel. *He notes: "October 31st is Halloween, or All Hallows Eve, when the dead are said to revisit their homes – a night for scary stories."*

Everyone is entitled to their opinion
a tip from Stephen Gallagher

If you create something, do it for the love of the work and not for the rewards you think it might bring you. Envy is OK, but jealousy isn't. Never reply to a critic.

Stephen Gallagher adds: You never know what the real rewards of your work are going to be, so getting fixated on any one particular outcome is bound to guarantee you a life of frustration. Everything's a long game, so try to enjoy the playing of it, because when you look back from the end, the playing is 90 per cent of what you'll have.

If someone does something that I admire and wish I could have done, I tell them. That kind of envy is a true compliment – it makes you feel good and it can make you look pretty good as well. Jealousy is the negative reaction – it sours you and takes nothing from the other person's achievement. Everyone is entitled to their opinion of what you do. Not everyone will love it, and that is something you have to live with. All that happens when you engage with a negative opinion is that you give it a validation that it didn't have before.

November 1

Professor Sir Hermann Bondi, KCB, FRS was born on November 1st 1919 in Vienna. He came to England in September 1937 to read mathematics at Trinity College, Cambridge. His move was due both to the anxiety Hitler's rise caused and to mathematical ambition. During the war he was first interned as an enemy alien (1940–41) and, soon afterwards, worked for the Royal Navy on radar research (1942–45). His career since has been first as an academic (Cambridge 1945–54, King's College, London 1954–67), then in public service, finally as an academic again as master (1983–90) and, since, as fellow of Churchill College, Cambridge. He has published numerous scientific papers and books on cosmology and relativity as well as an autobiography. November 1st is also his wedding anniversary.

We humans are social animals
tips from **Sir Hermann Bondi**

We humans are social animals. The chief pleasure in life is therefore interacting with other people, in the family, in work, socially. (I am not impressed by hermits or silent people.) One should therefore always strive to get the benefits of company, however unpropitious the circumstances. (I made life-long friends in internment and gave my first lectures there.)

My tip for the day is: Always try to get into conversation with the people you encounter. Do your best to make them talk about something that, perhaps to your surprise, you find interesting. Whatever job you have (except perhaps as solitary lighthouse keeper), you can talk to your colleagues and thereby take an interest in all aspects of their work and in them as persons. This is the surest way to prepare you to take wider responsibilities (whether in the same business or elsewhere) and so to go up in the world.

My second tip is not to overwork. In any job it is easy to bury oneself in detail, thereby not only missing the important things, but also pointlessly sacrificing one's free time and holidays. If you have people reporting to you, make sure that they do not overwork, or you will not get value from them. (In one very senior post I took up, my staff told me that my predecessor had spent 12 hours each day in the office and then taken a set of files home to prepare himself for the next day's work. My first words were "The new regime will be quite different". It was also, everybody said, a lot more effective.)

My third tip is to make sure you take holidays and enjoy them thoroughly.

Fourthly, never postpone decision-taking. You will not be any cleverer next week.

Don't press your interests on others
a tip from **Maurice Ash**

When I was 19, and about to embark on a voyage to India, my father gave me the advice: "Find out what other people's interests are: don't press yours on them."

Maurice Ash adds: This practical advice worked like a charm on shipboard, but I suspect it also nourished the growing doubts I was feeling over the Cartesian social science – that is, economics – I was then being taught. In turn, it underlay my refusal to accept the monstrous egoism of the Modernism of our times – whether in architecture, urban planning or the arts. And it led to an ever deepening interest in Buddhism, with its insistence on the non-substantiality of the self – and even to a slight comprehension of quantum mechanics.

November 3

Sir Ludovic Kennedy was born in Edinburgh on November 3rd 1919. For 35 years he was a presenter of television programmes and maker of television documentaries. He has written a dozen books, on miscarriages of criminal justice, naval history, Scotland and atheism. He was knighted in 1994 and has been married for more than 50 years to the former prima ballerina and actress, Moira Shearer.

If in doubt, don't
a tip from Sir Ludovic Kennedy

If in doubt, don't. Second thoughts are often best.

Don't take a girl to bed with you unless you, and she, are 100 per cent sure about it. Don't write an angry, apologetic or flattering letter which you think you may have cause to regret afterwards. Don't go along with the crowd on any matter if you feel it's against your nature. Don't do anything for a 'dare' or to impress, because to do so may well end in tears.

Sir Ludovic Kennedy adds: Where the tip came from, I've no idea, but I do know that if I'd followed it in my early life, I would have been spared much anguish, embarrassment, regret, remorse, etc. One learns as one gets older, but to learn young is a bonus.

Barbara Hosking was born in Penzance on November 4th 1926. She is deputy chairman of Westcountry Television. As she did not go to university, her honorary doctorate from the University of Ulster is doubly precious to her. She has worked for the Labour Party at Transport House; on a mine in the East African bush where she carried her own rifle; and for two Prime Ministers at No.10: Harold Wilson and Edward Heath. Her first broadcast was at the age of 16, her last on Any Questions *and, among other writing, she once had a poem published in* New Scientist.

Don't enthuse insincerely
a tip from **Barbara Hosking**, CBE

Say yes only when you mean it. Don't praise to be polite. Don't enthuse insincerely. Don't gush over other people's cooking and don't prevaricate to avoid giving pain.

Barbara Hosking adds: My worst vice is mistaken politeness. By overpraising I have acquired huge pieces of pottery which I can't hide, lose or break. And I once spent an atrocious weekend in a damp, draughty, isolated farmhouse because I said I loved Shropshire. I'm always eating second helpings I don't want through praising the food, while the avoidance of a firm no almost ended in a most inappropriate marriage. Learn from me that no is good and silence golden.

November 5

Alex Hamilton was born in Bristol on November 5th 1939, and almost immediately transferred to Brazil. An early life in South America gave him a painless way into being a polyglot and ultimately a professional travel writer. In this occupation he has won several national awards and edited the Guardian's travel pages for 15 years. Apart from several kinds of journalism he is the author of three novels and four collections of stories and is the editor of a miscellany of anthologies.

Handle advice carefully
tips from Alex Hamilton

Handle advice carefully: did you ask for it? Or is it a bombardment? Thus, from me:

When playing roulette, do not poach the favourite number of a gambler on a winning roll.

Kissing is more fun than boxing, but don't claim to be a heavyweight champion.

If you have something to say, it is your duty to say it – once.

The classics are politely waiting for you; don't let them wait too long.

Do not make jokes when going through customs, they don't find them funny.

Alex Hamilton adds: My uncle, a farmer, gave me much pithy advice, such as, "Avoid women who live on salads" and "Learn to thatch, then you can put a roof over your head." My father said, "The City would be a less precarious living than writing novels." A friend on the *Sunday Times* said, "*The Times* is the ideal paper with which to start journalism. You make your mistakes there, and move on." There is something in all of these, but none is an absolute truth.

Julian Litten was born on November 6th 1947. Ecclesiastical historian, writer and broadcaster, he is the founder of the Church Maintenance Trust and the Friends of Kensal Green Cemetery. His book, The English Way of Death: The common funeral since 1450, *is a standard work of reference.*

How everyone can win prizes
a tip from Julian Litten

The most genteel way whereby nobody wins and nobody loses, but all win prizes, is that environment where compromise reigns supreme. Remember that the other person's opinion is just as valid to them as is your own to you, and that the other person's right to an opinion is as strong as is yours. Ultimately, nobody is right and nobody is wrong, for the matter in hand already has its solution, all it is doing is waiting for both sides to realise that and to come up with the same answer.

Julian Litten adds: In 1990 I was asked my opinion on the proposed fate of a rather crude 1920s gothic revival chancel screen in a small village church. The incumbent wanted it removed so that the congregation could see what was going on in the sanctuary; a descendant of the donor wished it to stay *in situ*. Neither would budge, and a consistory court seemed likely. The vicar and the donor's descendant both had a point and, whilst the screen was not the best of its kind, it was, in general, worthy of a better fate than redundancy. I suggested that if the moulding above the central door was removed, and the two panels either side were cut vertically, then it could be hinged and folded back on a Sunday and drawn across during the week. Both sides were in agreement, the consistory court threat was removed and the monies each party had reserved for the court case were redirected towards the structural work on the screen.

November 7

Lucinda Green was born on November 7th 1953. A three-day event rider, she is six times winner of the Badminton Horse Trials, twice European champion and in 1984, a world champion and team silver medallist in Los Angeles. Lucinda now teaches cross-country riding and commentates for the sport of horse trials for the BBC. She also writes articles on racing and eventing for the Daily Telegraph. *She has appeared 22 times on the BBC sports quiz programme,* Question of Sport, *and is the longest serving panellist. She has two children, Freddie and Lissa.*

Don't worry about winning
a tip from Lucinda Green

Don't worry about winning. Worry about doing your best – but don't forget you do it for fun.

My father used to tell me the story of how before the war many flash young men flew light planes and crashed. He – as a flash young man – was determined not to fall into that trap, but to do things properly. That is all he ever asked of me – if you do something, do it properly.

Lucinda Green adds: This advice meant that I could live with situations when they didn't go my way and it meant that when they did go my way, they were doubly gloriously exciting.

Edward Goldsmith was born on November 8th 1928. He is the son of Frank Goldsmith and elder brother of the late Sir James Goldsmith. He is an author, publisher, campaigner and former editor of the Ecologist *(1970–89). He was awarded both the alternative Nobel Prize, the Honorary Right Livelihood Award Stockholm, and the Chevalier de la Légion d'Honneur in 1991. His books, as author or co-author, include:* Can Britain Survive?, The Stable Society *and* The Earth Report.

Question what you are taught
a tip from Edward Goldsmith

My advice to young people is to question what they are taught on all-important issues in their schools and universities.

Edward Goldsmith adds: The knowledge imparted to young people today is above all that which will rationalise and hence legitimise the policies that serve the immediate interests of large corporations and of the politicians who increasingly depend on them. This means that young people must develop the faculty to think things out for themselves.

November 9

Nicolas Freeling was born on March 3rd 1927. He has been writing crime novels since 1960. A European all his life, he is married to a Dutch woman and lives between France and Germany, but remains an obstinate Londoner. His books – which include Love in Amsterdam *(1960) and* One More River *(1997) – have been published, and are read, all over the world. Charles de Gaulle, who is mentioned below, died on November 9th 1970.*

Further up, less crowd
a tip from Nicolas Freeling

This aphorism was General de Gaulle's: "Further up, less crowd." The meaning is that you set your sights high. What you do is not for squalid material gain. If anything was won, it owed nothing to bribe or favour, falsehood or hypocrisy.

Nicolas Freeling adds: I have myself committed every idiocy known, and a great deal that was abject. What is essential – I am quite certain – is that we take responsibility. We are answerable for what we do, and this is what we must not forget, nor evade. 'Freedom' is not the liberty to do as we please and blame everyone else for the consequences. No doubt, you have also got drunk, committed adultery, stolen from the poor: just don't claim that you couldn't help it. If this sounds smug and priggish, very well, accept that too.

Jonathan Edwards, MBE was born in Westminster Hospital on May 10th 1966. He is a full-time athlete and the current holder of the world record for the triple jump. He was BBC Sports Personality of the Year in 1995. He married Alison on November 10th 1990 and they have two boys, Samuel and Nathan.

Think before you speak
a tip from Jonathan Edwards, MBE

"Do you see a man hasty in his words?
There is more hope for a fool than for him."

Proverbs 29:20

Jonathan Edwards adds: This verse from the Bible offers wise advice. I have lost track of the number of times I have opened my mouth and regretted it, and I am sure I am not alone in this. Once the words are out there is no getting them back – it's not like painting a wall one colour, hating it, then repainting it so as nobody will rumble your ghastly taste. The consequence of misplaced and thoughtless remarks endures, to both our own cost and those to whom the words were directed. I am all too quick to offer my opinion, often without listening to the opposing point of view; all too quick to assert my own wisdom over that of others. Socrates said: "He is wise who knows he does not know." Such a mindset is humble, recognising its own limitations and fallibility, and will rarely be hasty in its words.

November 11

Ronald Hayman was born on May 4th 1932. His books include biographies of Jung, Thomas Mann, Proust, Sartre and Kafka. His plays include Playing the Wife. *He broadcasts, appears on television and reviews books. He got married on November 11th 1969.*

Listening to the whisper
a tip from **Ronald Hayman**

Never ignore the small voice that's almost inaudible. It feels as if it's coming from somewhere inside the head, and maybe it comes from the unconscious or semi-conscious or the same twilight area you can explore late at night when you're almost asleep or in the early morning when you're not quite awake.

Ronald Hayman adds: The most serious mistakes I've ever made have resulted from ignoring this advice, though I first gave it to myself – by which I mean the whisper gave it to me – a long time ago. The good thing about mistakes that are serious enough is that not all the consequences are bad.

Philip Pullman was born on October 19th 1946. He says: "I write novels that are read by children and some clever adults. My books include Northern Lights, The Subtle Knife *and* Clockwork. *I live in Oxford with my wife Jude and our two sons, and I take no exercise." Van Gogh, who is mentioned in this tip, painted* Irises *while at the St Rémy lunatic asylum. The painting was sold for £30.2 million on November 12th 1987.*

Don't bother looking for ideas
a tip from Philip Pullman

Don't bother looking for ideas. You can waste more time waiting for inspiration than in any other way. The really important thing to learn is not how to have ideas, but how to do without them: how to write just as well when you're not inspired as when you are. And the only way to do that is to work.

Philip Pullman adds: I apply this tip on the 99 days out of 100 when no inspiration strikes. There exists a mythical condition known as 'writer's block'. It's just an important-sounding name for the fear of the empty page. But every page is empty before you fill it, and if you ever use writer's block as an excuse not to sit down and work, you're doomed. Remember what Vincent Van Gogh said: "It is the empty canvas which is frightened of the real painter, not the painter who is frightened of the canvas." Of course writing is difficult. So is any important work. But *do it*. Put some words down. Start. Any fool can write when they're inspired. You're not a fool, are you?

November 13

Libby Purves was born on February 2nd 1950. She is a journalist and Times *columnist, presenter of* Midweek *on BBC Radio 4, and bestselling author. Her novels include* Casting Off *and* Regatta. *Her non-fiction includes* How Not to be the Perfect Mother *and* Nature's Masterpiece. *She is also president of the Council for National Parks. She is married to Paul and they have two children, Nicholas and Rose. Robert Louis Stevenson, mentioned below, was born on November 13th 1850.*

Carry on the conversation once married
a tip from Libby Purves

The best bit of advice about marriage is: "Don't do it unless you can't bear not to." The best description of marriage is from Robert Louis Stevenson: "Marriage is one long conversation, chequered by disputes. Two persons more and more adapt their notions to suit the other, and in the process of time, without sound of trumpet, they conduct each other into new worlds of thought."

The only real essential is to carry on the conversation that you started.

Libby Purves adds: Sticking my neck out and with fingers crossed about my own life – Paul and I married in 1980 – in the centre of my book, *Nature's Masterpiece*, I risked an essay on the most contentious subject of all: marriage maintenance. The above tip is part of it.

Shân Rees was born on November 14th 1948. She works for the Greater London Forum for the Elderly; an organisation committed to empowering older people. She has been a freelance trainer since the mid-1980s, running courses in stress management and personal development, and is writing a book on women and ageing.

November 14

Be willing to shine
a tip from Shân Rees

Most of the shadows in this life are caused by standing in our own sunshine.

We can choose to emphasise the positive or negative in our lives and in ourselves. Oftentimes, people hide their best selves because they are afraid others will be overwhelmed, jealous, etc. And in some sense they are themselves more comfortable living in a limited way. We stand the best chance of being truly happy and fulfilled if we allow ourselves to shine.

Shân Rees adds: I have found, increasingly, that if I do or say something which is not true to who I really am, I feel out of rhythm and unhappy. When I am simply my best self, and not depending on being accepted, I feel a sense of integrity and inner peace – and shininess. And that has to benefit not only me, but also those with whom I come into contact.

November 15

Dawn Elizabeth Airey was born on November 15th 1960. She was first controller, then director of programme planning at Central Television until 1992. She then went on to be controller of daytime programmes at ITV Network Centre from 1993 to 1994, and between 1994 and 1996 she was controller of arts and entertainment for Channel 4. Dawn has been director of programmes for Channel 5 since 1996.

Self-confidence
a tip from **Dawn Airey**

Work like you don't need the money,
Love like you've never been hurt,
And dance like nobody's watching.

Dawn Airey adds: This piece of advice from my first boss was advocating total self-confidence in the face of adversity. Throughout my career, I have often found myself as the youngest and only female and subject to considerable scepticism and a certain degree of verbal abuse; but confidence in oneself always ensured success.

Marcus Braybrooke was born on November 16th 1938. He is a Church of England vicar who has taken a special interest in working with members of other religions. He is joint president of the World Congress of Faiths. He has written a number of books on Christianity, Judaism and about the co-operation of world religions. Mary, his wife, is a social worker and JP. They have two children and four granddaughters.

God-given time for the too-busy
a tip from the Revd Marcus Braybrooke

Remember God does not make mistakes. God gives you enough time to do what God wants you to do.

Marcus Braybrooke adds: When I am worried that there is too much to do and I won't get everything done in time, I try to remember the above words from a wise old priest. He also said that I should try mentally to make the various tasks queue up or stand in line and then concentrate on each in turn. Worrying about what you are not doing diverts your concentration and slows you up.

November 17

Mike Nicol was born on November 17th 1951. He has worked as a journalist on various South African newspapers and magazines and has contributed to some international publications. He is the author of a number of novels (including This Day and Age, *1992) and works of non-fiction (including his memoir* The Waiting Country, *1995) and two volumes of poetry (including* This Sad Place, *1993).*

The price of idealism
a tip from Mike Nicol

It's the money that counts, not the principle.

Mike Nicol adds: After firmly believing for most of my life that principles were more important than hard cash, a kind financial advisor persuaded me otherwise. It's a useful piece of advice, I'm sure, although it's made me no richer. But I can now accurately determine the market value of principles, for what that's worth.

Derwent May was born on April 29th 1930. He is currently a writer on books, birds and behaviour (human) for The Times. *He has also been the literary editor of the* Listener *and of the* Sunday Telegraph. *He is writing the official history of the* Times Literary Supplement *and is the author of a number of books, including four novels, and* Proust *in the Oxford Past Masters series. Marcel Proust died on November 18th 1922.*

Falling asleep
a tip from Derwent May

If you are finding it difficult to go to sleep, try to visualise a blank television screen, and stare at it with your eyes closed.

Derwent May adds: This is far more effective than counting sheep.

November 19

Robert Giddings was born on June 29th 1935. He is a professor in the School of Media Arts and Communication at Bournemouth University. He has been a college and university teacher since the 1960s, as well as journalist, author, scriptwriter and broadcaster. He contracted polio at 11 and was finally discharged from hospital aged 18. Since then he has been in a wheelchair. Educated at Bristol and Keele Universities, he has published some 20 books, including You Should See Me in Pyjamas *and* From Where I'm Sitting *(both autobiographies),* The War Poets 1914– 1918, The Classic Serial on TV and Radio *and* Imperial Echoes. *He has also contributed to BBC programmes and to periodicals. Edward Thring, mentioned below, was born on November 19th 1821.*

Anybody can learn
a tip from Professor Robert Giddings

"Anybody can learn. It just takes some people longer than others."

This was the dictum of Edward Thring (1821–87), eccentric headmaster of Uppingham, founder of the Headmaster's Conference and the public school mission to the London poor. He was a brilliant classical scholar with a devout belief in the moral purpose of education. Quite by accident I came across Thring and was inspired by his work when doing my professional teacher training. Thring argued against mistaking accumulated knowledge for innate intelligence and believed that given time, guidance and patience even apparently ungifted pupils could achieve high standards.

My own tip is: never give up on yourself or with others. Some people are gifted with an apparent immediacy of learning, others may take time. Give it time. Life is short. Don't shorten it by being impatient.

Robert Giddings adds: Hospitals and institutions prevented my having a secondary education. I was assessed as ineducable by an educational psychologist at a rehabilitation centre at 18. (He went on to become an Oxbridge don, a university vice chancellor and international authority on the rehabilitation of the disabled.) The local vicar encouraged me to go to the technical college in Bristol and do shorthand and typing. Here a wonderful English teacher (Mona Crombie) further encouraged me and eventually got me to university, where I failed my first term examinations. Professor L. C. Knights said it was simply ignorance – I didn't know enough, but that I should keep going. It seemed to do the trick. And I kept on trying to write. As a teacher I've endeavoured to adopt the same principle, and it works.

Lord Archer of Sandwell (Peter Archer) was born on November 20th 1926. He practised as a barrister and a QC. He was a member of Parliament from 1966 to 1992, having served as solicitor general in the Wilson and Callaghan governments and subsequently as a member of the Shadow Cabinet. He is now a life peer. He is the author of a number of books (including Communism and the Law, *1963 and* More Law Reform Now, *co-editor, 1984) and is a Methodist lay preacher.*

A word to the wise: the wisdom of silence
a tip from Lord Archer of Sandwell

Take a tip from nature – your ears are not made to shut; your mouth is.

First, you learn more from listening than from speaking and a good listener is less likely to say the wrong thing. No one ever listens themselves out of a prize.

Secondly, you can win more friends with your ears than with your mouth. The Golden Rule of friendship is to listen to others as you would have them listen to you.

Thirdly, silence is often the most effective answer. Chesterton called it "the unbearable repartee".

Peter Archer adds: For much of my life I have earned a living from giving advice. I found that the best advice depends upon first learning the facts and what the questioner most wants to achieve. I also learned as a politician that if I allow someone to talk long enough, they answer their own question.

November 21

Kate Clanchy was born in Glasgow on June 11th 1965. Her two collections of poetry, Slattern *and* Samarkand, *have won six literary awards. She lives in Oxford with her husband and son. She comments: "On November 21st 1997, in fear and trembling, I resign my teaching post. Years on, I still expect the deputy head to appear at my writing desk and tell me I should be covering 7A."*

Be wary of persuading yourself into a big acquisition
tips from Kate Clanchy

If you find yourself counting the merits of any big acquisition – an expensive shirt, a house, a marriage – and persuading yourself why you should like it, leave it alone.

Your most private and outrageous observation is also often the one most likely to be shared by others.

After the age of thirty, the path of excess gives you a much worse headache.

Kate Clanchy adds: I am rather bossy and like dispensing advice, but these are the only bits I could honestly say were useful.

Tim Beaumont was born on November 22nd 1928 of a long line of (mainly Liberal) MPs. After a delinquent youth, he was ordained into the Church of England, married and had four children. After his father's death, he became involved in publishing and politics. In publishing he provided a forum for the 'sixties ideas' which were slowly to revolutionise the Church of England; in politics he helped the just-surviving Liberal Party (five MPs strong) to survive and grow. As a reward or punishment for this, he was put into the House of Lords, where, he says, he has become steadily Redder and Greener as the years have gone by. He is the author of The End of the Yellowbrick Road (John Carpenter, £10). He is currently the only Green Party spokesman in parliament.

Spending pennies
tips from Lord Beaumont of Whitley

1) Follow the Duke of Wellington's advice and never miss an opportunity to have a piss.

2) Always carry handy coins to give to beggars (of a denomination which you would gratefully receive yourself if you were they).

Tim Beaumont adds: I have thereby preserved myself from embarrassment and returned plenty of nitrogen to the soil; and I have also kept my conscience alive and aware of the intolerable society in which we now live.

November 23

Francis King was born on March 4th 1923. In the course of a literary career that has now extended over more than half a century, he has published 43 books. Having been drama critic of the Sunday Telegraph for many years, he is now a regular novel reviewer for the Spectator. He is a former president of the writers' organisation International PEN and continues as one of its vice-presidents. King's tip is set in Japan. November 23rd is Kinrô Kansha-no-hi, Japanese Labour Thanksgiving Day.

A tip for tipping
from Francis King

In the early 1960s, I found myself escorting
Somerset Maugham around Japan – where I was
then resident. In a Japanese restaurant, he gave a
vast tip to our two charming and attentive
waitresses. Seeing that I was as astonished as they
were, he told me: "Never believe the idiots who
tell you that people despise those who overtip.
That's a fiction put about by the miserly.
On the contrary, people are always delighted if you
give them more than they expect."

Francis King adds: Since then, if I get better than usual service from a waiter or waitress, am specially
pleased by the way in which my hair has been cut, or have a particularly stimulating conversation with
a taxi-driver, I always tip more than 10 per cent or even 15 per cent. That way, I show my gratitude,
and the other party is encouraged to continue to give first-class service.

Elizabeth Filkin was born on November 24th 1940. She is parliamentary commissioner for standards at the House of Commons. She is responsible for: advising Members of Parliament about the code of conduct and rules for Members of Parliament, the public Register of Members' Interests and investigating complaints that MPs have broken the code or rules. She has worked in both the private and public sectors.

Never take a job you can do
a tip from Elizabeth Filkin

Never take a job you can do. Learning new things while trying to do the impossible makes work exciting, prevents boredom and usually encourages creativity.

Elizabeth Filkin adds: I've never had a job I felt I could do when I started it. When you ask lots of questions you can begin to contribute and you will start to understand who 'can do' in an organisation.

November 25

Paul Copley was born on November 25th 1944 in Denby Dale, Yorkshire. He is an actor and writer. He married actress Natasha Pyne in 1972. His theatre work includes: For King and Country, Rita, Sue & Bob Too, Other Worlds, Crossing the Equator, The Mortal Ash, Raping the Gold, Making Noise Quietly, German Skerries, The Servant, When We Are Married *and* Celaine. *Extensive TV work includes:* Days of Hope *(directed by Ken Loach) and, more recently,* This Life, The Lakes, Queer as Folk *and* Silent Witness. *Films include:* A Bridge Too Far, Zulu Dawn, The Remains of the Day. *Writing includes:* Pillion, Viaduct, Tapster *(Bush Theatre),* Calling, On May Day, Tipperary Smith, Words Alive *(BBC Radio).*

There is no indispensable man
a tip from Paul Copley

Some time when you're feeling important
Some time when your ego's in bloom
Some time when you're really convinced that
You're the best-qualified man in the room
Take a bucket and fill it with water
Put your hand in right up to the wrist
Pull it out and the hole that is left there
Is the measure of how much you'll be missed.

You can stir it around all you want to
Disturb it as much as you can
But you'll come to the inevitable conclusion
There is no indispensable man!

Paul Copley adds: This was advice from my beloved uncle, who loyally supported all my schemes and undertakings. With a twinkle, he would quietly start to recite this poem, origin unknown (to me), as I boasted of my prowess on my latest fast motorbike or revealed plans for grandiose adventures. His intention was not to dampen my spirit or sow seeds of defeatism but simply to try, in true Yorkshire fashion, to temper enthusiasm with common sense. He could have said (and probably did) "take nothing for granted" or "nobody has a charmed life" – but I wouldn't have remembered. This way, his advice still spurs me to greater thought and effort as I lurch through life.

Phil Cousineau was born in a US Army hospital in South Carolina on November 26th 1952 and grew up in the midwest hamlet of Wayne, Michigan. He is the author of more than a dozen books, including The Art of Pilgrimage *and* The Hero's Journey *and the screenwriter of more than a dozen documentary films, including* Ecological Design: Inventing the future *and* The Peyote Road.

Move slowly
a tip from Phil Cousineau

"When in doubt, move slowly."

Henry David Thoreau (1817–62)

Take time. Make time. Don't fake time. Don't pretend that you have more or less time than you really do. Slow down with your family and friends. Being present is more important than giving presents unless your present is time itself, for yourself or for your loved ones.

Phil Cousineau adds: As the world inexorably accelerates, Henry David Thoreau's nineteenth-century advice appears to me to be wiser and wiser. All my poor decisions were impulsive; all my best ones were intuitive, deliberate, thought-out. I am convinced that true happiness lies in the way we use our time, the way we honour the present, prepare reasonably for the future, but mostly how we dwell soulfully in the present moment. The best invention is still wisely-used time.

Whenever I think of Thoreau's other adage "As if you could kill Time without injuring Eternity", I want to shout with joy because he seemed to have prophesied our own era. The irony surrounding our obsession with newfangled timesaving gadgets is that we often fill up the saved time with more and more activities, thus unwittingly killing the very time we were trying to save. When that happens we are "injuring Eternity", meaning our very hearts and souls. "When in doubt, move slowly." Don't spend time, savour it.

November 27

Adam Thorpe was born in Paris on December 5th 1956 and brought up in India, Cameroon and England. After stints in theatre and teaching, he became a full-time writer and is the author of three books of poetry, three novels (including the bestselling Ulverton) *as well as plays for stage and radio, and a volume of short stories,* Shifts *(2000). He lives in France with his wife and three children. November 27th is his wedding anniversary.*

Hypnopompic advice
a tip from **Adam Thorpe**

If you're up against a snag in the free-flowing current of your personal life, try using the ancient hypnopompic method to find a way through – *hypnopompic* meaning anything to do with the process of waking up (*hupnos* is the Greek for sleep). Tell yourself, just before falling asleep (the hypna*gogic* state) that an answer to the particular problem will be given to you as you are waking up. Invariably the answer will appear in the form of a vivid dream or an actual phrase ringing in the head. The answer is almost always a lateral one, and way beyond what you might have discovered by more pedestrian methods. Then it's up to you whether you use it.

Adam Thorpe adds: As a writer, I frequently experience such snags in the creative current, particularly in relation to plot or character or sometimes (in a poem) to a particular line. I almost always solve them by the hypnopompic method. The last sentence in the central section of my novel *Pieces of Light* appeared in such a way, and it was used by a reviewer to sum up the novel: "A certain long moment lost in Africa." There is something strange and magical about it and I was very grateful when it sang through my emerging consciousness. The only two poems I have ever written in French appeared intact in the same way – and I didn't even ask for them.

Bob Alexander was born on September 5th 1936. He has been a barrister (QC) and a banker. He is currently president of the Marylebone Cricket Club and chairman of the Royal Shakespeare Company, chancellor of Exeter University and active in the House of Lords. Rudyard Kipling wrote the poem 'If–', mentioned below, for his son, John, on a Winter's day in 1910.

Study as if you will live for ever
a tip from Lord Alexander of Weedon

Live each day as if it's your last, but study as if you will live for ever.

Bob Alexander adds: Every day should be worthwhile and precious, whether at work or leisure. But one of the stepping stones highly relevant in these days of continuous education is the broadening of interests, horizons and knowledge. This advice is rather like Rudyard Kipling's 'If–' – a counsel of perfection. I have never lived up to it. But aspirations are exciting, which is why 'If–' was voted the UK's favourite poem.

November 29

Michael Robson was born on November 29th 1931. Following national service in the Royal Air Force, he read English at St Edmund Hall, Oxford. He is a writer of drama for film, TV, radio and theatre, and a writer and director of documentaries. He has reviewed regularly for the Times Literary Supplement *and* Books & Bookmen. *His screenplays include* The 39 Steps *and* The Water Babies. *His military documentaries include* The Battle of Arnhem. *He is passionate about the preservation of the disciplines of English Language and Literature.*

Never let your intellect slide into neutral
tips from Michael Robson

Never let your intellect slide into neutral.

Never assume that charm alone will win the day.

From adulthood, always recognise that at some time you may become very much a loner in life – and make provision for it.

If someone approaches you and begins: "I don't like to say this, but I feel you ought to know ..." – walk away from that person immediately.

Keep the heart endlessly affectionate. Remember that life is generally better than it is worse.

A fair way towards a sound marriage: stay apart by day and be together by night.

Michael Robson adds: As a writer I've always worked from home, and tend to regard home as my sole domain during working hours. I need the solitude. When my wife returns from her place of work, she's delighted to relax and we can exchange our individual news of the day. So our relationship remains fresh and unstressed.

Ray Lonnen was born on May 18th 1940 in Bournemouth. He became an actor before his 19th birthday and has played numerous roles with numerous theatre companies. He began his TV career in 1965 and has had leading parts in several series, including Z Cars, Honey Lane, The Sandbaggers, The Brief, Yellowthread St., Rich Tea & Sympathy and Harry's Game, for which he was nominated for an award. Ray has also played leads in West End musicals, including Leonard Bernstein's Wonderful Town opposite Maureen Lipman. November 30th is the birthday of Amy, Ray's daughter, who lives in Sydney, Australia.

Try to get things in perspective
a tip from Ray Lonnen

When you're holding your gas bill and you hit the roof, think of the person who'd *love* to be holding a gas bill but can't, because they have no hands. When you complain and say, "Have you seen this phone bill?", think of the person who'd *love* to see a phone bill, but can't because they're blind. When you say, "Ooh I'm starving", spare a thought for those who really *are*.

Ray Lonnen adds: Disabled and deprived people appear so brave and spirited. It always makes me feel humble and ashamed when I'm moaning my head off about something, and along comes a blind man tapping with his stick, or a limbless person cheerfully wheeling herself up the pavement. I know that what I've written above is a hard lesson to learn in life, but I always try to apply it.

December 1

Adrian Padfield was born on February 13th 1937 and studied medicine at St Bartholomew's Hospital. He qualified in 1961 and started to specialise in anaesthesia in 1963. In 1972 he became a consultant to the Sheffield teaching hospitals. He bought a 1927 Alvis sports car in 1961 and still drives it; he started canal cruising in 1962 and with his wife is now slowly traversing the canal system. He collects antique canal prints and maps and intends to catalogue British canal maps. G. H. Hardy, the Cambridge mathematician mentioned in this tip, died on December 1st 1947.

Teaching and learning
tips from Dr Adrian Padfield

Laziness is a symptom not a disease. Laziness is often evidence of a lack of curiosity, enthusiasm, or motivation for a task or subject. It may be the result of a hangover, unhappiness, sleepiness or impatience to get on with something else. A good teacher is capable of inspiring even the laziest of pupils and a good manager must be able to motivate his colleagues.

Experience is as to intensity not as to duration. This mathematical sounding aphorism applies in all forms of human learning. It can be used as an argument against unimaginative training programmes based on time serving rather than content.

Adrian Padfield adds: I coined the first tip when teaching medical students in the 1960s. Over the years it has been reinforced both in teaching and in the increasingly 'managed' National Health Service. It has also made me question the effectiveness of my scholastic education. My prep school was very inspiring, but looking back, my secondary school failed to teach me to learn and didn't stimulate.

I believe G. H. Hardy, one of the famous group of Cambridge mathematicians before the First World War, coined the second tip. Hardy befriended the Indian mathematical genius Ramanujan and also, as a lover of cricket, tried to clarify the mathematics of cricket ball swing. The truth of the tip became apparent to me during postgraduate training. I worked at the Brompton Hospital for a few months and learned more about cardio-thoracic anaesthesia (and surgeons) than I would have done in a year or more at other hospitals.

Janice Galloway was born on December 2nd 1956 in Ayrshire. She is the author of four critically-celebrated works of fiction: The Trick is to Keep Breathing, Blood, Foreign Parts *and* Where You Find It. *She has recently written* Monster, *an opera libretto for Sally Beamish and Scottish Opera. She likes cities and lives in Glasgow.*

It does you less harm to be kind
a tip from Janice Galloway

Don't judge, don't react without thinking, and don't drink yourself into thoughtlessness. Don't deny. Don't abuse power. Wherever possible, strive to be kind. In the end, it does you less harm to be kind.

Janice Galloway adds: This is as close as I can get to a tip that came from a man I met in HMP Dungavel during my time as a writer in four Scottish prisons. Serving a life sentence, he'd had plenty of time to think. He reckoned he'd seen a lot of cruelties, some outside prison and some in, and they invariably led to other cruelties. If he had the time to do again, he said, he'd try to be kind. It was harder than blindly reacting, he said, but more important. During the worst period of awfulness in my own life, this advice was invaluable in helping me keep calm and tick over. It helps you get by.

December 3

Naomi Gryn was born on New Year's Eve 1960. She is a writer and filmmaker, working in radio and television. She edited Chasing Shadows, *her father Hugo Gryn's account of his childhood, which was published posthumously. Rabbi Hugo Gryn,* CBE *was born in sub-Carpathian Ruthenia on June 25th 1930. He was deported to Auschwitz at the age of 13 and then transported to a German slave labour camp, where this story takes place, some weeks later. After the war, he came to Britain with a group of child survivors and then went to America to train as a rabbi. His first pulpit was in Bombay and later he became rabbi at the West London Synagogue, a post he held for 32 years, until his death in 1996. He was well known as a broadcaster, particularly as a regular panel member on BBC Radio 4's* The Moral Maze.

Choose hope
a tip from Hugo Gryn & Naomi Gryn

In 1944, the festival of Chanukah was early – the first week of December. The Jewish prisoners in our barracks – Block 4 – decided that we would celebrate it by lighting a menorah every night. Bits of wood and metal were collected and shaped into lightholders and everyone agreed to save the week's meagre ration of margarine for fuel. It was my job to take apart an abandoned prison cap and fashion wicks from its threads.

Finally, the first night of Chanukah arrived. Two portions of margarine were melted down and, as the youngest person there, I tried to light the wick, but there was only a bit of spluttering and no flame whatsoever. What the 'scientists' in our midst failed to point out was that margarine does not burn! As we dispersed and made our way to our bunk beds I turned not so much to my father, but on him, upset at the fiasco and bemoaning this waste of precious calories. Patiently, he taught me one of the most lasting lessons of my life and I believe that he made my survival possible.

"Don't be so angry," he said to me, "you know that this festival celebrates the victory of the spirit over tyranny and might. You and I have had to go once for over a week without proper food and another time almost three days without water, but you cannot live for three minutes without hope!"

Hugo Gryn, *Chasing Shadows*

Naomi Gryn adds: My father remained an incurable optimist for the rest of his life. He taught me to keep faith in eternity and never give in to despair. When I was badly injured in a car crash some years ago and had to overcome some difficult challenges of my own, I began to appreciate this legacy of indomitability. Since no one can tell what tomorrow will bring, you might as well choose to believe in happy endings.

Joan Brady was born on December 4th 1939. Formerly a dancer with the San Francisco and the New York City ballet, she won the 1993 Whitbread Book of the Year award and France's coveted Prix de Meilleur Livre Etranger for her second novel Theory of War, *an international bestseller translated into nine languages. She is also the author of short stories, newspaper articles, a highly acclaimed autobiography* Prologue, *a crusading novel* Death Comes for Peter Pan *and, most recently,* The Émigré.

Never argue the other's point of view
a tip from Joan Brady

Dr Johnson said somewhere that there is no meaningful discussion unless there is a foundation of agreement.

If such agreement exists, you don't have to argue the other person's point of view because it is basically yours already. But if agreement has to be fought for, never try to figure out *why* your opponent is arguing the way he is; if you do, you end up arguing his side against your own and you are sure to lose.

Joan Brady adds: My husband left me this most powerful legacy to help me deal with the world of business, where I started out as innocent and foolish as anybody could possibly be. Just recently, though, I managed to escape a producer's trap and win a case in a small claims court. I couldn't have done either without this piece of advice. If I learn to apply it fully, maybe one of these days I will even negotiate a decent book contract.

December 5

The Earl of Longford, Francis Aungier Pakenham, was born on December 5th 1905 and educated at Eton and New College, Oxford. In 1931 he married Elizabeth, Countess of Longford, who is the author of a number of biographies and historical books. He was first Lord of the Admiralty in 1951, Lord Privy Seal (1965–66) and Secretary of State for the Colonies (1965–66). He sits as a Labour peer in the Lords.

Use your luck to help others
a tip from **Lord Longford**

If you're lucky, you must reckon you are privileged and you must use your privilege to help other people. If you want to be happy, make use of such opportunities wherever you find yourself.

Lord Longford adds: I've been happily married since 1931 and have eight children, 26 grandchildren and six great-grandchildren. But that's just luck. I can't tell other people how to acquire this. I have been very privileged in a great many ways. I have tried to help other people. Even now in my nineties I visit prisoners at least once a week, but that doesn't mean that I'm better than other people. I've had more opportunities.

Sarah Woodward was born on April 3rd 1963. She is an actress, as are her father, mother and brothers. She trained at RADA, where she won the Bancroft gold medal, and went on to do seasons at the RSC and RNT. She has appeared in many West End plays and won an Olivier award for her performance in Tom & Clem in 1998. Her daughter Milly was born on this day in 1997.

Leg shaving
a tip from Sarah Woodward

Never shave your legs. Once you start you will never stop and it will become a complete bore. Shaving means darker, thicker stubble. Not shaving means lighter, finer, invisible hair.

Sarah Woodward adds: My mother said, "Whatever you do, don't shave your legs." Within 24 hours I did. I've regretted it ever since. I have a daughter now, I wonder if she will listen to me? Ha ha.

December 7

Anne Fine was born on December 7th 1947. She writes novels for both adults and children, including Madame Doubtfire *(1987, filmed 1993) and* Goggle-Eyes *(1989, adapted for the BBC). She has won the* Carnegie Medal *(twice), the* Whitbread Children's Book Award *(twice), the* Guardian Children's Literature Prize *and a* Smarties Medal.

The future will be much the same
a tip from Anne Fine

Remember that if you wouldn't feel like doing it tomorrow, you won't *ever* feel like doing it — however far in the future the invitation might be.

Anne Fine adds: This was a piece of advice given to me by my husband and it changed my life. It's so easy to say yes to things thinking, "Oh, that's miles away." Pretend to yourself that it's tomorrow you're agreeing to give that talk, drive that distance, go to that party, and it's a whole lot easier to have the courage to say no. To a novelist, this is *vital*.

Louis de Bernières was born on December 8th 1954. He had many dead-end jobs – including soldier, private tutor, mechanic and landscape gardener – before writing a novel whilst in plaster with a broken leg. He is now a full time writer, and "occasionally does things on the radio". Captain Corelli's Mandolin, his fourth novel, has sold over three million copies.

Don't let anyone else become your whole world
a tip from **Louis de Bernières**

Don't let anyone else become your whole world.

If you let someone else become your whole world, you will be heartbroken when they leave or when they die. There is no suffering greater than a broken heart, and sometimes the healing of it can take years. It is possible to love wholeheartedly with a sense of letting go, and you should spread your love amongst several people so that no one has to groan beneath the awful weight of it all. This is the kind of love that will bring happiness even after someone has gone. It is also the kind of love that makes it easier for others to love you in return.

Louis de Bernières adds: This is advice that results from the pain that I brought upon myself earlier in life by loving too clumsily and too powerfully. When I was about 32, I decided that I had had enough of being unhappy, and decided to give it up. I had to learn life from scratch – and the above is one of the things I learned.

December 9

William Roache was born the son of a doctor on April 25th 1932. He is an ex-army officer turned actor. Since 1960 he has been playing the role of Ken Barlow in the TV series Coronation Street. *The first* Coronation Street *episode aired on this day, December 9th, in 1960.*

You get back what you give out
a tip from William Roache

The human being is a complex, sensitive, electromagnetic organism which transmits and receives. If you give something out, a channel is opened which will also receive. You get back what you give out.

By being kinder to yourself, to others, to animals and to the Earth, not only will your surroundings be happier, but so will you.

William Roache adds: I used to blame others, the government, circumstances, but never myself for any misfortune. Then I realised that the only thing we can really change is our own attitude, and that we are responsible for how we think, act and feel. By being kinder, recognising kindness and understanding that kindness is love in action, my life changed.

Michael Irwin was born on June 5th 1931. Trained as a physician at St Bartholomew's Hospital in London, his career was mainly with the United Nations (in New York, Karachi, Dhaka and Washington). Since retirement to Sussex, he has been chairman of the United Nations Association (1996–98) and chairman of the Voluntary Euthanasia Society. December 10th 1948 is the day the Universal Declaration of Human Rights was adopted and proclaimed by the general assembly of the UN.

Wear out, don't rust away
a tip from Michael Irwin

Remember that, in the world's history, our individual lives are really only brief moments of activity between two periods of darkness – most of us are uncertain of any existence before birth and after death.

Throughout life we must ensure we act productively, campaigning for good causes, supporting families and developing communities, and not being distracted by acquiring too much material wealth or simply relaxing excessively.

Michael Irwin adds: The United Nations organisation may be far from perfect but it is the most effective instrument we have at present for international co-operation. I worked hard in the UN and ended my career there as its medical director. In retirement, I believe one should still work hard to improve our earthly existence. I believe passionately in human rights – the ultimate one being personal control of one's life and death when one's terminal illness becomes apparent. Thus I campaign vigorously for legalised voluntary euthanasia. In 1998 I founded Doctors for Assisted Dying, a group of physicians supporting a change in the present law, and willing to help each other now if the need should arise. Wearing out, rather than rusting away, may actually prolong one's life. If you do not use it, you lose it!

December 11

Jim Haynes was born in Haynesville, Louisiana on November 10th 1933, left five weeks later (in his mother's arms) and has been travelling ever since. He established the first paperback bookshop in Britain in 1959 and launched the Traverse Theatre Club (both in Edinburgh) in 1962. Later he co-founded the underground newspaper IT and the Arts Laboratory (both in London) in the mid-1960s. He co-launched the sexual freedom newspaper SUCK (1969) and the Wet Dream Film Festival (1970) in Amsterdam. Since 1975 he has been the host to a salon in Paris and in 2001 he helped launch the Paris Arts Club. December 11th was his father's birthday.

If you do someone a favour, forget it immediately
a tip from **Jim Haynes**

My father once said to me: "If you do someone a favour, forget it immediately. But if someone does something nice for you, never forget it."

Jim Haynes adds: I have attempted to do this all my life and have always appreciated this advice.

I might add that I have been happy all my life. I have realised that we must live every minute, enjoy every day, that this is IT. I refuse to be sad, to be upset by pain and injustice. One does all one can to make life better for others and for oneself. But one cannot solve every problem, right every wrong. When one realises this, it is not necessary to grieve. One does what one must do and that is that.

I have always believed that anything is possible. I purchased the property for my bookshop, The Paperback, simply by asking the proprietor if she would sell it and we agreed on the spot for the price. I rented the space for the Traverse Theatre Club by telling the owner that I could only pay him one shilling a year. And he accepted.

John Papworth was born on December 12th 1921. He was reared in an orphanage and at 15 was sent to work as a kitchen boy at Wentworth Golf Club. He served as a cook in the RAF, earning his matriculation through postal courses and gaining a degree in economic history at the University of London. In 1956 he founded the journal Resurgence *as a platform for the human scale concepts of Leopold Kohr, E. F. Schumacher and others. In the 1970s, he served as personal assistant to Dr Kenneth Kaunda, the President of Zambia, and was ordained as an Anglican priest. In 1981, he founded another journal,* Fourth World Review.

Self-governing neighbourhoods
a tip from John Papworth

I used to be bewildered by the validity or otherwise of arguments about politics or economics. It seemed to me that any proposition could be proved, even if it contradicted another equally proven.

I found a way out of this maze by always applying a proposition to the workings of my local neighbourhood on the assumption that it had the power to be self-governing.

For example, if somebody advanced all the arguments to prove motorways were necessary, efficient, economic and so on, I would ask myself whether my neighbours would spend our local currency on one – ditto with nuclear power stations, newspapers full of consumerist propaganda and TV full of moronism.

Abstract arguments about economic matters suddenly became translucent. Would we vote to do away with our local shops and shopkeepers in favour of a giant multinational supermarket in the next neighbourhood but seven? Would we watch our neighbours lead bleak lives because they were 'unemployed', when all we had to do was to print a little more of our money to set them to work on schemes which would improve neighbourhood facilities? If this caused modest neighbourhood inflation, would we not tax our better-off neighbours a bit more and make other minor adjustments? A lot of little inflationary ripples are easily managed, whereas giant national tidal waves of inflation cause untold havoc.

Medieval city states did just this and as a result they are still among the most beautiful urban centres on earth.

John Papworth adds: This concept stays in my head every time I read my morning newspaper.

December 13

Benedict Allen, born on March 1st 1960, is an author and modern-day explorer. He has written eight books about his expeditions through such varied places as the Amazon, New Guinea and the Gobi Desert, and he has filmed several of his lone journeys for the BBC. His most recent series, Last of the Medicine Men, *is an investigation into shamans, witchdoctors and medicine men worldwide. Laurens van der Post, who gave Allen his tip, was born on December 13th 1906.*

Make haste slowly
a tip from Benedict Allen

Make haste slowly. We all have struggles, we all have frustrations. But remind yourself of where you are intending to go, and slowly, steadily, keep striding onward. Don't allow others to distract you with their own ambitions for you, and one day you'll wake up to find that you are there.

Benedict Allen adds: The South African author Laurens van der Post once gave me this advice when I was faltering in my determination to pursue my own style of exploration. He scribbled it in a book he signed for me – this, a Zulu saying of some sort – and died before I had a chance to understand it fully. To me, making haste slowly is all about not being caught up in the hectic swirl of life, but steadily making your own path. It's not so easy to put it into action, but I've always, always found it a comfort to think of a young Zulu out there, striding across the *veld*, also mouthing such words.

Milena Petrova was born in Bulgaria on July 10th 1968 "during the dark ages of communism". She moved away from her parents at the age of 14 to study at an English language school in Plovdiv. The fall of the Berlin wall and the Bulgarian communist regime inspired her participation in various demonstrations and strikes. By chance, she got a visa to England and left with her boyfriend, with just enough money to cover two weeks' rent. Now at the linguistics department at the University of Southern California, she is in touch with a local 'tribe' of people that call themselves Gigsville, a community that inspires her with their creativity and support. Lester Bangs, mentioned below, was born on December 14th 1948.

Take liberties
a tip from **Milena Petrova**

My tip comes from Lester Bangs, the rock critic who died in 1982: "You may say that I take liberties, and you are right, but I will have done my good deed for the day if I can make you see that the whole point is *you should be taking liberties too*. Nothing is inscribed so deep in the earth a little eyewash won't uproot it, that's the whole point of the so-called 'new wave' — *to re-invent yourself and everything around you constantly*, especially since all of it is already the other thing anyway."

Milena Petrova describes one of her experiences of taking liberties — the Burning Man festival in Nevada: Came back this morning, after nine days in the desert. I had a great time, a healing experience and initiation into more of life's magic ... The first three days we were entertained by the weather jackassery: tents and shade structures were collapsing in the 100mph winds, people ran across the playa chasing trash, dust penetrated every fibre of my body, it was cold. My ticket said that I voluntarily assumed the risk of serious injury or death by attending. This was not the fun I was prepared for, but fun anyway, it made me feel strong and confident. I had arrived in Black Rock City, my home.

My most beautiful evening started with a 4pm communion in the church of Holy Fuckin' Shit and as dusk fell, we wandered around, admiring the culture that had emerged out of nothing. Illuminated towers, domes, art, fires, dust storm, there was so much mystique and magic in the air, Black Rock City was amazing. I was wearing my Desert Queen costume and hiding under the veil, feeling small amidst all that beauty, realising how quickly it becomes obvious in the desert what is good and what is bad, how used I had been to buying stuff and how much I really wanted to make art now, how much creation matters for our civilisation. Yes, out in the desert, away from all the cushions that the city life and the mass market had provided for me, there was nothing to take for granted, no existing culture except the one we had brought with us and were prepared to work on during the next seven days.

Pursuing intellectual goals and living inside my head for most of my life, I didn't have much time, or let's say confidence, for artistic creation. In the environment of Burning Man however, where there are no definitions, no boundaries and no judgement, I felt a strong urge to create something tangible, something which does not have to be processed in the context of history or intellectual theorising.

That's what the art of Burning Man is: direct and immediate. That night I also seduced a young guy :) Yield to change, yield to temptation, that's what the entrance signs said and I certainly followed. I also became more aware and involved in the creation of the community. With Gigsville, everyone had a number of unique, handmade costumes, art installations and events. I loved the organic entertainment, fire, fireworks, drumming, making stuff, acting, going away into the open and shouting and screaming, communing with the desert. Time for decompression ...

December 15

Diana Schumacher was born in Burma of English parents, lived her early life in India and read history at Oxford University. She is an author and passionately believes in making connections between the 4 Es – Energy Use, Environment, Economics and Education. She is a founder member of the New Economics Foundation, the Environmental Law Foundation, the UK Gandhi Foundation and the Schumacher Society. She lives in Surrey with her husband and has two married daughters. December 15th marks the birth of Diana's first child in 1967 – "at the moment one becomes a parent one becomes the bridge between the generations and hence one is responsible for passing on family knowledge and wisdom."

From generation to generation
a tip from Diana Schumacher

Ask questions and take note of the stories and remembrances of your family and loved ones *now* while they are still around. Don't wait for a more appropriate time or future occasion to give them your full attention. You may find that you never again have the opportunity. Our physical likenesses and family traits are passed down from generation to generation through our genes, but not the descriptions, memories, knowledge and experiences which make up the wisdom of a person's life. Ask now, listen carefully and maybe write something down for the next generation to experience and treasure. Keep a journal of your own life's journey with its highlights, learning points, insights and impressions – with your family's posterity in mind.

Diana Schumacher adds: As one whose own parents and grandparents are dead, I know too well the importance of asking all those often inconsequential questions while there is still time for them to be answered. My parents were pioneers who travelled extensively both independently and together. Each of their lives was a fund of experiences, adventures and meetings with remarkable people which, as a child, I took very much for granted. It was only after both parents had moved on that I came across a fascinating handwritten diary from my father's jungle trek from Burma to India fleeing the Japanese. There were many references to places and people which had been abbreviated and I realised there was nobody left to answer the questions. Who were the other 40 men, women and children led out from Rangoon? What became of the only man who reached Calcutta alive with my father? I had been told as a child that for nearly a year my mother had thought she was a widow, but the fact that both parents had survived their respective ordeals completely satisfied my childhood imagination, without need of further embellishment. Like most offspring, I was too occupied with my own youthful discoveries and living in my own present moment to pay much attention to their stories and reminiscences.

Sir Arthur C. Clarke, CBE, the science fiction writer, was born in Minehead, UK, on December 16th 1917 and now lives in Sri Lanka. While serving as an RAF radar officer in 1945, he published the theory of communications satellites, most of which operate in what is now called the Clarke Orbit. He has won three Hugo and three Nebula awards for his science fiction, and shared an Oscar nomination for the movie based on his novel 2001: A Space Odyssey. Aged 81, he wrote: "I have been affected by Post-Polio Syndrome since 1984 and can only manage a ten-hour working day," assisted by "nine secretaries in three continents".

Exploit the inevitable
a tip from Sir Arthur C. Clarke, CBE

A pragmatic piece of advice: exploit the inevitable.

Sir Arthur C. Clarke adds: This advice may explain the usually optimistic and upbeat outlook I have towards not only the present, but also the future – a subject about which I have written occasionally. I've applied the advice in all sorts of situations over the decades. For instance, owing to a missed connection, I was once stranded at a remote Indian airport for a couple of days. So I used the opportunity to write a synopsis, which turned into one of my most successful books.

December 17

David Kherdian was born on December 17th 1931. Although best known as a poet, he is the author of over 50 books that include poetry, novels, memoirs, children's books, as well as critical studies, translations and re-tellings. The Road From Home, the biography of his mother – a survivor of the Turkish genocide of the Armenians – has been published in Asia and England, as well as most European countries, and has never gone out of print. He has been nominated for the National Book Award, and his many honours include the Jane Addams Peace Award and the Friends of American Writers Award.

Set the right precedents for yourself
a tip from **David Kherdian**

Be careful not to set a wrong precedent for yourself; finish whatever you start that is finishable, or worth finishing (almost everything is); never let yourself off for any other reason, eg it's too hard, no one cares, what difference will it make. Work to awaken your conscience, in this and other ways, and you will never be in need of an outside agency to guide you in your life.

David Kherdian adds: Jake LaMotta, the boxer, was taking a pounding in the ring at the end of his career. He was knocked down repeatedly but kept getting up, with the fight going the entire 15 rounds. He lost, but not by a knock-out. Afterwards he was asked why he didn't stay down till the count of nine, after being knocked to the canvas, so he could rest. He replied, "I didn't want to start any bad habits." This from a fighter who probably never fought again. At the time (I was a teenager) all I knew was that I wanted to be a writer, but with no idea how to begin. Now I knew: Don't start any bad habits, i.e. don't set a precedent for failure because if you do, each time you fail it will make it that much easier to fail again – and again.

Sheila Thompson was born on June 18th 1927 in Dundee. When not working as a group psychotherapist and psychiatric social worker, and writing a number of books, she travelled the world with her husband and brought up her children in Kenya and then in New York. She now lives in Islington. Sam Wanamaker, US actor, director, producer, had a dream to rebuild Shakespeare's Globe (mentioned below) at the site of the original theatre and eventually raised the money to make it possible. He died on December 18th 1994. The new Globe Theatre officially opened in 1997.

December 18

There is no such thing as bad weather, only the wrong clothes
tips from Sheila Thompson

Remember that there is not such a thing as bad weather, only the wrong clothes. I only wish I had absorbed this pearl of wisdom when I was younger. It would have kept me from a number of sartorial disasters not to mention nasty colds. Like many tips, it is essentially a reframing exercise, reallocating responsibility and putting oneself back in control.

Take short views of human life – never further than dinner or tea. This is one of the nine bits of advice that Sydney Smith, 18th-century clergyman and wit, gave to a sad young lady. Though maybe not of universal application, it can help in times of difficulty by focusing the mind on the immediate and the possible. I find that the older I get, the more valuable this tip becomes.

When faced with a big cock-up, stop and think how you can turn the situation to your advantage. Advice given to me by a friend in UN peacekeeping, who claimed that this always works (and who must have often been in a position to test it out).

Sheila Thompson adds: Tip 1) I was reminded of this when at Shakespeare's Globe recently, in an evening of continuous downpour (for which, as it happens, I had come well provided), the groundlings in plastic capes with hoods were also thoroughly enjoying the play. But the ill-equipped were having a miserable time and expending a lot of negative energy in looking balefully and accusingly at the skies. Many of them left at the interval.

Tip 2) This advice recalls another quotation, source lost, "I have had many troubles in my life and most of them have never happened."

Tip 3) I recall a formal 'duty' dinner party where there was a power cut just as the food was being put in the oven. When the hostess had dried her tears and reassessed the possibilities, an array of candles was quickly assembled, pizzas were sent for and some hoarded champagne brought out. That party is still remembered with great pleasure.

December 19

Pat Hartridge was born on October 13th 1934. In Oxford she spent a year as PA to Robert Maxwell before starting a family. She ran the Sunday Times Bestsellers List from its inception in 1974 until her resignation when Rupert Murdoch took over the newspaper. On this date, December 19th, in 1984 she was told that she had contracted Legionnaires' Disease and that she was lucky to be alive. The disease took ten years to recover from. Her experience of an isolation ward convinced her that the introduction of wildlife (butterflies, birds, etc.) close to wards would be beneficial. The idea became a national project, Hospital Wildlife Gardens, in 1988. She now maintains (physically and financially) such a wildlife garden at the Churchill Hospital in Oxford.

Believe in yourself
a tip from Pat Hartridge

Have absolute faith in yourself and only discuss your idea or dream with people who also have faith in you and with the sort of people the Americans call 'can do' people.

Take advice, but match it to your gut instincts. See criticism as a useful tool and use it positively to improve your idea. If you meet rejection from one quarter, approach the project from a different angle – if you feel the objection is valid.

Pat Hartridge adds: I have been lucky. I had a father who believed I could do anything, a history teacher who had confidence in me, and at 17, straight from school, I was thrown all sorts of work by a boss who assumed I would be able to do it – so I did. From the moment when I was told that blood tests showed the mysterious illness I had was Legionnaires' Disease, I really tried to seize the day. The diagnosis gave me permission to convalesce – and that long convalescence gave me time to develop my latent interest in wildlife – albeit from a bedroom window. The hospital garden scheme seemed impossible to launch as I was so tired, but I won the Ecology prize from the Institute for Social Inventions in 1986 which gave public validity to the idea. With the prize came practical advice and publicity which I then used to push the idea as a national project. But even without the prize, I would have still believed in the idea. I'm just stubborn I suppose.

Uri Geller was born in Israel on December 20th 1946 and was wounded as a paratrooper in the Six-Day War in Israel in 1967. He first became aware of his psychokinetic powers at the age of five, "when a spoon curled up in my hand and broke". As an adult "he could stop a cable-car in mid-air or an escalator in a department store" using only the power of his mind – and he claims to have stopped the Big Ben clock of London's Houses of Parliament on three occasions. Controlled experiments in which, for instance, he guessed eight out of ten die-throws, were described in a paper in the journal Nature. He says he can detect oil and precious metals. He is a 'mind power' coach in sports and business. He lives in Berkshire, is the father of two teenagers and the author of 14 books, including the novels Ella and Dead Cold. His website is: www.urigeller.com

My top ten steps to success
tips from Uri Geller

1. Wake up your willpower by writing down exactly what you want to achieve. Word it clearly. This is the target.

2. Repeat the target over and over. Believe in it.

3. Forbid all other ideas to distract you from the target.

4. Imagine how life will be when you achieve the target. Picture and visualise the details vividly, with tastes, sensations and sounds.

5. Create a movie in your head and watch yourself achieving your own aim and hitting the target.

6. Visualise how others will react to you when you have achieved your target.

7. Speak out clearly. Never mumble. How else can the world hear you?

8. Before you sleep, run the target words three times through your mind like a hypnotist.

9. Always believe in yourself. You have the mind power.

10. Only you can achieve your target. No one else can do it for you. Seize the responsibility. Go for it. Be positive and always optimistic. Believe in yourself.

Uri Geller adds: One occasion for me of awakening my willpower was in the mid-1970s. I was on a massive ego-trip, being mainly focused on fame and fortune, and I became bulimic. I was killing myself slowly but surely, simply because I could not handle my success. One day I could not get out of my car I was so weak. I knew that I had to awaken my willpower to change and I did so in the middle of the street in Manhattan. Summoning up all my strength I shouted out "I must stop this". And stop it I did. The mind is so powerful it can order the body to do certain things in order to change your life for the better. People generally do not use their mind power.

December 21

Anthony Howard was born the son of a farmer on December 31st 1937 and lives on a smallholding in the New Forest with his wife, Elisabeth. He has written ten books about the English countryside and is the chief executive of Countrywide Films Ltd. He writes, produces and directs films and programmes for British television. Since 1983, the Country Ways *series has made over 200 films and is probably the longest-running regional documentary series in the country. Howard says, "December 21st was Tommy Beeton's birthday and, incidentally, 'doubting' Thomas' saint's day. A well-remembered date because it was the day after my dear old Dad's birthday, December 20th, and, during the war years, we had a double celebration full of games, fun and innocent pleasures."*

Beware compulsive liars
tips from **Anthony Howard**

Slow and steady wins the race. Remember that the best work is almost always done steadily and methodically. Rushing at things or even working too fast can be a kind of laziness and is usually counter-productive.

Beware compulsive liars. Seldom if ever believe anything that anyone in authority says to you. They are almost always compulsive liars and usually have a hidden agenda.

Anthony Howard adds: I learned the first tip from Tommy Beeton, a Suffolk tractor driver, who could neither read nor write. He was my best friend when I was young and I called my dear son, Tom, after him. Tommy was a perfectionist and achieved his wonderful results by going calmly and gently at everything he did. He ploughed the straightest furrows I have ever seen.

To the second tip I would add that throughout my life I have found again and again that grandees and members of the ruling classes, who speak to you with born-to-rule voices and effortless superiority, are not to be trusted. If a gentleman's word is his bond, these characters are certainly no gentlemen – or ladies come to that.

Paul Henry was born in Aberystwyth on December 22nd 1959. Originally a singer-songwriter, he is one of Wales' leading Anglo-Welsh poets, combining freelance writing with part-time work as a careers advisor. Now living in Newport with his wife and three sons, his most recent collection is The Milk Thief *(Seren).*

December 22

Know your lover's past
a tip from **Paul Henry**

Know your lover's past. Unromantic and seemingly unreasonable this, but establishing a few basic facts, early on in a relationship, apropos old flames – their temperaments, beliefs and whereabouts – could prove a lifesaver.

Paul Henry adds: As a student, I had a brief affair with an Italian dancer. All very innocent really, the stuff of crass poems and incense. She was much older than me and perhaps because of this and also the language barrier, I failed to follow the above advice. Anyway, one candlelit night in her flat, I had just finished singing her a terrible song called 'Brittle Love' when a rockery stone smashed through the window behind me, courtesy of her Sicilian ex, who then proceeded to take an axe to the front door. I remember her bundling me out of a back window, miming that everything would be fine but that it might be better if I got out of town, and her life, on the next train.

December 23

Colin Luke was born on January 24th 1946. He is a documentary director who runs the TV production company Mosaic Pictures. He used to travel widely around the world making documentaries. Now he is more likely to send others to do them. December 23rd is his wedding anniversary.

Never travel without a book
a tip from Colin Luke

Never travel without a book, something warm to wear and enough money to get home. Keep a packing list with every possible item you are likely to need on it. It means you can pack on autopilot.

Colin Luke adds: Travelling with a book was my mother-in-law's advice and it has often come in handy, especially when planes are delayed. A good novel can help you switch off from the problems of the day and transport you back home very fast. When working in third world countries I recommend the novels of Anthony Trollope. It puts other things in perspective when you can lose yourself worrying whether the parson's daughter will marry happily.

John Bowker was born on July 30th 1935. He was Professor of Religious Studies at Lancaster University before returning to Cambridge to become dean and fellow of Trinity College. He is at present a fellow of Gresham College in London, and adjunct professor at North Carolina State University. He is the author of many books, including Problems of Suffering in Religions of the World, Is God a Virus? Genes, culture and religion, Voices of Islam, *and* The Meanings of Death, *which was awarded the biennial HarperCollins Prize in 1993 for the best academic book. His most recent books are* The Oxford Dictionary of World Religions, World Religions *and* The Complete Bible Handbook *(the last two by Dorling Kindersley).*

Feed the hungry
tips from **John Bowker**

Feed the hungry and give to the thirsty something to drink. Welcome the stranger. Clothe the naked. Care for the sick. Visit those in prison.

John Bowker adds: These tips, from Jesus in Matthew 25, change the way we live – if we live them. They are extremely simple and at the same time extremely difficult, but without them we would not know what it means to love God and to love our neighbour.

December 25

Professor Christopher Frayling was born on December 25th 1946. He is an historian, author of 12 books, an award-winning broadcaster on TV and radio, and since 1996 has been rector of the Royal College of Art – "the only wholly postgraduate university of art and design in the world".

Keep your exit clear
a tip from Professor Christopher Frayling

There is a road sign which reads *do not enter yellow box unless your exit is clear*. It is a useful sign for life as well. The exit need not be obvious, but it should always be there. Otherwise you might find yourself trapped in the yellow box. This thought protects one from dogma and enables one to think about both strategy and tactics.

Christopher Frayling adds: I first saw this road sign in the early 1970s and it struck a chord. It has since helped me out of several tricky situations. It has also encouraged me always to have an 'A' movie and a 'B' movie running simultaneously in my career: at present, rector of the RCA and broadcasting. I don't like being boxed in.

A. D. P. (Tony) Briggs was born on March 4th 1938 in Sheffield. After studying at Trinity Hall, Cambridge and the School of Slavonic Studies in London University, he taught for 20 years at Bristol and then became Professor of Russian Language and Literature at Birmingham. His special field is Russia's best-loved writer, Alexander Pushkin, about whom he has written and edited several books. He likes radio, and has done over 100 broadcasts for the BBC. A great poetry lover, he has also edited five volumes of poetry for Everyman.

December 26

The Magic Holiday Box
a tip from **Professor A. D. P. Briggs**

The perfect way to stop children getting restless on a long car journey, especially when going on holiday: prepare in advance a *Magic Holiday Box*. It's slightly expensive, but worth it.

Buy six or seven small presents for each person, beginning with little things like a comb or a Mars bar and culminating in, say, a paperback book or something else worth about a fiver. Wrap, label and number ('James 2', 'Mum 5', etc.). Put them all in a gaily-wrapped box two days before departure; note the admiration and curiosity. Stow in car with kids and dog. Open presents with great fuss and fun every half hour or so during the journey.

Tony Briggs adds: We adapted this idea from something heard years ago on *Woman's Hour*. There's a huge disparity between the smallness of the gifts and the degree of excitement. Rummaging and opening are as important as receiving. As an experiment we started a Boxing Day *Magic Holiday Box* – the same game played all day – and now we can't stop. The game was used on many family holidays. It is remembered with affection, and will go on down the dynasty (our grandchildren are now getting old enough to appreciate it). It is almost too popular. Will it never end?

December 27

Tim Hunkin, engineer and cartoonist, was born on December 27th 1950. After a scholarship reading engineering at Cambridge, he became a cartoonist for the Observer, writing and drawing a strip called 'The Rudiments of Wisdom' for 14 years. He then made three TV series for Channel Four called The Secret Life of Machines. He currently designs and curates exhibitions for museums.

Choose minor B projects
a tip from Tim Hunkin

For creative freedom and an easy life, when working with large companies or institutions, choose minor B projects that don't seem important or interesting to the people in charge. They will be much less closely scrutinised.

For prestigious A projects, try to get involved at the last minute. Everyone will then be in a panic to complete everything on time and happy to accept anything.

If all else fails, aim to be 'second quote' – it's often much more fun dreaming up daft ideas than actually having to build them.

Tim Hunkin adds: This tip applies to most of the projects I've ever been involved with. Failures include various high profile TV series and large millennium projects. I became involved at an early stage, but the projects were often frustrating and none got anywhere. Successes include my TV series – started in an early evening education slot, but moved to peak time – and my gallery in the Science Museum, 'The Secret Life of the Home', which started as low-cost refurbishment to avoid embarrassment to a major rebuilding project alongside, but is now one of the most popular galleries.

Flora Maxwell Stuart was married to Peter Maxwell Stuart, the twentieth Laird of Traquair – Scotland's oldest inhabited house. They opened it to the public and worked there together for 35 years. She is a practising Roman Catholic. She writes: "December 28th is the date of my second marriage. To my surprise at the age of 64 – after being widowed for ten years – I fell in love again and was married to Robin Crichton. In the same year my widowed daughter also remarried."

"Be still and know that I am God"
from Flora Maxwell Stuart

"Be still and know that I am God."

Psalm 46:10

Flora Maxwell Stuart adds: It took me many years to know the true meaning of this phrase. I had always been inclined to think that I was responsible for many things and worried about them, not realising that they were mostly beyond my control. When my first husband died of cancer I even felt that in some way his death was my fault. After my newly-married son-in-law died at the age of 42, leaving a three-month-old baby, and my younger brother who was very close to me was killed in a car crash, I began to realise that life was not under my control. It made me stop worrying so much and I let go with a great sense of relief.

December 29

Sir Samuel Brittan was born on December 29th 1933. He writes:
"I am a columnist on the Financial Times *and have written several*
books – which ought to be better known than they are! – including
Capitalism with a Human Face *(1995). I received a knighthood*
for being wrong about the pound sterling and became a Chevalier
de la Légion d'Honneur for being wrong about the French franc. I
still prefer to receive correspondence by old-fashioned post."

Perils of prophecy
a tip from **Sir Samuel Brittan**

Never trust an economist – or any other kind of
prophet.

Explanation: It is hopeless to expect people to realise
that economics, and social science in general, have
nothing to do with historical prophecy. But anyone
who happens to be interested should read Popper's
Poverty of Historicism.

Sir Samuel Brittan adds: This tip came in good stead just after the 1973 oil crisis. A New York pundit was
embarrassing a group of British 'Great and the Good' by asking what plans they had to cope with the
oil price of $100 per barrel. I said I just didn't believe it would happen. Collapse of pundit.

As I have said elsewhere, "the key to understanding many economic pronouncements is that they belong
at least as much to the entertainment as the information industry" (*The Economic Consequences of Democracy*,
1977).

Morton N. Cohen was born on February 27th 1921. He is professor emeritus at the City University of New York. He writes fiction, children's books and travel pieces. He has also written books and articles on H. Rider Haggard, R. L. Stevenson, Lewis Carroll and Rudyard Kipling. Kipling was born on December 30th 1865.

December 30

Don't let it get to you
a tip from Professor Morton N. Cohen

When your motor car breaks down on the M25, when you find that the venison stew that you planned to serve to your special date burns, when you get home from the supermarket and find that you have been overcharged on three items, when the public phone box swallows your coins and doesn't connect you – *don't let it get to you.* Just step back and say, "It isn't worth getting depressed or having a heart attack. It's the price I pay for my style of life." Just push ahead, onward and upward.

Morton N. Cohen adds: In this mad, mad world of ours, I find people's fuses to be very short. Everyone is ready to fly off the handle. So I've resolved that I'll try not to do the same. Instead, I talk to myself. "Don't let it get to you" is a wonderful cliché, but it works for me. Look, I'm still here.

December 31

Trevor Phillips was born on December 31st 1953. He is managing director of Pepper Productions. He is also an award winning TV producer and journalist, best known for Windrush, Britain's Slave Trade *and* The London Programme. *He is chair of the London Arts Board and is a board member of several arts and charitable bodies. He was Frank Dobson's running mate in the year 2000 London mayoral elections and he is now the Labour chairman of the Greater London Assembly.*

Greet defeat with a smile
tips from Trevor Phillips

Try not to persuade yourself that the world will stop without you or your opinions.

Be ready to take risks; if you fail, you can try again.

If you bear grudges, do so in private, or better still, get over it.

Greet defeat with a smile.

Treat your enemies with grace – you will one day have the opportunity to dispose of them quietly!

Allow your parents and your children to tell you your faults – they will speak the truth out of love.

Trevor Phillips adds: This is the accumulated wisdom of a lifetime of competing against other people's presumptions and prejudices. If you allow anger to rule your life, it will consume you. Excessive worry about other people's opinions of you can leave you paralysed.

Acknowledgements

The editors are grateful to Anita Roddick for her foreword; to Brian Eno for his introduction; to Mary McHugh for her work on contacting possible contributors; to all the team at the Institute – Nick Temple and Retta Bowen (who both helped with proofreading), Neel Mukherjee, Francis Bickmore and Poppy Aza-Selinger; to Richard Dykes for the loan of his copy of Debrett's *People of Today* (which seems to have turned into a gift); and to all those who kindly contributed tips, whether or not their tip made it through to the final edit.

The Institute is especially grateful for advice and contacts received from: Liz Attenborough, Dame Beulah Bewley, Peter Boizot, Dr Branko Bokun, Geoffrey Burgon, Frances Burton, Lord Butler of Brockwell, Dr John Campbell, Andrew Castle, Samuel Cavnar, Chris Charlesworth, Helen Cresswell, Gillian Cross, Mark Curry, Sarah Curtis, Timothy Easton, James Galway, Stephen Garrett, Dina Glouberman, David Hamilton, Jeremy Hardy, Gerald Harper, Sandra Harris, Tony Hawks, Anne Hooper, Joyce Hopkirk, Sir Michael Jenkins, Sarah Lee-Barber, Maureen Lehane, Frank McLynn, Somerset Moore, Dr Margit Nofer, Karen Pickering, Duncan Poore, Baroness Prashar, Edith Ryan, Alan Sillitoe, Colin Smythe, Arlen Dean Snyder, Nathaniel Tarn, Alan Titchmarsh and Heather Waddell.

The Institute gratefully acknowledges permission to use material from *The Road Ahead* by Bill Gates, Copyright © 1995 by William H. Gates III (used by permission of Viking Penguin, a division of Penguin Putnam Inc.); from *Letters of Rainer Maria Rilke*, Jane Bannard Greene & M. D. Herter Norton (trans.) (W. W. Norton & Co., New York, 1972) from *Chasing Shadows*, Hugo Gryn with Naomi Gryn (Penguin Books Ltd., 2001); and from *I Know Why the Caged Bird Sings*, Maya Angelou (Random House, Inc., New York, 1970).

Index

The Institute for Social Inventions

The Institute for Social Inventions, a charitable project based in London, receives all the royalties from *Seize the Day*. The Institute's aim is to encourage innovative solutions to social problems.

Whereas technological inventions tend to be new patentable products, social inventions are new social services, or new and imaginative solutions to social problems: new laws, new electoral systems, new projects, new organisations, new ways for people to relate. The Institute provides an opportunity to tackle social problems before they become crises, through encouraging public participation in continuous problem solving – and through the promotion of small-scale innovative experiments.

Founded in 1985, it acts as a think tank and an international suggestions box, giving awards and £1,000 in prize money to the best ideas and schemes sent in by members of the public or by its correspondents around the world.

Previous award winners include the Forest Garden; the Prison Ashram project; a Community Balance Representation electoral system for Northern Ireland; and a self-taught computer literacy scheme for children in a Delhi slum.

These schemes are all described in detail on the web, in the Institute's Global Ideas Bank (at www.globalideasbank.org).

This vast online encyclopedia of social inventions receives about three million 'hits' a year and contains over three thousand entries. The public can vote on these schemes, with the result that the best ones come democratically to the surface.

The Institute helps to carry out some of the best ideas as projects. One of these projects – the Natural Death Centre is described on the following page.

There is an annual published compendium of the best social inventions, available in printed form for subscribers (£15 per annum) who also have access to a social inventors' club for meetings or when travelling.

The Institute's patrons include musician Brian Eno, industrialist Sir Peter Parker, authors Fay Weldon and Colin Wilson, Diana Schumacher of the Schumacher Society and Anita Roddick, founder of the Body Shop. The Institute's fellows include Lord Young of Dartington, Tony Buzan and Edward de Bono. The Institute is a part of the Fourth World Educational and Research Association Trust, registered charity 283040, of which the trustees are Lord Beaumont, Sir Richard Body, Edward Goldsmith and John Seymour.

The Institute for Social Inventions, 20 Heber Road, London NW2 6AA, UK (tel. 020 8208 2853; fax 020 8452 6434; e-mail: rhino@dial.pipex.com; web: www.globalideasbank.org).

The Natural Death Centre

The Natural Death Centre was launched by the Institute for Social Inventions in 1991. It is not, as some assume, a centre for euthanasia. The name came about by analogy with the natural birth movement, which supports home births, since the primary aim of the Natural Death Centre is to support families looking after somebody dying at home or trying to retain family control over the funeral arrangements.

To this end, the Centre has published an encyclopedic *New Natural Death Handbook* (available for £13.50 incl. p&p with update sheets and forms from the Centre or from its website at www.naturaldeath.org.uk) which is like a *Which?* magazine consumer report, with recommendations and best buys, but only to do with death and dying.

The subjects covered in this book include: Living Wills, Death Plans, Advance Funeral Wishes Forms, preparing for dying, looking after someone dying at home, the laws surrounding private land burial, arranging a funeral with or without funeral directors, setting up a woodland burial ground, the 130 or so existing woodland burial grounds (described in detail), the varieties of cardboard and other coffins available by mail order, recommended funeral directors, cemeteries and crematoria.

The Natural Death Centre gives awards to the funeral trade. For instance, a recent national winner as representing best value in the woodland burial ground category was Greenhaven burial ground, on New Clarks Farm near Rugby, which for £570 offers a service including the grave, the digging of the grave, a tree over the grave, a biodegradable coffin and collection of the body, even from as far away as London.

The Natural Death Centre has started an Association of Nature Reserve Burial Grounds, which sets criteria for the woodland burial grounds of the UK to follow, so as to provide some protection for the public; and a Befriending Network which trains volunteers who visit those who are critically ill in their homes (this latter is now an independent charity with its own website at www.befriending.net).

The Centre provides training sessions for nurses, doctors and palliative care workers and runs workshops for the general public on themes such as 'Accepting Death & Living Fully' and 'Living with Dying'.

Each year, on one Sunday in April, the Natural Death Centre organises a National Day of the Dead, where families are encouraged to light a candle during the meal for a family member who has died and then to go round the table telling stories about this person. Woodland burial grounds are open to visitors on this day and there are various exhibitions and seminars at the Centre.

The Natural Death Centre, 20 Heber Road, London NW2 6AA, UK (tel. 020 8208 2853; fax 020 8452 6434; e-mail: rhino@dial.pipex.com; web: www.naturaldeath.org.uk).